THE

SECRETS

OF

LOST

STONES

THE
SECRETS
OF
LOST
STONES

MELISSA PAYNE

LAKE UNION
PUBLISHING

Published by Lake Union Publishing, Seattle

www.apub.com

Amazon, the Amazon logo, and Lake Union Publishing are trademarks of Amazon.com, Inc., or its affiliates.

ISBN-13: 9781542006286 (hardcover)
ISBN-10: 1542006287 (hardcover)
ISBN-13: 9781542041942 (paperback)
ISBN-10: 1542041945 (paperback)

Cover design by David Drummond

Printed in the United States of America

First edition

For my family

CHAPTER ONE

JESS

A gas station. That's all she needed, and then Jess Abbot could get out of this backwoods mountain town and return to the highway. If she had known the actual town was fifteen miles from the exit, she would have kept driving. But the sign for Pine Lake had appeared just when she noticed the needle hovering over empty, and she'd taken the exit, assuming any place this far from Denver would have to have gas. The engine gave a weak cough, and her hands gripped the wheel. She'd bought the car for in-town errands, had never intended to test it on steep mountain passes. Her back muscles twitched, and she shifted in her seat, the pleather slippery and uncomfortable. This was almost her worst decision of the day. She gritted her teeth. Second only to driving a hunk of rusted metal into the mountains with no plan other than to get as far as she could from home.

The double yellow line she used to keep from losing sight of the road faded under a thick fog. It rolled through the air in meaty patches, enveloping her car in a grayish white that slowed her speed to a crawl while she navigated the switchback curves. An ache developed in her upper back from sitting hunched and tense behind the wheel. Where was the damn town? She was considering giving up and turning around when shapes with substance and edges began to form within the gloom. She squinted. Log buildings, squat with red metal roofs. She breathed out. Pine Lake. The gas station couldn't be far now.

The fog broke apart enough to allow her to see a large concrete dam where the town appeared to end—no gas station in sight. She groaned and considered pulling over to ask for help, but Pine Lake was nothing more than a road lined on either side with raised wooden sidewalks and storefronts that stared back at her with empty and darkened windows. It couldn't be much past three in the afternoon, yet it was deserted, empty of people and cars, the sky matching the air, gray and heavy. Hopefully, she'd have enough bars and minutes left to use the map function on her phone. But it lay just out of reach, nestled between the bonsai trees in a small cardboard tray on the passenger seat. She grasped it with the tips of her fingers, and it slipped and tumbled to the floor.

"Damn it!"

Her decision to leave that morning had been impulsive. For God's sake, it wasn't the first time she'd found an eviction notice taped to her door. Her thirty-two years were a patchwork of bad decisions compounded by jobs that paid shit and managers who sometimes fired at will. It also hadn't helped that today marked eight years since the night she'd lost everything that mattered, leaving her edgy and tense and maybe looking for a reason to run from the only home she'd ever known.

Holding the wheel steady with her left hand, she stretched her arm long and reached for the phone. She'd taken her eyes off the road for only a second when a small figure in a bright-red sweatshirt darted in front of her bumper, the headlights flashing yellow against his dark jeans.

Jess lurched upright, gripped the steering wheel, and slammed on the brakes. Her heart pounded, vibrating almost painfully against the bones in her chest.

A boy? Had it been a little boy?

The muscles in her throat constricted until she felt like she couldn't breathe. She'd almost killed him. Sweat trickled from her armpits as she scanned the street, the wooden sidewalk to her right. Empty. The boy was gone.

She tried to relax her grip on the wheel. He was fine and, most important, alive. Probably ran straight home, terrified himself. She wanted to feel relieved, except she couldn't move, frozen with her foot pressed so hard on the brake her toe touched the floorboard.

She closed her eyes, waiting for her racing pulse to slow, but thoughts of Chance pricked at her like the shards of glass that littered the floor of her apartment. That morning she had crumpled the eviction notice into a tiny ball and had opened her apartment door, intending to move on like always—find another job, get a crappier apartment, whatever it took. But then her eyes had landed on a school picture of Chance taken when he was in second grade. Her son looked at her with his bright eyes and impish smile, and something came unhinged inside her. He'd given her life meaning, and when he had needed her the most, she'd failed him. Her hands shaking with a familiar rage that sprang from her heart, flooding her body with a horrible impotence, she'd thrown the frame against the wall, and the glass shattered, spraying the carpet in small pieces. The slivers pricked her skin when she rescued Chance's picture from the mess, but she knew what she had to do: leave and never look back. It had taken only a few minutes to pack a duffel bag and load the old car with the few items she cared about. The landlord could figure out what to do with the rest.

The flashing dash light brought her back to the present, a blinking reminder that she was alone in this quiet town with eighty bucks to her name. She ran the car to empty enough to know that once the orange low-fuel light started blinking, the tank was on nothing but fumes. She eased her foot off the brake, the car inched forward, and Jess scanned the road ahead. There had to be a gas station here; this town was too far off the highway to be without one. A full tank would buy her a few more hours. Maybe enough to get her to Grand Junction? Not that she knew anyone there, but it was a place that she and Chance had planned to visit one day so he could see the Native American petroglyphs he'd learned about at school. They'd had so many plans. Like visiting the Four Corners Monument, where Chance wanted to straddle Arizona and Colorado while Jess did the same with New Mexico and Utah. Their own version of Twister. Her eyes stung, and she swiped at them with the back of one hand. Thoughts of all the adventures that had been stolen from Chance coiled around her body and squeezed until she thought her pent-up grief and sorrow and anger would melt out of her pores, leaving her as empty and scarred as she felt. She pressed her lips together and kept driving. There was no turning back time—or her car. All she could do now, all she could ever do, was move forward. Today that meant finding a gas station and getting the hell back to the highway.

The car had moved only a few feet when her headlights dimmed and a metallic shriek sounded from under the hood. A heavy odor of burnt oil wafted from the vents and stung her nose. She groaned. The car had needed an oil change months ago, but she'd ignored it because she hadn't had the money to spare. Without a high school diploma, Jess worked to pay her rent and eat, which usually left her no more than a couple of months ahead of broke.

Smoke drifted from under the hood, disappearing into the gray air. Could nothing go right today? She pulled into a parking spot on the street, but before she could turn the car off, the engine sputtered and died.

"Damn, damn, damn." The flesh across her wrist burned with a sudden itching that made her scratch the skin until it turned a bright pink. Alone and stranded in a cowboy ghost town. She slumped forward under the weight of everything she had lost this year alone: her job, her apartment, Mr. Kim—the first friend she'd bothered to make in eight years. Her forehead dropped to the steering wheel, and the plastic felt cool against her skin. She hit the dashboard with a balled-up fist. "Damn!" she said again.

A heavy bang, like a door being slammed shut, sounded from a store immediately to the right of the car. She lifted her head to look around. A café, a coffee shop, and what looked like a secondhand store lined the still-empty sidewalk, all with black-and-white CLOSED signs turned outward. *Very weird.*

She looked through the passenger window and up toward a glass door with the words MOUNTAIN MARKET spelled out in white lettering. The same CLOSED sign hung on the door, tapping the window as though it had just been turned. A small face appeared from inside the darkened market, and she jumped, startled. Was that the boy she'd almost hit? Today had been a crap day, but at least she could do something right; she could talk to the boy about darting out in front of cars. She swallowed hard. Might save his life one day.

She stepped out of the car, walked up the wooden steps to the market, and paused a moment to look around. The sidewalk was empty, not a soul in sight. She shook her head. Instead of spending time lecturing a kid about road safety, she should focus on finding someone who could fix her car.

The bell rang softly above the door, which she noticed stood open a crack. The market must not be closed after all.

"Hello?" she called. Where had the boy disappeared to? She reached for the door handle, but her leg muscles twitched, and she fought an overwhelming urge to return to her car. The boy was probably playing with her. She gave a soft grunt. Chance had been a bit of a prankster too. This kid needed to understand the dangers of running in front of a car. She pushed the door open a bit more, poked her head inside. "Hello?" she called again.

Dim light filtered from the back of the store, and a woman's voice, strained thin, like it took effort to call out, said, "Be right there."

Jess stepped inside and rubbed her arms at the goose bumps that spread up to her shoulders. She wished she hadn't left her coat in the car. It wasn't spring at this altitude; here the air was still crisp with winter cold.

The interior of the market was about what Jess expected based on what she'd seen of the rest of the town during her short drive down its main street. Small, with four dimly lit and narrow aisles, the air tasting of dust and vinegar, giving the entire space the feel of a neglected storage room rather than a place to buy milk and toilet paper.

Late-afternoon sunlight broke through the low-hanging clouds outside and shot through the window, brightening the front of the store but creating dark pockets in the far corners. The glare highlighted a thick layer of dust that coated a shelf with cereal boxes and stale-looking bread. Her nose tickled, and she sneezed three times in a row, muffling it into the crook of her elbow. When she looked up, she noticed a slight figure standing at the end of one of the darkened aisles.

The boy from the street. She softened. He looked even smaller than she'd thought.

"Hey there, bud," she said. "You should really be more careful when you cross the street. I almost hit you."

He stood so still she almost wondered if the light had played tricks on her. She squinted. No, that was him: red sweatshirt, dark jeans. From his size he looked to be about seven or eight. She blinked rapidly, pressed a palm to her chest.

"I'll be right there," the same voice she'd heard before said from somewhere in the back of the store.

The boy hadn't moved, and Jess felt a prickle of annoyance at how effortlessly he ignored her. And with his head angled toward the shelves of food and the hood of his sweatshirt pulled up, she couldn't see his face. She tried to soften. *Just a local kid trying to be funny.*

She took a step toward him. "Just look both ways next time, okay?" Her mouth had turned dry, papery. She cleared her throat.

He turned and came toward her, carefully placing one foot in front of the other like he was walking a tightrope. His head hung down, eyes trained on the floor. Jess took an involuntary step back and tried to ignore the sweat that had gathered in her armpits despite the cool air. There was something off about his behavior.

"Hey, bud," she tried again, and this time the boy stopped dead in his tracks.

A rustling came from the back of the store and then the woman's voice again. "You're here!"

The boy sprinted past Jess, trailing his finger along one of the shelves as he ran. Cans of food and packages of noodles tumbled to the floor with a crash.

"Hey!" Jess yelled, hurrying after him, but the little vandal had already disappeared outside. The bell above the door gave a shrill ring when it slammed shut.

A hoarse feminine chuckle sounded from behind Jess. "Guess he didn't want to stay for the blueberry muffins."

Jess turned and tried not to let her mouth hang open at the sight of the woman wearing an outfit better suited for Halloween than a Wednesday afternoon in May. Her black dress looked like it belonged in a museum, with a skirt billowing around her ankles and a high neck edged in lace that brushed along her jawline. The color was severe against the old woman's pale, wrinkled skin, which stood in stark contrast to her tight bun of flaming-red hair.

"Excuse me?" Jess said.

"It's Wednesday," the woman answered, as though that were explanation enough.

Jess pointed down the aisle. "He knocked those things off your shelves."

The old lady smiled, and the effort deepened the wrinkles around her cheeks and eyes. She had to be at least eighty, and that might be too generous. "Never mind about the boy," she said. "Some of them like to have a bit of fun with me." She stared at Jess with eyes so blue they seemed almost transparent and tapped her chin. "I thought you'd be younger," she said.

"O-kay." Jess had heard jokes about backwoods mountain towns and the people who lived in them, but she'd only ever lived in the city and had thought the jokes were mostly from city snobs. She studied the woman in her black dress with the full skirt and high neck, thought about the empty streets and closed businesses outside. Maybe the jokes weren't too far off the mark.

"I was expecting a girl."

Jess was at a loss for words. The woman reminded her of Mr. Kim. With his effortless smile and sharp wit, Mr. Kim made it easy to grow fond of him at the nursing home where she'd worked. Mr. Kim was one of the few residents who had retained the majority of his faculties, except for the occasional slip from reality, which made him all the more endearing to Jess. The elderly were like that for her: interesting, nonthreatening, and good companions during her long shifts. She felt a pang. She'd loved that job.

But this was not a nursing home, and this woman either worked here or was as lost as Jess, so Jess smiled and held out her hand. "I'm Jess. I was looking for a gas station, but my car broke down."

Instead of shaking her hand, the woman covered it between her small, soft palms. "I'm Lucy," she said, winking, "and I know things."

Jess laughed. Lucy definitely reminded her of Mr. Kim. "Well then, Lucy, do you know anyone who can fix my car for less than sixty bucks?" Leaving her twenty dollars to do what? Buy a quarter tank of gas and a pack of gum? She groaned inwardly. *Stupid* was too kind a word for the predicament she had gotten herself into.

Lucy's face brightened. "That's the right question." Then she turned from Jess to the counter by the door and began to riffle through a stack of newspapers beside the register. "Where is it?" she mumbled.

Jess's chest tightened with a swell of pity. Lucy looked suddenly lost and unsure of herself. "Can I help?" she asked, and joined the woman at the counter. The papers were all crossword puzzles—folded in half, most of them blank, a few filled in with one or two words. "You like crossword puzzles, Lucy?" she said with a soft smile, then shifted her gaze outside. Why was the older woman all alone in this store? Or, for that matter, the entire town? "I noticed all the stores are closed. Is there somebody I can call for you?"

Lucy halted what she was doing to stare at Jess. "Nothing's open today, dear. Everyone thinks the ice on the lake is finally thin enough."

"Thin enough?"

"For the ice-melt barrel to fall through, of course." She winked. "It's been a long winter, so there's a fair amount of money riding on when it falls through the ice. Quite the to-do up here every spring."

Jess rubbed the back of her neck. In her experience, there were no days off, no holidays, no sick leave, and definitely no celebrating a barrel falling through the ice when she could be working. She gestured around the store. "Yours is the only store open in town. Why aren't you watching the ice melt too?"

Lucy's smile stretched the folds of skin around her mouth. "Because it's Wednesday, dear. I only open the store on Wednesdays." She turned back to the pile of papers, pulling one page loose from the stack. "Here it is!" She lifted a pair of reading glasses from a chain around her neck and settled them on the bridge of her nose. Her finger ran down the page, paused; she read, "It's good when a batter does it on the field, but not on the road." Her eyes met Jess's, huge and shockingly blue behind her black-rimmed glasses. "Well?"

"Um . . ." Jess stumbled over her words. Lucy spoke as though they were longtime acquaintances picking up halfway through a conversation. It made her head spin.

Lucy frowned, looked down at the paper again. "Hmm. Multiword. We're not ready for that one yet, are we? Let's see." Her finger ran down the page. "How about this one? Eight letters. Having nowhere to live."

Her smile warmed Jess, like how a grandmother must make her grandchildren feel, deserving of attention.

"I know this one," Lucy said. "Homeless."

Jess watched as her gnarled fingers carefully wrote each letter inside the boxes. The paper shook, and Jess wasn't sure if it was from the old woman's excitement for the game or an unsteady hand. Whatever the cause, it made Jess want to reach out and help.

Lucy squinted down at the puzzle, then raised her eyes from the paper to look at Jess. "Four letters. The sun, for example." She hovered her pencil over the paper, waiting, Jess assumed, for her to come up with the answer.

Jess pulled at the sleeve of her shirt, touched by Lucy's enthusiasm for the game and for Jess's participation, even if she was a total stranger. Mr. Kim hadn't been a crossword puzzle enthusiast, but he had loved his bonsai trees. They had covered his room and were his favorite topic of conversation. Jess had a bonsai tree too—one that someone had given to her son—and beyond all odds the damn thing still lived. It was why she had connected so easily with Mr. Kim. She thought of the trees in her car right now. Her own plus the two from Mr. Kim's collection that she'd been able to save. Seeing his prized trees in the garbage had given rise to an anger so deep inside it had taken even her by surprise. It was the reason she'd been fired and why she was standing here trying—and failing—to answer crossword puzzle clues. "I'm sorry," she said at last. "I'm not very good with word games."

Lucy tapped the eraser side of the pencil on top of the counter while she silently studied Jess. After a few seconds, Jess grew uncomfortable.

"Maybe you're not the right one," Lucy said quietly. "But so often it doesn't make sense until later." She squinted. "There's something about you, though. Something familiar."

The woman seemed not entirely in her right mind, and Jess couldn't bear the thought of a worried family member or caregiver looking for her. She opened her mouth to ask again whether there was someone she could call, but a word bubbled to her lips and she blurted it out before thinking. "Star!"

A slow smile spread across Lucy's face. "What's that?"

It was quite possibly the only thing she remembered from sixth-grade science. She pulled her ponytail tight, crossed her arms. "The sun is a star," she said. "That's your answer."

Lucy scribbled the word into the boxes. "Well done, Jess." She gestured toward a small round table underneath the storefront window. "Have a seat. I'll bring you one of my famous blueberry muffins and a cup of coffee."

Jess started to protest, but Lucy had already disappeared behind a curtained doorway in the back of the store. She stood for a moment, unsure what her next move should be, then shrugged and took a seat at the table. As the day wore on, it seemed unlikely that she'd be leaving anytime soon. Might as well have a cup of coffee and something to eat.

She gazed outside. The fog had completely burned off, exposing a deep-blue sky. Snowcapped mountains ringed the town, and at the end of the short main street, Jess glimpsed a concrete dam with what appeared to be a mostly frozen lake above. She grunted. Didn't look like the barrel was falling through anytime soon.

It was a beautiful place, though; she'd give the town that. Her visits to the mountains had been limited to a handful of field trips in elementary school when they'd studied Colorado history. She could never afford to ski or take time off work to camp or hike; the gas to get there alone cost more than her mother made in an entire day. Those activities weren't for people like Jess and her mom. She'd lived her entire thirty-two years within the same fifteen-block radius in Denver, poor and always one job away from losing everything.

She sighed and turned from the rugged beauty outside. This morning it had felt like a plug had been pulled inside her, and she had finally realized just how tired she was. Tired of pretending that losing her son hadn't leached the color from her life or turned her numb. Those years after Chance was gone, every child reminded her of him. A little boy on the RTD bus, his caramel curls dancing above the seat in front of her. A boy at the grocery store on a late-summer night in Chance's favorite *Transformers* pajamas. He was everywhere for her, and it nearly shattered her. She'd become a robot, unable to talk to anyone, drowning in the memories and haunted by one thought: it was her fault.

Her fault that her eight-year-old son had been in the path of a car whose driver either didn't see him or didn't care. Her fault that he'd died cold and alone and in his *Transformers* pajamas.

Afterward, there had been a few friends who'd tried to help her through her grief. Like her neighbor Marissa, who brought her dinner every single night in small Tupperware containers until Jess, in a moment of gut-wrenching anger at everything and everyone, screamed at her to stop. Or her old friend Juanita from the group home. They'd been pregnant together. Juanita's little girl must be fifteen by now. Jess wrapped her arms around her stomach and rounded forward over the table. Juanita had invited her to church every Sunday until Jess finally told her she didn't believe in God. Because if God existed, he would have taken Jess, not the boy with the soft brown eyes and the sweet heart who saw the good in everything and everyone. Besides, Jess didn't deserve any of their attention. She deserved to be exactly where she was—alone.

The earthy aroma of brewing coffee filtering in from the back room brought her back to the present, and Jess breathed it in along with the sweet smell of blueberries. Today her head seemed filled with ghosts.

There was a light touch on her shoulder, and Jess turned to look behind her, expecting Lucy, but she found only the empty market. "Lucy?" she called, and stood. Memories and the guilt attached to them created a giant sinkhole below her feet that threatened to swallow her whole. She had to move forward and stop thinking about the past.

"Almost ready, dear!" Lucy answered from the back room.

Jess glanced outside. The sun had already begun to slide behind the tallest peak. She looked toward her car, half expecting to see smoke still pouring from under the hood of the boat-size sedan that was about as old as her and rusted through in several spots. Her shoulders slumped. She'd never have enough money to fix whatever had just killed her car. She thought she recalled seeing an RTD bus stop sign on her way down the main street. Her best option was to dump the car and grab a bus back to Denver, start from scratch—but her stomach knotted at the prospect. There was nothing for her there but memories and ghosts.

Surely Pine Lake had a diner. Jess had been a waitress for much of her working life, and those jobs always seemed to be available. Maybe she could get a job here, build back her savings at least to the point where she could make a real plan. She rubbed at her face. Where would she stay? She eyed the car, shrugged. She'd lived in a car once before; she could do it again. A bulletin board by the front door caught her eye—surely there would be job openings listed there. Flyers covered the board. Most of them advertised local music, pet sitting, and other services, but a plain white flyer pinned to the top of the board caught her eye.

LOOKING FOR A CHANGE? OR A SECOND CHANCE?
YOU CAN FIND IT IN PINE LAKE!
CAREGIVER NEEDED FOR OLD, SLIGHTLY DAFT WOMAN WITH POSSIBLE DEMENTIA!
RESPONSIBILITIES INCLUDE: HOUSEWORK, COOKING, ERRANDS, AND DOCTOR VISITS!
EXPERIENCE A BONUS, BUT SENSE OF HUMOR A MUST!
ROOM AND BOARD, USE OF CAR.
MUST BE WILLING TO RELOCATE!

Jess read it again. No name, just the letter *L* scrawled across the bottom of the page in delicate handwriting.

"I see you found my advertisement," said Lucy from behind her.

Jess turned, held out the flyer. "This is yours?"

Lucy nodded and set a cup of coffee and a plate with a large muffin on the table.

"You think you have dementia?"

A shrug. "Perhaps. But in case you hadn't noticed, I'm old, and Phoebe thinks I need some help around the house."

"Phoebe?"

Lucy took the flyer from Jess's hand and crumpled it into a ball before dropping it in a trash bin by the door. "I'm closing up now. Let's walk up to my house."

Lucy turned, and her long black skirts spun with her.

Jess stood rooted to the spot. It was too good to be true—a job opportunity with a place to live. But after everything that had happened today, why would she second-guess a bit of good luck? Only minutes before she'd been considering sleeping in her car. "Wait," she said.

Lucy turned back and folded her hands in front of her.

Jess rubbed the back of her neck. Did she really think she had a better option? "I, uh, I've worked in a nursing home facility for the last four years. I can provide references if you need them." She pulled at the end of her ponytail. "Actually, I don't know why I said that. I don't have any references."

Lucy raised an eyebrow. "Why?"

Jess sighed. Might as well come clean. "I was fired for locking a resident's relatives out of the building. I was—the resident and I were close. I mean, we talked, and I liked to listen to him." Mr. Kim had deserved so much more than his arrogant son and self-absorbed grandson who visited no more than twice a year. "Anyway, Mr. Kim died one night." She hesitated, her heart heavy with memory. "I didn't know. No one thought to call me. So when I came in for my next shift, his son and grandson were already there, packing up his room and going through his things like they were having a garage sale. I could have ignored them except for one thing."

Lucy raised her eyebrows, and Jess took a deep breath and hoped that her honesty would count for something. "Mr. Kim loved his bonsai trees like they were his children. They covered his room—literally covered the floor and any open shelf space he could find. But the day after he died, they tossed the bonsai into a huge black garbage bag like they meant nothing. He'd worked on some of them for years, and all that was left were broken pots and spilled dirt." Her hands curled into fists. Her own anger had taken her by surprise that day, but the bonsai trees weren't just special to Mr. Kim; they were special to her too. "I was sad to see how little they knew about him or cared. So I made them leave," she finished lamely.

"That's it?" Lucy said. "You made them leave?"

Jess felt her cheeks warm. "Not exactly. First I dumped the contents of Mrs. Harrington's bedpan on the man's head."

Lucy didn't react, and Jess deflated. Honesty was a terrible policy. Too late to take it back. She straightened her shoulders. "I've also worked in housekeeping at a hotel in Denver. I cook, I've never had a speeding ticket, um . . ." She paused. Lucy's face was smooth, indifferent. "Don't you have any questions for me?" She had no hope of getting this job now, and it surprised her how suddenly she wanted it. How much she wanted something to change in her life.

Lucy tilted her head to the side. "I think you're the one who's supposed to ask the questions, dear."

It was like no job interview she'd ever experienced. Lucy leaned heavily against the door, waiting for her. It was obvious to Jess that the woman probably did need a bit of caretaking. Maybe this was exactly what Jess needed too. Mr. Kim's friendship had filled a small portion of the hole inside her, even if it was only for a little while. She missed him. "Do you have grandkids?" she asked.

Lucy's laugh was hoarse and scratchy. "No, dear. No kids at all. Life had other plans for me."

Jess relaxed. That was good. Chance would be a teenager by now, and it stung to be around kids that age. Any age, really. She closed her eyes, shook her head to clear it. "So you live alone?"

"For now I do, but that can always change." Lucy nodded as though decided. "I don't use bedpans, so any visitors I have should be safe from you. The job is yours if you want it." She pulled a set of keys from a pocket in her dress and walked out the door, holding it open for Jess, eyebrows raised expectantly.

With a quick glance toward her sad car, Jess nodded and stepped outside. She helped Lucy lock the door and followed her down the sidewalk and up a hill behind the market. For the first time that day, a beat of optimism curled her lips into a small smile. She had found a job.

CHAPTER TWO

STAR

Between the slats of her concrete bench, Star could see the outlines of city buildings stretching high above her, their jagged tips stabbing a dark-blue sky. It was May in Denver, but spring was slow to warm the ground. At this time on a Saturday morning, the streets were quiet, regular people at home and probably still snuggled under their comforters, asleep. She yawned, curled into a tighter ball, and rested her cheek in the cradle of her palm. With her spine wedged against the farthest solid edge under the bench, only her knees stuck out the open side. She dug out the bits of crust that had gathered in the corners of her eyes during the night.

It was early morning, time to start the day. Except Star wasn't ready to face the long hours ahead of her, not just yet. She slid her hand deep into her coat pocket and rubbed her finger across her rock, feeling it strengthen her resolve. After getting busted for stealing the dad's stupid watch at her last foster home, Star knew that her next stop might be a state-run kind of place. Escaping the entire system for the streets had been her best option. She rubbed her eyes with the heels of her palms. They felt gritty and dry, sticking to the fleshy insides of her lids every time she blinked. Living on her own might be a slight improvement to foster care, but surviving the streets as a fifteen-year-old girl consumed her thoughts and fueled her nightmares, making sleep nearly impossible. It was wearing her down.

An empty potato chip bag skittered across the pavement, and Star watched it skip and hop, crinkling lightly as it danced by her hiding place. The breeze that pushed it snaked under the bench and through the holes in her coat until her bones ached with cold. It stirred the air, peeling unpleasant smells off every surface: the stench of old cigarettes ground into the smudged concrete and the musty, slightly sweet odor that rose from her pillow of matted hair. Her stomach turned, and she shivered. One hundred and ninety-two days since she'd climbed out the bedroom window while her foster parents were sleeping, and she still wasn't used to the stink of being homeless. She sniffed, buried her face into the crook of her arm. Better to stink than to live another minute as a foster kid. She was getting too old for it anyway. Nobody wanted a kid her age. Her last foster mom had frowned when she opened the door to Star and her caseworker. *I thought we'd get a baby this time,* she'd said.

From behind her bench came the sound of the Sixteenth Street shuttle slowing to a stop with an electric whir. The doors opened, breaking the quiet with regular-people chatter. Saturday mornings brought the tourists along with the few commuters who didn't get their weekends off. They thumped past her head in tennis shoes and dull leather work boots. She sighed. The buses were running. Time to get up. She waited for the sidewalk to clear, watching their feet as they scurried off to shop or eat breakfast or whatever the hell they had planned for a lazy Saturday. She shook her head, snorted. Clueless fucks, all of them, with no idea who watched them from under benches or in doorways.

When their shoes disappeared from her view, Star yawned, stretched, and crawled out from under the bench. Her left foot had fallen asleep, and a thousand little bees stung her skin as it tried to wake up. She winced, sat down on the bench, and rubbed it hard until the feeling returned.

A stooped figure in a wool coat approached her, pushing a shopping cart that wobbled over the pavement, two wheels jerking uselessly back and forth. Mel, the old man who slept in a doorway half a block from her bench. The one who, on a cold night this past winter, had pulled out a heavy coat from his shopping cart of treasures and slid it under her bench. She liked Mel, even if his trash bags did smell like pee.

The cart gave a catlike shriek when Mel stopped in front of her. He stared at her, his face weathered and dirty, cracked lips sucked in over toothless gums.

She gave a small wave. "Hi, Mel."

He squinted, then grunted. Mel wasn't known for conversation; Star didn't mind. She preferred this bench because it wasn't far from the doorway he normally camped in at night. It was stupid, she knew, because Mel constantly reeked of alcohol and was never without a brown paper bag clutched in one hand. Still, just the fact of his presence made her feel the tiniest bit safe. He wasn't a bad guy. She pulled the coat tight across her chest. She should know. There were plenty of bad guys here.

Mel turned to his cart, stuck a hand inside one of the thin garbage bags, pulled out a long piece of fabric, and laid it beside her. A scarf. Or what had once been a scarf, anyway. She picked it up, poked her fingers through several big holes. Her throat grew tight; she smiled. "Thanks, Mel." She wrapped it twice around her neck. "I love it."

He grunted again, nodded, and had started to turn away when the whir of skateboard wheels rolling over cracked pavement came from down the block. Star stiffened, tried to grow smaller, pulling inside her too-big coat like a turtle in her shell. She knew the sound. Street kids, like her. And drug dealers, like her father.

From the corner of her eye, she saw a tall kid in a baggy sweatshirt, greasy yellow hair poking out of his wide-brimmed hat, flanked by two boys and a girl. The tall boy was Shred, and Star had learned quickly that he was dangerous. In her months on the street, she'd tried to make herself invisible, staying away from his places, going in a different direction whenever she could. Despite her efforts he'd noticed her, and she could feel him staring at her now. The muscles in her legs cramped, and her skin crawled. It was only a matter of time.

The skateboard wheels faded down the street, and Star looked up to find that Mel had stood in front of her the entire time, nearly blocking her from view. Something twisted in her chest, and she had to look away.

She smiled into her hair when she heard Mel grunt a final time, and then the squeal of his cart started up again. When she finally looked up, his hunched form was crossing the mall.

Another bus pulled up and unloaded more people. Time to get moving. She stood and headed down Sixteenth Street Mall, letting her long black hair swing around her face as she walked. Her favorite place to hang for the day was directly across from a gourmet chocolate shop. While its out-of-the-way location didn't make it the hottest spot to beg, the odds of someone buying her a hot chocolate were pretty good.

Her boots made dull thumping noises on the pavement. She'd hoped that if she kept to herself the other kids would leave her alone, let her do her time until she was eighteen. Then she figured she could win the lottery, go back to school, and buy sheets for her very own bed in her very own apartment. She wasn't stupid, but she needed to dream or this place was going to tear her apart.

A little while later, she inhaled the sweet aroma of chocolate and for the moment let herself forget whatever Shred might or might not want. She took a sunny spot on a low garden wall and leaned back on her hands. A man jogged past in dark-gray sweatpants, earphones in, eyes glued to the phone in his hand. He was followed by a young woman pushing a little brown-haired girl in a stroller. The girl was sound asleep; her mother glanced nervously at Star and walked faster.

Star shrugged, slid her hands under her thighs, and bounced her heels against the garden wall. The woman's reaction didn't surprise her anymore. She was used to making people uncomfortable.

Girlish laughter and the soft strumming of guitars drifted from a spot just past the chocolate shop. She looked over her shoulder. Two girls sat cross-legged on the ground, guitars in their laps. One with dreads poked the other one in the shoulder, and they both laughed again. Star knew the type—band followers who ran out of money and got stuck. Probably had two parents, a little sister with shiny pigtails, and a golden retriever waiting for them back home in their four-bedroom mansion with a pool. Star couldn't relate; she'd never had a pool. But once upon a time she did have two parents and a pretty decent house.

She sniffed, looked away, and scooched farther back on the wall so that she was partially hidden behind a leafy green bush. Thinking about what she didn't have did nothing to get her through the day, so she focused on the guitar music that had started up again and listened as one of the girls began to sing in a voice that slipped over the words like ribbons of honey.

Star relaxed, tilting her head to let the weak morning sun touch her face. A glint of scarlet flashed in the corner of her eye, and she turned to see a woman with bright-red hair staring at her from across the street.

She crossed her arms and stared back. When the woman didn't look away, Star bristled. *Rude.* She hopped up from the wall, making a beeline across the street. If the old lady was gonna stare like that, then she might as well give her some money.

As Star drew closer, the little hairs on the back of her neck stood on end. Her feet dragged. Maybe she shouldn't bother with this one. The woman's dress made her look out of place: long with a big black skirt, more like a costume. She was probably mental.

The girl's singing faded into silence. Despite the alarm bells clanging in her head, Star couldn't stop herself, and soon she stood opposite the old lady. The woman continued to stare, her eyes wide and unblinking. This woman couldn't possibly have money to spare.

Then Star noticed the little boy partially hidden behind her skirts. He was small, seven or eight, and stood unnaturally still. He'd pulled the hood of his red sweatshirt over his head and cinched it so tight she couldn't see his face. Star pushed a ratted strand of hair behind one ear and gave him a small smile. He didn't move.

She sighed, planted her feet, and straightened her spine. Maybe the old lady would be extra generous to impress her grandson.

"Excuse me." Star held her hands out in front of her, palms spread wide. Up close, the woman looked even older, the skin of her face crisscrossed with deep lines. They ran across her forehead, shot out from her eyes, and fell down her cheeks, where they disappeared over the flabby jowls hanging from her jaw. Man, this woman was *old*.

The woman's eyes shifted, and she turned her head to look down at her grandson. The boy hadn't moved, and his stillness left Star cold. She slid her hands into her pockets, fingering the rock.

Her stomach growled, and she sighed. She needed the money. "Hey," she said, and the woman jerked her eyes away from her grandson. "I was wondering if you'd spare some change? I need to catch a bus so I can go see my parents. They live outside Durango."

The old woman moved forward until the hem of her black skirt swung close to Star's leg. "I'm Lucy," she said in a voice that sounded soft but scratchy, like silk over sandpaper.

"Okay." *Great, a first-name basis.* Lucy was probably a do-gooder who thought *having a conversation* would make Star feel more human. Like it was better than money. Star crossed her arms. Food and water beat conversation any day. She'd better cut to the chase before the old lady asked for her favorite color. "Listen, Lucy. I don't have parents in Durango. The truth is I don't have parents at all. At least not anymore. But I do need money. And that's something I never lie about."

Lucy raised a gnarled finger toward Star's chin, but when Star flinched, she took her hand away, staring. Star couldn't look away from Lucy's eyes. The color was like nothing she'd ever seen—the bottomless blue of a glacier with hunks of amber and emerald that seemed to spin. Her stomach churned, and a tremor ran through her legs, making her knees wobbly.

"Just a few dollars," Star said, her voice shaking along with her body. "Nothing that'll break the bank." But Lucy still didn't respond, and all Star could focus on were the spinning flecks of color in the old woman's eyes, making her feel dizzy. She gripped her toes into her shoes to steady herself.

"Another loose end," Lucy whispered.

Star opened her mouth to speak. What could this crazy old bat mean? Her bones felt welded together at every joint. With great effort, she finally wrenched her feet from the ground and stumbled backward. No amount of money was worth this woman's kind of crazy.

But when she turned to go, she noticed the little boy in the red sweatshirt had disappeared, and she felt a pang, thinking of a kid that young getting lost on the streets. She pointed behind Lucy. "Your grandson."

Lucy waved her hand dismissively. "He'll be back," she said.

Two women walked down the sidewalk and came to a stop on either side of Lucy, a pair of bookend bodyguards. One wore denim overalls and had her curly gray hair tied into pigtails. She grasped a to-go cup of coffee in each hand and gave Star a friendly half smile. The other was much younger. Her dark-brown hair was pulled into a tight ponytail. A deep frown wrinkled the skin between her eyes.

"Make a new friend, Lucy?" the young one asked, her voice soft and kind.

Star crossed her arms, narrowed her eyes. She didn't need their pity.

"Is this the girl, Luce?" asked the woman with gray hair, who gave Star a wide, easy smile.

Star shifted her weight. She wanted to leave this odd trio behind and find someone else to pester, but her feet wouldn't move.

Lucy tilted her head to the side, and to Star it looked like she was straining to listen to something only she could hear. Then she gave a slight nod, and the corners of her mouth turned down in a frown. "You're in danger," she said. "I don't understand yet, but it's not safe for you here."

Star felt her body relax, and for the first time she wanted to laugh. Of course she was in danger. She was a teenager living on the streets. Now she understood Lucy's weird outfit; she was one of those fake psychics who told paying customers the obvious. Maybe the old woman would ask *her* for money. "Lady," she said, "no disrespect, but that's not exactly news to me."

Lucy shook her head vigorously from side to side, looking confused and upset, and for a moment Star almost felt sorry for her. The younger woman placed a hand on her arm. "Should we go?"

Lucy shook off the woman's hand. "Not yet, Jess." She stepped toward Star, her gaze so intense that Star lifted her chin and backed away, her hands balled into fists by her sides.

"He says you're a loose end."

Star shivered. "I don't need this," she muttered, and hurried across the street. Lucy's last words followed her as she half walked, half stumbled back to her spot on the garden wall.

"I take care of all my loose ends, girl."

CHAPTER THREE

JESS

She stared at the yellow sticky note clinging to the bathroom mirror. *Wash your hands!* Jess pulled off the note, turning it upside down to rest on the counter while she cleaned the mirror. She scrubbed at the spotless surface, wiping along the edges, imagining stubborn water spots and smears of toothpaste. Studying the mirror, she nodded. *Check that off my list.* With just the two of them and four bathrooms to choose from, it had already been clean. Now it just looked cleaner, but Jess didn't mind, even if it was Sunday and Lucy had tried to get her to take the day off. She enjoyed the work and preferred doing something to nothing.

She stuck the note back onto the mirror and checked her watch. It was nine o'clock. Time for breakfast. It was staggering how her life had changed since Wednesday, and Jess was surprised at how quickly she had grown comfortable in her new role and with Lucy. It was hard not to like the old woman, even if she was an odd mix of fairy godmother and witch.

On that first afternoon in Pine Lake, after she'd accepted the job, she'd followed Lucy up the road behind the market to a large gray Victorian home perched on a hillside above town. Jess found the style of the house at odds with the western buildings that lined Main Street, but Lucy informed her that it was a town original, built by her parents when they moved from Boston.

She put the cleaning supplies away and headed down the wide staircase, trailing her hand along the smooth wood of the banister. The bottom of the stairs opened into the high-ceilinged foyer, where the staircase curved outward on either end. Jess's favorite detail in the house was the elaborate lamps affixed to the end of each banister. They were identical, each a mirrored iron sculpture of a scaled serpent nearly swallowing a yellow globe in its mouth. At night the lamps glowed yellow, reflecting against the parquet wood floor and casting warmth that spread throughout the house. Lucy had called them newel lamps and said they were original to the house.

Jess wasn't used to big houses like this one. She'd only lived in tiny apartments with one bathroom and a kitchen with a two-burner stove. Lucy's house felt cavernous with only two people inside. It didn't help that it seemed to move and breathe like it was alive. The floorboards creaked, the walls groaned, and doors slipped open on occasion, even after Jess made sure to pull them shut until she heard a click. Bad hinges, Lucy had assured her. For the most part, though, Jess was learning to ignore the home's odd quirks in favor of a job she enjoyed very much.

She touched one of the globes as she passed—it was cold, the light turned off until the evening—and crossed the foyer, her feet making light tapping noises as she walked. At the doorway to the kitchen, she hesitated. Her back tingled; she felt like she was being watched. She tensed, turned. Someone stood at the end of the narrow first-floor hallway, reaching for her with long, thin arms. She gave a strangled cry and stumbled backward. With her heart racing, she shook her head and looked again, laughed weakly. No, not a person—an antique coattree with long metal arms that held several of Lucy's black wool coats. Goddamn, she was jumpy. It wasn't the first time she'd imagined seeing something here. With its tight corners and muddled lighting, Lucy's house played tricks on her.

She crossed the kitchen to where a paper calendar hung on a push-pin next to a flesh-colored phone. The ancient wall-mounted phone had a cord that stretched to the floor, where it lay across the laminate tiles like unspooled intestines. It was the only one in the entire house, and it hadn't rung once this week. Jess had even put her ear to the receiver to make sure it had a dial tone.

Lucy had informed her that whatever she had planned for the day would always be on the calendar, and she insisted that Jess check it every day, sometimes more than once. Lucy was serious about her schedule. But on Friday night, Jess had forgotten, and when she woke up yesterday morning, she'd found Lucy waiting for her in the kitchen, jangling the car keys in her direction. *Where are we going?* Jess had asked.

Lucy pursed her lips, shook her head, and rolled her eyes toward the calendar. *I like to people watch in Denver. Phoebe usually drives, but I told her that you could do it this time.*

Lucy had raised her eyebrows as though expecting Jess to protest, but as much as she didn't want to go back to the city, a bigger part of her was curious about what Lucy did with her time. Jess sighed. As it turned out, Lucy had a soft spot for street kids, even talking to one girl who ran off, probably spooked by Lucy's clothes and eyes. Jess rubbed the back of her neck, trying to ignore the prickle of guilt. She'd lived in the city for years, but there was something about going back as a visitor that had made the contrasts sharper; an old woman huddled in a doorway with red, chapped lips and a sign that read HAVE NOBODY, NEED MONEY and more teens than she remembered with broken teeth and yellow skin hanging in loose groups or alone, like the girl, while people walked past in shoes without holes, eyes trained on phones.

When they got back to Pine Lake, Jess had sipped in the mountain air, relieved to be back.

She ran her finger over the squares of the calendar until she located the one for today, Sunday. Lucy's handwriting filled the square.

Clean under beds, be careful.

Jess wrinkled her forehead. Statements like these were as common to Lucy as her sharp wit, and it was a bewildering blend that both amused and worried Jess.

She turned to open the refrigerator and paused. A dozen or so yellow sticky notes covered the front, each one with a directive.

Eat breakfast!
Put away the milk!
Don't drive!
Take a coat!

She sucked in her bottom lip. Lucy had notes like these scattered all over the house. Her memory did seem to blur at times, but to Jess it appeared as though she simply lost herself in a moment. Her spells, as Jess had come to think of them. Because for an eighty-five-year-old woman, Lucy was physically strong and sharp as a tack.

While the scrambled eggs cooked in a cast-iron skillet, she reached for a wooden tray above the refrigerator, scraped the eggs onto a small plate, and added a side of buttered toast and a glass of orange juice. After years of waitressing, Jess knew how to handle a tray.

She tapped on Lucy's bedroom door. "Breakfast." She waited, but after no response, her heart missed a beat. The juice sloshed over the side of the glass, staining the cloth napkin a bright orange. "Lucy?" She pushed open the door with her hip to find Lucy sitting up in bed, the covers tucked around her waist, her back resting against the headboard of a massive four-poster bed. Awake and smiling.

Jess relaxed. Lucy's spells lasted only a few moments, and for the time being, she didn't think there was cause to be too concerned. But as Jess was the first caregiver Lucy had hired, she felt the responsibility for her health resting heavily on her shoulders. She'd already planned to speak with Lucy's doctor.

"Have you checked the calendar, Jess?"

Jess pulled the legs down on the tray and placed it across Lucy's lap. She smiled, nodded. "I'll get to the beds right after breakfast."

Lucy waved a hand in the air. "Not that. My visitor. Is she coming?"

Jess shook her head. "Phoebe? She didn't mention anything about stopping by today."

"Not Phoebe." Lucy turned to gaze out the window.

Jess pressed her lips together, feeling like she'd entered the conversation late. She felt that way a lot. Trying to change the subject, she asked, "Have you lived alone your whole life, Lucy?"

Lucy folded her hands in her lap. "Not my whole life. I lived with my mother until I was eighteen. But then she died and . . ." She paused. "Well, let's just say it was much harder being on my own than I thought it would be."

Jess nodded. She'd been on her own at that age, too, a young, single mother with no one to help her but herself.

You will get an abortion. Her mother's words had shattered whatever scrap of hope Jess had that maybe, just this once, she would be the kind of mother Jess had always wanted. Someone to tell her it would be okay, someone who made her feel like she mattered, someone to love her. She'd pressed her palm against the flat space below her belly button as though her mom's words had teeth that could rip away at her flesh. Jess didn't want to be pregnant—she was only sixteen—but when she saw the two lines on the test, her heart fluttered against her rib cage and she knew that it was no mistake. She was meant to have this baby, meant to love this baby.

I won't, she'd said softly, but with a firmness she felt in her bones.

Her mother's lips had thinned with contempt, and she'd stared at Jess with tired, red-veined eyes, her cheeks sallow under the fluorescent light. *Then get out.*

"I understand," Jess said to Lucy past the tightening of her throat. "I've been alone most of my life."

Lucy raised an eyebrow. "Most?"

Jess felt her shoulders tense. As close as she'd been to Mr. Kim, he'd never known about Chance. As their friendship grew, she wanted to share it with him, but having kept to herself for so long, she was out of practice. Besides, a part of her didn't feel like she deserved his sympathy or his friendship. But there was something about Lucy, even having known her for only a few days, that put Jess at ease, made her want to pry open the place inside her where she put her secrets. "My mother kicked me out when she learned I was pregnant. I lived in a group home for a while after that."

Lucy tilted her head to the side, and her eyes were a soft blue that made Jess look away. "That must have been very difficult."

Jess nodded, swallowed hard, and noticed that Lucy didn't ask about the pregnancy. For that she liked her even more. "What happened after your mother died?" Jess asked.

Lucy cleared her throat. "This house and the market were all left to me." Lucy looked down at her right hand, turned it so that the palm faced up, and traced a line with the pad of her finger. "But it was the loose ends that were the most difficult to handle on my own." She lapsed into silence, her eyes trained on her palm.

Jess studied the old woman. Lucy had mentioned loose ends frequently during the past few days and spoke about them as someone might when mentioning something troublesome. Like they were errant toddlers she couldn't control. Jess had asked Lucy about it a few times, but she had waved her off as though the effort to explain was too much. Jess figured she'd get an answer in time.

With a start, she noticed how Lucy's mouth had slackened, and her eyes looked dull and watery. Jess moved quickly to her side.

"You doing okay?" She pressed two fingers along the vein in Lucy's wrist. Her skin was cool, smooth. "Lucy?" she said. "Can you answer me?" Jess reached for her phone, her fingers hovering above the emergency call button.

"You don't need to make such a fuss, dear," Lucy said, and Jess exhaled with relief.

"Why didn't you answer me?" she asked.

Lucy smiled. "I couldn't hear you." She bit into a piece of toast, and butter squished from the bread, glistening white on her lips. "It was very loud."

Jess stifled a sigh and tightened her ponytail until the corners of her eyes inched toward her scalp. The woman's vagueness could be frustrating. "What was very loud?"

"The boy," Lucy said, and gestured toward the floor, raising her thin eyebrows comically.

Something hit the toe of Jess's boot. She yelped, pressed a hand over her racing heart, and looked down. A small rock, more like a pebble, lay by her foot. She knelt down to pick it up, but a sound from under the bed stopped her, and then the red-and-gold bed skirt bulged, emitting what looked like the tip of a small finger.

Jess froze. Her throat went dry, and she blinked several times. But when she looked again, it was gone. She almost laughed out loud at her reaction. A mouse, of course, not a finger. Lucy's fanciful talk had her seeing and hearing things.

She got on her knees and carefully lifted up the bed skirt, resting her cheek on the carpet to look under the bed. The opaque blackness inside made her scalp prickle, but she shook it off and waited for her eyes to adjust to the dark. There was nothing under Lucy's bed but the fuzzy carcasses of dust bunnies. She exhaled forcefully and let the bed skirt fall back into place. This old house had century-old doors and windows. Perfectly drafty and full of rodent-size holes, no doubt.

Get mousetraps, she added to her mental to-do list, and picked up the small rock as she stood. She'd found a number of rocks around the house and figured they had been tracked in from outside. Once she'd stepped on one in her bare feet, and it had dug into the tender spot in the ball of her foot, making her cry out. She wouldn't want Lucy to step on one too. The rock made a soft clunk when she dropped it into the trash bin. Maybe sweeping once a day would keep the floors clear of the small stones. Another item for her to-do list. Her chest tightened at the ease with which she planned her time caring for Lucy. Living in the old woman's house and caring for her was a more intimate experience than working at the nursing home. And the last time she'd lived with and cared for someone had been when she was a mother. She pressed a hand to her heart and tried to push away her memories, but they were always there, like the phantom pain from a missing limb. Visions of Chance threatened to pull her apart at the seams. She inhaled and could nearly smell his skin after a bath, like soap and coconut shampoo. Her face was wet, and she realized with a shock that she was silently crying. "I'm sorry," she said, and wiped at her eyes with the sleeve of her shirt. "Allergies. Must be from the dust under the bed." She finally met Lucy's steady gaze and managed to give her a weak smile.

Lucy took a sip of her orange juice. "There's no shame in a good cry," she said.

The doorbell rang, and her shoulders slumped with relief at the echo of the heavy front door opening and closing.

"It's just me!" came Phoebe's voice from the foyer.

From what Jess had seen, the woman was one of Lucy's closest friends. She stopped over frequently to visit or play cards. Phoebe was a Grateful Dead fan who seemed to think that most of life's questions could be answered with a Dead song or a Jerry Garcia quote. Jess enjoyed her visits.

A few moments later Phoebe's smiling face appeared in the doorway, and she took her usual seat in the chair by the large window that overlooked the lake. She wore a tie-dyed winter hat over gray curls and her customary denim overalls. Her cheeks were ruddy from the cold temperatures outside. "Feels like spring today!" she said, rubbing her hands together.

Jess shot a dark look at the bare aspen branch outside the window. "You call this spring, Phoebe?" It was May, but the light-green buds that had already started to show themselves in Denver had yet to make an appearance at this altitude.

Phoebe laughed. "I love when flatlanders come up here. You sure know how to pick them, Luce. But I've already told you, Jess, please call me Ebee. Only my mother and Lucy call me the other."

The two women laughed as though sharing an inside joke. Although more than two decades and vastly different senses of style separated them, Lucy and Ebee were good friends. The witch and the hippie was how Jess had affectionately come to think of them. Yet they seemed to understand each other in a way that Jess had never shared with anyone in her life.

She set herself to clearing Lucy's tray; then she helped her out of bed and to the chair by the window and opposite Ebee. Lucy might not act her age, but after a night of sleep, she rubbed at her knees and fingers, her eyebrows knitted together. She never complained; Jess saw her fatigue in the way her back curved inward, as though to shield herself from the pain. Over the last few days, Jess had encouraged her to ease into each day at a slower pace, and Lucy seemed grateful for the routine.

"Are you two planning another outing to Denver?" Jess asked. She had enjoyed being with the two of them, and their presence had taken some of the sting out of being in the city.

"No," Lucy said. "I think my trips to Denver are done for now."

Ebee raised her eyebrows. "Is that so?" she said. "You seemed to think she was the right one."

33

"I have a note," Lucy said abruptly, and laid a white envelope on top of the table.

Jess stood by the door of the bedroom, breakfast tray in hand, wondering at their cryptic conversation. She often had no idea what they were talking about and had decided to chalk it up to the fact that they had been friends for so long. With a sigh, she turned from the room.

"Can you run an errand for me, Jess?" Lucy called.

"Of course," she said, and set the tray on a hallway table. "What do you need?"

Lucy held up the note. "Please deliver this to the girl by tomorrow morning."

"The girl?"

Lucy nodded. "Yes, of course, the girl."

Jess pressed her lips together to keep from vocalizing her frustration. It wasn't fair to make someone as old as Lucy feel bad for her inability to express her thoughts. She took the envelope, flipped it over. Lucy had written a single word in her loopy handwriting across the front: *Star*.

"It's for the girl we met in Denver," Ebee clarified.

"The girl who asked you for money?" Jess asked, eyebrows raised. She thought of the girl Lucy had spooked yesterday and felt a twinge. Her clothes had been dirty and oversize, but it didn't hide the fact that the girl's frame was small, too skinny. "Her name is Star?"

Lucy stared at her with a look that bordered on exasperation. "Yes, you figured that out already, remember?" Then she slid her reading glasses on and picked up her crossword puzzle as though the matter were closed.

Jess looked helplessly at Ebee, who shrugged. "You get used to her after a few decades."

Jess gave Ebee a small smile before turning to Lucy. "I don't think it's a good idea to give her money." When Lucy looked sharply at her over her glasses, Jess added, "If she's really homeless, it would be better to call social services, help her get into a home is what I mean."

Lucy sighed. "The girl needs to have that envelope, Jess, and you need to be the one who delivers it."

Jess started to say something but stopped. Lucy's firm tone and stern look made her realize that for now there was no arguing with her. Besides, Jess didn't want to do anything to jeopardize this job. She thought of the gaunt angles of the girl's face, the haunted, hollow look in her eyes, and shuddered. The streets weren't safe, and at the very least Jess could offer her the numbers of a few shelters that provided safe places for teenagers like her.

Lucy had picked up a pencil and was focused on her puzzle again. "Seven letters," she said. "A kamikaze mission."

Jess moved toward the door, feeling dismissed, the note heavy in her pocket. "Lucy," she said, "how will I find her?"

Lucy looked up from the paper, her eyes a swirling blue. "Good question." She tilted her head to the side. "Chocolate," she murmured, and then she spoke louder. "She loves the smell of chocolate."

Jess flattened her lips. Not an exact address, but it did make sense. Most of the homeless, particularly the kids downtown, hung around the Sixteenth Street Mall. There were two chocolate shops on the mall, and Jess believed she remembered the girl being close to the one on the south end.

"Suicide!" Ebee cried out suddenly. She slapped her knee and smiled at Jess, then Lucy. "Suicide," she said again.

The eraser of Lucy's pencil bobbed up and down as she wrote. "Too easy for you, Phoebe."

Jess backed into the hallway, picked up the breakfast tray with one hand, and closed the bedroom door with the other. Her legs felt rubbery, weak, and she fought the urge to charge back in there and haul them both to a hospital or a home of some kind. Instead, she cleared her throat, gripped the tray, and headed downstairs, trying to ignore the way the skin across her wrists burned and itched.

CHAPTER FOUR

STAR

She leaned against the brick garden wall by the chocolate shop with her knees drawn up, arms wrapped around her shins. The stubborn spring air hadn't let go of winter's chill, and a constant drip from her nose had created a split in the very corner of her nostril that made her eyes water. This morning she'd woken up to find it tender and bleeding. She'd used the scarf to dab at it gently, but her breath fogged in the cold air, and her nose ran freely, making it hurt even worse. The ground felt hard and cold through her thin leggings, and a dull pain had begun to spread behind her eyes. Today she felt weak and small and very, very alone.

"Star?" A woman's voice.

She pressed her forehead into her knees, let her hair fall over her face, and breathed out. Her stomach somersaulted. She'd often wondered when social services would catch up to her, and on a day like today she felt extra vulnerable. But she'd sworn she'd never go back to being a foster kid. She'd been one since she was eight years old, and she was so fucking tired of the system, tired of the families who didn't want a sad teenage girl with klepto issues sleeping in the room next to their precious blonde-haired daughter, even tired of the ones who at least pretended to care but, when shit got hard, didn't actually care enough. She dug her nails into her thighs. Star was convinced that her mother would never have let the world fall apart the way her dad did. Sometimes at night she dreamed about her mom. Her memories were small pieces that didn't always make sense: a whiff of cinnamon, the soft grittiness of soil between her fingers, her cheek resting against a pillowy chest. She'd been only five when her mom got sick, but the one thing Star did remember was how safe she'd felt back then. Safe and warm and loved.

The woman cleared her throat, shifted her feet. *Good, she's uncomfortable. Serves her right.* Star rubbed her nose across her leggings, dug her fingers into her legs. This woman would have to drag her back into foster care, because no matter how cold her ass got, Star was not moving from that spot.

"I have something for you," came her voice again, and this time Star thought she recognized it.

She peered over her knees. The younger woman from the other day stood opposite her, brown hair pulled back into the same tight ponytail. She had a look about her that Star knew. An emptiness that made her eyes dull. It was a look Star saw often enough on the streets and before, when her dad was still alive. She shivered and pushed the thought of her dad out of her head. She was eight when he died, and unlike her mom, those memories had sharp claws that tore away at her. Right now she had too much to deal with.

"I'm Jess," the woman said.

Star crossed her arms, narrowed her eyes. What did she care? "Unless you have a twenty and a soda, I'm not interested."

Jess turned her head and looked around and behind Star, like she was searching for someone. She frowned. "Where do you live?"

Nosy, that's what she was. "Lady, that's none of your business." She picked up her cup and got to her feet, taking a seat on the garden wall opposite Jess. "Your grandmother is creepy."

Jess chuckled softly. "You're not wrong there. And you're a bit of a smart-ass, huh?"

Star raised her chin and gazed at Jess, unblinking. "You bet."

Jess opened her mouth, then shut it. She held out a small white envelope. "Here, this is for you."

Star didn't move from her spot. "What's that?"

"It's a note." Jess stepped forward, placed it on the brick wall beside Star. Star noticed how she rubbed at her wrist with the fingers of her other hand, back and forth, like one of those worry stones. "It's from Lucy, not me."

Star shrugged, ignoring the note beside her, even as a burning curiosity made it difficult not to ask Jess a billion questions.

Jess smiled. "Lucy is unusual, Star. I can't argue with you about that. But that probably makes whatever she says in your note worth reading."

Star thumped her heels against the brick wall, pretending she didn't care, but a panicky feeling expanded inside her. What did Jess want? Or the old woman? What could they know about her? If they'd ever seen her caseworker's file on Star, then they'd know she was prone to stealing, hard to love, and even harder to place. But a wrench in her gut told her that the old woman knew something else. Star's chest tightened. There were worse things about her than what her caseworker knew. She tried to glance casually down the street, gauging how quickly she could run and disappear if she needed to. "How do you know my name?"

Jess's forehead wrinkled. "I don't—I mean, not really. I just guessed at Lucy's crossword puzzle . . . I mean . . . Lucy must have known it somehow." For a second Jess looked confused, her face scrunched up like she was thinking too hard. It made Star want to laugh.

"You must have told Lucy or something," Jess continued. "Anyway, you left an impression on her, so she asked me to give that to you."

"What is it?"

"I have no idea. To tell you the truth, I've known her only a few days myself. But what's the harm in reading it, Star?"

Hearing her name spoken again in Jess's firm but soft voice felt comforting in a way that made Star's eyes itch. She trained her gaze on the ground, shrugged.

Jess's feet moved back and forth, but she didn't leave right away. Star sensed she wanted to say something more. Jess sighed and stepped so close that Star smelled a light citrus scent. She picked up the envelope, and Star heard the scratching of pen on paper.

"I don't know your situation, Star, but if you're alone and need help, I know a couple of shelters that only take kids. They're safe places." Jess set the envelope back down beside her, and from the corner of her eye Star noticed a couple of names and addresses written in black ink. And then on top of the envelope Jess placed a twenty, followed by another twenty.

Star's eyes bugged wide. Forty dollars!

"Take care of yourself," Jess said. "The streets are no place for a kid like you." She hesitated, mumbled, "Or for any kid."

Jess's boots disappeared from Star's view. She lifted her gaze and watched her walk away, shoulders hunched, one hand rubbing the other wrist, back and forth, back and forth.

Star pocketed the cash and picked up the envelope. A chill raced along her shoulder blades at the sight of her name written across the front.

She ran her fingertips along the pointed edge of the envelope, then slid her finger underneath the flap. It opened easily. Inside was a folded sheet of paper that matched the envelope. Smooth and thick. But when she unfolded the note, a thin rectangular piece of paper fell from its folds and fluttered to the ground.

A bus ticket.

Star hopped down from the wall and snatched the ticket off the ground. She stuffed it back into the envelope and shoved the envelope deep into the pocket of her coat. Lucy had sent her a bus ticket.

Guitar music and laughter floated from behind her. The same two girls who'd camped by her spot the other day sat cross-legged on the ground with their guitars. They must like the smell of chocolate too. Star sat down so that her back rested against the wall and listened to the music.

She wanted to read the note. Her fingers reached into her pocket, touched the stiff edge of the envelope, hesitated. What good could possibly come from some old lady? More than likely she wanted to help her find her parents or call her caseworker, or maybe she was a front for a sex trafficking ring. Star gave a bitter laugh. Those fuckers preyed on girls like her, but an old woman like Lucy really didn't fit that mold. She slid her hand out of her pocket and shoved it under her thigh. Maybe she'd read it later, or maybe she'd throw it away.

For the rest of the day, she managed to ignore the note. She bought a hot chocolate with the money from Jess and sipped it, trying to savor every bit of chocolate and sugar that touched her tongue. It went cold before she reached the bottom, but even cold it was still good. When the streetlights flickered on that night, a thin layer of coins and a few crumpled bills lay piled in her paper cup. Along with the remaining money from Jess, it wasn't a bad day. Satisfied, she pried apart her little fabric change bag, slid the money inside, and tucked it under her shirt.

The night air held a deep chill that poked through the thin spots in Star's wool coat. Three sizes too big, it did little to keep her warm anyway, but it was all she had. She pulled it tight to her body, shivering, and moved quickly down the street. Night made her feel visible to all the wrong people.

Just before the sun dropped behind the mountains, Star wolfed down a fast-food hamburger and drained a small cup of water, tossing the trash into the bin before flinging herself under a bench. When she curled up against one end, her entire body was almost hidden from view, making her feel protected and safe. The wide bench had three sides made of solid concrete, and with her small frame, she could almost pretend she was alone. Except for the guys sitting on a bench on the opposite side of the street, talking to one another, their voices raised. They sounded high or drunk or both, but they didn't seem to know she was there, and that was good.

She tried to tune them out, but when she did her thoughts went immediately to the note. It felt heavy in her pocket, as though it were made of metal instead of paper. When she couldn't fight her curiosity a minute longer, she dug her fingers deep into the pocket of her coat until she touched the small plastic flashlight, the kind someone might put on a key chain. Then she pulled out the bent and crumpled envelope. The thin beam of the flashlight shook. She tightened her grip to stem the trembling in her hand and pulled open the note. In the same delicate script, it read:

Dear Girl,
Here is what I know:

1. You watched your best friend die.
2. You are not a liar unless you need to be.
3. You are not an addict, but you do let something rule your life. Fear.
4. You think you are better off alone.

Everyone deserves a second chance. Consider this your invitation to come and stay at my house. Use this ticket to take the 401 to Pine Lake. From the bus stop, walk west on Main Street for one block, take a right at the Mountain Market. Follow the path to the house at the top of the hill that overlooks the lake. Ring the doorbell.

Lucy

The letter turned blurry, and Star was surprised to find she was crying. She wiped her eyes on her shoulder. For a second she felt a lightness touch her heart at the thought that somebody, even an old-ass lady, had noticed her. But it was gone just as quickly. She hadn't just watched Jazz die. She'd been the cause of his death. And she deserved everything that had happened after that night.

She reread the note. *You think you are better off alone.* Lucy was right there. Star deserved exactly that. She crumpled the letter into a ball and shoved it into her pocket, then took out the paperback book she kept tucked inside her coat. Reading helped her disappear into a pretend world where her own didn't exist. She flipped to a dog-eared page and began to read, trying to push the invitation to Pine Lake out of her mind. However sincere Lucy's offer, it was nothing more than a fantasy. So she began to read, huddled under her coat, using her hair as a pillow, until her eyelids grew heavy and she fell asleep.

Star woke up to a muffled sound from outside the bench. Something was wrong. The air still had the bite of darkness. Too early to wake up. She was curling deeper into her coat when she felt something touch her knee. Her eyes shot open. A face peered at her through the open slats.

Before she could cry out, a hand grabbed her ankle, and Star flew out from under the bench, her skull scraping across small pebbles on the pavement. Two forms huddled above her, faces in shadow beneath wide-brimmed baseball caps.

They grabbed her clothes. Tugged her coat aside. One knelt on her shins while the other straddled her waist. He pushed and prodded, then fumbled with the hem of her shirt. She screamed, and he covered her mouth and nose with the moist palm of his hand. She kicked her legs, tried to buck them off, but she couldn't breathe from the weight of their bodies trapping her to the ground. Her pulse throbbed in her neck, her body stiff with panic.

She felt the sharp point of a blade press into her cheek, and time seemed to stand still. She'd been lucky so far, stayed low, kept to herself.

It was a risk to be alone on the streets, but it was one she'd been willing to take. Now she wanted nothing more than to be anywhere but here. Fear lodged itself in her throat, made her want to cry and scream at the same time.

In the dark, she couldn't make out the face that swam into her line of vision. All sharp angles and deep hollows that made it look like a mask. Breath that smelled like skunk and onion. And then he spoke, and her stomach churned. "I see you, bitch." Shred.

Her skin went cold, and she again struggled against their weight, trying to free her arm or foot, anything, so she could dig her fingernails into his eyes, knee him in the nuts. Shred laughed, and the sound made her scream into his hand. She was trapped.

His fingers tugged at her coat, found the string around her neck, and pulled; the bag slid easily out from under her shirt like a traitor. Tears slid down her cheeks, but she couldn't cry. She felt everything and nothing, and with his weight on her chest she couldn't get enough air to keep her thoughts from scattering. Through black spots in her vision, she saw him slash through the cord, look inside, and grin.

Star moaned. Her money, all her money. As he shoved the bag into his pocket, she felt something expand inside her chest, pushing against her insides, squeezing her heart until it burst like a balloon. Her head fell to the side, and she closed her eyes. Her will to fight rushed out of her in a whoosh that left her limp. This was it; he would do with her whatever he wanted, take whatever he wanted, because he could. She was nothing but a street kid. Nobody cared what happened to her. Nobody. The truth of it slithered through her insides until she felt empty.

Cold air swept down and around them along with the sound of feet thumping on the pavement by her head. Her eyes flew open in time to see a round black object launch out of the night and hit Shred in the temple.

"Ow! The fuck?" he said, and kneed her in the groin when he stood. She whimpered in pain.

Shred and his buddy loomed above her and stared into the alley. With their attention diverted, she scrambled to her feet, gasping for air. She looked frantically down the dark street. If she ran, they'd follow, but for the moment she was free, and it buoyed her enough to make her want to fight. Maybe today Shred would be satisfied with just stealing her money. She straightened her spine and raised her fists, but then she noticed a little boy standing in front of Shred. Her scalp tingled. It was hard to tell in the dark, but it looked like his sweatshirt was red. She squinted. It couldn't be the same boy she saw with the old lady. He stood facing Shred, hands shoved into his sweatshirt pockets, head pointed down. He kicked something black and heavy between his feet like a soccer ball.

"You want to die or something, shithead?" Shred took a step closer, his hands balled into fists.

The boy darted behind a dumpster. Star inhaled sharply. *Run, kid!* She wanted to yell, but fear squeezed her throat shut. Shred glanced at her over his shoulder as though to remind her that he hadn't forgotten. A thin black line inked down the side of his face. She felt cold all over. He'd kill the boy for that.

When Shred approached the dumpster, the knife gripped in one hand, a shopping cart loaded with black trash bags appeared from the other direction. It wobbled erratically over the pavement before smashing into his knees. He sprawled forward and landed with a grunt on top of his buddy, his knife clattering to the ground. The cart toppled, scattering bags across the pavement. One split open, and the smell of unwashed wool coats, cotton gloves, and hats filled the air.

A hunched form appeared beside the cart, bearing a baseball bat raised high above his stooped shoulders. Star sucked in a breath and lowered her fists. Mel. The tails of Mel's black trench coat brushed the ground when he brought the bat down onto Shred's calf. Shred howled in pain.

Mel's eyes were huge beneath his tight black skullcap, red rimmed and watery, giving him the look of a charging bull. He bent down and picked up the knife, sliding it into his pocket. As Shred's buddy rose to his feet, Mel pulled the bat to the side, the tip swinging in the air, ready to take another swing. The guy took one look at the bat and Mel, and he ran, leaving Shred writhing on the ground alone.

Mel lowered the bat until it rested on the back of Shred's neck. He looked up at Mel through the corner of his eye, his back rising and falling with his rapid breaths. "That fucking hurt, man." He started to rise but halted, his eyes locked on something behind Star.

She turned. From the other side of the street, she saw two dark, hulking shapes advancing toward the three of them. The homeless men from the bench. Mel lifted his chin in their direction, and they halted. Shred noticed, and his head dropped to the pavement with what Star thought might be defeat. Mel lifted the bat and pointed it down the street. "Go," he said in a deep, cracked voice.

"Fuck, man, you're not my problem—she is." Shred scrambled to his feet, stumbling on his injured leg, and shot Star a burning look before limping into the night.

Her legs gave way then, and she sank to the bench. She let her fists relax until her fingers spread wide, and she stared at the way the blood flowed back into her hands, turning the flesh a light pink. She shoved her right hand into her pocket and to the very bottom, where her rock lay snug against the polyester lining. Her thumb sought its smooth surface and rubbed along a much-worn path. Thoughts crowded inside her head, pushing to get out. Shred. The boy. Her money. She tried to stitch the fragments together into something coherent. But it was all too much, and her mind emptied until she was numb.

She watched Mel collect the spilled garments and stuff them into trash bags, tossing them one by one into his cart. When he was finished, he ambled closer to her and carefully laid down a pair of gloves beside her on the bench. She stared at the gloves and listened to the cart rattle down the street, rusted wheels squeaking in the silence that followed.

The sun stabbed holes into the night sky, and from the street behind her came the screech of brakes, the puff of doors opening. The buses were running. Time to get up. She pulled her coat tight around her body, and with a final wary glance in the direction where Shred had run, she hurried down the street with no plan, her heart pumping so fast it left her breathless.

A cold breeze moved through her hair, lifting its tangled knots away from her face and bringing with it the heavy scent of chocolate. Instead of lifting her spirits, it assaulted her—clinging to the skin inside her nose, coating her throat, and stinging her eyes. Reminding her of everything she didn't want.

The whine of a city bus rumbled past, emitting a puff of black exhaust that knifed through the suffocating aroma. She leaned against a parking meter, staring at her scuffed boots over the ratty hem of her coat.

I don't want to be alone anymore.

She squeezed her eyes shut, shook her head. It didn't matter what she wanted. But the loud crunch of brakes weakened her resolve, and her eyes flew open in time to see a bus sliding to a stop a few feet from where she stood.

The 401.

She touched the pocket with the balled-up letter and crinkled bus ticket.

The bus doors inched closed. She curled her hands into fists, bit her bottom lip.

I'm tired of being alone.

Star lurched forward and ran, thumping on the glass door with one hand. The driver pressed his lips together as he eyed the ticket she held against the window. Despite the suspicious squint of his eyes, he opened the door. She jammed her ticket into the slot and stumbled to the very back, where she fell into a seat and rested her forehead against the greasy window, her heart pounding in her ears.

When the bus jerked forward, acid bubbled up from her throat, and she winced. What had she done?

~

An hour and a half later, the bus pulled to a stop in the middle of a two-lane street. The driver twisted around and said in a flat voice, "Pine Lake." She didn't move at first, frozen to her seat with her thoughts spinning. Outside the bus the world had never looked so different. A blue sky clear of buildings and billboards and power lines. Squat buildings with colorful painted signs surrounded by steep mountains carpeted in green pine trees. Her hands shook as she took out the note and read it one more time. Lucy knew something, and Star was going to find out what. She stuffed the letter inside her pocket and felt her back relax, filled now with a new kind of determination. Maybe it was time for her to stop running from the truth.

She made her way to the front, gave the driver a half-hearted wave, and stepped out of the bus. The quiet that followed seemed unnatural, devoid of the constant hum of people and cars and machines. She stood on a wooden sidewalk, breathing in cool air that tasted like water and wood mixed with the sour smell of her wool coat and unwashed hair. Star had never breathed in anything so clean or ever felt so filthy. She looked up the mostly empty street to see a wooden sign hanging over the walkway with the words MOUNTAIN MARKET.

A man in a red flannel shirt and work jeans passed by, barely containing his interest or the wrinkle of his nose. Star shrugged, shoved her hands into her pockets, and ran her fingers over the rock. She pulled out the envelope and scanned the letter one more time, straightened her shoulders, and began to walk down the uneven sidewalk.

CHAPTER FIVE

JESS

"Did you check the calendar today?" Lucy's voice came from behind her.

Jess glanced over her shoulder. "First thing this morning, but since the day looked free, I thought I'd give my bonsai trees a little attention." Jess stood in front of her bedroom window, where she had placed the trees. She held a pair of scissors in her hand, trying to mimic what she'd seen Mr. Kim do on pruning days. He'd made it look effortless and easy, but to her the tiny trees looked too delicate. Jess had no idea what she was doing. Chance's bonsai tree had never seemed to need anything other than the occasional watering and picking of dead leaves. Now, seeing Chance's tree side by side with Mr. Kim's trees, she realized just how poor a job she'd done. Instead of shiny leaves, the tiny branches had grown thin and bare. Compared to the others, it looked overgrown and gangly.

"She's coming," Lucy said.

"Ebee?" Jess said, half listening. She set the scissors down, picked up a wet cloth, and began cleaning dust off the small leaves. The bonsai as a whole weren't doing well; their leaves had turned dull, and she'd found a handful each morning on the table and floor. She couldn't bear the thought of watching them die because of her ineptitude. She rubbed a cloth over a dull leaf. The small plant had been a gift to Chance from one of his friends. Jess didn't know who. He had loads of friends at school, but he seemed to keep to himself at home, content to play in his fort, read books, and bake cookies with Jess. She felt a sharp pain in her chest. The last time they'd made cookies together had been on his birthday. It was the night he died. Something felt stuck in her throat, and Jess had to swallow hard.

"They don't look so good, Jess." Lucy stood beside her now, her black skirt swinging close to Jess's boot. Jess inhaled; she loved the way Lucy smelled, a mixture of orange peels and lavender that made Jess relax.

"I wonder if it's the altitude," she said.

Lucy pointed a long white finger, touched the thin trunk of Chance's bonsai. "What happened to this tree?"

Jess sucked in her bottom lip. She found herself sharing bits and pieces with Lucy, sometimes about Chance and sometimes just about herself in general. Lucy still hadn't asked anything more about her son than Jess was willing to offer, and Jess suspected that it was her way of giving her the space she needed until she was ready. Jess was growing very fond of Lucy and her ways. "That tree was my fault. I don't have much of green thumb, and I had no idea the level of care a bonsai needs until I met Mr. Kim."

Lucy didn't respond right away, and they stood in silence, contemplating the bonsai.

"It belonged to your son?" Lucy said quietly.

Jess stiffened, her mouth dry, and wrapped her arms tight across her chest, trying to push back the sorrow that filled her body like sand. "I found it after everything happened . . ." Her voice trailed off, ragged. She coughed and tried again. "It was next to the oatmeal raisin cookies on the kitchen table. A beautiful little plant on top of a birthday card someone had made out of pink construction paper, glitter glue, and stickers." She laughed softly, but it came out broken and sad. She ran a finger under each eye and continued to stare at the tree because she knew that if she met Lucy's gaze, she'd start to cry.

"It was from a friend," Lucy said.

Jess nodded. "I guess so."

"Was there a name?"

Jess was taken aback. An odd question that seemed intimate and irrelevant at the same time. "Um, no, it wasn't signed. It was just a picture of two stick people and a rainbow."

Lucy threaded her arm through Jess's and leaned heavily into her as though she'd grown suddenly very tired. "Yes, yes, that makes sense," Lucy said, but her words came out garbled.

Jess sprang into caretaker mode, relieved to end the conversation but also worried about Lucy. "I think you may need to sit down, okay?" She led the elderly woman down the hall and to the deep leather chair in her bedroom. Lucy sat down but clasped Jess's hands between her own, searching Jess's face with her blue eyes.

"She'll be here soon," she said. "And she's going to be hungry."

Jess gently pulled her hands out of Lucy's surprisingly strong grasp and patted her arm. "I'll make those cucumber and sprout sandwiches she likes." Jess had learned quickly that Ebee was a lifelong vegetarian after serving her a bacon, lettuce, and tomato sandwich the first time they met. "Why don't you rest for a bit until she gets here? I'll bring up one of your crossword puzzles."

The deep lines in Lucy's face relaxed. She nodded and settled back into her chair. Jess breathed out, relieved to see that whatever it was had passed. She tightened her ponytail and resolved to make Lucy a doctor's appointment. They needed to find out what was causing these episodes.

~

Lucy had ended up lying down, obviously exhausted, and since Ebee had yet to show up, Jess set to cleaning that morning's breakfast dishes. She loaded plates and silverware and a frying pan into the sink along with a squirt of dish soap. When the bubbles grew higher than the dishes, Jess slipped her hands into the hot water.

Lucy had asked twice more if Jess had checked the calendar, and it was still early morning. She'd gently reminded her that the calendar was blank. *Maybe Ebee has other plans,* she'd suggested.

Lucy had looked at her like she'd grown two heads and said, *Of course Ebee has other plans.* Jess had just smiled and shaken her head.

Cool air tickled the backs of her arms, like someone had left a door open. She yanked her hands out of the water, splattering soapsuds across the counter. Had she forgotten to close the front door after she took the trash out that morning? She turned from the sink and stopped cold. An uneasy feeling rippled across her skin. She tried to ignore it as she approached the calendar.

Lucy's small script filled the once-empty square. Jess blinked. She had been in the kitchen or close by for the last hour. When had Lucy written that? She shook her head—she must have been looking at the wrong square—and peered closer to read.

10:00, *will ring doorbell*

She picked up her phone, checked the time—9:59 a.m.—and laid it back on the counter. Before the screen dimmed, the time changed—10:00 a.m.

A shrill *rriiinngg* cut through the silence of the big house. She jumped, hand to her chest, finding it hard to get a deep breath. God, she was jumpy. She pulled her shirtsleeves down and made her way to the foyer. The inner door stood partially open. She frowned. She'd have to remember to pull it tight next time or Lucy's heating bills would go through the roof.

She stepped into the enclosed porch and with both hands took hold of the heavy outer door. Her breath frosted in the air, and her skin prickled at the sudden chill that permeated the unheated porch. It was May, but she was quickly learning that in the foothills the spring thaw moved on its own timeline. Through the colorful window she caught the outline of a small figure standing just outside the door. She hesitated, thinking of the boy at the market. *Don't be silly—the kid's not following you.*

She pulled open the door, gave a soft gasp. Star, the girl from the street, looking much the same as she had yesterday, if with darker circles bruising the skin beneath her eyes. Her wild hair sprang from her head in a cloud of tangles that fell across her face in clumps, and she wore clothes that were nothing more than layers of stained and ill-fitting rags, well past an expiration date.

Jess softened. The girl acted brave, with her chin held high and her arms crossed tight, but Jess could see apprehension etched in the crease between her eyes. What was she doing in Pine Lake? "Hello, Star," she said, and scrunched her eyebrows together. "What a surprise. I wasn't expecting you."

Star tightened her fist around the note. "Lucy invited me to come," she said from behind a strand of hair.

Jess gripped the doorknob tight. What was Lucy thinking? She could get in trouble for bringing a runaway kid here instead of calling social services. Or, Jess hoped, maybe that's what Lucy intended to do. Maybe she just wanted to get Star off the streets first. Jess pressed her lips together, stunned by her own inaction yesterday when all she had offered was a couple of phone numbers on an envelope. How could she have walked away? Her face burned with shame. At least Lucy's heart was in the right place.

Star shifted her feet and lifted her chin a little higher, and Jess felt something hard lodge in her throat. How had this girl survived even one night on the streets? She was small, tiny in fact, her features delicate and completely dwarfed by her mane of uncontrollable hair. From her size, she appeared to be no more than a child, but from her confidence and the way she held herself, straight backed, almost proud, Jess suspected she was older.

"Aren't you gonna say something?" Star's words were tough, but her voice quavered just the tiniest bit.

Jess's mind had emptied, and her skin suddenly felt too tight across her back. She rolled her shoulders and tried to relax. She knew she was being insensitive by not inviting Star inside right away, but something kept her hand on the doorknob, her body blocking the way in. She couldn't explain how a girl so small could make her uneasy, but something about her did. "How old are you?" she said at last.

"Fifteen."

The number hit her with a force that made her heart expand momentarily, releasing bits of sorrow stuck into its deepest cavities. This girl was nearly as old as Jess had been when her mom kicked her out. Had she looked this young when she became a mother?

The desire to be away from Star clutched at her throat, and a sharp pain at the base of her hand sent a tingling numbness creeping up her arm. She glanced down and stifled a gasp. Her nails had left puffy red marks across her wrist. She looked up to find Star staring at where the inflamed flesh bunched up and around silvery white scars.

Star's eyes widened. "Whoa," she said. "Is that what I think it is?" She reached out as though to touch her, but Jess pulled her sleeves down past her palms and crossed her arms.

When Star raised her eyes, Jess saw a softness touch her face that hinted at understanding. Jess stepped onto the porch, opening her mouth to say something kind or welcoming—what she should have done to begin with—but she was overpowered by an odor that filled the enclosed space. "Oh," she said, and covered her nose with one hand before realizing where the smell came from. "It's you—I mean, damn it, I'm so sorry," she said. "I didn't realize . . ."

Star's face hardened again. "No shit, Sherlock." Her deep-blue eyes stared defiantly back. "Homeless people stink."

A lightness bubbled up from the pit of Jess's stomach that erupted in a hiccup kind of laugh. Something bad had sent Star running to the streets, but it hadn't taken her sense of humor. She smiled at the girl, abashed. "I'm so sorry, Star. It's been that kind of week, I guess."

Star raised an eyebrow. "The kind where you laugh at sad teenagers?"

That only made her laugh again. Jesus, it felt like she'd come unglued. "Only the smart-ass kind," she said, and now Star smiled.

"She's here!" came Lucy's voice.

Jess turned. Lucy stood at the bottom of the stairs dressed in her usual black gown, her hair pulled into a bun at the base of her neck.

"Yes, what a surprise. Why didn't you tell me you'd invited Star to Pine Lake?"

Lucy smiled wide. "I told you she was coming."

Jess sighed and wondered briefly if Lucy's vagueness was purposeful. From the porch behind her, Jess heard Star sniff and shift her weight. She stepped away from the door and said in a low voice, "Shouldn't we call social services?" Lucy pressed her lips into a thin line. "Look, I'm not trying to be the bad guy here—"

"Then don't." Lucy walked around Jess and spoke to Star. "Come in, girl. You are very welcome here." She tilted her head to the side, her face clouding with what looked like confusion. "At least I think you are." She swatted at the air as though aiming for a fly, then gave Star a wide smile. "But that's something we can figure out later." Without another word, she disappeared down the hall and into the sitting room.

Star hadn't moved from her spot on the porch. It must have taken quite a bit of courage for the girl to come all the way to Pine Lake. Jess couldn't very well send her away, especially without trying to help her first. It was the right thing to do. Jess gave her a soft smile and a shrug, then opened the door all the way and gestured for her to enter. "Come in. Lucy's been waiting for you all morning. She said you'd be hungry.

I've got cucumber and sprout sandwiches—" Jess scrunched up her nose. Star was a teenager who probably hadn't eaten a proper meal in some time, not a sixtysomething vegetarian. "I can make you anything you like," she said.

Star hesitated, indecision clear in the way her eyes darted between the door and her feet. Then Jess heard her take a deep breath. "I'll eat anything," she said, and stepped inside.

CHAPTER SIX

JESS

Before joining Lucy in the sitting room, Jess made Star a turkey sandwich and had her eat it at the table in the kitchen while she made tea. Jess could tell Star was nervous from the way her knee jiggled up and down, and she figured it would calm her nerves to have something in her stomach. When Star was done eating, Jess picked up a tray loaded with a white ceramic teapot, three cups, a small bowl of sugar, and a tiny pitcher of cream and led Star to the sitting room, which was down the hall and to the right of the staircase. Lucy liked tea and had asked her to serve it formally whenever she entertained a guest. But halfway through the foyer, Star paused. Her eyes swiveled around the room, taking in the grand staircase and then the oversize brass chandelier with the etched glass shades that hung above her.

"Uh, wow," she said, her eyes so wide they seemed to take up half her face.

Jess laughed. Star's reaction wasn't far from her own when she'd first walked inside. "This place is something else, isn't it?"

"Fuc—" Star's face reddened. "I mean, heck yeah. Is Lucy like a queen or something?"

"Not that I know of, but I'll tell you what I do think."

Star narrowed her eyes as if she thought Jess was going to say something unpleasant. Jess felt a pang. The girl was guarded and suspicious. What kind of life had she lived? She smiled. "I think she's a really lovely person who seems to care about everyone."

Star dropped her gaze to the floor and mumbled, "Oh."

They entered the sitting room, where Lucy sat in her favorite wingback chair with the gold thread and smooth wood. Lucy pointed to a matching chair across from her. "Have a seat, Star." Star perched on the edge of the chair, her fingers stuffed underneath her legs, shoulders tense, as though she might shoot out the door at any moment.

Jess set the tray on a gleaming walnut coffee table and took a seat on the elegant sofa that stretched between the two chairs. The sofa was long and patterned in a cream fabric that Jess suspected might be silk and trimmed in a dark gleaming wood she'd polished just yesterday morning. She cringed when Star moved in her chair, worried that the girl's clothes would leave marks on the pristine furniture. But Lucy seemed unaffected by it, so Jess relaxed. If Lucy wasn't going to worry about it, then the last thing Jess wanted was to make the girl any more uncomfortable than she already was.

Star sat quietly in her chair, shoulders slumped, and stole glances around the room with the same wide-eyed look she'd had in the foyer. The silence between the three of them stretched long, and just as Jess began to wonder if she should start the conversation, Star piped up. "You look like a witch," she said to Lucy.

Lucy's face lit up, her lips pulling wide. "I've been told that before. Not to my face. Most kids don't have the courage. But behind my back they call me the Witch of Pine Lake." She laughed, smoothing out the wrinkles in her skirt, her fingers bone white against the deep black fabric. "You're here."

"You invited me." The toes of Star's boots rested on the floor, and her heels flopped back and forth.

"I did."

"Why?"

Lucy shrugged, sipped her tea. "I just did."

Jess asked the question she'd been wanting to know since she opened the door. "How did you get here?"

"The 401."

"What about your family?" Jess tried to keep her voice gentle, but she knew her questions sounded like an interrogation to Star, who seemed suspicious of adults. Jess glanced at Lucy to see her reaction, but Lucy gave her a placid smile, as though this had all been Jess's idea to begin with. "Or . . . do you have a caseworker we could call for you?"

Star's mouth hung open, and her eyes shifted from Jess to Lucy and back to Jess again. "I didn't ask to come here, you know." She pointed at Lucy. "*She* invited me."

Lucy's attention had drifted back to a crossword puzzle, and the sound of her pencil on the newspaper grated in the quiet that followed Star's words. The girl stared at Lucy, her face a tight mask that showed little of what she must be feeling. She was tough. Jess pulled at the sleeve of her shirt. Tough in a way that reminded her of herself when she was pregnant and living in a group home with absolutely no idea how she was going to support a baby. Jess couldn't help but feel a flutter of admiration for Star. She understood more than most what it took for the girl to have survived this far on her own.

"If you're calling social services, I'm leaving." Star scrambled to her feet. "I don't need this."

Lucy looked up from her crossword puzzle. "But at least have tea before you go," she said, and rose slowly to her feet. "I'm quite tired from our exciting morning. If you'll excuse me, I think I'll have a rest."

Jess felt her mouth drop open. She was as surprised as Star by Lucy's quick exit.

Star's hands curled into tight fists by her sides. "Wait! Please. You sent me that note." Her bottom lip trembled, and Jess realized she was nervous, maybe even terrified. Why? For allowing herself even the smallest strand of hope that someone cared? For thinking she could start over? Jess knew only too well that there was no reset button when it came to a shitty life. She clasped her hands in her lap and fought an urge to put her arms around the girl, because she had no words of encouragement when it came to shitty lives. Her only example was her own, and that was nothing but a merry-go-round of bitterness and unbearable loss.

Lucy paused at the bottom of the staircase. "The note." She drummed her fingers along the railing.

A soft pink stole across Star's cheeks. "About a second chance." Her voice quavered, but she stood with her feet planted firmly apart, back held stiff.

Lucy tilted her head the way she did when she was working on one of her crossword puzzles. "Chance," she murmured, and her eyes found Jess. Jess swallowed, trying to ignore the hard knot that had formed in her stomach.

Star folded her arms, lifted her chin. "You told me to come."

Lucy pursed her lips and nodded. "I did. But you'll have to have patience, dear. Sometimes I can be as blind as everyone else." She started up the stairs, her back stooped as she climbed. "Show her to a shower, please, Jess. She smells like death."

∼

"You doing okay in there?" Jess tapped on the bathroom door for what must have been the tenth time. She understood the need for a hot shower, especially for a street kid like Star. But after thirty minutes, Jess had a hard time believing there could be hot water left anywhere in Pine Lake. "Star?" she called.

The pipes in the walls popped.

"There are towels underneath the vanity and—" The door creaked open, and Star poked her soaking head out. Water dripped down her face and over her shoulders.

"Do you have scissors?" She tugged at a strand of hair, clean now, but matted into fuzzy knots.

"Sure, give me a minute."

"Here you are, dear," Lucy said, appearing at the top of the stairs.

Jess's eyes widened. "Lucy! You were just resting on your bed. I thought you were asleep."

"Yes, well, the girl in the bathroom needs these." She held out a pair of black-and-silver clippers with a thick rubber cord that trailed the floor.

Jess stared at the clippers, momentarily lost for words. Lucy had an uncanny ability to anticipate what a person might need or want. She'd done it with Jess on more than one occasion. When it came to Jess's past, Lucy just seemed to know what to say—or more importantly, what not to say. Jess shook her head and took the clippers.

"Her name is Star," Jess said.

"Whose, dear?"

Jess eyed Lucy for a long moment, trying to decide how much she was being played with this whole memory thing. Lucy smiled sweetly back.

"The girl in the bathroom," Jess said. "The one who smells like death?" Lucy blinked. Jess pursed her lips and continued. "The one you sent a note to and who's staying for tea? Her name is Star."

"Yes, well, give Star those clippers. She needs them."

Lucy turned, and Jess watched her make her way downstairs, grasping the railing as she navigated each step.

The bathroom door creaked open, and Star poked her head out. Her hair wasn't dripping all over the place anymore, but it looked as tangled as a bird's nest. Star raised her eyebrows when she spied the clippers and, without a word, grabbed them out of Jess's hand and closed the door.

CHAPTER SEVEN

STAR

Black hair filled the bathroom trash can. It looked like a small animal had crawled in and died. She studied her reflection in the mirror, running her hand along the side of her head. A girl who worked at the chocolate shop had a hairstyle like this, shaved on one side and long on the other.

It had taken forever to scrub the grime from her skin and under her nails, but based on how clean the girl in the mirror looked, it had been worth it. Star frowned at her reflection. It was familiar to her in a way that made her dig the jagged tips of her fingernails into her palms.

She looked like her father. Not in her features so much, although she thought she had his nose. Maybe. The details had blurred over the years. It was in the way her flesh stretched thin across jutting cheekbones, her eyes dull, the skin below bruised from lack of sleep. That's how she remembered her father. Tired and high.

Her eyes burned. The first time her dad had overdosed, she was seven years old. It was a memory that hadn't faded with time, no matter how much she wished it would. If she turned around, she was sure he'd be sprawled across the floor of this bathroom, his vomit squished beneath his pale cheek. She squeezed her eyes shut and tried to ward off the memory, but it bloomed anyway, staining her mind with images she'd rather forget. When she couldn't wake him, she had knocked on Mr. Ahmed's door, and he had sat with her in the hallway, his long legs folded under him like a giraffe, until the paramedics arrived. He spoke very little, but his stoic presence was a comfort anyway, even if Star remembered her insides shaking so bad she couldn't speak.

At the hospital, Star sat by her father's bed, where he lay hooked up to machines and tubes, his eyes closed. She sat in a plastic chair on the other side of the room because she didn't want to go near him. The only shoes she had at the time were a pink Dora the Explorer pair. They were so dirty that they looked brown against the gleaming linoleum. It made Star's face get hot. While the machines beeped and squawked, she licked her finger and tried to clean a black stain off the white rubber. It was the first time she remembered feeling embarrassed.

Later, a nurse moved her to a waiting area and sat her in a chair across from a uniformed policeman. *This nice officer has offered to sit with you until social services gets here.*

The policeman's eyes crinkled with his smile. *I heard you had a rough morning, kid,* he said, and when he moved, Star noticed how his face scrunched up like it hurt.

Star's father didn't have nice words to say about police officers, so Star knew to stay silent. *Shy?* the officer said. *I understand. You're smart to be wary of strangers. But see here*—he pointed to his badge, a gold five-pointed star pinned to his dark-green shirt—*this means I'm one of the good guys.* He shifted in his seat and groaned.

Star knew the sound of pain. *Are you hurt?*

He smiled. *That's why I'm here, kid, but it's nothing the doctors can't fix. Like your dad too. I heard them say he's going to be okay.*

Star shrugged, and her eyes trailed along the lines in his badge, following them up and to each point of the star.

Do you like my badge?

It's a star.

He chuckled. *Why, yes, it sure is.*

She avoided looking him directly in the eyes, but his voice was kind and sad, and it made her want to give him something. *My name is Star,* she offered.

You certainly don't meet many Stars. From the corner of her eye, she saw him hold out his hand. *My name is Ben.*

Her dad did get better that time, and social services didn't take her away from him. Thinking back to everything that had happened afterward, Star wished they had. It might have made all the difference.

She ran the cold water, splashed it across her face, and rubbed it vigorously with a towel, turning her cheeks pink. The last time she'd seen her reflection had been earlier that winter, when below-zero temps had forced her to sleep in a shelter. Come to think of it, that might have been the last time she'd showered too. She ran her hand up the soft skin of her arm, inhaled soapy perfume, and smiled. It felt good to be clean.

The sour smell of old cheese rose from the pile of her clothes. She glanced at the rags and scrunched up her nose. Jess was right—she did stink. She considered her choices. She didn't want to put those disgusting rags back on, but she sure as hell wasn't going to leave the bathroom wearing only a towel. The bathroom door rattled softly. Star wrapped the towel tighter. Her heart beat fast against her chest. She'd locked the door, but still.

A square yellow note lay on the floor, the edge of it wet.

You can keep the dress, it read.

"What dress?" she wondered aloud, and flicked the paper over to find more writing.

The one hanging on the outside of this door.

Star hesitated. What did she know about Lucy? Nothing, except that she lived in this tiny mountain town in a big, weird house. She thought of the note that Jess had given her. Lucy knew things about her. How? And what about Jess? At first Star had thought she was Lucy's granddaughter, but she acted more like a housekeeper. Jess didn't seem to fit into Pine Lake any more than Star.

A yellow dress hung from the crystal doorknob with a plastic bag looped around the hanger, and a pair of black Doc Martens sat on the floor. She reached through the crack and grabbed them before quickly locking the door. Another note had been stapled to the bag.

Leave your clothes outside the bathroom.
Jess will wash them for you.

Star stared at the pile of rags. What was the worst that could happen? If Jess stole her clothes, Star could always trade the dress in for something better at a secondhand shop. She shrugged, kicked her clothes into the hallway, and placed Lucy's note on top of them.

Her plan was to get dressed and eat as much food as they offered. Maybe she'd stay for one night. Treat Lucy, Jess, and Pine Lake like nothing more than an overnight shelter. She'd seen a dozen or so expensive-looking antiques since she entered the house. She could swipe one or two—the old lady would never notice. That would more than make up for the money that Shred had stolen.

A packet of new underwear and a sports bra lay inside the bag, along with a toothbrush, toothpaste, and floss. Lucy had been confident she'd accept her invitation. She ran her finger over the dress's stiff material. Star hadn't had a new dress since she was five and it was Easter. But that one had bows and tulle in spring shades of pink and green, and her mother had worn one with colors that matched. She remembered because she'd eaten a chocolate bunny from her basket and accidentally smeared chocolate across the skirt. Instead of getting angry with her, Star's mother had laughed and wiped the brown smudge off as best she could, then hugged Star and said, *Well, the silly bunny should have left a napkin too.*

Star blinked hard to keep her eyes dry and pulled the dress from Lucy over her head. Unlike her Easter dress, this one was simple and unadorned. She zipped up the side—a perfect fit. Star picked up the rock she'd left resting on the bathroom sink along with the note from Lucy and slid them both into her sock. The rock was cool and hard, but it was the only thing that felt familiar.

CHAPTER EIGHT

JESS

Jess poured the last of the tea into Lucy's cup and watched as she took a careful sip. "Would you like me to make a fresh pot?" she said, reaching for the cup.

"This is fine." Lucy held firm to her cup, shaking her head. "The girl will be down soon anyway."

"Star."

"That's right." Lucy smiled. "Star. What a beautiful name."

"It's probably a street name," Jess explained.

"Still beautiful." Lucy stared at Jess over the rim of her cup, her eyebrows raised.

Star entered the room, and Jess gasped, spilling her cold tea.

"Well, well," Lucy murmured.

Jess blotted her jeans with a cloth napkin, trying to hide her surprise at Star's dramatic transformation. Her overpowering cloud of black hair was gone, buzzed from the sides of her head until the soft pink of her scalp lay visible beneath the short black strands. She had left the top longer and wore it swept over to the left, where the tips grazed the top of her ear. She wore a mustard-yellow seventies-style minidress, oddly fresh alongside her severe haircut. Teen punk glam. Jess softened. Without the rags and all that hair, Star looked even smaller than before.

But the girl had not moved since entering the room, balancing on the balls of her feet as if prepared to turn and flee at any moment. She held her chin high. "The dress was on the door," she said.

"It looks very nice on you." Lucy nodded her approval. "Sit down."

Star tiptoed to the chair opposite Jess and Lucy, shoving her hands under her thighs. Her feet barely touched the ground.

Tears pricked Jess's eyes. The girl unearthed dark memories.

"You have no family, is that right?" Lucy asked, staring hard at the girl like she was solving one of her crossword puzzles. "All alone. An orphan. Little Orphan Star."

"Lucy," Jess said quietly, wondering at the woman's taunting words.

Star knitted her eyebrows together. "What of it?" she said.

Jess stared at her hands. Star looked vulnerable and young, but with a membrane of pure toughness. Like Chance. Jess had loved him with her whole being, but she hadn't always been able to provide for him the way he deserved. They'd lived day to day, and there had been times when that meant rice and beans for every meal or sleeping in two pairs of socks and a winter coat because she couldn't afford the heating bill. But Chance had never complained. Her throat closed, and she pushed to her feet. She shouldn't leave, not now, but she had to get away. "I'm sorry," she mumbled, and hurried past Star's chair. "I have to go . . ." The room blurred, and she touched the wall with her hands to steady herself, feeling their eyes follow her to the hall.

"It's not a street name."

Jess halted, her head hanging low, eyes squeezed shut. Her wrist ached from an itching so intense she wanted to rip her skin off, and a deep tiredness had seeped into her bones. "What did you say?"

"I said it's not a street name. It was my mother's name for me. She said I was her wish."

CHAPTER NINE

STAR

After Jess disappeared, Star turned around to find Lucy watching her. She stuck a thumb toward the ceiling. "She do that often?"

Lucy sat straight up in her seat, legs crossed at the ankles, hands folded in her lap, and stared at her with those eyes. It made the skin on the back of Star's neck prickle, and she doubted her intention to stay even one night with this woman. She turned her head to look out the window. It was early afternoon, probably still plenty of time to catch the evening 401.

"Your note." Star swallowed hard. "How do you know about my friend?"

Lucy raised her eyebrows, shook her head, then picked up a folded newspaper. "A Japanese art form." She looked expectantly at Star.

"What are you talking about?" The glimmer of hope she'd had this morning when she jumped on the bus, the faint belief that maybe something could go right for a change, grew cold. There was nothing for her here but a demented old woman.

"Six letters, dear." Lucy held out the paper, pointed to a row of boxes. A crossword puzzle.

Star shook her head. "I-I . . ." Her bottom lip trembled, and she felt her eyes get wet. *No, no, no.* She would not cry. She pressed her lips together, waited for the moment to pass, then stood straight and crossed her arms. "You know about the accident?"

Lucy shook her head.

"Then how do you—" Star's voice faltered, and she cleared her throat. "What do you want?"

Lucy sat back in her chair, resting her hands on the padded armrests. "Those are excellent questions, Star."

She waited for her to continue, but Lucy tilted her head and gazed intently over Star's shoulder. Her scalp tingled the way it might when someone stood just behind her. "Then why aren't you answering me?"

Lucy smiled, piling the loose skin of her cheeks into soft folds around her mouth. "Give me time, girl. I don't always understand what they want at first."

Cool air brushed across her neck. She shivered. "What who wants?"

Lucy waved a hand in the air. "Never mind that for now. But you can trust me, Star."

She snorted. "You want me to trust you? Then tell me why you want me to stay here. And how you know all those things about me. Tell me something."

Lucy nodded. "I can't tell you much yet, but I do know that the pieces are finally coming together, and I can promise you that it will all make sense in time." Without another word, she rose from the couch and swept out of the room, her black skirts swinging, leaving Star to ponder her cryptic words.

She should have left right then. Grabbed a handful of jewelry and sprinted for the bus stop. But she didn't. She sat as though glued to the chair, her stomach twisted into knots.

Lucy returned carrying a small plate crowded with buttered toast, fresh strawberries, and a ramekin of yogurt. She set it on an oval table beside Star, along with a cup filled to the brim with amber liquid. "Do you like tea?" Lucy said.

Star nodded and stared at the food. It looked too fresh, too clean—the butter glistening a creamy yellow, the strawberries impossibly red and plump. Her mouth watered, and her stomach growled. She wanted to hold the plate above her head and let the food fall into her mouth all at once. Instead, she forced her fingers to pick up a single piece of toast, and she took a small bite.

Lucy watched, her eyes bright with amusement.

Star ate until her plate was empty of everything but the leafy part of the strawberries. "What's wrong with Jess?" she asked at last.

Lucy hummed softly to herself.

"Lucy?"

"Yes?"

"About Jess? She ran out of here like she was mad or something. What's wrong with her?"

"I hardly know her." Lucy glanced past her into the hallway where Jess had been a few minutes ago. "But she lost someone too." She frowned.

A small, dark figure darted past the entrance to the sitting room, making Star cry out in surprise. Was there another kid living here? A puff of icy air tickled the exposed skin of her neck. Maybe Lucy was some kind of nut who collected street kids. Her full belly turned suddenly nauseated.

Lucy's shocking blue eyes widened. "You too," she said so quietly Star almost didn't hear her.

"Me what?"

"So angry." Lucy tapped her chin. "But with whom?"

Star's heart hammered in her chest, and she bolted to her feet. She needed to get out of here. "Listen, lady, I don't think—"

From somewhere above her head came a loud crash that shook the lights on the walls, and Lucy was halfway up the stairs before Star could utter another word.

CHAPTER TEN

JESS

Their voices drifted up the stairs and into her room, her only sanctuary here. She closed the door to shut them out and sat on the edge of the bed, her arms folded across her stomach, her eyes closed tight.

But the room felt stuffy and hot, and her wrist had begun to throb with the near-constant itching. She traced the scars with her finger and felt shame burn her skin.

It was at her lowest point, a year after Chance died, when she couldn't find the answers to the questions that plagued her or stop the nightmares that woke her every single night. Why did Chance leave the apartment? What was he doing outside on a night thick with snow and slush, the streets wet and slippery, in nothing but his pajamas with the red and blue and yellow Transformers? Too many unanswered questions except for one: At a moment when her son needed her the most, why wasn't Jess there? And then he was gone, and the absence of him and her failure to protect him were simply too much.

When she'd noticed the knife sitting out on the cutting board, she'd seen a way out, and then she was sawing at her wrist, tears streaming down her face as she cried and screamed and the blood snaked hot down her fingers until everything went black.

She woke up in the hospital, her wrist bandaged in white, to find her mother sitting beside the bed in a yellow chair that wobbled and squeaked when she shifted forward in her seat. It had been years since she'd last seen Joann, first because her mother wanted nothing to do with Jess and her mistake and then because Jess wanted nothing to do with the woman who'd abandoned her and her son.

Why, Jess? Her mother had coughed, a phlegmy, hoarse sound that filled Jess's mouth with the sour taste of cigarette smoke.

Leave. Jess turned her head to the wall, pulling the blanket tight around her body like a shield.

I tried to be part of your lives, Jess, but you kept me out. Maybe if you'd let me into Chance's life, maybe none of this would have happened.

Jess's stomach burned with a rage that curled her fingers into claws. She yanked her body around and for the first time looked at her mother. Hair more gray than brown, eyes sunken into dark circles, her thin lips a straight line. Jess's body vibrated with a festering rage. She threw the covers to the floor and stood, not bothered by the cotton edge of her hospital gown flapping against the backs of her thighs. She lifted one arm and pointed to the door. *Get out.*

Her mother hugged her bag to her chest, pursed her mouth. *You're a suicide risk, Jess. You need me now. They say you can't be trusted to be alone.*

All these years later, Jess could still feel the way her anger had crawled just under her skin, biting at her until she was screaming in a voice that grew higher in pitch and made her eardrums tingle. *Get out, get out, get out!* Her screams sent two nurses rushing through the door, hands stretched in front of them like they intended to tackle her. Joann backed out of the room, and suddenly Jess's bones felt too heavy for her body and she crumpled to the bed, curled into a tight ball, and closed her eyes. It was the last time she saw her mother.

A stinging sensation in her arm brought Jess back to her room in Lucy's house with the window that overlooked the sparkling lake and the warm wood planks that soaked up the afternoon sun. She looked down, shocked to find her wrist a mass of red lines from her incessant scratching, and pressed her cool palm over the hot marks. It seemed to itch more now than when it had been healing.

She pulled her sleeve down to hide the scars. The only reason she didn't finish what she'd started was because of Chance. If she died, then her son would truly be gone. Who else would remember the boy who'd loved Matchbox cars and snuggling and eating cookies after bad dreams? She pressed her arms into her belly, waiting for the urge to throw up or cry to pass, and when it finally did, she rose from the bed, pulled her ponytail tight, and smoothed her shirt. She couldn't hide up here forever. A homeless girl who'd experienced God knows what was downstairs in a yellow dress, and she was probably starving. And Lucy seemed to be having quite a few episodes today. Jess needed to get back to work.

She crossed the room and noticed the top drawer of her dresser hanging halfway off the tracks, the clothes inside crumpled and unfolded. She rubbed the back of her neck. *Odd.* She was a tidy person who kept her room clean and her clothes folded. Had Lucy been in her room? When she moved to push the drawer in—she'd have to refold everything later—she noticed Chance's picture, the school one, sitting on top and in the center of her messed-up clothes. Her hands shook. She had been intending to buy a new frame for it, but so far her days had been full. She grasped the drawer's delicate crystal knobs and tried to push it back in, but it was stuck and wiggled loosely like it was off the track. She bent down to figure out how to fit it back on and froze when the skin across her exposed neck prickled like she was being watched. She twisted around, small white spots, like tiny feathers, flitting at the edges of her vision. Empty. She shook her head—of course the room was empty—and with a forced laugh turned back to fix the drawer. But she must have unintentionally pulled it out too far; before she knew what was happening, the entire drawer slid off the tracks and tumbled out, landing hard on the floor and upending her clothes.

"Damn it," she said, and as she bent to pick everything up, the door was flung open.

CHAPTER ELEVEN

STAR

Lucy had already disappeared up the stairs. Man, that old woman could move. Star darted from the sitting room and toward the front door. Her hand rested on the knob, but she couldn't make herself turn it. She chewed on her lip. If she left now, she could be on a bus back to Denver soon. Besides, Jess had probably already called social services.

But the image of Shred hovering above her last night, his knees pinning her to the ground, stopped her. She shuddered at her pathetic helplessness. Whether she stayed or returned, it seemed like everyone but her got to decide her future. Her hand released the doorknob. *Fuck it.* She'd hang here, fill her belly with food, and split when she was ready to go.

Muffled voices filtered down from the second floor, and Star felt a magnetic pull lure her up the stairs and to an open door at the end of the hallway. She peered into the room.

Jess knelt on the floor with her back to a tall dresser. An upended drawer lay beside her, clothes strewn across a ruby-and-navy-blue wool rug.

"What were you going to do?" Jess said to Lucy. "Try to pick me up yourself?"

Lucy sat on the bed. "You looked like you needed a hand."

Jess pushed to her feet, and Star noticed the color had drained from her cheeks. "Thank you," she said to Lucy in a gentler voice. "But you're one of the only eighty-five-year-olds I know taking nothing but vitamins. I don't want to add pain pills because of my clumsiness."

Star snorted. "Yeah, 'cause when the painkillers stop working, it's heroin all the way."

Both Jess and Lucy turned to stare at where she hovered just outside the room. The silence that followed made Star shift her weight from one foot to the other. Jess's eyes widened, and her mouth hung open slightly. Lucy raised an eyebrow.

Star sucked in her cheeks. These two were a pair. Old maid Lucy and bipolar Jess.

Star moved into the room and lifted the drawer, sliding it back into the dresser. When she picked up a thin blouse, something fell from its folds. She squinted down at it. A picture. But she caught only a glimpse of the back of it before Jess snatched it off the floor.

"I got this," Jess said in a strangled voice, and stuffed the clothes into the drawer.

"How did the drawer fall out?" Star asked.

A long piece of Jess's brown hair had pulled out of her ponytail. She pushed it behind one ear, blowing out a forceful breath. "It had shifted off the track somehow, and it fell when I was trying to fix it. Just lost my grip on it, I think." She bent over to pick up a shirt from the pile and began to fold it.

Star figured Jess wasn't too old. But since she'd first stepped through the front door just a few hours ago, she hadn't seen the younger woman smile much. Something told her that was normal. When Star turned to leave, she caught sight of three bonsai trees on a narrow table behind Jess. Her breath caught in her chest, and for a moment she couldn't speak. When she noticed Jess staring at her, she pointed at the small plants. "Your bonsai trees are dying."

Jess's shoulders slumped when she looked at the trees. "Yeah, I noticed," she said with a frown.

"Bonsai! Aha!" Lucy chirped, and pulled her crossword puzzle from a pocket in the folds of her dress. She scribbled across the paper with her pencil.

Star shook her head and almost smiled. Lucy was crazy. Then she walked over to the table and looked closely at the trees. "Your problem is that they're either getting too little sun . . ." She pressed a finger into the soil of one. Dry. "Or too little water." A few dead leaves lay scattered across the table. "Or both." Jess was looking at her as though she'd spoken an alien language. Star's gaze fell on the one in the middle; it looked different from the others, bigger, scrawnier, and less full of the tiny leaves. She rubbed her finger along the smooth trunk. A static shock ran through her hand, and she jerked it back, her heart beating a little too fast. That was weird. "That one is overgrown." Jess studied her, head tilted, and Star shifted her weight, wishing she'd kept her mouth shut. "My mom loved bonsai," she said simply, hoping nosy Jess wouldn't ask a million questions now. She didn't like to talk about her mom; it hurt too much.

Jess blinked. "Oh, Star. I'm . . . I—"

Star tensed, tried to come up with something sarcastic to say to change the direction the conversation had taken. But Lucy very loudly cleared her throat, interrupting whatever might have come next, and Star exhaled with relief.

"Star!" Lucy said, and rose to her feet. Star could have sworn she heard her bones pop.

"Yeah?"

"I have a job for you." Lucy took Star's hand and led her down the stairs without a word to Jess.

"A job?" Star pulled her hand away. "What kind of job?"

"Not just one job, dear." They stopped in the foyer, and Lucy turned to face her. "But one main job." She winked. "It's Tuesday. I like to walk the lake on Tuesdays."

Star waited for her to continue, but Lucy was busy rummaging through a hall closet. She pulled out a long black coat and slid an arm inside, twisting around to reach for the other half. It kept slipping down her back. Watching Lucy struggle with the simple act of putting on her coat gave Star a twinge, and she took hold of one side and held it out. Lucy peered at her over one shoulder, smiled, and slid her other arm through.

"You want me to walk with you?" Star said.

"On Tuesdays."

"You want me to walk with you on Tuesdays?" Star repeated. This morning she'd been nobody. Now here she stood in the foyer of a massive and ancient home, in a town she'd never heard of, clean, not hungry for the first time in forever, wearing a dress, and taking an old lady for a walk.

"Yes, Tuesday. But only on Tuesday." Lucy reached back into the closet and pulled out a worn green army coat, handing it to Star. "You'll want to take this. May's always colder than it looks."

"What about Jess?" Star asked as she opened the door. "Doesn't she walk with you?"

"No, of course not. I hardly know her."

They walked side by side down the pockmarked cement steps to the dirt sidewalk. Below them and past the town, the icy lake shimmered, reflecting the green of the pine trees that surrounded its banks. Beyond the trees, Star could make out the tips of even higher mountain peaks, frosted white with snow.

She turned to Lucy. "But you hardly know *me*."

Lucy smiled. "Then stay, and we can all get to know each other better."

～

They walked down the hill to the corner on Main Street and stopped by the Mountain Market just as a small white van with the words FOOTHILLS TAXI pulled to a stop in front of them. A town this small had a taxi service?

The driver's door popped open, emitting a tall, skinny kid with curly hair and a wide grin. He jogged around the van and opened the front passenger door with a flourish, his arm extended, head bowed.

"Lucy," he said in a deep, formal voice, and took her hand.

"Jeremy." She acknowledged him with a nod and entered the van with her head held high.

"And who is the young lady accompanying you today?" the kid asked, giving Star a quick glance.

"This is Star from the city," Lucy answered. "She's my Tuesday girl."

He gave a solemn nod. "'Bout time you had a Tuesday girl." He flashed Star a quick smile before opening the sliding door for her. "Nice to meet you, Star." The door slid shut, leaving Star to wonder whose tripped-out dream she'd stumbled into.

They drove a short distance through town, giving her a chance to see Pine Lake again. It felt as though she'd landed in the Old West. Squat, wood-frame buildings with rusted metal roofs ran along either side of the main street. Covered walkways lined the two-lane road, with colorful signs boasting a coffeehouse, saloon, and gift shops.

They drove past a small dam situated at the far end of Main Street. Water from the lake poured over in icy streaks, falling into the pond in arcs of misted rainbows. Star sighed. She could be happy here. But the thought of being happy anywhere hit her like a blow to the stomach.

Jeremy pulled the van into a parking spot near the lake house. He jumped out and opened Lucy's door with as much dramatic flourish as before. He was younger than she'd guessed at first, not much older than Star, but old enough to drive. Her door slid open, and he extended a hand to her. She ignored it and climbed out, joining Lucy.

"Happy Tuesday," he said.

"Same to you," Lucy responded.

"Take care of our girl, Star." He winked and hustled back to the van.

"O-kay," Star mumbled to his back. People in the mountains were weird.

They stood alone in the middle of a deserted trail. Had she ever been to the mountains before? A vague memory came to her of snuggling into her mother's lap in front of a hot campfire, hands sticky from marshmallow, a million stars sprinkling the sky above. She could almost taste the sweetness of melting chocolate on her tongue mixed with the sharp tang of bug spray. Then it evaporated, leaving Star colder than before. She glanced into the dark woods surrounding the lake. The openness of the mountains made her feel conspicuous, exposed, and her back itched from a strong sense that something lingered between the trees. Maybe she actually preferred city life. She shrugged. It would make leaving that much easier.

Lucy had ambled ahead, and her stooped figure moved at an unexpected clip. Star hurried to catch up. They followed a gravel path that cut around the boathouse to the wider dirt trail circling the lake. It felt good to stretch her legs, and the uneven ground made for a challenge she hadn't had during her months on pavement.

She studied Lucy from the corner of her eye. Today she wore another black dress that buttoned up to her neck with a skirt that brushed the ground. The dark color did nothing for her skin, pale as it was and littered with age spots. And her hair. Star's grandmother had died when Star was a baby, and the only old people she knew were drunk, homeless, and mostly mean. She didn't know what to make of Lucy, who was the most bizarre person Star had ever met. And considering Star's circumstances, that was saying something.

They walked in silence. Star had little experience with old people and had no idea what to say. They rounded the farthest point of the trail where the path switched back in the direction of the boathouse.

Lucy walked on, placing one foot in front of the other as she carefully navigated the uneven trail.

Star surprised herself by talking first. "Jeremy's . . . interesting," she said.

"Who, dear?"

"The kid who drove us here."

"Ah yes, Jeremy. Always there when I need him."

"So you don't drive anymore?"

Lucy turned her head sharply and stared narrow-eyed at Star. "That's the right question."

"Okay."

"But you're right, I don't drive anymore."

"Because you're old?"

Lucy laughed then, a sound so light and airy it made the corners of Star's mouth lift.

"Yes and no," she said. She began to walk again, but her pace had slowed, and Star noticed how she worried the hem of her sleeve with her fingers, rubbing back and forth across the cuff. "I stopped driving because something bad happened with my car."

"What happened?"

Lucy waved a hand in the air. "Nothing, really. I pushed the gas instead of the brake and took down my mailbox." She sniffed. "Benjamin thought it best if I retired from driving after that, and I suppose he was right, but . . ." She trailed off, her eyelids lowered, and for a second Star thought she'd fallen asleep in the middle of their conversation.

"Lucy?"

A look of confusion drew Lucy's eyebrows together. "I didn't see it coming when I should have. Mother always said I could be blind when I wanted to be."

Star waited for her to say more, but Lucy lapsed into silence, her eyes trained on the path, her back rounded a fraction more than before. She suddenly looked very old.

The conversation stalled there, and when they came to the end of the loop, Lucy took a seat on a bench and looked out over the lake. Star followed her gaze, and her eyes widened at the sight. The icy water sparkled like someone had spilled a million diamonds across its surface. Flapping wings sounded above her, and Star gasped when she saw a big black bird with a long skinny neck skim across the still surface. It dove gracefully through patches of melting ice and into the water, disappearing briefly before it burst out with a watery spray a few feet away.

After the bird flew beyond the lake, Star turned back to Lucy, who sat straight backed on the bench. Star shifted her weight from one foot to another. The silence was both awkward and comfortable, but Star was growing impatient. She shook her head and blew out through her teeth. "Why am I here?" she blurted out.

Lucy sat very still, her cheeks flushed a faint pink from the walk, and Star wondered if she'd heard the question at all or was ignoring her. She mentally reviewed places along Main Street that would do as a temporary bed.

"Ever since I was a very little girl," Lucy said, "I could see them. But it was my mother who taught me how to understand them."

"Understand who?" She slumped onto the bench. Getting a straight answer out of Lucy obviously took some time.

Lucy turned to her. "The loose ends, of course. That's how I like to think of them."

"I don't understand."

Lucy studied her. "Of course you don't, dear. It's my gift to see them and my job to help. Sometimes it's unfinished business or forgiveness." She frowned. "Sometimes they want revenge." Her lips flattened into a thin line. "I don't like those." She sighed. "But I've learned to be patient with the things I don't understand because often all that is needed is time."

"Time for what?"

Her eyes were like blue fire, and her smile made Star feel important in a way she couldn't explain. "It takes time for all the loose ends to be in one place, but once they are, things tend to move very quickly."

Star peered over her shoulder toward the parking lot, hoping to catch sight of Jeremy or his van. Lucy sounded mental. And Star didn't care about her "loose ends." She cared about what Lucy knew about her and Jazz. "The letter you sent me. You know about the accident. You know I was there." Saying it out loud stung, and she blinked rapidly, turning her face toward the lake. "How do you know about that?"

Something brushed across her wrist, and Star looked down to see Lucy's fingers covering her hand. Her skin was smooth, soft as velvet, and the tenderness of her touch scratched at the hard layer that protected Star's heart. She pulled her hand away and stuck it under her thigh.

"I don't know much yet, except that this one is yours," Lucy said.

"What's mine?"

"It's your loose end." Lucy's hand returned to her lap. "And his. And hers. And . . . it's hard to see. Something's different about it . . ." She trailed off, and Star noticed how Lucy's jaw had slackened, her eyes faded to a dull blue.

"Are you okay?"

Instead of answering, Lucy slipped her fingers into a pocket hidden among the folds of her dress and pulled out a handkerchief. The old woman's skinny forearm trembled when she patted the cloth to the back of her neck. Only then did Star notice a thin sheen across her forehead. Her pulse sped up. What would she do if Lucy passed out?

"I think we should call someone," Star said. "You should get back to your house and—"

"I don't always understand myself, you see," Lucy said.

A hint of color returned to the folds of the woman's wrinkled cheeks, and Star exhaled.

"Since I was a very little girl, I just knew." She laughed softly. "I was only eight years old when I told my mother that I'd helped Mrs. Holland from the bank tie her shoelaces. Oh, how she laughed, and she said that's exactly what we do."

"Huh?" What the heck was the old woman talking about? Star was beginning to think she was even crazier than she looked.

Lucy waved a hand in the air. "Oh, not literally, dear. Mr. Holland was a real scrooge, and after he shot himsel—" She pursed her lips and gave Star a look. "Well, let's just say that after he was gone, Mrs. Holland was in quite a financial predicament. So I told her where he'd buried all their money." The wrinkles in Lucy's face seemed to smooth out as though the memory made her younger. She winked. "Under his mother's headstone, if you're curious. So, ever since then, that's just how I've seen it. Because once I understand a person's loose ends, well, to me they're just like untied shoelaces, and I'm sure you can imagine that."

"Imagine what?"

"That sooner or later you'll trip."

Star fidgeted in her seat. "I don't understand, Lucy."

Lucy blinked. "Don't worry," she said, and let out a soft grunt when she pushed to her feet. "Sometimes the answers only make sense after all the questions have been asked." She looked past Star. "Ah, just in time."

Star turned to see the Foothills Taxi van pull into a parking spot on the other side of a low wooden fence. Even from this distance she could make out Jeremy's tall form and mop of curly hair in the driver's seat.

Lucy walked toward the van, paused, and turned around. "Are you coming?"

Star sucked in one side of her cheek. An afternoon bus would put her back in Denver by nightfall. She could leave this weird woman who knew too much, and her sidekick who asked too many questions, and the house full of nice things. Pine Lake was beginning to feel less predictable than her life on the streets. Except the thought of going back made her wrap her arms tight across her stomach, and she slumped forward. "I need you to tell me something first. How do you know about the accident?"

Lucy looked skyward, blew air out of her mouth. "Such a good question, Star. But I don't know much, only what I read in a newspaper article years ago. I just knew that it was important somehow." Lucy smiled. "That's how it works for me sometimes."

"What newspaper article?"

"The one about the accident. It was in the *Denver Post.*"

Star dug her fingers into her thighs. She was too young to remember everything that had happened that night. Was it possible that someone had seen her? "How can you remember an article from eight years ago?" It didn't make sense—nothing made sense—and the thing that bothered her the most also made the least sense. "Why do you even care, Lucy?"

Lucy shrugged. "So many great questions, and I'm really sorry that I can't give you a better answer, Star. I simply don't have enough information yet, but if you're patient, I will answer you in time. For now, I can offer you food, safety, and a place to stay for however long you'd like. If you can be okay with that, I'd very much enjoy your company."

A breeze rippled across the water, moving through the branches of the trees above her. Star tilted her head, closed her eyes, and felt the sun trace the lines of her face, then filled her lungs with the musk of water and earth. It was getting late, and while her mind spun with questions and uncertainty, she knew for certain that finding a new bench to sleep under was always easier in the daylight. She sat up straighter. One night. She'd leave first thing in the morning.

Star opened her eyes, ran a hand through her short hair, and jumped to her feet. "I liked being your Tuesday girl," she said. "But I'm really curious about Wednesday."

CHAPTER TWELVE

JESS

Jess thrummed her fingers in a nervous staccato on the kitchen table, her knee jiggling up and down. She'd finished straightening her room and had come downstairs expecting to see Lucy at the kitchen table working on a crossword puzzle. But she was nowhere to be found. Jess checked all the rooms, even peeking into the attic and tiptoeing into the basement. But there was no sign of Lucy or Star. Where could they have gone?

She spied the silent phone. The receiver was in her hand, and her fingers dialed 9-1-1 before slamming it back down. What was she doing? Reporting that Lucy had left the house without telling her? She let her head drop into her hands. In one day, a homeless girl had appeared on the doorstep and Lucy had vanished. What would the girl do if Lucy had another one of her spells and needed help?

The keys to Lucy's Cadillac hung on a hook by the door. Jess grabbed them as she headed outside. She'd drive around town until she found them. They couldn't have gone far.

But when she walked outside, her pulse quickened at the blare of a siren drifting up from Main Street. The siren grew louder until a white van pulled to a stop by the front walkway, followed by a police cruiser.

The two vehicles crowded the small road, lights flashing on the squad car as the whine of the sirens slowed to a stop.

A tall boy popped out of the van and jogged over to open the passenger-side door. There was Lucy. Jess almost doubled over with relief. The boy took Lucy's hand and helped her step down.

"Lucy!" she called. "Where did you go?"

The door of the police car opened, and a tall middle-aged officer got out. He strode up the driveway and fell in step next to Lucy. "Is everything okay?" he said to her.

Lucy smiled up at him. "Benjamin Watts, what a nice surprise!"

The three of them reached the bottom of the porch steps, where Jess stood trying to make sense of what had happened. Had Lucy been hurt? Jess's pulse sped up when she realized who was missing. Star. Had she taken off? Hurt Lucy in some way? She scanned the area. There, in the van, was the girl, hunched down so low Jess almost missed her. Obviously hiding. The boy seemed to notice, too, because he'd fallen back to where the van was parked and stepped in front of the window. His tall form hid her from view.

"I'm here because you called 9-1-1, Lucy," the officer was saying.

Lucy sniffed. "I did nothing of the sort. It's Tuesday. Jeremy took me to the lake for my walk."

Jess felt her cheeks warm. She cleared her throat. "Sorry, Officer, that was me. I didn't know she'd left, and I got worried."

The officer seemed to notice Jess for the first time. "And you are?"

Lucy answered first. "Jess is my live-in caregiver."

Benjamin frowned and studied Jess for a moment too long. She crossed and uncrossed her arms, feeling like she'd done something wrong. He turned to Lucy. "I didn't realize I'd been fired," he said.

Lucy touched his arm. "Now, Benjamin, you have a job." She tapped his badge. "An important one too." There was real affection in Lucy's voice that made Jess realize that Lucy and the officer knew each other well. "I couldn't burden you any longer with my shenanigans."

Benjamin gave her a half smile. "You're not a burden." He eyed Jess again, his face friendly enough, but the lines around his mouth were tight. "You're not from around here." He made it a statement, an obvious fact, she supposed, in a town this small.

"Denver. I was just passing through, but my car broke down, and then Lucy offered me a job. So, well . . ."

His eyes narrowed, and Jess was struck by how ridiculous it all sounded. If she were him, she'd be suspicious too. But then his face relaxed, and he laughed. The sound caught her off guard. He glanced behind him. "That sounds like our Lucy, doesn't it, Jeremy?"

Jeremy nodded from his place by the van and grinned. "It sure does."

Benjamin rubbed his chin with one hand. "So that's your beater that's been parked outside the market all week?"

Jess nodded, tightened her ponytail. "It needs to be towed. I just didn't have enough . . ." She trailed off, humiliated to have to admit how desperate she'd been and also surprised at how quickly she'd settled in here. She hadn't thought about the broken car or leaving Pine Lake in days.

"But you fix cars, Benjamin," Lucy said, and began to rummage in the pocket of her dress. She pulled out a handkerchief, a pencil, and finally her crossword puzzle. She squinted at the paper. "Eight letters," she mumbled. "No, that can't be." She looked up at Ben, and Jess noticed how her eyes had grown dull and her shoulders sagged as though the effort of standing had suddenly become too much. Jess gently took her by the elbow. Poor Lucy was exhausted. "Maybe we can go inside and have some tea, Lucy?" She glanced at Benjamin. "Would you like a cup, Officer?"

Benjamin had taken off his hat and held it between his hands as he studied Lucy, his forehead creased with concern; then he nodded. "That would be great, but please call me Ben."

~

Inside, Jess followed Lucy to the sitting room and helped her get settled on the small couch. She peered through the tall front windows to the driveway outside. Jeremy hadn't moved, standing like a soldier in front of the van. Jess shook her head. "Who's the boy?" she asked.

"That's Jeremy. He gets me where I need to go."

"Like to the lake for a walk?" Jess said with the tiniest hint of sarcasm. The least Lucy could have done was to leave Jess a note before she left the house with two teenagers.

"Exactly," Lucy said with enthusiasm. "Always there when I need him."

Jess bit her bottom lip, deciding to let the matter go for the moment. She'd been working for Lucy for only a week, so she couldn't expect to know all of the woman's routines yet.

"Tea for our guest, Jess?"

"I'm sorry?" She turned away from the window. Ben had joined them, standing in the doorway, his shoulder resting against the frame. She stiffened when she realized why Star was hiding. A police officer would be obligated to call social services. She glanced out the window—the van had disappeared.

"I said, why don't you make a pot of tea?" Lucy pointed toward Ben. "For our guest."

"Of course," Jess answered. "Tea." And she headed to the kitchen to brew her second pot of tea in one day.

CHAPTER THIRTEEN

STAR

The minute the van pulled up to the house, they'd been tailed by a police car with sirens wailing. She pressed her arms into her stomach, told herself not to panic. Jess had called the cops, of course. Her betrayal stung, but what had Star expected? Jess owed her nothing. And Star knew better than to expect anything more from an adult.

As soon as Jeremy stopped the van, she flung herself toward the door. She'd run back to Denver if that's what it took to get away.

"No, Star." Lucy's calm voice eased the panicky feeling that ran circles in Star's stomach. "He's not here for you. Stay in the van."

She let go of the door handle and hunched low. Her muscles tingled, making it hard to sit still.

Lucy eyed Jeremy, who was staring at Star with his mouth hanging open. Star glared back. "My door, please, Jeremy," Lucy said.

Without a word, Jeremy hopped out of the van, but Star noticed how he stood in front of the window, hiding her from the cop. Did he know how much she wanted to run? A few minutes later, Lucy, Jess, and the policeman disappeared inside the house.

"Coast is clear," Jeremy said through the glass now. "Mind if I come in?"

"It's your van," she said, and pushed up from her crouch to sit on the bench seat.

Jeremy slid into the seat, started the van, and without a word drove quite a distance down to where the road ended, then turned the van around so that it faced Lucy's house up on the hill. "We can see when he leaves from here," Jeremy explained.

Star ripped the top layer of a fingernail off with her teeth.

"I'm coming back there," he said, and without waiting for a reply climbed into the back, settling his tall frame beside her on the fabric bench. His long skinny thighs rose high above the seat, his knees jammed into the back of the driver's seat.

Star bit off another nail and twisted around so that her body faced away from Jeremy.

"You know you've got loads of bacteria underneath your fingernails?"

Star halted midbite and turned to stare at him.

"Not yours specifically. In general." He held his hands out in front of him, peering underneath his short nails. "Even mine." He waggled his long fingers, and that's when Star noticed his nails: painted with a clear coat, tiny white pieces of glitter embedded in the polish. "Too much?"

She shrugged.

"Then maybe I can paint yours sometime," he said. "I'm in desperate need of a girlfriend."

Star stiffened and inched her hand toward the door handle.

"Not that kind of girlfriend, Star." He half smiled, his jaw tense.

She shrugged. "Okay." So he was gay. What did she care?

"It's a small town," he said, and peered dramatically over his shoulder, continuing in a terrible country accent. "Some folks say there's a camp, deep in the woods, where they send kids like me. It's called Camp WeCanChangeYou. They have crafts."

She laughed, and the sound was so foreign to her ears she almost choked. "I guess it's a good thing I hate crafts."

He smiled and relaxed into the seat.

"But I don't care," she said, crossing her arms.

He looked at her for a long moment. "Thing is, there aren't kids like you around here." He studied his nails. "I should know."

She bristled, sat up straighter in her seat. "Like me?" What could he possibly know about her?

He held his hands up. "Easy there, Tuesday. It's not hard to tell you don't live here. And there's something about you—an edge, I guess. The kids here, well, most of them are as stereotypical 1960s as they come. So I thought I'd just lay it out there, see if my theory about city kids is true."

"What theory?"

"That you're not small-town stupid."

She took another nail in her teeth and, while she stared at him, tore it off. He smiled back. "Plus, if Lucy likes you, well, that's endorsement enough for me. Lucy knows how to pick the good ones."

They sat for a few minutes. Star didn't know what to say to this boy. He was so different from any of her foster siblings or the kids on the street. Weirdly open. And from the way he'd protected her from the eyes of that cop, he'd obviously guessed she had a reason to hide. But he didn't pepper her with questions. She sat up a little straighter in her seat. "How come you're not in school?" she ventured.

"I graduated early."

"You graduated early so you could drive a taxi?"

His eyes narrowed. "How come you're afraid of cops?"

"That obvious, huh?"

His floppy curls danced as he laughed. "Nah. Weird caregiver lady definitely noticed, but I think Ben was focused on Lucy."

"You know him?"

"Small town, remember?"

Star didn't respond. She'd never lived in a town as small as Pine Lake. Once she'd lived in a suburb with green lawns and a park, but that had been when her mom was alive.

"So cops scare you?"

She sighed. "They don't scare me," she said, and let it drop. They'd never rescued her from a single one of her abusive foster homes, though. And they'd dragged her back every time she ran. But that wasn't any of Jeremy's business. "What's your story?" she said, trying to change the subject.

"You want to know my story?" He threw his hands up in the air with a smile. "Why not? Who can't trust a Tuesday girl? Besides"—he pointed to her hair—"I like your style. It's fierce."

Star ran a hand along the side of her head.

"The truth is that I haven't graduated yet. I'm homeschooled, so my hours are very flexible," Jeremy said.

"That sounds cool."

He snorted. "I'm sixteen and the oldest of eleven kids. My youngest brother still craps his pants. I go to school in a nursery. But I'll tell you a secret." His eyes shifted from side to side. "It's not really a job. I just drive Lucy around whenever she needs me."

"But you have a decal and everything," she said.

"I sometimes go a little overboard."

His openness caught her off guard, made her uncomfortable and curious. The kids she knew were guarded and suspicious. Jeremy was none of those things. He was so *normal*.

He clasped his hands behind his head. "Your turn, Tuesday."

She stared down at her lap. Sharing personal bits of information was something friends did. And the last real friend she'd had was Jazz. She shuddered, hugged her arms into her chest, and fell quiet. Maybe Jeremy would get the hint and go away.

But he stayed seated beside her, apparently waiting for her to talk, thrumming his glitter nails across his thigh.

She turned back to face him. "I'm not afraid of cops," she said, and his fingers halted. "But I don't trust them either. I'm a foster kid—or was."

Jeremy shifted, cleared his throat. "What happened to your family?"

She paused and studied her fingernails—ragged tips but clean now. "My mom died when I was five and my dad when I was eight."

"Oh man." Jeremy swallowed, and his large Adam's apple moved visibly up and down. "That's . . . really sad. So your foster family moved to Pine Lake?"

"No, I don't live here, and I'm not a foster kid anymore."

Jeremy scrunched his eyebrows together in confusion. His eyebrows were thick, like two caterpillars, and combined with his flop of curly hair the effect was clownish. "So where do you live?" he said quietly.

"On the street," she said. "Take your pick—I'm homeless, a street kid, a fucking nuisance."

Jeremy didn't respond, but his face had lost the comical expression from before. He stared at her until she began to fidget, rapidly regretting her candor.

"I'm sorry," he said.

She bristled. "What?" Her life was her own, and she didn't have to explain it to anyone. She was tough. And she didn't need some spoiled small-town kid taking pity on her.

"I'm really sorry," he said again.

"What the hell are you sorry for?"

"That it took this long for Lucy to find you."

Star opened her mouth, closed it, felt her face grow hot. Find her? Like Lucy had been looking for her? Like she wanted her? A warmth trickled inside, tiny fingers of hope creeping toward her heart. But then she thought of Jazz, and the warm feeling turned cold. She kicked the seat in front of her and turned to look out the window again. If Lucy wanted to find her, it wasn't because she cared. Nobody cared about a girl like Star.

CHAPTER FOURTEEN

JESS

She took a seat opposite Ben, who sat in the same chair Star had perched on earlier in the day. His bulk made the chair look comically small, his hands swallowing the delicate teacup. She waited for Lucy to say something, but the older woman's attention was again on her crossword puzzle.

Lucy tapped the tip of the pencil on the paper. "A nine-letter word for a confirmed habit." She peered at Ben above the rim of her glasses.

He chuckled and said to Jess, "Lucy and her crossword puzzles. I've always been terrible at those."

"Me too." She gave Lucy a fond smile. "I'm afraid I'm not much help."

Ben fell silent and looked around the sitting room. He rapped the arm of his chair and jiggled one knee up and down. It was an awkward silence that made Jess feel as though she'd intruded.

He cleared his throat. "You doing okay, Lucy?"

"I'm doing fine," Lucy said. "Still old and senile."

Instead of smiling, Ben leaned forward, his forehead creased, and again addressed Jess. "Has Lucy been having trouble?"

Jess bristled at the way he talked about Lucy like she couldn't hear or understand. It reminded her of Mr. Kim's son. But Ben had obviously been caring for Lucy. He was nothing like that man. "Trouble?" she said.

He shifted in his seat and glanced at Lucy, who continued reading her crossword puzzle like the two of them weren't there. "Look, Jess, I've known Lucy a long time," he began.

Lucy set the puzzle down in her lap. "I caught Benjamin trying to steal my car," she said.

He gave a deep, rumbling laugh and seemed to relax for the first time. "I was only going to take it for a joyride. And it's hardly stealing when you leave your keys in the ignition. Besides, that car was missing a battery and a hood. It wouldn't have started anyway."

Lucy tilted her head to the side. "Was that the car you fixed up your senior year?"

Something flickered in Ben's eyes, and his smile faded. He coughed and set his cup on the table. Tea sloshed over the side.

Jess grabbed a few napkins and wiped up the tea. She'd prefer to let Lucy visit with Ben on her own so she could get dinner started, maybe check on Star. Besides, Jess wasn't much of a social person. But Lucy gestured for Jess to sit, so she did, the soggy napkins still gripped in her hand.

"Ben was fourteen when I found him behind the steering wheel of my old car."

"It was a bet!" Ben protested, smiling again. He turned to Jess. "She's the Witch of Pine Lake, you know." Lucy laughed. "And I was a stupid kid." He clasped his hands behind his head. "My family was dirt poor," he said. "Two sets of clothes, no winter coat kind of poor. I thought stealing a car would prove something. I passed Lucy's house one day and saw this old, unused car just sitting in the driveway. I can still remember thinking how unfair it was that some lady had two cars while my family had nothing." He gave a rueful smile and pointed at Lucy. "She was the only good that came out of my short career as a thief."

"How?" Jess asked.

"First, because she scared the hell out of me," he said, grinning. "She told me that car was going to ruin my life. I believed her, so I gave her back the keys and promised I'd never try to steal a car again."

"I scared you?" Lucy said, sounding not at all surprised.

"Of course you did! You had on that black cape, your hair looked like it was on fire, *and* you held a broom in your hands!"

"I was sweeping the kitchen, Benjamin Watts."

"Or about to fly to a witch convention . . ."

"Your hands shook so bad . . ."

"I was terrified! And you acted like you'd been expecting me."

"Of course I was. It was on the calendar."

Their familiarity made Jess feel like a third wheel, and she took the opportunity to glance out the window to see if the van had returned.

A small, pale face pressed against the window, features blurred by the thick glass, peering inside at the three of them.

Jess gasped, and the face vanished in a blur of red as she shot to her feet. The boy from the market, she was sure of it. Did he live around here? She hurried to the door, urged by an unexplainable desire to find him. Find out why he was playing games with her. Maybe speak to his parents.

"What's her deal?" she heard Ben say to Lucy.

But she was already in the foyer and flinging open the front door before she realized that she should have excused herself. Said something before she fled the room.

Outside, the low-hanging sun turned the pine needles an inky black. Shadows coiled and stretched across the ground. There was movement out of the corner of her eye, and she turned to see the heel of a dirty shoe disappear around the side of the house.

"Hey!" she called, and followed, stumbling over a thick tree root.

A small path led to the overgrown flagstone patio on the side of the house where Lucy's huge library windows faced. An aspen branch clicked against a window. The boy was nowhere to be seen. Was he hiding? From the hill behind the home came the sound of a metal door banging shut. She looked up. An old shed sat on the only bit of flat land on the sloped property. The boy stood beside the shed, staring down at her. She squinted, but the failing afternoon light plunged his face into shadow. He turned and disappeared inside the shed.

A breeze kicked up then, whooshing through the pine trees and causing the shed's thin metal door to flap against its frame.

"Hey, kid!" she called, and began to carefully pick her way through a patch of thistle. The shed appeared when she reached the top, rusted and sunken, as though it had grown out of the ground. But the thing that made her breath catch in her throat was the door. Closed and locked with a heavy iron padlock.

Her shoes crunched the dry grass as she approached the shed. It was loud in the stillness. "Hello?" No reply. She reached out to touch the lock, and her fingers left prints in the heavy dust that coated it. It looked like it hadn't been opened in years.

"What are you doing up here?"

Jess yelped and spun around, her palm flat against her chest. "Ben," she gasped. "You startled me."

His eyes narrowed. "Startled you? Looks more like I scared the hell out of you. You're white as a ghost." He pointed behind her, a crease in his forehead. "Did you need something out of Lucy's old shed?"

"No, I just saw—" What was she going to say? *I think I saw a boy run into this locked shed?* Through the sleeve of her shirt she rubbed the puckered scar across her wrist. She felt . . . off. Like the earth had tilted ever so slightly off its axis. Ben stood with his feet planted apart, hands on his hips, and the way he looked at her made her feel like she'd done something wrong. "I-I thought I saw a bear," she said.

He stood just below her on the slant of the hill, looking up at her from under the wide brim of his hat. The dim glow of the sun hit the sharp angles of his face, giving him a hollowed-out look. "Don't see many bears in Denver, huh?" He gestured for her to follow him back to the house. "Lucy said you might want to get dinner started."

She walked past him and down the hill, hugging her arms across her chest to avoid the bite of the thistles. At the patio she stopped, turned. "What's in there, anyway?"

Ben hooked his thumbs through the belt loops of his pants and sighed. "I suppose it's filled with a bunch of Lucy's old antiques. It's been locked for as long as I can remember, so I guess I don't really know. Why do you ask?"

"Oh, no reason," she said casually. "Just wondering."

Ben continued past the house, and a moment later Jess heard the thump of the front door closing. She glanced once more at the shed and shivered. The building looked frail, like a stiff breeze could knock it down, but remembering the boy disappearing inside left her cold. Could she have imagined that? A tickling sensation inched across her wrist, and she began to scratch at her scars. Scratch, scratch, scratch. She watched her fingers move across the skin, thought about the night it happened, and knew deep in her heart that she was capable of imagining all kinds of things.

~

She closed the front door softly and froze when she heard Lucy's and Ben's voices coming from the kitchen.

"Who is she, Lucy?" Ben said quietly.

"A loose end." Lucy's familiar words, a mantra.

He sighed. "We've talked about this before, remember? Not everyone's a loose end. Some people just have bad luck, and it's not your job to help them."

"I helped you, didn't I? Although I'm not sure it made a difference . . ." Her voice trailed off.

Jess hovered in the enclosed porch, the inner door to the house cracked just enough for her to see the edge of Ben's wide-brimmed hat where he stood in the kitchen.

"You did help me," Ben said flatly. "And look at me now, one of Lucy's kids all grown up."

Jess could hear his voice edged in what sounded like anger. She shifted her weight from one foot to the other. She shouldn't be eavesdropping, but she was trapped, unsure whether she should go inside or slink back out the door.

"I'll always appreciate what you did for me when I was a kid, but I've worked hard to be the man I am today." He paused, and Jess heard him sigh again. "I'm not trying to make light of the things you do. Hell, you've done something for just about everyone in this town. But, Lucy, I'm worried about you. The house is too big for you, and I think this 'loose ends' stuff is starting to mess with your—oh damn it, how do I say this?"

"Say what, Benjamin?"

"I brought you those brochures on that new place over in Georgetown."

"The assisted living facility? I've already told you, I'm not moving out of my house."

"Is that why you went behind my back and hired that woman?"

She heard Lucy sniff. "She answered my ad at the right time."

Ben blew out a loud breath. "Is she qualified to take care of you? Has she found you wandering around your yard at two in the morning yet? Damn it, Lucy! Why would you keep something like this from me? I've only been trying to help you!"

Silence filled the kitchen, and Jess tried to quiet her breathing. The emotion in his voice struck a chord in her. He cared for Lucy. She took a deep breath and pushed through the door. "I looked all around the outside. No bear. Guess I scared it off."

Ben turned to her, his eyebrows knitted together, no doubt wondering how much she'd heard. Lucy sat at the kitchen table, her shoulders hunched forward, and Jess felt a strong urge to put her arm around the old woman. "Are you staying for dinner, Ben?" she asked, hoping he'd say no.

He shook his head. "I need to get going, but it was nice to meet you. My house is the one through the pine trees up behind Lucy's house, so don't hesitate to call if you need anything." He patted the doorframe once, gave Lucy a quick glance, and left.

CHAPTER FIFTEEN

STAR

Jeremy's words hung in the air. *That it took this long for Lucy to find you.* She thought again about the note from Lucy. What could she know about the accident? Star squeezed her eyes shut. She'd met Jazz when everything had fallen apart, after her mother died and her father buried himself in addiction. She was only seven, but she was lonely and sad all the time. Jazz was the brightest spot in her life, and his friendship made her think that maybe things could change for the better. And then he died because she let the ugly black spots of her life bleed into his.

Voices floated from the direction of Lucy's house, and Star opened her eyes. Jess and the police officer stood outside the house, talking. Star's heart pounded, and she slid down in her seat until she was huddled on the floor of the van. Jeremy had put some distance between the van and the house, but the cop only had to glance down the road to see it.

A few minutes later, Star relaxed when she heard the whine of an engine, followed by the crunch of tires as the car drove. The van engine started back up, and with Star still crouched low, Jeremy drove back to the house. Lucy's wrinkled face appeared in the van window.

"He's gone," she said. "Come inside." She nodded formally. "Jeremy."

"Lucy," he said in an equally serious tone.

Lucy turned and walked slowly up the stairs and into her house.

"Ready, Star?" Jeremy said.

Before she could answer, the driver's door creaked open, and a moment later Jeremy slid the side door wide. Star blinked up at him. He extended one arm and bent forward in an exaggerated bow. Star stared at his hand. Then Jeremy lifted his head, peering up at her through the strands of his hair, and gave her a lopsided grin. Something inside her softened a bit; he was a good guy. Still, she ignored his hand and climbed out on her own.

"I'll see you . . ." He paused, staring down at the ground. "Look at that." His slender frame bent in half, fingers reaching out to pinch something between his thumb and forefinger.

"What is it?" she asked, distracted. Her eyes scanned the road to make sure the cop was long gone.

"Here." He took her hand, and the contact made her jump.

"Sorry, I'm just not used to people . . ." For some reason, her face reddened. She'd already told him she lived on the streets.

"Check this rock out," he said.

She inhaled sharply. He held her rock. The one painted red with gold stars that had been a gift for her seventh birthday. She tried to steady her shaking hand as she took it from him. It must have escaped her shoe. "It's mine," she said, trying to steady her voice. "I guess I dropped it."

He pointed to an indentation in the rock. "It's a heart," he said. "Must be a good luck charm."

She nodded, her throat fused shut. His shoes crunched the gravel when he walked to the van, but she couldn't tear her gaze away from the rock.

"Hey, Tuesday," he called. She looked up. His hair fluttered around his face in the light breeze. "I hope I see you next week."

~

Dust floated in the air after Jeremy left. Star sat on the front steps and pulled her shins in close to her body. The rock had been a gift from Jazz for her seventh birthday. They had just met, and it was the only birthday gift she got. She squeezed her fist. The stone pressed into the tight flesh of her palm, smooth and cold. Jeremy was like those girls with the guitars, sheltered and naive. He was wrong—the rock wasn't a good luck charm. She'd kept it by her side all these years as a reminder that life was cruel and unfair and she'd be stupid to expect anything different.

Not like Jeremy could understand that. He probably had a mom who made him a hot breakfast every morning and told him she loved him every night.

She wrapped her arms across her belly. Her mother had been like that, from the little Star could remember. She knew that things had been good once, because her very early memories, while fuzzy, made her feel warm.

Like the bonsai trees. Seeing them in Jess's room had flooded her with memories. The color of her mom's hair. Black as night. The way her skin smelled like cinnamon rolls. The sound of her voice rumbling softly against Star's ear just as she was falling asleep.

A bonsai tree needs lots of love, she'd told Star once.

Why, Mommy?

Because it wants to grow bigger. But if I keep it close and give it my attention, then I can keep it small and perfect. Like you. She tweaked Star's nose, and Star gave a bubbly kind of laugh.

But then one day her mother couldn't get out of bed anymore. Star tried to take care of her trees, but her chubby hands were small and clumsy, and the trees began to die. Weeks and then months passed, and her mother grew so thin it bleached the color from her cheeks and sucked the brightness from her eyes. Star curled inside her thin arms and pressed her ear to the bones of her chest. And then one day, her mom died too.

Star slipped the rock inside her sock and stood up, wiping an arm across her eyes. She straightened her spine and for the second time that day rang the doorbell.

"You don't have to ring the doorbell," Lucy said, waving her in. "You're staying here now. Think of it as your house too."

"I'm only staying for one night," she blurted.

"Come in, then," Lucy said, and turned back to the kitchen.

Star stood in the unheated porch, her foot hovering over the threshold to the inner foyer.

Jess appeared from the kitchen and walked across the gleaming parquet wood of the foyer to the bottom of the stairs. She gave her a small smile. "Close the door before you let the bears in."

Star pictured the slatted roof of her bench, smelled the mixture of urine and moldy cheese that wafted from the concrete, felt the clammy hands of the boy who had attacked her tugging at her shirt.

Her feet crossed the threshold.

Lucy sat at the table with a newspaper folded into thirds and lying in front of her. A pair of black reading glasses rested on the tip of her nose.

Star cleared her throat. "Um, thanks for today, Lucy," she said, pressing up and down onto the balls of her feet. "For the food and the clothes and the walk."

Lucy took a pencil from behind her ear and scribbled something across the paper. Then she brought the paper close to her face and read out loud. "A six-letter word for accidental, serendipitous. Do you know the answer, Star?" she asked without looking up from the puzzle.

Star hadn't been in Pine Lake for twenty-four hours, yet in some ways it felt like she'd always been here. And that it was here she should stay. She rubbed her arms. One night, she repeated silently, because once Lucy figured out why her friend had died, she wouldn't want Star anywhere near her.

"Star?" Lucy said.

She breathed out, squared her shoulders. One night with the feel of her body sinking into a mattress and the warmth and security of a heavy comforter. "If I'm going to sleep in your house tonight, Lucy, I need to be honest about something."

Lucy raised her eyebrows. "Go on."

"I hate crossword puzzles."

"Too bad," she said, her attention drifting back to the newspaper in her hand. "They make you smarter." She gestured toward the stove. "Jess left you a dinner plate. I hope you're not disappointed."

"By what?"

Lucy smiled. "Her cooking."

"I heard that, Lucy." Jess's voice drifted from somewhere on the second floor.

Lucy made a face, and Star smiled.

She wolfed down three tacos and a bowl of rice and beans in silence, washing her plate in the sink and setting it into the rack to dry. "Um, Lucy?"

Lucy set the paper aside, folding her hands on top of the table. "Tired?"

Star nodded.

"Well, don't stay awake on my account." She winked. "Top of the stairs, first bedroom on the left."

Star wandered out of the kitchen and had one foot on the first step when she heard Lucy's chair scrape across the floor.

"Do you hate reading too?"

She turned. "I love to read."

Lucy pointed past the staircase to a short hallway. "Then you'll like the room at the end of the hall. It's full of books. Take whatever you like. Books are good company."

Star's face burned; the offer stirred something deep inside, reminding her that her only company in the long months she'd spent on the streets had been the occasional book she found left behind on the free shuttle. And books reminded her of her mother, who'd often read to Star when she was too sick to do anything else. She mumbled, "Thanks," hurried up the stairs, and locked the door behind her.

She studied the room. It was nice, with old polished furniture. Small trinkets straight out of a history book adorned bookshelves and side tables. She traced the edges of a wooden jewelry box, the top inlaid with a thin strip of pearl. Lucy's antiques must be worth a lot of dough.

A length of thin white fabric had been laid across the middle of the bed. She picked it up and held it to her shoulders. A nightgown with a hem that reached her ankles. It looked like something a settler living in a one-room mountain cabin might have worn. The voluminous folds of material brushed against her skin when she pulled it on.

A few minutes later, Star snuggled under the comforting weight of the quilt. Her body sank into the mattress, and she stretched out her legs, wiggled her toes, and tried to absorb the sensation of something soft beneath her bones.

The floor outside her door creaked from labored footsteps, and her eyes flew open, her body tensed. She curled her hands into fists and inched up into a sitting position with her back against the headboard and her eyes trained on the door. She didn't fall asleep until the house had been quiet for hours.

CHAPTER SIXTEEN

STAR

In the morning, she pushed the covers aside, yawned, and wiggled her toes. Sleep hadn't come quickly, but when it had, she'd slept hard without waking until her eyes fluttered open to the glow of an early-morning sun. That kind of sleep didn't happen on the streets. Not when the nights were fractured by voices raised in anger or frigid air that froze her fingers or the stinging heaviness of a numb foot.

She yawned, stretched her legs long in front of her, and shook her head; without the weight of her hair, the air brushed easily across her scalp. Her eyes roamed, taking in the dark wood wardrobe, an antique mirror, and heavy silk curtains that covered the floor-to-ceiling window.

From the door came a soft rustle, and she scooted her feet back onto the bed. A yellow square of paper inched under the door and into the room. Lucy was a big fan of notes.

Star set her feet on the wood floor and tiptoed across the room. A sticky note with black script in Lucy's unmistakable handwriting read:

Open the door

She put a hand on the knob, hesitated. What would today bring? There was only one way to find out. She squared her shoulders and opened the door. Another dress hung from the doorknob. She pulled it into the room and shut the door, twisting the lock closed.

Stuck to the dress was a sticky note.

For you, it read.

The dress was blue with tiny green flowers scattered across the cuffs and hem and cinched at the waist by a thin leather belt. She swallowed. She understood suspicion and mistrust. But this? She shook her head. She had little experience with kindness. After her mom died, her dad was lost, unable to pay all the hospital bills. The bits and pieces she remembered were soaked in the sweet musk of liquor coming from her dad's breath. It didn't take long before he stopped being kind the minute the bottle was empty, and then later, when the drugs wore off. The foster homes weren't all bad, some better than others, but there were so many of them, fifteen in all by the time she decided to run.

She looked at the dress again, shrugged. Then again, who was she to turn down free clothes? The dresses were impractical for the streets, but she would change back into her other clothes before she left that afternoon.

She tightened the belt of the dress, slipped the rock and the note into her sock, and opened the door. From downstairs came the clink of pans and the hiss of popping grease. The sweet aroma of frying sausage made her mouth water. She hurried to the stairs, but a soft thump, followed by Lucy's muffled voice, stopped her. She pulled herself away from the direction of food and walked lightly toward the bedroom where the noise had come from. She peered inside.

Lucy stood beside a huge four-poster bed. Her hair floated around her head, and a black nightgown draped her stooped frame. It looked very similar to the white one Star had worn last night. Lucy bent over, one hand resting heavily on a side table, her other hand reaching toward the floor to where an oblong eyeglasses case lay half under the bed by her feet.

Star moved swiftly into the room. "I can get that for you," she said.

Lucy eased her body into a chair by the bed. "Be careful, then."

Star narrowed her eyes at Lucy's odd warning. But the old woman had busied herself with a crossword puzzle, and when Star bent down to pick up the case, she gasped. It was gone.

She pulled up the red-and-gold bed skirt to look under the bed. There it lay, just out of reach. Lucy must have kicked it when she sat down. Holding the bed skirt up with one hand, Star slid her fingers under the bed, feeling around for the smooth leather case. But all she felt was empty space and the carpet beneath her fingertips. She bent lower to get another view, but the case appeared to have moved farther away.

Some trick of the light, she figured, ignoring the way her scalp prickled. She lay on her belly and stuck her head and then shoulders under the frame. But the distance lengthened like in one of those mirrors where the proportions were all wrong, and the floor beneath the bed felt cold through the thin fabric of her dress.

She fought the urge to retreat, but the case was within reach now, so she moved forward, propelled by a sudden desire to do one good deed for Lucy.

Something slid over the scratchy wool rug. Her ears tickled with the sound. She wasn't alone. Her head shot up and banged against the metal support of the bed. "Ow!" she said, and the sound of her own voice made her feel silly. Why was she acting like such a child? She and Jazz used to play hide-and-go-seek all the time, and her favorite place to hide was inside a small space. She was so small then that she could curl up into a tiny ball. Jazz almost never found her. But she was bigger now, and the confined space and darkness suffocated her, made her pulse beat in her ears. It was so dark that the only light was a thin line shooting out from under the dust ruffle. Silly or not, she wanted to get out of there.

She scrambled backward, unmindful of her skull cracking against the heavy side rail. When she finally emerged into the warm light of Lucy's bedroom, she rolled onto her back, one hand to her chest, her breath coming in ragged huffs. Lucy stood above her, staring at her with bright-blue eyes.

"Thank you," Lucy said.

Star stared up at her, dumbfounded. "For what?"

Lucy pointed to the floor. "My case."

She turned her head to the side. The glasses case lay beside her on the floor.

Lucy chuckled and reached for the case. Star handed it to her with shaking hands as she sprang to her feet and backed away from the bed.

"I told you to be careful," Lucy said, and settled into her chair.

Tremors racked Star's body, and she tried to make sense of what had happened.

Lucy perched her glasses on the tip of her nose and read from the paper in her hand. "A six-letter word for an unnatural ending . . ." She pursed her lips, looked up at Star. "Oh, that's right. You don't like puzzles."

Star's tongue felt swollen and stuck to the roof of her mouth. She pointed to the bed. "I-I thought something was under—"

"Some*one*," Lucy said.

Star rubbed her arms. The room felt electric. "What did you say?"

"A boy, to be exact." Lucy tilted her head to the side. "Do you know what he wants?"

Star backed farther away until her hips touched the doorframe. Her leg muscles twitched. "What he wants?"

Lucy tapped the eraser end of her pencil on the newspaper. "He's here because of you, Star."

"B-because of me?"

Lucy sighed, tapped the tip of her pencil on the arm of the chair. "A loose end is always more complicated than it first appears." Her attention fell back to the paper in her hand. With another sigh, she scribbled letters into a row of small boxes. "I can help you find out," she said.

Star clenched her jaw. She should run—flee from this woman and her haunted house and from whatever Lucy thought was hiding beneath her bed. If she were a normal kid like Jeremy, maybe she would. "H-how can you help me?"

"He wants something from you." Lucy's eyes were trained on her crossword puzzle. "I can help you find out."

"What does he want?"

Lucy tapped a finger on her chair. "Exactly!"

A coppery tang stung the tip of Star's tongue. Without realizing it, she'd ripped a fingernail past the quick. Star bent forward, placed her hands on her knees. An image popped into her mind of the boy playing hide-and-go-seek behind Lucy the first time she met her and the boy who threw a rock at Shred and then disappeared behind the dumpster. She shook her head to try to shake the stupid thought loose.

But then she recalled Lucy's words from the day before. *It's your loose end.* Lucy claimed to see things. But what kinds of things? Star shivered and glanced at the bedside clock. Enough time to catch the morning bus if she left now.

"You're safer here, Star, than out there."

"Safer here?" Her finger shook when she pointed to the bed. "From what?"

Lucy waved a dismissive hand at the bed. "From all of it."

Star opened her mouth. Then shut it just as quickly. How could Lucy promise her that? Her options were limited. She thought of the attack and the boy, Shred, who wouldn't leave her alone now if she went back. She'd been so stupid to think she was better than those kids. Her father hadn't been. What made her think she was any different? Her eyes darted to the bed. Lucy said she could help find out what the boy wanted. Star shook her head. Impossible. There was no boy. Star had just scared herself under the bed, and Lucy obviously had a screw loose. There was nothing more to it than that. Except how could she explain the note? *You watched your best friend die.*

Star breathed in, lifted her chin. "How did you know about my friend?"

Lucy stabbed her pencil into the air. "That's the right question!"

Star sucked in her bottom lip. "Did you talk to my caseworker?" Brenda had been the latest one, young, shiny red hair, stylish black-framed glasses, wore a new outfit every time they met. Nice enough and convinced she could change the world, or at least Star's world. She felt a little bad for Brenda. But she didn't know about Jazz. At least Star didn't think she did.

"I've already told you," Lucy said, interrupting her thoughts. "It's what I do."

"What is?"

Lucy sighed and set the paper in her lap. "The loose ends." She tapped her temple. "I see them. And you have more than one. Now that one"—she nodded toward the bed—"is nothing to worry about. At least, I don't think so." She raised her eyes to look at Star over her reading glasses. It made the wrinkles in her forehead spread up and out. "But if you'd like some advice from an old lady, stay a little longer and see what happens. I'd like to help you if I can." She smiled, then lowered her eyes to the puzzle, her lips moving as she read herself a clue.

Star smoothed the dress that Lucy had given her, thought of the walk around the lake yesterday, the full night of sleep, and—her stomach rumbled—the food. Lucy might be a little off her rocker, but Star knew for a fact that there were crazier people on the streets. With nothing good waiting for her in Denver, why would Star leave the one person in the world who wanted to help her?

She bit the inside of her cheek. The truth was that she didn't want to go back. Even the thought made her stomach turn. Despite everything she couldn't explain about Lucy, Star didn't want to sleep under another bench tonight. Not yet, anyway. "Okay, I'll stay for now," she said. "But only for a little while."

"You told her she could stay?" came Jess's stunned voice from behind her.

Star turned to find Jess standing in the middle of the hallway, clutching a white tray with a plate of scrambled eggs and sausage and a glass of orange juice. Jess stared past Star, her skin pinched into frown lines around her mouth. "You don't know anything about her, Lucy."

Lucy's face lit up, and she laughed. "I know!"

A chill rippled across Star's skin.

She was staying.

CHAPTER SEVENTEEN

JESS

She scrubbed at the frying pan, pushing hard against the metal to dislodge bits of sausage stuck to the bottom. She was speechless after hearing Star tell Lucy she wanted to stay. Just that morning, before Star woke up, Jess had made a point to talk to Lucy about the girl. To convince her that there was a system in place for kids like her and that it would be in everybody's best interest to call the authorities.

Somebody's worried about her, Jess had argued. *We should encourage her to contact her family. Or at the very least, let them know she's okay. Any mother deserves at least that,* she'd said, and her voice sounded small and broken when she said it.

But Lucy just shook her head. *Nobody's missing that girl,* she'd said almost cruelly, and turned back to her crossword puzzle. Matter closed.

And now Star wanted to stay, and from the way she flitted about the kitchen, she was happy with her decision. After wolfing down her breakfast in minutes, Star paced about the kitchen in a restless dance. She fingered the Post-it notes on the fridge, pulled at the phone's long cord, and finally paused in front of the calendar.

"What's the Mountain Market?" she asked.

Jess scrubbed harder at the pan. She had mixed emotions about Star's presence. She couldn't send the girl back to the streets, but legally she was a runaway, and Lucy could get into trouble for not calling social services. Besides, someone had to be looking for Star. Like her mother. The thought made Jess's eyes itch.

Lucy was offering Star a safe place to stay, and while Jess had no problem getting the girl off the streets, she hated that Lucy was misleading her. Star couldn't stay here. To Jess it felt wrong to dangle the promise of a home in front of a kid who'd hit rock bottom. Especially when that promise couldn't be kept.

She felt a tap on her shoulder. "Hard of hearing, Jess?"

Jess turned the faucet off, wiped the pan dry, then set it on the rack next to the sink. Star stood behind her, leaning her hip against the counter. Despite her rough existence, her skin still had the vulnerable glow of youth.

"I asked you about the Mountain Market."

Jess nodded. "It's a small grocery store on Main Street. You must have seen it when you came into town yesterday. Lucy owns it, but today is the only day of the week she opens it for business."

"That's weird."

Yes, it was. Jess had been to the market only once more since she first arrived. Lucy had taken her for a couple of hours on Friday morning to give her the lay of the land before the big day. Jess had spent the time cleaning, organizing shelves, and wondering how many customers came into the rustic market. Judging from the amount of dust and the expiration dates, not many. But a few did trickle in, acting surprised but happy to find the store open. Like the woman in a blue winter hat and sunglasses who'd entered through the back door when Jess was making coffee. Jess had jumped, spilling the coffee grounds across the white counter.

Sorry, the woman had said, frowning, then entered Lucy's office without even knocking. She'd left thirty minutes later without the hat or sunglasses on and her face split into a grin. Jess had given her one blueberry muffin to go, wrapped in a paper towel as Lucy had instructed her to do with all her customers. Except, like that woman, not a single customer who came in that morning purchased anything.

When she'd asked Lucy about her visitors, Lucy said simply, *Just a few folks who needed my help. Nothing too big.*

Star tapped her foot, opened her eyes wide as though Jess were the slowest person in the world. When Jess began to speak, a thought unfolded that stuck inside her throat, made her heartbeat weak. What would Chance have been like at Star's age? She pressed a hand against her chest, pushed the thought away. She'd never know, and it was pointless and painful to guess. She tried to smile at Star, but her lips felt stiff. "Anyway," she said at last, "you don't need to worry about the Mountain Market."

"Oh, but she does!" came Lucy's voice as she swept into the kitchen.

"Why?" Star asked.

"It's Wednesday."

"And?" Star looked to Jess as though hoping she might translate.

Jess shrugged.

"And you said you were curious about what I did on Wednesdays," Lucy said.

"Am I walking you to the store?"

"Walk me to the store?" Lucy shook her head. "What an absurd job. No, you'll help Jess make blueberry muffins and serve coffee."

Star's eyes shifted from Lucy to Jess, until finally her face broke out in a wide grin, making her look even more like a child. "That's so weird," she said.

Something twisted in Jess's chest, and she turned back to the sink. She cleared her throat and tossed the drying rag across the counter. "Let's go, then. The store's not going to open itself."

~

It had happened last Friday when she opened the door to the market—the feeling that someone had just left, a shifting of the dark, the way the shadows crawled to the corners when she flipped on the overhead lights. But it looked exactly the way she and Lucy had left it last week.

Star wandered the store while Lucy disappeared into the back room. If it was like last Friday, Lucy would sit at an oversize wooden desk, flip through ledgers, and take notes. Maybe have another "customer" or two. Jess followed her, closing the door that separated her office from the kitchenette. She paused by the desk. "Lucy?" she said.

"Yes?"

"How is the store able to stay in business without customers actually buying anything?" Jess assumed that Lucy was well off financially, but what if she was holding on to the store for personal reasons? It could be a financial drain, for all Jess knew. Jess had never run a business, but she understood that inventory plus no customers did not equal sales.

Lucy rapped the desk with her fingers. "The customers come when they need something."

"But do they ever buy anything?" Jess asked.

Lucy continued to tap the desk with her fingers. "You are very closed off to possibilities."

Jess pressed her lips together. If evasiveness were a sport, Lucy would be a gold medalist. "What do you mean?"

"I think you know."

Jess shifted her weight and tightened her ponytail, having no idea how to respond.

Lucy sighed as though disappointed. "When customers need something," she said, "they come to the market. Sometimes they come for flour or sugar, but mostly they come for my help."

"Your help?"

"The loose ends. I've talked to you about this already." Lucy picked up her eyeglasses and set them on the bridge of her nose, leaning forward to study a calendar on the desk in front of her.

The gesture made Jess feel dismissed, but she wasn't about to give up that easily. "You don't like loose ends. I know. But what are they?"

Lucy sighed and folded her arms, sitting back in the chair. "It's a family trait to see them. My mother and her mother before her and so on. They all had the gift." Her face clouded. "But I'm the last. Maybe that's why it's so strong in me."

"What's so strong in you?"

"Seeing them. They're everywhere, and it's my business to help them. And when people in this town need my services, they come to me." She squinted at Jess over the rim of her glasses. "And I'm only open one day a week because I'm old, Jess."

Jess gritted her teeth and rubbed the back of her neck roughly with one hand. Did Lucy enjoy confusing her? From what she had come to understand, Lucy was a sort of grandmother to the people in town. Jess figured they came to her for advice and that Lucy liked to refer to it as her gift. And Jess couldn't disagree; listening was a gift not given to many people. Her mother certainly didn't have it. She briefly wondered what her life might have looked like if she'd had someone like Lucy back then. "Lucy, I—"

"Like I said, you're very closed off to possibilities." Lucy dismissed her with a wave of her hand. "Which is surprising, considering."

Jess stiffened. "Considering what?"

Lucy sucked in her bottom lip and tilted her head to the side. Then she shook her head and let her eyes drop to the desk. She pulled out a leather-bound book, opening it to a page in the middle, and began scribbling across the paper. When she didn't lift her head again, Jess realized that was all she had to say.

With a sigh, she backed away from the desk and slipped between the curtains into the main store. Star stood by the cash register at the front.

"This tuna looks like it's been sitting on the shelf since I was born." Star blew across the top, and dust rushed into the air. "Pretty sure that means it's expired." She scrunched her nose and squinted her eyes. "What does she do here every Wednesday?"

Jess sighed and walked past Star to the area behind the counter. "It's her routine," she said, and grabbed two black aprons from metal hooks.

"Huh?"

"Elderly people sometimes hold on to a routine. It's comforting. I think the market does that for Lucy. Plus, I think that people like to talk to her." She tossed an apron to Star. "Time to make the muffins."

"People come in here for muffins and coffee?" Star asked, tying the apron behind her waist.

Jess smiled, enjoying Star's bewilderment. At least she wasn't the only one in the dark. "Yep."

Star released a low whistle and shrugged. "Show me where to start."

"Don't get excited. The muffins are a mix from a box."

While Star made the muffins and coffee in the kitchenette, Jess wiped down the small round table by the front window, swept the floors, dusted the counters, and reorganized the toiletry section.

The ring of the front door and then Ben's voice interrupted the quiet morning. "Hello? Jess?"

He stood by the door, holding his wide-brimmed hat between his hands.

"Good morning," she said.

"See any bears today?" His smile softened the hard lines of his face. He was a tall man with big hands and wide shoulders that filled the room.

"Can I help you with something?"

"All business, aren't you?" He set his hat on the counter. "Is Lucy here?"

"She's in the back," Jess said. "Would you like me to get her?"

"Actually, I stopped by to see you."

Jess felt her shoulders tense.

"I know I came off a bit rude yesterday. I was surprised, I guess, because Lucy didn't talk to me about hiring an in-home caregiver." He scuffed the floor with the toe of his boot. "Lucy's been more of a mother to me than mine ever was, and I always assumed she'd want my help when she got to this stage of life."

She thought of Mr. Kim and understood exactly how Ben felt. Even though she'd been his paid caregiver, it had stung when nobody thought to call her at his passing. For as close as Lucy and Ben seemed, part of her wondered why Lucy hadn't talked to Ben about her plans too.

"I stopped by to see you because I want to make sure that you've got the full picture about Lucy."

She raised her eyebrows.

He looked up at the ceiling as though searching for his next words. "Lucy says she knows things."

She laughed. "She told me that when I first met her."

"You don't understand." He pointed a finger at his head. "She thinks it's a gift."

"Like a psychic?"

He shook his head. "Not really. More like an intuitive."

"What does that mean?"

Ben shifted his weight. "She thinks that she can help people find answers, solve problems. And she does—that's the crazy thing. But I've always believed it just comes from Lucy being a nice person. She's helped find lost pets or brought two people together, and she has a particular fondness for lost kids. Like me, for example. She didn't have to buy my practice gear for football or pay my college application fees. But she did because that's the kind of person she is."

Jess wrinkled her nose, confused. She didn't see the problem. "Those are all really nice things," she said.

"They are. But as she's gotten older, I think she's begun to believe the hype about her in town."

Jess couldn't help but smile. "That she's a witch?"

"Not so much that, although she does enjoy dressing the part." He smiled. "But now . . . she's beginning to lose track of time. I've found her a couple of times in the middle of the night wandering around her yard in her nightgown, confused and disoriented."

"You're worried there's something wrong with her?"

He nodded.

She took a deep breath. It was good that he told her. "Thanks, Ben. This is the kind of stuff I need to know if I'm going to be of any help to her. We have an appointment with her doctor soon, and I'll be sure to speak with her about your concerns. In the meantime, I can help Lucy go through the house, prepare for the day if it comes." It made her sad to think of Lucy having to leave the home she loved, but that was exactly where Jess could help her. "Maybe we'll start with that old shed of hers and . . ." At the look on Ben's face, she trailed off. "What's wrong?"

"Benjamin Watts, how many times do I have to tell you? I'm not and will never be leaving that house."

Jess turned. Lucy stood just behind her, her eyes glowing blue.

Ben twirled the edges of his hat. "Now, Lucy. I'm just making sure Jess has all the information she needs to do her job. I've already offered to buy the house from you. You wouldn't even need to do anything to it. I'll take it as is."

Lucy pressed her lips into a flat line.

There was a tension between them that made Jess edge around Lucy and head to the back of the store. "Coffee, Ben?"

"Yes, thank you."

She pulled the curtain closed behind her. "Star?" she hissed. She searched the office opposite the kitchenette, but that was empty too. The girl must be hiding again.

She poured coffee into a mug and was setting a warm muffin onto a plate when the screen door to the alley rattled against its wooden frame.

She walked over to the door. "Star?" The porch was empty except for a few stacked crates and boxes.

When Jess turned to leave, she heard a tapping on the doorframe. She peered over her shoulder, expecting to see Star. Her hand flew to her chest. "You again," she breathed.

He stood on the other side of the door with his hands pressed into the screen until it seemed his flesh might pop through the webbing. He tilted his head toward the ground so all she could see was the top of it. A little prankster, that's what he was. Her shoulders slumped with relief. She wasn't crazy after all.

She started to say something, hesitated. He was familiar in a way that made her chest tighten: his size, the way he stood with his toes pointed slightly out, jeans that fell just short of his ankles.

Her eyes burned. She felt hot and dry, feverish. But she approached the door, reaching for him with the hand that grasped the full coffee mug. "Hey, buddy," she croaked. A rush of frigid air blew across the back of her neck.

She felt a sudden urge to tip his chin up, a desperate need to see his face. Her hands began to shake, and black coffee dripped over the side of the mug. His utter lack of movement made her legs feel watery, insubstantial, and she almost dropped to her knees. Her reaction to this kid was ridiculous.

But being around a little boy again brought on a rush of memories that assaulted her. Chance's skinny arms around her neck when she tucked him in, the velvet softness of his cheek when she kissed him good night. The card he made for a classmate whose dad died in Afghanistan, the way he smiled, even if he was sad.

Then a thought came to her, and the memories faded. Ben said Lucy had a soft spot for kids. Maybe this one needed her help.

"Hey, bud," she said, louder this time. Without responding, the boy turned and bolted away. "No, wait!" she called, and pushed open the door with her hip. Hot coffee splashed across her skin, and the liquid collected into muddy rivulets in the dirt at her feet. "Ouch!" she cried, blowing on the angry marks across her hands.

Ben swept through the curtains, and his eyes surveyed the room. "I heard you yell. Everything okay?"

"There's this boy I keep seeing . . ." She frowned at the soggy muffin and the half-empty cup.

Ben leaned against the doorway, grinned. "Sounds like he's trying to see the Witch of Pine Lake."

She laughed. Of course. She returned the wet plate and half-empty cup to the counter. A kid that age would be fascinated by the stories of Lucy.

"Something wrong with your hand?"

"What?" Without realizing it, Jess had been scratching at her wrist again, so hard this time a tiny bead of blood welled from a particularly deep scratch. She pulled her sleeve down and pasted a smile on her face. "How do you take your coffee?"

Ben stared at her for a moment. "Black," he said. "Listen, Jess, I wouldn't worry about the boy. He'll either lose interest or finally get the nerve to speak to Lucy instead of trying to scare you."

She tried to laugh, but her mouth felt too tight, her nerves thin and shaky from the morning. "I want you to know that I'll take good care of Lucy."

He knocked back the rest of his coffee and set the mug on the counter. "I'm around if you need me," he said, and tipped his hat before leaving the kitchenette.

She leaned against the counter; she could feel herself coming unhinged. Whether it was from the boy who seemed to be waiting for her around every corner or Star's youthful presence in the house, Jess felt her thoughts continually dragged backward to the night her son died, to finding him sprawled in the street. Telling herself as she ran, her heart in her throat, her feet slipping across the icy street, that he must have tripped and fallen, except she was already screaming, a shriek that echoed against the building, disappeared down the empty street. She knew he was gone, could feel it in the way her insides had wrenched apart, forming a hole so big she thought she might disappear inside. She knelt beside him on the pavement, her jeans soaked to the knees, and sobbed into his curls.

She pulled in a ragged breath that came out as soft moan, tightened her ponytail, and began cleaning the coffee mug and plates, trying to focus on the here and now. It was the only way she had survived, by moving forward. Tomorrow she would confirm Lucy's doctor's appointment, organize her cavernous and trinket-filled basement, and convince her that Star would be better helped by professionals.

Lucy walked into the kitchenette then, her gaze running across the room.

Jess straightened her apron and pointed to the back door. "The boy was back," she said.

Lucy nodded once. "The boy. Yes, well, we already know about him."

CHAPTER EIGHTEEN

STAR

When the police car pulled up to the Mountain Market, Star was outside, throwing away the trash. The metal lid banged heavily when she closed it, causing the man to glance in her direction. She jumped between the dumpster and the hill behind it, trying to hold her breath. Rotting meat tinged the air, and the moist ground felt like a sponge beneath her feet. With her body pressed against the damp hillside, she waited for his footsteps to come closer.

Her pulse raced. It would end as it always had—with the cops taking her back to the foster family.

She remembered the first time she ran away. She'd been in foster care for two years and was already on her fourth placement. The family had been fine. But Star didn't want *fine*. She wanted her mother.

So one night, when everyone in the house had been asleep for hours, she pulled a packed pillowcase from under her bed, slipped into a coat, and walked out the front door. She slept under a yellow plastic slide in a play park that night and woke up to a red-haired toddler with a runny nose poking her in the stomach. When the cops showed up, she was on a swing, pumping her legs with her eyes closed and her hair flying around her face.

I like the park, she told them.

They took her anyway.

The ding of the front door sounded, and the memory dissolved. The cop had gone inside the market. She slumped against the prickly earth but didn't move from behind the dumpster. She wasn't taking any chances on him finding her.

Ten minutes later came the cough of the squad car as the engine started up. She tiptoed to the back door and stopped in her tracks. Her skin prickled. She was being watched. Shoes inched out from behind a box. Next came the tip of a small finger. She shook her head, squeezed her eyes shut, and hurled open the door, locking the deadbolt with trembling hands.

"Did you see it?"

She whipped around to find Jess studying her with pinched lips.

"See what?"

"That damn raccoon. He keeps finding a way into the dumpster." Jess's eyebrows scrunched together. "You put the bar down and locked it, right?"

"What?" She frowned at Jess. "Yeah, I locked up your garbage."

A few hours later, Lucy poked her head between the curtains. "That's all for today. Let's go home."

CHAPTER NINETEEN

JESS

It was after five when they returned from the market. Lucy immediately retired to her room, leaving Jess and Star in the small kitchen. Jess tried to make conversation, but she was distracted by the memories of Chance that had continuously plagued her all day, and with the weight of figuring out how to best help Star and her concern for Lucy's overall health, she just didn't have it in her for small talk. Star seemed to be in her own world, too, because the silence stretched between them until Star made a beeline upstairs.

Jess stood in the middle of the quiet kitchen. After the chaos of the past few days, a slice of alone time might restore her equilibrium. There'd been a bite in the air on the way home from the market. She opened the refrigerator door and pulled out ingredients for chili. Making dinner would occupy her hands and mind.

Her thoughts went to Star. What had she eaten on the streets? Where did she sleep? When she thought of the girl alone and probably terrified, she found it hard to breathe. How had she survived at all? Jess peeled an onion and slid the knife easily through its layers. It stung her eyes. She used her shirtsleeve to wipe the tears away, and with her eyes closed she wasn't in Lucy's kitchen anymore. She was in the apartment she'd shared with her son, standing in the tiny kitchen with the single fluorescent bulb that flickered and buzzed whenever Mrs. Rodriguez from next door dried her hair.

Why do you have to go to work so late, Mama?

She didn't want to leave him, especially on the night of his birthday, but Mrs. Rodriguez—who usually stayed with Chance—was at the hospital with her husband, who'd had a heart attack two days before. She could have told Tony she couldn't take the shift, but she'd missed so much work when she got the flu in January and then more when it morphed into pneumonia. Saying yes tonight would put her back in Tony's good graces, at least until the next crisis.

Chance had sat at their tiny kitchen table in his *Transformers* pajamas, his chin resting on his forearms, yawning. He could come with her, but the sidewalks were slick with ice, the night black and moonless and cold. He was eight, old enough to stay alone for a little bit. Jess had when she was his age.

Don't answer the door. She'd always made him promise.

I won't.

And don't leave the apartment.

Never.

She smiled and kissed the shallow dimple on his cheek, inhaled the sweet scent of chocolate, tasted a light dusting of sugar. He ate the hot chocolate mix by the spoonful when he thought she wasn't looking, but she didn't say anything. *Happy birthday, handsome. I love you.*

I love you too, Mama.

She remembered hesitating at the door so clearly it pierced her heart; something had twisted deep in her gut, mother's intuition. *Don't go.* But then she eyed the stack of envelopes in the middle of the table—rent, electricity, water—and stepped out into the hallway, closing and locking the door behind her.

A sharp pain made her eyes fly open; the knife had slipped over the wet skin of the onion and bitten down into the bony part of her finger.

"Ow!" she cried, and sucked on her finger, the sharp bitterness of the onion and the tang of her blood mixing on her tongue. She grabbed a paper towel and wrapped it around her hand before collapsing into a chair. Her breathing was shallow, stuck in her throat while she tried to keep from crying.

Despite what her son had promised, he had opened the door that night and left the apartment, and she never knew why, because the next time she saw him he was in the middle of the road outside her apartment building. She leaned over her knees, gripped her head between her hands, and willed the memory of that night to go away.

But she saw him in the face of every child she passed on the street, or standing by her bed when she woke up screaming from a nightmare, or in the mirror just beyond her reach.

"Is the chili ready, dear?"

Jess's head shot up. Lucy stood in the doorway to the kitchen, her head tilted to the side and a look of such compassion on her face that Jess had to look away.

She smoothed her jeans, tightened her ponytail, and stood. "Not quite." She held up her hand. "Had a little medical emergency." Lucy had a faraway look in her eyes, and Jess noticed how she leaned heavily against the doorframe. "Is everything okay?"

"I think the better question is, are you okay, dear?"

"Me? I'm fine."

"It's okay to cry, you know," she said.

Jess wiped at her face, tried to laugh but couldn't. "That was the onions."

"If you say so."

Lucy had caught her crying twice now. Trying to change the subject, she said, "The little boy who keeps showing up . . . what do you think he wants?"

Lucy wagged her finger toward Jess. "That is the right question."

Jess muffled a groan. "He acts so odd. Do you know him?"

"No, dear, I don't know him. Or not very well, I should say. But I am surprised he keeps coming to you."

"For what?" Food, maybe. Could he be hungry? Poor, like Ben's family had been?

"That's what I still don't know." Lucy smiled. "But don't worry. He'll be back."

Jess nodded, thinking she understood. Sometimes at the diner Tony would leave out day-old rolls or sandwiches for a homeless woman who slept in the alley. Was the boy homeless like Star? She felt a twinge. Maybe next week she'd leave a few muffins out back. "I'll keep an eye out for him, then," she said.

Lucy nodded. "That's a good idea. I'll take my dinner in my bedroom tonight, if you don't mind." She turned and started up the stairs, her back stooped, fingers white from her grip on the railing.

A little while later, the simmering chili filled the kitchen with the sweet tang of tomatoes, garlic, and cumin. Jess filled a bowl and took it upstairs to Lucy, passing Star's door along the way. It was cracked open, light from inside falling in a rectangle on the hallway floor. Jess couldn't help but glance inside. The unmade bed was empty, her clothes scattered across the floor by the door. Jess snorted. Teenagers.

The walls popped, and from behind the closed bathroom door the rush of water stopped. Thinking of how filthy Star had been when she showed up yesterday, Jess understood more than most how the girl must feel to be clean again. She could still recall her first shower after her homeless stint in a car when she was just a girl herself. The warm ribbons of water slipping over her soapy skin, the way it turned brown before gurgling down the drain, leaving her skin a light pink. She smiled to herself. Star deserved to shower as much as she wanted.

Jess sat with Lucy while she ate her chili, then turned down her bed. Lucy insisted that it was unnecessary, but Jess enjoyed spoiling her when she could.

"I'll be downstairs if you need me." She was closing the door when she heard a rustling sound from the direction of her bedroom. A heated mist floated from the open bathroom door. She squinted. Were those wet footprints on the wood floor? She took a step down the hallway. Why would Star be in her room?

"Jess," Lucy called, "I'd like a glass of ice water, if you don't mind."

She poked her head inside Lucy's room. "Of course," she said, and started down the stairs, then hesitated. She thought about knocking softly on Star's door, but the girl probably needed her own bit of alone time.

A deep tiredness had sunk into her bones, and suddenly all she could think about was bed. After giving Lucy her water, Jess cleaned up the kitchen, left some food out for Star in case she came down later, and headed back upstairs to her room. A good night's sleep would clear her thoughts, help her to focus on the more pressing needs. Like Lucy's health and Star's future.

CHAPTER TWENTY

STAR

She lay on the bed, reading, thoughts about the day crowding her head until she finally rested the book on her stomach with a sigh. Her mouth watered at whatever Jess was cooking, but she stayed in her room, not ready to go downstairs and risk Jess asking her questions about her past. She was interested, Star could tell, and not because she was curious. Star snorted. Poor clueless Jess. She must think there were "Missing!" posters with Star's picture and a mom and a dad waiting for her to come home and feed the golden retriever.

It had been awkward sitting in the kitchen with Jess after the market. Star was curious about the woman, and she found herself wanting to ask questions. Instead, she bit her tongue and stayed silent.

She kicked off the thick comforter, suddenly hot under its weight. There was something about Jess that seemed motherly—not that Star had much experience with that—but it was in the way she cared about stupid things. Like at the market today, Jess had taken the time to show Star how to fold the can of blueberries into the muffin mix. *So they won't break apart,* she'd explained. *Here.* She handed her a plastic spatula. *You try.* She did as Jess instructed and tried to ignore how her wet eyes made the blueberries blur into a thick glob.

A faint odor rose from her armpits, and the smell darkened her mood. It reminded her how gross she'd feel in only a couple of days on the street. While she was here, she might as well stay as clean as possible.

In the bathroom she sat on the edge of the claw-foot tub, dipping her fingers in and out of the flow of water. When it was warm enough, she took off her dress and stepped in. The water slipped smoothly over her skin, and she slid down until it rose to her neck, the warmth giving her the sensation that she was enveloped in a cocoon. She'd locked the door as always, but she wasn't staring at it like someone might try to open it at any moment. An unfamiliar feeling let her eyes droop closed, and she breathed out. She felt . . . safe.

Her jaw clenched. She couldn't let herself get too comfortable here, no matter how much she wanted to. It wasn't permanent. Lucy was old, and Jess thought she belonged back in foster care.

Besides, Lucy knew things she shouldn't. Star shivered despite the heat of the bath. How could the old woman know about the accident? Star's memories were pitted, fuzzy from lack of details surrounding that night and especially the days and weeks that followed. Had anyone else seen the two of them running across the street? Did Star tell someone? She had never thought so, but Lucy's note made her realize that there was so much she didn't remember.

Star slid farther into the tub until the water closed over her head. The longer strands of her hair floated around her face, caressing the skin of her cheek like fingers. Everything that had happened that night was her fault. She'd gone down to visit Jazz because she wanted to do something nice for his birthday. She didn't have anything to give him, except for one of her mother's two remaining bonsai trees, and she couldn't think of anyone who deserved it more than Jazz. He'd been her best friend when nobody else cared.

She held her breath, letting little bits of air escape through her nose. Small bubbles floated to the surface. The water darkened, and then a face appeared above her, distorted by the water so that the angles of his cheeks sloped down, his brown eyes pulled apart at the corners. She opened her mouth to scream, and water rushed in, filling her lungs. Shooting up from the bath, choking, coughing, she squeezed her eyes shut, gasping for air. Her skin crawled with the feeling that someone stood beside her, and in her panic she slipped on the wet floor, cracking her knees when she fell on the hard ceramic tiles. Her eyes flew open, and she scrambled to her feet, pressing her back against the door, fists raised.

The bathroom was empty.

Her heart raced so fast she could feel it pulse in her throat. Why did she keep imagining him? With all her talk, Lucy was making her see things. She grabbed a towel and wrapped it around her shaking body.

Something rubbed against the door, and she flinched, goose bumps spreading down her arms.

"Yeah?" she called out.

From somewhere down the hall she heard Jess's muffled voice, and Star opened the door, hoping that if she saw Jess then she could forget whatever she thought she saw in the bathroom. The hallway was empty, but Jess's bedroom door, which was directly across from the bathroom, stood wide open. She tiptoed across the hallway and peered in. The air inside her room was cool, making Star keenly aware that she stood in the hallway in nothing but a towel.

She shivered and turned to go, and then she noticed a dresser drawer, the one Jess was trying to fix yesterday, hanging from its rails. She hurried over and shoved it in all the way, making the dresser wobble on the uneven floor.

Her hand brushed something pointed. One of Jess's bonsai trees. She stared at the little tree. After her mother died, there had been nothing left. No money, no house, her father broken. But she'd been able to keep something when they left the mint-green house with the white trim—two bonsai trees. The ones her mother had nurtured for as long as Star could remember.

Inhaling, she felt a current of anger rush from her chest and down to her toes, and her fingernails bit into her palms. Fucking bonsai. She moved one of the plants close to the edge of the table. Closer still, until the curve of the pot hung over space. One more nudge and the tiny plant would fall to the floor and the ceramic planter would shatter, spilling dirt and leaves.

From outside the room came the creak of a door opening and Jess's voice from the hallway. "I'll be downstairs if you need me."

She jerked her hand back. What was she doing? Star pushed the plant back onto the table and balanced on the balls of her feet. Should she hide or stay where she was and face Jess? If Jess found her in her room, what would she think? Her jaw tightened. She'd think what everyone always thought—that Star was a thief, a liar, a bad seed. Being a foster kid had been a stamp on her forehead that warned everyone: *Beware, not to be trusted.*

Her heart fluttered painfully. It felt different here. Special even. The way Lucy wanted to help her, even how Jess treated her like she was a regular kid. It was the most comfortable Star had felt anywhere. Almost like she was meant to be here. She bit her lip hard. *Stupid, stupid, stupid.*

Then Lucy's voice. "Jess, I'd like a glass of ice water, if you don't mind."

The stairs creaked as Jess went down. Star bolted from the room, eyed the puddles of water she'd left in the hallway, grabbed a towel from the bathroom, and swiped it across the wood planks. *Good enough.* Her bedroom door clicked behind her, and she slid to the floor, breathing hard, cold beads of water sliding down her wet hair and dropping onto her shoulders.

CHAPTER TWENTY-ONE

STAR

The clock on the bedside table said it was only nine o'clock, but Star was used to crawling under a bench soon after the sun went down, and in the dead of winter that could be early. Tonight it didn't seem to matter, because the face from the bathroom hovered behind her eyelids, and she tossed and turned until finally she gave up and pushed the covers to the side.

Jess had come up the stairs a half hour ago and paused to check on Lucy. Star heard their murmurs through her door. Then Jess had done something that felt at once familiar and uncomfortable all at the same time: When she'd left Lucy's room, her footsteps made the wood floor creak. They stopped outside Star's door like she stood on the other side, hesitating. But for what?

Star's heart pounded, and she stared at the door. Her skin warmed with the faint memory of her mother doing something similar. Except her mother would have walked inside her room and pressed her lips to Star's forehead in a quiet kiss while Star pretended to be asleep.

The floor creaked again, followed by the soft click of Jess's door closing. Star wiped a hand across her eyes. Stupid memories.

The aroma of cut onions and minced garlic from earlier hung in the air. Her stomach rumbled almost painfully. She'd been hungry a long time.

She tiptoed down the stairs, feeling like an intruder in the dark and quiet house, the only light a dim bulb above the stove in the kitchen. She'd planned to scavenge the pantry for chips or cereal, but she spied a bowl of chili sitting on top of the stove. Small serving bowls of shredded cheese, sour cream, and green onions sat beside it. Her mouth watered.

It took only minutes before her spoon scraped the sides of the empty bowl. She drank a glass of water and sat back in the chair, her belly full.

After washing the dish and setting it to dry on the rack beside the sink, she remembered Lucy's invitation to borrow a book. Her old one lay on the bedside table in her room next to the rock and note. She should throw the note away. She didn't need it anymore, but something made her keep it. Like it was a golden ticket that gave her permission to be here.

She ran upstairs and grabbed the book. She'd add it to the collection and take one of Lucy's in return. The thought of snuggling underneath the covers tonight with a new story made her smile. She wandered down the hallway to the left of the staircase, her bare feet slapping across the wood floor. She kinda liked having the place to herself. At the end of the hallway was a door with a slim gold plate that said **LIBRARY**.

She pushed open the door, flipped on the light switch, and gasped. The room was huge, rising two stories above her head. From the center of the domed ceiling hung a tiered chandelier that bathed the space in a soft rainbow. She'd never seen anything so . . . rich.

The walls were covered in dark reds, forest greens, matte whites, and other colorful spines of books lining every inch of vertical space.

Attached to rails that ran the length of the wall was a brass-handled ladder with wheels that rolled it back and forth along the shelves.

Star thought of where she'd slept only two nights ago, and the difference in her surroundings made her giggle like a little kid. She moved lightly across the rug to the nearest wall, running her fingers along the books, pulling out one, then another, finally settling on a silly children's book of poems—one she remembered reading over and over when her dad didn't come home or the noises outside their apartment door made her hide under the covers with a flashlight. She sank into the deep cushions of a worn leather couch and read until her eyes grew heavy and she fell asleep.

~

She was a little girl again, sitting cross-legged on her cot in the living room and staring at her father. His skin had gone yellow like a banana, and the color crept up his cheeks, turning the whites of his eyes dull. There was a knock on the door that made the entire apartment shake. Her body went rigid at the sound because it meant her father had a visitor, and his visitors scared her.

He pinned her with his watery gaze and pointed down the hall. "Go," he said. "Do not come out. Understand?"

She nodded, scrambled to her feet, and raced for the bathroom, peeking over her shoulder in time to see her father open the door and a tall man, his face shadowed by the brim of a baseball hat, step into the apartment. She slipped inside the bathroom, heart racing. Had he seen her? They weren't supposed to know she was there, and if the man saw her, her dad would be angry. She peeked through a crack in the door. She could see the man's face now in the light from the kitchen, and she felt her breath whoosh out in a relieved sigh. She remembered him from the hospital—he wasn't like the others. She closed and locked the door anyway, like her father always told her to do when someone came over.

She climbed into the grimy bathtub, pulled the torn plastic curtain shut, and counted the drips from the faucet until her father knocked on the door. The bare light bulb above the sink buzzed and flickered. She stared at it through the thin plastic and listened to the water plink into the tub. One. Two. Three. From outside the bathroom came raised voices, one begging, one angry. She curled into a tiny ball and covered her ears with her hands, rocking back and forth, her pajamas wet, her feet sliding on something slimy.

Wake up, Star. Wake up. Wake up.

The door flew open, hitting the edge of the small bathroom counter, and her father stood on the other side of the curtain. The metal rungs scraped across the bar when he opened the curtain. He loomed large above her, his chest heaving, hands held out in front of him. His head dangled at a sick angle, his neck a pattern of black-and-blue fingerprints. His mouth twisted into something ugly, and he stepped toward her saying the same thing over and over.

Your fault. Your fault. Your fault.

Star screamed, and everything went black.

CHAPTER TWENTY-TWO

JESS

She sat on the edge of the bed, rubbing lotion into her hands and massaging the scars on her wrist. She frowned. Her bonsai trees had gotten worse, their color dull and the edges of the leaves thin and browned. Had it been only yesterday when Star pointed out that they were dying? In some ways it seemed like the trees and Star had been around for a long time.

She slid under the covers and let her head fall back into the pillow with a sigh. Tomorrow she'd move the plants to the sitting room, where the light was better. She yawned and closed her eyes, and her last thought before she fell asleep was of Star and her mother and bonsai trees.

In her sleep, the scream was muted and soft, and it took her a while to shake the thickness that fogged her mind. But when it came again, Jess sat bolt upright. Her heart pounded against her chest, and she scrambled out of bed, stumbled to the door. The screams quieted into pathetic whimpers that seemed to come from every corner of the hallway. Lucy? She ran down the hall and flung open her door. Lucy lay facing her, covers pulled up to her chin, eyes closed. Snoring lightly.

Jess closed the door and shook her head. Had she been dreaming? Then the scream again. A girl sounding shrill and terrified. Star. Jess hurried down the stairs, heart beating fast. The kitchen was empty, the sitting room dark. She must be in the library. She rushed to the door and twisted the handle, but it wouldn't budge. Locked.

Keys. Lucy had a master set of keys in a drawer in the kitchen. Jess hurried to the kitchen, pulled out the drawer under the calendar, and grasped the keys with shaking hands. The hollowness of Star's cries sucked the air from the room. Jess fitted a key into the lock and turned. The library was pitch black. When she flung on the overhead light, the darkness seemed to resist it until eventually the room filled with a warm glow.

She found Star on the couch, lying on her side and curled into a fetal position. One hand covered her cheek and eye. Jess knelt down and pushed Star's hair away from her forehead.

Asleep. The girl was asleep.

CHAPTER TWENTY-THREE

STAR

A warm glow lit the insides of her eyelids, turning them a bright red and waking her up. Immediately she thought of her father, and a sob caught in her throat.

"Are you okay?"

Her eyes flew open. She lay on the couch with her feet on the rolled leather arm and the chandelier above spraying the room in light. Jess sat on one of the wide fabric chairs, her hair falling around her face and spilling over her shoulders, wearing blue pajama pants and a long-sleeved cotton shirt. She was really pretty, Star thought.

The deep wrinkle between Jess's eyes made her look worried. "You were screaming. Did you have a nightmare?"

Star nodded but found she couldn't quite form words yet, the dream of her father too real. She pulled a pillow into her lap and cradled it against her stomach.

"The door was locked," Jess said.

Star shrugged. "I didn't lock it." She yawned and tried to find a clock in the room, but only books filled the walls. "What time is it?"

"Eleven thirty. Is everything okay, Star?"

The way she asked, with a hint of genuine concern, made Star almost break down. Almost. But what was the point in telling Jess anything about herself? She breathed in and felt stronger. Telling Jess wouldn't change anything, but it would have her calling the cops in a heartbeat.

"I'm good, just fell asleep and had a nightmare—you know, like your average homeless teen invited to a mansion in the mountains by an old witch." Star grinned, and the side of Jess's mouth rose.

A moment later a look came over Jess's face that made Star squeeze the pillow tight and jut her chin up. "What?" she said.

Jess cleared her throat. "Where did you sleep the night before last?"

Star straightened her shoulders, held Jess's gaze. "Under a bench." "Why?"

Star was thrown by her question. It sounded like Jess thought she'd had a choice. "Because it's where I belong."

Jess gripped the arms of her chair and said so softly that Star almost didn't hear, "You belong in a family."

"Most families don't want a girl like me." Star looked down at her hands, pulled at the tips of her fingers. "And not everyone deserves a family anyway." It had slipped out so fast. Star fought an urge to clap a hand over her mouth.

"Kids do," Jess said softly.

Star kept her eyes trained on her hands, and the silence between them lengthened.

Jess stood suddenly. "I have a job for you."

Star snorted, looked up. "You want me to walk you around the lake too? Aren't you a little young for that, Jess?"

She smiled. "Smart-ass. No, I'd like you to save my bonsai trees." Star swallowed hard. "What?"

"You said they were dying, and I don't want them to die. The other day it seemed like you knew a thing or two about bonsai, certainly more than me. So I figured it couldn't hurt to ask. My thumb is more brown than green." Jess gave her a soft smile.

She felt her cheeks heat up and her eyes burn. She couldn't save Jess's bonsai trees any more than she could save her friend. "Sorry, I don't think I can help. It's probably too late to do anything for them anyways."

Jess sighed. "You could be right. But I'm moving them to the sitting room tomorrow, and if you feel like it, you can take a look at them. Who knows? Maybe they're not totally past saving." She stood and moved toward the door. "Hungry?"

Star's stomach growled in response. "Starving."

"I make great pancakes." She checked her watch. "And they happen to taste even better at midnight. C'mon."

CHAPTER
TWENTY-FOUR

JESS

The next morning Jess knocked on Lucy's door, breakfast tray in one hand, the *Denver Post* rolled and tucked under an arm.

"Come in, come in," Lucy called.

"Good morning." She was surprised to find Lucy out of bed and sitting by the window that framed the lake. The ice-melt barrel had, in fact, fallen through on her first day in Pine Lake, and she had noticed that when the lake began to melt, it melted fast. Today was a clear day, and the water, poking through the last remaining bits of ice, sparkled like a jewel. "You're up early." She set the tray on the small table by the chair, smoothing out the paper before handing it to Lucy.

"How did our girl do on her second night?"

"Other than screaming so loud she nearly woke the fish in the lake?"

"It didn't wake me." Lucy smiled and sipped her coffee.

"She's still sleeping." Jess had rapped on her door early this morning when she passed it on her way downstairs, but Star had yet to emerge. "Or she took off during the night with the good silverware."

Lucy clucked her tongue. "You don't care for her?"

"It's not that at all." She looked down at her hands. "If she were my daughter . . ." Her throat closed briefly, and she paused. If Star were her daughter, Jess would wrap her arms around her, pull her close, and tell her everything would be okay. After hearing Star's pitiful screams last night, she'd had to fight the urge to do just that. Jess felt her face harden. She used to lie with Chance at bedtime while he said his prayers and afterward when she kissed him good night, tucked the comforter under his arms and legs, and told him she loved him with all her heart. He'd blow her a kiss and tell her she was the bestest mom ever. She swallowed hard. She'd loved being his mother, but she would never do it again. She didn't deserve to be someone's mom.

"I'm worried for her, Lucy. What if her mom is out there wondering if she's okay, waiting for her to call and come home?" Jess thought of her own childhood, closed her eyes. That wasn't fair of her. She knew better than most how unfeeling a mother could be. "Besides that, she's a minor, a missing person. You could get into serious trouble for having her here."

Footsteps sounded from the hallway and then Star's voice. "I don't want to get you in trouble." She leaned against the doorframe, her small form enveloped by her long white nightgown. "I'll leave today," she said.

"No, you won't." Lucy's voice was firm. "I invited you here, and here you will stay." She jerked a thumb in Jess's direction. "Ignore my jailer."

Jess crossed her arms. Lucy didn't see the whole picture. "Your heart's in the right place, Lucy. I know you're trying to do the right thing." She turned to Star. "But there must be someone out there worried about you, and if home isn't a safe place, there are systems in place to help you. Lucy and I would make sure that you get all the help you need."

Star entered the room, kneeling on the floor in front of Lucy and ignoring Jess. "Thank you for everything, Lucy. I haven't had two nights of sleep like that in a long time. But I'm okay on my own."

Echoes of Star's cries from the night before and the image of her small body curled into a protective ball overcame Jess. Luck was the only thing that had allowed Star to survive homelessness. "There must be someone worried about you," she said in a softer tone. "Do you really prefer the streets to your home?"

Star rose to her feet and whirled around, her eyes dark blue and hard. "You don't know anything about me."

The words were tough, but she winced at the way Star's voice cracked, and Jess couldn't fathom sending her away. Yet staying with Lucy was a false hope that would eventually drain whatever reserves the girl had used to survive on her own. "Someone will question who you are," she said gently. "What happens then?"

"Not if you don't tell them," Lucy said.

"What?"

"Lie," Lucy repeated. "Make up a story; nobody here knows her."

"But you hardly know her—"

"You really don't," Star agreed, and Jess looked at her in surprise, noticing how the stiffness in the girl's shoulders had relaxed as though she was relieved. "But to be fair"—she gave a half smile—"for all I know, you're both witches who want to try me out in some great new recipe."

Lucy stood, her face split into a broad grin. "It's settled, then. We hardly know one another." She walked out of the room, and her voice trailed from the hallway. "Come along, then. I think you should check the calendar. You two have a busy morning ahead of you."

Jess pressed her lips together.

Star stared after Lucy with her eyebrows raised. "She's a little bit crazy, isn't she?" she whispered.

"Yes, I think she might just be. Or maybe we all are." She picked up the tray of untouched food. Pine Lake was the kind of town where everyone knew each other. But nobody here knew Star, or Jess for that matter. She thought of the way Star's bony shoulders poked out of the nightgown. Could it really hurt to keep her here for a while? She heard the rumble of Star's stomach and cocked an eyebrow in her direction. "Hungry again? I've got waffles downstairs."

Star's face lit up, and she sprang to her feet, the ridiculous nightgown billowing behind her. Jess smiled and followed her into the kitchen. She'd have to be made of stone not to be charmed by her unsettling mixture of tough girl and guarded innocence.

"Phoebe is coming over this morning." Lucy was peering out the window when Jess walked into the kitchen. "She'll be here any minute."

"Phoebe?" Star spoke around a mouthful of waffles and strawberries.

"Yes, she comes over to play cards once a week," Jess offered. "But she's told me to call her Ebee, so I suspect she'll tell you the same."

At her narrow-eyed look of confusion, Jess clarified, "She was with us that day we met you." She coughed, finding it hard to reflect back on the first time they saw Star because it made her face what she hadn't let herself believe then—that the girl had no one.

Star took another bite of waffle, seeming not to care one way or another.

The doorbell rang, and Lucy shuffled out of the kitchen to answer it. Moments later she returned with Ebee, who wore a yellow-and-blue tie-dyed shirt under her denim overalls. Jess smiled. She enjoyed Ebee's wardrobe as much as her company.

Jess handed her a cup of coffee. "Almond milk this time. I remembered."

"Just the way I like it. Thank you." Ebee turned to Star. "You're here."

Star pushed her empty plate away and wiped her mouth. "I was invited," she said, and crossed her arms like she expected Ebee to dispute the fact.

Ebee nodded, her eyes bright with amusement. "And you are very spirited. I like that about you."

Star shrugged back and drank the rest of her orange juice. "Ebee's a weird name."

Ebee laughed. "I know! But my younger sister couldn't figure out how to say Phoebe when she was little, so she started calling me Ebee, and I guess it stuck." She studied Star, who ran a finger through the syrup on her plate, then licked it off. "But you can call me Phoebe if you'd like. Lucy does."

"Ebee's cool," Star said, and licked another glob of syrup off her finger.

Ebee smiled at her. "Good, glad we have that settled. I have a few things for you." She handed over a small grocery bag, winked. "Lucy said you might be a tad low on clothes. It's not much, just a shirt and a pair of jeans."

Star's face reddened when she took the bag. "Thanks," she mumbled.

Jess sucked in her bottom lip. Her friend Marissa from across the hall used to give her clothes she claimed she didn't wear anymore, even though some still had tags on them. And Tamara from 3C would leave freshly washed and folded boy's clothes outside her door a few times a year. If she wanted to keep both her and her son in clothes that fit and weren't thin with holes, Jess had to accept their gifts. But it wasn't easy. She understood Star's embarrassment more than most.

Star pulled out a pink-and-purple tie-dyed shirt emblazoned with a pair of dancing bears and held it up to her face, inhaled, and smiled. "It smells like dreadlocks and laundry detergent," she said. "It's perfect." She studied the shirt and frowned. "What's the Grateful Dead?"

"Lucy!" Ebee said. "Shame on you! You bring this child into your home, but you don't give her a musical education?"

Lucy laughed. "She's only just arrived, Phoebe. And I'm too old to be hippie-dippie like you."

Ebee turned to Jess. "I understand that the plan is to keep Star's visit on the down low, is that right?"

Jess raised her eyebrows. When had Lucy had the chance to tell Ebee their plan? "For the time being," Jess said, without looking at Star. "Until we can find Star a more permanent place to stay. For now, the only people in Pine Lake who know are you, me, and Lucy."

"And Jeremy," Star said in a small voice.

Jess breathed through her teeth, turning to Lucy. "What about Ben?" The police officer seemed to have a vested interest in Lucy. But Jess was sure that if he found out, this whole idea would end quickly.

Lucy nodded as though Jess had correctly answered a trivia question. "Yes! What about Ben?"

Jess narrowed her eyes. Did she really need to spell out the obvious? "He's law enforcement. I doubt he'll be able to ignore the fact that Star's a runaway, no matter how close the two of you are."

Lucy frowned, turned her gaze to Ebee. "We were close," she said. "But I didn't help him the way I was supposed to." She rubbed the pale skin on the inside of her wrist, mirroring Jess's own habit.

The light dimmed, like a cloud had passed over the sun, and the temperature in the kitchen plummeted. Jess shivered and tried to rub the gooseflesh from her arms. This old house invited the cold inside.

"Help him how?" Jess asked.

"You always said it would work out in time, Luce," Ebee said in a low voice. "Maybe it's just not been his time yet."

Lucy and Ebee stared at each other, and to Jess the pair appeared to be locked in a silent argument. Star shifted beside her, and Jess noticed how she twisted the dancing bears shirt in her hands and stared at Lucy, who had turned so pale her skin looked almost gray against her bright-red hair.

"Lucy?" Jess said. "Are you okay?"

Lucy ignored her and began to circle the kitchen, touching the counter, the cabinets, running her fingers along the squares of the paper calendar. Her brow furrowed as she studied the calendar, causing the lines in her face to deepen further. "I couldn't find it because it wasn't there," she said.

"Find what?" Jess said, struck by the way Lucy hunched forward, making her look sad, defeated.

"His loose end." Lucy flicked her hand toward the calendar, and the bottom corner of the page fluttered.

Jess stepped forward. Why hadn't she noticed how the past two days had exhausted the old woman? She reached out to take Lucy by the elbow, but her fingers only brushed the sleeve of her black dress because Jess's legs buckled as though she'd been kicked.

She crumpled to the floor.

"Jess!" Star cried and dropped to her knees beside her. Her eyes were huge in her small face. "Are you okay?"

But the pain that stretched across her wrist kept Jess from answering. It pierced her skin with hot nails, and she clutched at her arm, gasping. She squeezed her eyes closed to ward off the tears and laid her head back to get control of herself when the floor beneath her hardened into the icy pavement of a city street. The tip of her nose dripped from the cold, and her heart thumped hard against her chest. What was happening? The glare of a stoplight bathed her skin in red, the light reflecting like blood off the freezing puddle of water beneath her. She was back to the night of the accident. She opened her mouth to scream, but her chest only rattled, a horrible hollow sound that slithered into her ears. *No, no, no. Not here.* She tried to close her eyes but not before she saw his shoe lying upside down in a black puddle.

Then the pavement morphed into tile, and the stoplight dissolved into the white ceiling of Lucy's kitchen. Star held her hand, and Lucy and Ebee hovered above her, their expressions flat and unreadable.

"Jess?" Star said.

Jess pulled her hand out of Star's grip, sending another wave of stabbing pain through her arm. She filled her lungs and pushed the air through her body. Her eyes itched with unshed tears. Was that how her son had felt? The unbearable thought made her want to curl into a ball and wrap her arms around her head. To hide from Lucy's eyes and pretend it had never happened.

But Lucy stared at her and also past her, as though seeing something else.

A strong hand took her by the elbow and pulled her to stand. Ebee. "Fall much?" she said with a lightness that made whatever had just happened fade. It had seemed so real—the street, the bitter cold of that night, the stoplight—but Jess knew better. It was nothing but her grief that made her see those things. Nothing but her guilt that on that night her son was alone and she couldn't help him.

She turned from their stares to brush at imaginary dirt on her jeans. She felt short of breath, on the verge of panicking, and forced herself to take long, even breaths. "I must have hyperextended my knee or something. I'm used to walking every day—probably just need to exercise my legs a bit more."

Lucy made a *tsk tsk* sound at Jess. "That's why I walk around the lake, dear. Keeps me young." She clapped her hands, then placed one on Jess's shoulder and the other on Star's. "Speaking of walking, you two had better get going. That coffee's not going to drink itself."

Jess's mouth fell open. She wavered between asking Lucy if she'd completely lost it and taking the first bus out of town. But the thought of starting over was too much. "What are you talking about, Lucy?" she said.

Lucy pointed behind her. "It's all on the calendar, dear," she said, "as usual." Then to Ebee: "Let's play in the library today."

"I don't think I should leave you . . ." Jess stopped. Lucy had already swept out of the kitchen.

"I'll be with her," Ebee said with a smile. "No need to worry. You two should get out of the house for bit." She made to leave, hesitated, then turned back to face Star and Jess. "I've known Lucy a long time, and I can assure both of you that you are exactly where you're supposed to be." She nodded at each of them. "And Lucy says you're not alone, Star," she said.

"I-I know that." Star's voice quavered. "You're here, and Jess and Lucy."

Ebee nodded, her mouth lifting on one side. "I think you know what I mean." She turned to Jess. "And neither are you." Ebee nodded again, squinted at the calendar, and smiled. "Shopping day. Better do what the calendar says."

CHAPTER
TWENTY-FIVE

JESS

They walked down the steep hill from the house to Main Street, pausing at the Mountain Market to get their bearings. Lucy didn't require Jess to be by her side every minute of the day, but Jess liked to stay busy, and with a house as large as Lucy's it wasn't difficult to find odd jobs to do. She'd never been much of a social person, so Jess had limited her Pine Lake outings to the market and hadn't taken the time to explore Main Street. It appeared to be nothing more than a typical strip of trendy boutiques and restaurants more suited to an idle tourist than someone from town.

"Lucy wants us to get coffee and then do what?" Star wore the Grateful Dead T-shirt and a pair of jeans that looked to be about three sizes too big. They had both left their coats at home, enjoying the unexpected spring temperatures.

"She wants me to take you to a consignment store. You need more clothes to replace the ones I threw away."

Star stopped walking. "You threw them away?" She glared at Jess. "Those were mine."

"It's for the best, Star. They were pretty threadbare, and I doubt they'd have made it through the spin cycle intact."

Star was upset, and Jess understood why. Jess had assumed she knew what was best for her without ever thinking to ask Star what she'd want. Her own mother had done the same thing to her. Made her choices for her, even telling her to get rid of the baby. Jess had hated her for that.

She'd thought she was doing Star a favor by throwing those rags out, but she should have given her the choice. What if someone she loved had given her those clothes? "I should have asked," she said. "Were they special to you?"

Star stared at her for a moment, her eyes giving nothing away, her mouth pressed into a firm line. Then her lips quirked up at the ends. "Yeah, they were real special. I traded sex to get those clothes."

Shocked, Jess missed the uneven wooden slat sticking out of the sidewalk and tripped, stumbling forward until she caught herself on a railing. She blinked hard before turning around. "Oh, Star, I'm so sorry," she said. Star's head hung down, and her shoulders shook lightly. Jess stretched her hands toward the girl, touched her lightly on the shoulders. "I didn't mean . . . that's so awful. I . . ."

But when Star lifted her face, Jess yanked her hands away. The girl was laughing so hard she clutched at her stomach. "You should see your face." She wiped the back of her hand across her eyes. "Oh my God, I can't believe you fell for that. That was so funny!"

Jess's nostrils flared. "So you didn't trade sex for clothes?"

"What? Hell no! I only did that for drugs."

Jess crossed her arms. "That wasn't funny. At all."

A more serious look crossed Star's face, and she fidgeted, looking at the ground and then back up again. "I guess not," she said, biting on a nail. "I've never really known how to joke with normal people."

Jess relaxed her shoulders and tried to smile. If it hadn't been so shocking, it was *kind of* funny, she guessed; then she shuddered. No, not funny when it was probably close to reality. "C'mon," she said. "Let's find that coffee shop."

Up ahead she spied a sign swinging in the light breeze. Muddy Buck. Star fell into step beside her, and their shoes thumped across the wooden sidewalk. She couldn't help but wonder what had landed Star on the street in the first place, and she winced, thinking how close to the truth her joking might be.

"What's wrong with your wrist, Jess?"

Star's question surprised her, and she self-consciously pulled down her sleeve. "Just an old injury."

"It doesn't seem old. You scratch at it all the time."

Jess rubbed the back of her neck. Star was straightforward in a way that Jess found familiar. Tough childhoods could strip inhibitions from children pretty fast. "That's just lately," she repeated in a firm voice. "It's the dry air or something."

"Okay, okay," Star said, and left it at that.

They were almost to the Muddy Buck when a familiar voice called to her. "Hi, Jess."

She turned. Ben and another uniformed police officer were walking toward them. She heard Star's sharp intake of breath. The girl hunched forward, making herself look even smaller than she already was. Jess felt a twinge and moved so that she partially obscured her.

The officer beside Ben gave her a big smile. "Hello," he said. He was older than Ben by a few years, with a rounded stomach that spilled over the top of his uniform pants like stuffing. "I'm Matt. New in town?"

Ben answered first. "You haven't heard the big news in Pine Lake, Matt? Lucy hired a caregiver. This is Jess."

"Good for Lucy!" Matt bellowed. "She should have some company in that big house of hers."

Jess smiled in return, her mind running through a list of excuses to end the conversation before the questions about Star began.

Too late. Matt peered around Jess to address Star. "And you are?" he said.

Jess stepped to the side and saw that Star stared down at the ground and pulled at the cuff of her sleeve. She swallowed over a sudden lump. She'd come to think of Star as a wisecracking tough kid. But the girl standing beside her now looked small and helpless. Protectiveness surged through her, and she slung an arm around Star's shoulders, pulled her close. "This is my niece," she said. "She's come up to Pine Lake to visit me."

Star relaxed under Jess's arm. "Nice to meet you, Officer . . ." She trailed off, squinting as she studied his name tag.

Matt laughed. "You can call me Officer Matt." The skin around his eyes tightened, and in a more serious tone he said, "Unless you get mixed up with the kids who smoke weed by the boathouse. Then you'll have to call me *sir*."

Star's body stiffened, and Jess gave her shoulder a light squeeze.

But Matt was laughing again, his belly moving in time. "So, you're staying with the Witch of Pine Lake, huh?" He gave Star a playful wink. "Have you seen any ghosts in that old house of hers?"

"All the time," Star said in a serious tone that made Matt laugh even more.

Ben, who had been silently observing their exchange, cleared his throat. His forehead wrinkled. "Your niece? I didn't know you had family in town."

"I don't. She's not from here."

"And Lucy's okay with this?" Ben studied Star with an intensity that made Jess fidget. Had he seen her face on a missing kid poster?

"Is she okay with what?" she said.

"With you bringing your niece to live here?"

She bristled at the tone he'd taken, as though Jess were taking advantage of Lucy, and she said the first thing that popped into her mind. "It's only for the summer," she said, trying to keep her irritation from bleeding into her words. "And I cleared it with Lucy first. I'd say she's more than happy with the arrangement."

"Of course she is!" Matt bellowed. "Lucy loves kids, Ben, you know that. Heck, she's taken in half the kids in this town at some point or another."

But Ben kept staring at Star, making Jess uneasy. Did he suspect they were lying? "You seem familiar," he said quietly.

Star shrugged, crossed her arms.

"She's a teenager," Jess said. "Don't they all kinda look the same?" She reached for Star's hand and moved them toward the door of the Muddy Buck. "You'll have to excuse us, but we haven't had our coffee yet this morning, and my niece is a real bear if she doesn't get her caffeine. Nice to meet you, Ma—"

"What did you say her name was?" Ben interrupted.

She hesitated a moment too long. "I didn't." She glanced at Star. The girl's face had gone very still. Jess's mind was a blank, and no other name would come to her. "Her name is Star," she said finally, when the pause had stretched too long.

"Star, huh?" Ben said, fingering his badge. "That's not a name you hear every day."

"Yeah," Jess said with a laugh, pointing to Star's tie-dyed shirt. "Her parents are old-school hippies."

"Well then, you'll feel right at home here. We've got plenty of old hippies." Matt dipped his head. "Welcome to Pine Lake, ladies. We'll see you around."

The men walked away, their boots striking across the old sidewalk. Star slipped inside the coffee shop as soon as they left, but Jess hesitated outside. Through the glass door she saw Star slink to the very back of the Muddy Buck and plunk herself down onto the cushions of a large chair. She flipped open a magazine, and for a moment she could have been a regular kid. But as she looked over the top of the magazine and through the window, her eyes big and haunted, the reality of the girl's situation became painfully clear.

Star caught sight of Jess standing outside and gave her a small wave. Jess's heart puffed momentarily, then quickly deflated. She gritted her teeth and pushed open the door. Her job was to be Lucy's caregiver. She was not about to add a child to that list. That was a road she could never take again.

~

After coffee, they headed farther down the sidewalk to a small shop on the corner with a sign that read SECOND CHANCE CLOTHES in purple and yellow letters. A pair of headless mannequins draped with that day's fashionable ensembles stood guard on either side of the door. Incense drifted from inside, nearly overpowering the heady musk of densely packed racks of used clothes.

Jess entered with Star following close behind. She'd been quiet ever since the run-in with the officers, but Jess couldn't blame her. It must wear her nerves thin not knowing when she could be picked up and returned to a system she hated enough to escape.

A woman in a black-and-white polka-dot shirt with a red bandanna tied around her neck waved at them from behind a stack of clothes piled so high on the counter they nearly hid her from view. "Welcome, ladies! I'm Savanah. You must be Jess and Star. Lucy told me you were coming in today."

Jess sneaked a glance at Star, who was staring back at her from the corner of her eye. When their eyes met, Star shrugged and giggled. Jess smiled back in understanding. Lucy was something else.

Savanah came around from behind the counter in black cropped pants and ballet flats that made her look like she'd stepped straight out of the fifties, even though she couldn't be more than twenty-five. She approached Star. "Lucy has store credit here, and she said to make sure you got whatever you needed!" Savanah winked and smiled so wide her eyes almost crinkled shut. She clapped her hands. "Girls' shopping trip!"

she sang out. "If you need anything, I'll be sorting through clothes. So have at it and have fun!" She returned to the counter, and the store filled with the soft crooning of Elvis joined by a high-pitched and slightly off-tune voice that Jess could only guess was Savanah singing along.

Jess shook her head. "Okay, then. Since it's still spring and the weather is all over the place, why don't you pick out a few shirts, jeans, shorts—like Lucy said, whatever you'd like."

But Star stood in the doorway, pulling at her fingers and not moving.

Jess tilted her head. "Don't you want to get some new clothes?"

Star shook her head, sucked in her cheek. "Yeah, it's just a lot to take in right now, you know?" She looked down at her hands. "I don't know my size or anything like that."

Jess felt a lump rise in her throat. "Why don't we start with jeans?" She pointed to a circular rack. "I'm guessing you're a zero in women's sizes? Let's start there."

Star joined her at the rack, and Jess began to pull a few jeans, holding them up for Star to see. A dark-blue pair. "This one?"

"Sure."

A light-washed pair with brightly colored patches on the thighs. "Is this your style?"

"Yeah."

Black jeans with a thick white stripe down the outside seam. "How about these?"

"Yep." Star folded them over her arm with the other two.

Jess hesitated before pulling the next pair. "You know you have a choice, right? You don't have to try on anything you don't like."

Star shrugged.

"Or because Lucy is paying. She still wants you to choose." It pained Jess to see Star's confidence drain out of her during a time when she should be having fun. Most girls her age would love to be on an all-expense-paid shopping trip. Jess sucked in her bottom lip. Star wasn't a regular teenager. She was a girl who chose to sleep under a bench. "Why don't you pick out a few things yourself?" she suggested.

Star shook her head, took a step back from the rack. "I don't care, Jess."

"About the jeans?"

"About any of it. I literally don't care what I get. I'm just—"

Star's eyes were so bright they glowed, and for the first time since she met her, Jess thought the girl might cry. She put her hand out, laid it gently on her shoulder. "What's wrong?"

Star wiped at her eyes, but Jess noticed they were dry, and she softened. Such a tough girl.

"No one's ever done this for me." She hugged the jeans to her chest, swayed back just enough so that Jess's hand fell from her shoulder. "I mean, my mom bought me stuff, I guess, but I don't remember her so much anymore. And at all the foster homes." She lifted her chin. "I wasn't at any of them long enough. If I needed new clothes, they were just there. No one—" Her voice grew hoarse, and she paused, then said, "No one's ever asked me before now."

"Oh," Jess said, and her shoulders sagged from the weight of Star's admission. The girl stared at the floor, the back of her neck exposed, making her look painfully vulnerable. More than anything, Jess wanted to comfort her; she felt it in the way her arms tingled from an instinct to wrap the girl in a hug. The feeling hit Jess square in the chest. She had loved being a mother. Instead she stuck her hands into the pockets of her jeans. She had no right to offer Star that kind of comfort.

"Well, we're asking now, so . . ." Jess tried to imitate the shop-keeper's singsong voice. "Girls' shopping trip!"

"Woo-hoo! That's right!" came Savanah's voice from behind the stack of clothes at the counter.

Star pushed a strand of hair behind one ear and gave Jess a small smile. "Girls' shopping trip!" she said softly, and turned to the rack of jeans, replacing the black ones and pulling out a cute pair of acid washed.

CHAPTER TWENTY-SIX

STAR

For the third morning in a row, Star awoke buried in the folds of a thick comforter, in a room with a door that closed and locked.

Yesterday with Jess had been nice. Jess was a private person, and at times she seemed wound pretty tight, but she was also kind in a guarded way. Star tried to resent her for constantly looking for a reason to make her leave, but in her heart she really couldn't blame her. Besides, Star sensed that Jess hid something painful. Her life had made her an expert on recognizing that in others.

And yesterday when Jess collapsed in the kitchen, her cry had been horrible—empty and so sad. Star recognized that sound too.

She pulled the covers under her chin, letting her feet search for pockets of coolness in the warmth of the bed. If this were a foster home, she would've already been looking for a way out. She wiggled deeper into the bed and pulled the comforter up until it covered her head. The truth was that she liked it here, and the feeling scared her. The air beneath the covers grew thick and hot, and she flung the comforter away, taking in sips of cool air.

A quick knock rattled her bedroom door. "Star?" called Jess.

"I'm getting up," she said, and reached for the bag of clothes from their consignment shop trip. She rifled through the bag, settling on a pair of acid-washed jeans and the dancing bears tie-dye shirt from Ebee.

"Can I come in?"

Star gripped the doorknob and hesitated. Jess had been open about her desire to call social services. Was today the day she'd win that battle with Lucy?

The door rattled with another knock. "Star?"

She opened the door. "Yeah?"

Jess knelt in the doorway, tying up the laces of a pair of athletic shoes. She wore loose black yoga pants and a long-sleeved apple-green top, her hair pulled back in her normally too-tight ponytail. She looked up at Star, frowning. "We went shopping yesterday so you wouldn't have to wear the same thing every day."

With the mention of their shopping trip, Star breathed out. Jess hadn't come here to send her away. At least not yet. She looked down at her shirt. "Well, *Aunt* Jess, it's a hard habit to break, I suppose. Besides, I like these little bears—they're so cute."

Jess rose to her feet and crossed her arms. "Just Jess works fine."

"Got it. Just Jess it is!"

Jess's mouth twisted into a bemused expression. "You are such a smart-ass."

She grinned. "I'm a teenager. It's our natural state."

Jess stepped away from the door and leaned over to touch her toes, stretching her hamstrings. "So, listen. I want to go for a walk around the lake. Now that this crappy mountain winter is finally coming to an end, I thought it'd be a good time to go." She gestured toward Star. "And with you here, I feel okay leaving Lucy for a bit."

"You trust me with Lucy?"

"Well, as Lucy says, we hardly know one another. I figure you have as much to lose as any of us."

Star squinted at her. "You do know that children are the future, right? You're supposed to lift us up with words of encouragement and praise. Tell me I can do anything I set my mind to. Fly, little bird, fly. You know, that sort of thing."

Jess rolled her eyes. "You can do anything you set your mind to." She smirked and turned to walk down the stairs.

Star hurried to the landing. "Wait, Jess! What do I do? Wake her up? Feed her with a spoon? Keep her away from sharp objects?"

"Toast and scrambled eggs for breakfast, and knock on her door at nine o'clock. You can do this, little bird." The door closed behind her.

~

"I'll be downstairs if you need me." Star closed the door to Lucy's room, proud of herself for making breakfast and delivering it to her by nine o'clock on the dot. It felt good to be doing something for someone else. But when she passed the sitting room on the way to the kitchen, a whispering sound stopped her cold.

A blast of frigid air blew against the spiky ends of her hair. She took a tentative step toward the room, gritted her teeth, and peered inside.

Her eyes widened. A rose-patterned bedsheet stretched across the backs of the two fancy chairs where she and Lucy had sat on her first day here. It lay awkwardly over their wooden arms and seats, making what looked like a small tent. She stared at the bedsheet. Was this how Lucy did her laundry or something? But Lucy had been in her room all morning, Star was sure of it. The space between her shoulder blades tickled. She wasn't alone. She backed slowly away until her heel hit the wall behind her, bringing her to a stop. Her eyes scanned the room. Empty. Yet she couldn't shake the feeling that something watched her. Her knees weakened, and she had to press her palms against the wall to keep from sinking to the floor.

"A fort," came a voice from the staircase above her head. Star's head shot up, and she found Lucy halfway down the stairs and looking over the railing.

"What did you say?" she said.

Lucy pointed her curved, bony finger into the living room. "It's a fort."

A fort. "But, Lucy," she said, "how did you—"

"He thinks the other one was much better."

Star's blood turned to ice. "He who?" she croaked, although a voice inside her whispered that she already knew the answer.

Lucy had descended the stairs and stood beside her now. Her skin glowed white against the black fabric of her dress. "His fort under the stairs. He thinks it was better."

Her legs trembled, and she shook her head. *No, no, no.* Lucy couldn't know anything about that, but she couldn't stop herself from asking. "Whose fort?"

A smile lifted the corners of Lucy's mouth, showing her teeth, small and antique like her house. "Your friend." Lucy squinted into the sitting room. "But he's very young." She frowned. "Oh dear. And very dead."

The room began to spin, and Star gripped the wall to keep from toppling forward. The fort had been where she and Jazz met every Saturday. She pressed her palm against her chest. It had been their safe place.

"This was in her room." Lucy handed her a white rectangle.

Star grasped it with her fingers and flipped it over. A picture. Her eyes widened. The small face that smiled up at her sent her stomach into free fall. Jazz. "Wh-where did you get this?" But her thoughts had already landed on the fallen drawer in Jess's room and the picture partly hidden among her scattered clothes.

"Jess's room, of course. But she can't talk about him yet, poor thing."

With trembling hands, Star pulled the paint-flecked rock from her sock, held it even with the picture, and memories she'd tried to bury hit her like a fist.

~

It was the morning of her seventh birthday when she awoke to her father retching in the toilet of the bathroom, the open door giving her a view of him on his knees, his face disappearing beneath the plastic seat.

She pulled a hand towel from a stack on the floor and tossed it to him, holding her nose as she did, then closed the door all the way and headed to the kitchen to make his coffee. This had been their routine for the past few months: her father with his head in a toilet or a needle in a vein, and Star trying to pretend everything was normal.

She set a mug of coffee on the thin green carpet outside the bathroom, pulled on her shoes, and left the apartment to wander around the third floor.

"Hey," someone called out to her.

She ignored the call and kept walking. She didn't know the other kids in the building well, preferring to be on her own most of the time.

"Hello! Hi! *Hola?*"

The voice was right behind her now, and she turned around to find a boy about her age, with skin the color of caramel syrup and light-brown hair that clung to his head in tiny curls.

"Hola," he said again. *"¿Cómo estás?"*

"I'm sorry," she answered. "I don't speak Spanish very well."

He grinned. "Neither do I! But when you didn't answer me, I thought maybe you did."

"Okay, well, bye." She turned and pushed through the door and into the stairwell.

"Wait!" He followed, walking beside her down the stairs.

She kept her eyes down. The stairs echoed metallically under their feet.

"What're you up to?" he said.

She didn't answer, hoping he'd get the hint and leave her alone. She didn't have friends in the building because friends asked questions about her dad that she couldn't answer.

"My mom and I just moved in," he continued. "It's a lot nicer than our last place."

Her foot hovered in midair. The Lancaster apartment complex was not nice at all.

"Our last place was a car."

She nodded in understanding.

"Anyway, so I thought we could play or something," he said. "Except I can only play on Saturday mornings."

"How come?" she asked. If Star wasn't at school she was here, in the apartment. There wasn't anywhere else to go, not even a park close by, just miles of city and sidewalks and people.

He rolled his eyes, giving her a goofy, gap-toothed grin. "My mom," he said. "She has stuff for me to do every day of the week except for Saturday mornings. She says every kid gets one morning a weekend to do nothing, or watch TV, which she says is the exact same thing."

"Okay." She began to walk again, taking the stairs one at a time. She didn't want to hear about his mom.

"So I usually watch *Transformers* because it's the best show and I think robots are awesome. Jazz is my favorite." His eyes got really big, and Star thought the show must be something she should know about, but they didn't have a television. It didn't seem to stop him. "Anyway, everyone always loves Optimus Prime, but I think Jazz is the best because he's small like me but really, really brave, you know?"

She shrugged.

"But I know a really cool place we can hang out," he said, keeping pace with her steps. "What's your name? My mom says I can't play with strangers, but if I know your name then you're not a stranger. And plus, you're a girl and you're my age, so I think that makes you not a stranger. Right?" He was winded, having raced ahead of her, jumping down two stairs at a time. But when he hit the ground level, he turned away from the exit door and disappeared into the space underneath the bottom flight of stairs.

She hesitated for a moment, curious, but then she pushed against the door handle with her hip.

He called to her again. "Hey, come here and check out my fort. I bet you're gonna love it!"

She backed away from the door and walked toward his voice. A sheet had been taped to the bottom of the metal stair rail; it hung low, partially obscuring the space behind it. She pushed aside the sheet and peered in. An old comforter covered the stained cement floor, with a few books and games scattered across the top of the red-and-yellow print. The boy sat in the middle of it, his shoes pushed off to the side.

"My name is Chance," he said. His brown eyes were soft and warm. "But you can call me Jazz, 'cause that would be awesome. He's the best, and my mom says he's a real talker like me, and I think I can be brave like him." He stopped, breathing a little heavy from all his talking. It almost made Star giggle.

She looked back at the exit door, wondering if it was safe to go back to the apartment yet or if her father's friends would be there. She chewed on her lip. She hated when those people came over. The boy sat very still, his eyebrows lifted high, waiting for her answer. She breathed out and stepped inside.

"My name is Star," she said in a voice so soft she almost couldn't hear herself.

"Wow! Cool name." He stuck out his hand, and she noticed they were scrubbed clean, his fingernails white. "Hi, Star. Nice to meet you." She settled on the blanket across from him and shoved her hands under her legs.

But he only laughed and kept his hand hanging in the air. "We're friends now, so we have to shake on it."

She pulled her hand out from under her leg and held it out, keeping her eyes lowered. He grabbed it and pumped their hands up and down until she laughed.

"It's my birthday today," she told him.

His eyes grew wide. "It is? Wow! How old are you?"

"I'm seven years old."

"Just like me! Then you have to check this out! I found it outside in front of the building." He searched behind him, pulling up the edge of the comforter, then picking up something before turning around to face her. "Look at it," he said, extending his hand toward her.

Nestled inside the center of his palm was a painted rock. Tiny, hand-drawn stars sparkled gold against the red.

"Here," he said, and raised his hand up, holding it close. "Take it."

He placed it in her hand. She pinched it between her thumb and index finger and flipped it over. The letters *CA* had been written on the back. Then she noticed the small dip in the top of the rock.

"You see it too, don't you?" he asked. "The heart?"

She nodded—a perfect heart—and handed it back to Chance, but he just smiled and shook his head.

"Keep it," he said, closing her hand around it. "My mom said it would bring me a friend. Happy birthday, Star."

CHAPTER TWENTY-SEVEN

STAR

After giving Star a glass of water and a light squeeze on her shoulder, Lucy quietly slipped from the kitchen. Star heard her heavy tread on the stairs a moment later and released the breath she hadn't realized she'd been holding. She was grateful to be alone. She sat at the kitchen table and stared at the picture in her hands. On the back, in neat print, it read, *Chance, Second Grade*. She brought it to her chest. He'd asked her to call him Jazz, but Star had always loved his real name. One his mom had chosen, Jazz had told her, because she said he was her chance to be a good mom. Star wrapped her arms across her stomach and fought the urge to throw up. Jess had picked his name. Jess had been his mom. Even then, Star had been happy for him to have a mom who loved him. But now she knew that Chance had had the best kind of mom. He'd had Jess. Her head hung with the truth—she had taken everything from them.

She stared at the picture, and something heavy settled on her chest. Chance. He'd been her best friend. Her only friend. A small voice screamed inside her, *He can't be here. He's dead.* Except a bigger part of her knew with a numbing certainty that Chance was here. Had felt it all along, even if the rational part of her brain had fought against it.

She covered her face with her hands, still clutching the picture between her fingers. Her stomach soured, and her mind filled with images of the night he died.

It had been a black night that froze the snot in her nose and made the street slick with puddles of slushy ice. They were running so fast her tennis shoes kept sliding across the sidewalk. Chance was crying, tears streaming down his face, and holding her hand, pulling her to her feet every time she fell. *Hurry, Star, hurry!* The lights were blurry through her tears. He pulled her into the intersection, but then he moaned, let go of her hand, and pushed her so hard she flew back and cracked her skull on the pavement. Her scream caught in her throat and choked her. Chance stared at her from the middle of the road, his eyes so dark they looked like black holes; a white glare painted the side of his face. Her last thought before the car came with a sickening crunch was that he looked like the moon.

She tried to push down the sting of bile that rose into her throat. For years she'd tried to forget about what had happened, but forgetting was impossible.

The front door opened and closed with a heavy bang that echoed from the end of a long tunnel. Star couldn't move. She stared at the picture, traced her finger across the curls on his head. Tears pooled in the corners of her eyes. He would never have been out that night if it hadn't been for her.

The picture was snatched from her hands, and she looked up to find Jess standing above her, face bone white, eyes wide. "Did you go through my things?" she said through clenched teeth.

With Jess so near to her, it hurt to breathe. Star kept her eyes lowered. A trembling had begun inside her that spread out until her knees jiggled up and down. She sneaked a look at Jess, who stared at the picture with her eyebrows scrunched together.

"Did Lucy—" She looked at Star. "I keep this in my room . . ."

Jess's mouth was still moving, but a roaring sound filled Star's ears, and she couldn't hear her anymore. She stumbled to her feet, her skin cold and tingling. Jess was Chance's mother. The thought ran a loop in her mind, each time bringing with it another wave of coldness.

"Star?"

She pushed past Jess and ran upstairs to her room, closing the door and pulling the covers up and over her head while her thoughts tumbled around, getting caught on the words Lucy had repeated since the first day they met. *Loose ends.*

The boy was Chance. Jess was his mom. And they were all here.

CHAPTER
TWENTY-EIGHT
JESS

She stood in the kitchen holding the picture of her son and staring at the spot where Star had been sitting. The girl had run away like something chased her. Why did she have the picture in the first place? Jess shook her head, confused and feeling like she had so often since arriving in Pine Lake. Like she was missing something important. She didn't keep anything valuable in her room, except for Chance's picture, and she doubted that Star would have pulled this out of her drawer and brought it down here. Why would the girl care about a school picture anyway?

Now, Lucy, on the other hand, had a tendency to wander the house, and Jess had already found her inside her bedroom, staring at her bonsai trees or looking out the window. It was possible, she guessed, that Lucy could have found the picture during one of those visits. The damn drawer kept sliding out. She'd had to push it in a number of times already.

Jess stared at Chance's face in the photo and softened. She'd forgotten it was picture day, and he'd gone to school with his hair a mess of unkempt curls. She touched his face, felt a fresh wave of grief wash over her. It never got easier. He smiled up at her, his curls dancing above his wide, nearly toothless grin. She smiled back. He'd lost his four front teeth in a two-week span, leaving him with a gaping hole. He'd gone around for a week smiling and poking his tongue through the hole at Jess. Echoes of their giggles hit her like shards of glass. She closed her eyes, held the picture to her heart, and could almost feel the weight of his body leaning into the crook of her arms while she read him a book.

From the hallway came the light patter of footsteps. Star? She ducked her head around the corner. The foyer was empty. She rubbed her eyes with one hand. She wasn't sleeping well, and her tiredness had become a persistent partner, muddling her thoughts and making her see things wrong, like the mouse under Lucy's bed and the coat-tree in the hallway.

She was turning back to the kitchen when she noticed the music. It floated down the hall from the direction of the sitting room. Her leg muscles twitched, pushing her to where the music grew louder. She peered into the sitting room. The music came from a vintage radio that sat on a table by the window. She cocked her head and tried to pick up the tune, but the volume was so low she couldn't make it out. She pulled at her fingers as she made her way across the room and the notes began to make sense. "Me and Bobby McGee." The song was one she knew by heart, one she'd sung to her colicky baby because it was the only thing that would quiet his cries. One she remembered her mother singing after dinner, after half a bottle of gin and before she passed out on the sofa in front of the television.

She wrapped an arm across her stomach, squeezed. She hadn't told anybody about Chance's funeral—she couldn't bear the thought of sharing her grief with people she hardly knew. After Chance was born, she wasn't interested in friends; she was focused on being Chance's mother and working every minute she wasn't with him to give him a life far better than her own. So it was just her and the small black casket and the minister. Afterward she sat huddled on the ground beside his grave, her eyes dry and sticky, her face chafed from the wind and the tears that came in waves. And she sang to him one last time, a song she'd never wanted to hear again.

A surge of rage rushed through her body, and she fumbled with the dials on the radio until she turned the right one and the radio darkened, taking the last few lyrics of "Me and Bobby McGee" with it. Jess was left in a silence so thick it felt as though she stood at the bottom of a deep sea with miles of water pressing against her eardrums.

Her wrist burned, and she looked down to see that she'd scratched it hard enough to leave red marks again. She studied the silvery white lines, ran her finger across the puckered flesh. The year after the funeral was gray and dim. She worked. She slept. She ate. She saw her son everywhere. And when she couldn't take it anymore, she tried to join him. A sharp pain flashed across her wrist, making her gasp. The paramedics were at her door before she could do the other one. A fluke, because it was Mrs. Rodriguez who'd called 9-1-1 for Mr. Rodriguez, who was having another heart attack. The paramedics had busted through the wrong door. And Mr. Rodriguez had only had bad gas.

She didn't know how long she stood there, but the shadows outside had lengthened, which meant it was well past lunch. She inhaled sharply, surprised. It was unlike her to lose track of time like that. She hurried from the room and up the stairs to check on Lucy.

CHAPTER
TWENTY-NINE

STAR

She'd never met Chance's mom. He'd wanted to introduce them, had invited Star over on more occasions than she could count for mac-and-cheese or pancakes shaped like snowmen and smiley faces. But she missed her own mother in a way that made her chest hurt. Chance eventually stopped asking, until one day he showed up at the fort with pancakes and warm syrup and a can of whipped cream. It was her favorite day.

She rocked back and forth on the bed. Chance and his mom had been the perfect family. Star pressed her eyes into her palms, then shot to her feet. She shouldn't be here. She grabbed an armful of clothes and stuffed them into her shopping bag from the other day. Her rock sat next to the note from Lucy on the bedside table. She reached for them both, paused, then swept the note and rock into the top drawer and stood undecided in the middle of the room. She'd leave as soon as Jess went to bed and—

A soft knock rattled her door. "Star?"

Her shoulders slumped. "What do you want, Jess?"

She paused for so long, Star thought she might have left.

"Can I come in?"

She stashed her bag under the bed, checked her face in the mirror to make sure it didn't look like she'd been crying, and, satisfied, opened the door.

Jess stepped inside, and they stood facing each other, an awkwardness flaring up between them. Jess rubbed the back of her neck but didn't speak. Star chewed on a nail, waiting. She couldn't help but notice how the shape of Jess's face mirrored the boy in the photo, her eyes the same soft brown. It was so obvious now.

"I'm sorry for accusing you earlier," Jess said. "I think Lucy probably found the picture in my room and unintentionally brought it downstairs."

Star looked down at the floor. She knew she should tell her who she was, but she was afraid that after Jess learned the truth, Star would disappear back into the system, where nobody cared about her like they did here. And that scared her more than anything. But Star couldn't explain why Chance was here, could hardly believe it herself, despite what she had seen. Goose bumps raced down her spine. What did Jazz—Chance—want?

"That picture you found . . ." Jess sighed.

Star's pulse thundered in her ears; she wasn't ready to talk to Jess about Jazz. It was too much, and her spine curved forward from the heaviness of knowing. "I'm sorry about the police officer," she said, hoping to change the subject.

Jess scratched her head. "What? Why?"

"For making you lie when I know you didn't want to. I've been thinking that maybe you're right about me."

"How so?"

"That I should leave Pine Lake before I get Lucy in trouble."

Before Jess could answer, the antique lamp with the frosted white shade on the bedside table flickered on and then off in rapid succession. Star clasped and unclasped her hands. Jazz.

Jess walked over to the lamp. "What the hell?" she said, and pulled the small chain, but the light grew even brighter until the bulb popped.

A chill rippled across Star's skin.

"That was weird," Jess said, unscrewing the blackened blub.

"Yeah."

"Is that yours?" Jess murmured and bent over, peering at something on the floor.

Star's rock, the one she'd just put in the drawer, lay on the rug. She reached down and snatched it off the floor. "Yeah," she said, and closed her hand around it.

Jess stared at Star's fist.

"It's just some rock I found when we went to the lake," she said. "It has sparkles in it."

Jess shook her head, blinked, and her face softened into a small smile. "Hey, listen. You're not a problem. In fact, Lucy perks up when she's around you. I think you're good for her." She moved back toward the door. "I'm just worried that someone is missing you."

"Nobody's missing me, Jess."

Jess nodded, and her mouth turned down at the ends. "I find that hard to believe."

"Believe it."

She brought her hands up, palms out. "Okay, okay. We'll table it for now," she said. "Hey, I saw that teenage cabdriver when I was coming back from the lake this morning."

"So?"

"He asked how you were doing. And if he could stop by and hang."

Star crossed her arms, pursed her lips. "With you?" she said.

"Smart-ass," Jess said with a smile. "He seems like he'd make a nice friend."

Star's hand tightened around the rock.

"Didn't you have friends on the street, Star?"

The question took her by surprise, and Star struggled to keep her emotions inside. "Not really." The rock felt heavy in her palm. "I kept to myself."

"That must have been really lonely," she said with so much compassion it made Star look away.

If Jess knew the truth about her, she wouldn't be so nice; Star knew that with a certainty that tied her stomach into knots. "I don't need friends," she said, but her voice carried with it a pathetic hoarseness.

"Everybody needs a friend, Star."

She pressed her lips together, stared at her hands.

Jess cleared her throat. "I've been homeless too."

"You have?"

She nodded. "Twice. Once when I was a kid with my mother. We lived in an old van. It was only for a few months, but it wasn't easy."

"And the second time?" But she already knew. That time had been with Jazz—no . . . Chance—right before they moved into the Lancaster.

Jess hesitated. "The second time was my own damn fault. I got fired from a waitressing job after the owner grabbed my ass."

"Can they do that?"

Jess smiled. "They could after I broke his nose with a serving tray."

Star gave her a tight smile. "Bet he deserved it."

"He did, but it put me three months behind on my rent. We got evicted."

They both grew quiet. Guilt gnawed at her, making it hard to keep from blurting everything out. Star held her breath, hoping the conversation would end there.

Jess turned to leave, and Star felt her shoulders round forward. She opened her palm, stared at the rock, thought of Chance. Was he angry at her? Or, a small, hopeful voice asked, did he want to help her? She shivered. Lucy would know, and sooner or later Star was going to have to find out.

Jess was looking at her, and for a moment Star felt her eyes get wet again. Chance had always smiled when he'd talked about his mom. She must miss him so much. She breathed in and tried to make the tears go away. "H-he died." The words fell out so quickly Star wasn't even sure if she'd said them out loud.

Jess cocked her head to the side, looking confused. "Who died?"

Star took in a ragged breath. She couldn't believe she was saying it out loud, but she also couldn't seem to stop herself. "The only friend I've ever had."

Her dad had been jittery that night, smoking one cigarette after another until a layer of smoke hung heavy in the apartment. It made Star's eyes water and her nose itch. Her father paced the small apartment, his movements jerky, like he was one of those puppets with strings and someone else controlled him. *Bastard owes me money,* he mumbled, and gripped Star by her shoulders, the heated red glow of his lit cigarette inches from her cheek. *Do not speak to him. Understand?* He spoke through his teeth and had a look in his eyes that made her think of the stray dog who lived in the alley behind the building. Hungry.

Before she could answer, he jerked away from her and disappeared into the bathroom, the door cracked just enough for her to hear him talking to himself. She'd thought of Chance then. Just that morning he'd told her that he was going to make oatmeal raisin cookies with his mom for his birthday. Her mouth watered. She'd never had a cookie like that. She glanced nervously toward the bathroom. The toilet flushed. Before she could change her mind, she grabbed the card she had made him and the only present she had, one of her mother's bonsai trees. With the tree clutched to her side, she sprinted out of the apartment, not even bothering to close the door behind her, and into the stairwell, taking the stairs as fast as she could without falling or dropping the plant. Her heart had beaten so loud she could hear it thump in her ears.

It was late at night; she didn't know how late, but enough so that the apartments she passed were quiet, TVs turned down or off. She found herself standing in front of Chance's apartment door. She brought her fist up to knock, hesitated, and dropped it back to her side. When did normal kids go to bed? If she woke him up, would his mom get mad?

But Chance had said his mom was the nicest mom he knew, and besides, Star hadn't wanted to go home. So she'd raised her fist again and knocked.

Jess's hand touched Star's shoulder, making her jump. The rock lay in the center of her open palm. Had Jess seen it? She closed her hand and looked up, but Jess seemed not to have noticed the rock, staring down at her with her forehead creased, eyes bright with pity.

Star clenched her jaw and stood. She didn't deserve pity from Jess. "Guess what?" she said. "I'm hungry."

Jess's face relaxed, and she smiled. "Shocking," she said, and gestured for Star to follow as she left the room and walked downstairs.

CHAPTER THIRTY

JESS

She placed the last bonsai tree on a table in the sitting room, wiped the dirt from her hands, and stood back. The trees were soaked by the sun's afternoon glow. She frowned. The light highlighted how lifeless the leaves had become. Something needed to be done, or she was going to lose all three. Maybe Jess should ask Star again if she'd help. It would probably be good for her to have something to focus on.

Since Star had arrived, all Jess could think about was getting her back to where she belonged. But when she had offered to leave Pine Lake, Jess felt something tug at her heart at the girl's stricken face, and in that moment, she couldn't let it happen. At least not yet. Besides, Star's youthfulness was good for Lucy; that was the truth.

The doorbell rang, and Jess opened the door to Jeremy, who gave her a sheepish grin, his hands stuck into the front pockets of his jeans.

"I know, I know," he said quickly. "I'm a stalker."

She leaned against the door and smiled. He'd stopped by to see Star three times in the last two days. Star had turned him away each time. "You do seem to be trending in that direction," she said.

"Hey, but at least I stalk the old-fashioned way."

"As opposed to?"

He rolled his eyes. "Duh, Jess, online. C'mon, you're not that old. I'm sure even geezers like you stalk people online just like us young people."

He pantomimed snapping his suspenders, or at least that's what Jess thought he was doing. She shook her head with a sigh. "You're an old soul, Jeremy," she said, and opened the door all the way. "Star's in the library with Lucy."

He hesitated, losing his playfulness for a moment. "Shouldn't you ask her first?"

"Nah. I think she just needs a little push. Go on, surprise her."

He rocked onto his toes, looking unsure of himself.

She smiled. "Are you scared of her or something?"

His Adam's apple moved slowly up and down his long throat. "Can I tell you a secret?" he whispered. "I think I am. She's lit, you know?"

Jess raised an eyebrow. "No, I do not know."

He clapped a hand to his forehead. "Cool—it means she's cool."

She sighed and gave him a half smile, gesturing for him to come inside. "Get in here before I close the door."

He hopped inside, flashed her a wide smile, and loped down the hall. Jess shook her head and went into the kitchen to see what she could pull together for dinner. A few minutes later she heard the faint echo of Star's laugh and was satisfied she'd done the right thing.

She was wiping down the kitchen counters when Lucy appeared with Star and Jeremy tagging behind. "We'll be back," she said to Jess.

"Where are you going?"

Lucy looked skyward. "Why does nobody check the calendar?"

Jess sighed—that damn calendar—and squinted at the small square. *Dinner, movie.* She pointed to the refrigerator. "But I made lasagna."

"It'll keep," Lucy said with a pat on her shoulder.

"You could come with us," Star suggested.

Jess tried to hide her surprise at the offer. It would be nice to get out, to do something other than work. But one glance at the hopeful look on Star's face and Jess shook her head. She had to be careful how close she allowed herself to get to the girl, because neither one of them could afford the heartbreak that would happen when Star had to leave. "No, thanks. I'd like a quiet night here."

Star slumped.

"Do you have a phone, Jeremy? In case Lucy needs me for some reason?"

He pulled out a slim black phone and waved it in the air. "All set."

"Very well then," Lucy said with a wave of her hand. "But if you're in the mood to let loose," she said with a wink, "I keep some liquor stashed in the library."

Jess couldn't remember the last time she'd had a drink. Work always came first, and drinking never put her in a good place anyway. "Thanks, Lucy, but a good book will be all I need tonight."

After they left, she wandered into the library, hoping she could lose herself in a story for at least a little while. As she pushed open the door and flipped on the light, her eyes caught the corner cabinet to her left. A wineglass sat on a small silver tray next to a chilled bottle of chardonnay. Lucy.

She walked over to the bar, intending to put the wine away, but she noticed that it had already been uncorked. Oh hell. Why not? She poured herself a glass before wandering over to the wall of books that towered above her head. She pondered her choices, feeling out of her depth. Reading was a luxury she didn't often have the time to enjoy. She chose a slim volume at random and returned to the couch, book in one hand, wine in the other.

A couple of hours later, she was two glasses in and well into the story when the library window rattled as though hit by a gust of wind. Then a light *clack, clack, clack* of something hitting the glass.

She rose to her feet and felt the wine go directly to her head. "Oops." It was a light buzz, but it made her feel weightless, like she had detached from her body and now hovered suspended inside it.

She ambled to the window and pulled the heavy gold cord to open the curtains. To her surprise, it was fully dark outside, and her own reflection stared back at her. The clacking had quieted. Must have been the wind knocking the branches of a tree against the house. She studied her reflection, ponytail pulled tight, lines around her eyes. She wasn't that old, but sadness left marks, and she bore plenty of them.

A puff of frigid air tickled the back of her neck, and she gasped. Reflected beside her in the window was a little boy, the one from the market—she could tell by his red sweatshirt, the hood pulled up and cinched tight.

She whirled around, eyes wide open, but the room was empty, of course. Cold beads of sweat formed in her armpits. "Jesus, Jess," she berated herself. "What the hell is wrong with you?"

She shook her head. Her imagination had grown too active in Pine Lake. Time to put the wine away for sure. When she moved to return to the couch, her toe hit a small black stone on the rug, and she groaned in frustration. The damn rocks were still being tracked in daily, making it quite a chore to keep the house clear of them. Bending down, she picked it up, but the shape of it in her palm stopped her cold. She opened her hand and inhaled sharply. A perfectly heart-shaped rock.

She held it to her chest. Chance had loved looking for heart-shaped rocks, and it didn't matter if they were an actual heart or more of an impression of one. To him, most of them were close enough. Biting the inside of her cheek, she tried to push away her memories, but they were always there, like the phantom pain from a missing limb. It took only the thought to conjure Chance to her side, feel the light press of his bony shoulder into her hip. She could reach out and tousle his curls, and he would look back at her with his gap-toothed smile, skin the color of butterscotch, his eyes lit with excitement, small fingertips grasping a rock. Her chest tightened. She'd told him they would bring him good luck because they were hearts. And that the heart was where love lived. And that love was magical.

She closed her eyes and let the rock drop into a wastepaper basket by the couch. Her memories did nothing but hurt and make her wish for things she couldn't have.

The clacking started up again with such force she thought the window might explode.

Jess rushed over to the window and peered outside. The boy stood on the patio directly across from her. Her breath came hard and fast, fogging the glass. He raised his arm and threw something at her that landed with a clack on the window. And then another. *Clack!* And another. *Clack!* The kid was throwing rocks.

She rapped on the glass. "Hey!" she yelled. "Stop that!"

He turned and bolted into the thistles. She let the curtains fall together and rushed from the library. It was time she confronted the boy.

The minute she stepped outside, she wished she'd grabbed a coat. The night was moonless and cold. She picked her way around the side of the house, stumbling over unseen tree roots and toe-stubbing rocks. She shivered. Something urged her forward despite a growing desire to go back inside where it was warm and light.

She made it to the relative flatness of the side patio and stopped in her tracks. The similarity to the other day made her heart jump into her throat. There he stood beside the old shed on the hill above her, his sweatshirt hood pulled up and over his head, hands shoved deep into the pockets. Unmoving.

"Hey, kid," she called, but she'd begun to shiver from the cold and her voice shook. "What do you want?"

He raised his arm and let something sail from his hand. She shrank back, hands over her head. He was throwing rocks at *her* now? What was the kid's deal? The object tumbled onto the patio and rolled, lopsided, until it clattered to a stop at her feet. She stared at it, and for a second she lost the sense of the ground beneath her, the feel of her skin, the need to breathe.

It was a rock, and she knew even before she picked it up that it was heart shaped.

Her strength left her in a whoosh, and she sank to her knees on the hard stone, mindless of the jagged pain it sent up her thighs. *Breathe, Jess. Breathe, damn it.* The rocks, her wrist, the dreams about her son. It felt like she was reliving that year all over again. But the boy was real, wasn't he? Hadn't Lucy seen him too? She looked up the hill, squinted in the dark; he was gone.

From the thick woods to her left came a heavy crashing of leaves and branches. She sprang to her feet, chest heaving. What the hell was that? Even in the black night she could make out low-hanging pine branches thrashing back and forth, and she heard a deep huffing sound. Bear.

She backed away from the trees, but the huffing grew louder until it seemed like the animal was running full tilt and straight at her. In a panic, she hurled the rock toward the sound and turned to run, but in her haste she tripped and fell to her hands and knees. Her racing heart beat loud in her ears as the air filled with an animal stink.

Jess clasped her hands across the back of her head, bracing for a claw to rip through her skin, but then the sound of someone running through the dry grass behind Lucy's house brought her head up. A figure darted down the hill.

"Hey, bear!" came Officer Ben's voice. "Hey! Go, bear!" Ben tore down the hill, sidestepping the patch of thistle, arms raised high over his head and waving back and forth. "Hey! Go, bear!" He ran past Jess and stood at the tree line, arms still raised, his voice deep, guttural, and authoritative. "Hey! Go away, bear!"

The thrashing faded, and the night became quiet again. Jess pushed to her feet and wiped dirt from her jeans, her hands still shaking from the encounter. The wildest animal she'd seen in the city had been a large and very scary-looking raccoon scavenging in the dumpster behind her building.

"Thanks," she said. "It's a good thing bears obey cops too."

He smiled, still breathing hard.

A bead of sweat dripped down her back. She rubbed at her arms and shivered; she felt hot and cold all at the same time, and her pulse still raced. "What are you doing here?" she asked, trying to think about something other than how she'd nearly been eaten by a bear. Ben stood in a wide stance, his eyes trained on the forest. Jess noticed that he wasn't in uniform, and like her, he also wasn't wearing a coat.

He pointed past the shed at the slope behind Lucy's home, where Jess could just make out the glow of house lights between the tree branches. "That's my house up there. I was getting firewood when I heard you yelling. There's been a mama bear and her cubs spotted a few times already. When I heard you scream, I figured mama bear saw you as a threat." He glanced into the woods again. "Guess I was right."

"Thanks again. Would you like to come inside for tea"—she thought of the wine—"or a drink?" Part of her hoped he'd say no; she'd prefer to avoid the uncomfortable chatter that inevitably came with small talk. But another, surprising part of her thought it might be nice to spend some time getting to know someone new. Pine Lake was changing her.

"Sure, that sounds nice." In the dark she couldn't see his face well, but she could feel him staring at her, as if he was measuring her up. "Mind if I ask what you were doing out here this time of night? Spring's an active time for animals, and with the thaw the bears are waking up, and they're hungry."

"I saw a bo—" At this point she wasn't sure how much she could trust her own perception, and she certainly didn't want Ben to think she was unstable or fragile. She suspected he only needed a reason to suggest to Lucy that Jess was unfit for the job. Something told her that he'd been deeply offended, maybe even angry, when Lucy took matters into her own hands. "I thought I saw a bear from the library window."

He chuckled, shook his head. "Again, huh? Looks like you were right this time, but how about next time you stay inside so you can watch from the safety of the house?"

She laughed. "Good idea."

CHAPTER THIRTY-ONE

JESS

He followed her inside and to the library; she pointed to the cart in the corner. "Help yourself. I just learned today that Lucy keeps liquor stocked in here."

He crossed the room to the small bar. "I know all about Lucy's stocked bar." He opened the cabinet door, took out a crystal tumbler, and poured three fingers of whiskey into the bottom.

Jess felt her cheeks warm. "I'm sorry, I didn't mean to sound like I knew more—"

"She caught me sneaking a sip of whiskey when I was fourteen," he said with a smile, and Jess relaxed.

"What did she do?" She returned to her seat on the sofa, closed the book she'd never finish. She'd never been much of a reader anyway—didn't have the time. Magazines were easier and faster.

"She said that whiskey is a man's drink, and a real man doesn't have to sneak around to drink it." He took a long swallow.

"Did that stop you?" Ben had a weathered look to him, the planes of his face deep, angles sharp, which made it hard to imagine him as a teenage boy.

"Hell no. But something else did."

"What?"

"I was around your niece's age, right? So I was young, maybe a bit naive."

She tried not to react to the mention of Star as her niece, feeling bad for the lie. "Okay, so?"

"And maybe a little drunk, because when she found me the second time, I had just downed an entire shot glass of whiskey. She swept through that door with her eyes closed and came right up to me. I was shaking so badly the shot glass slipped through my fingers and fell to the floor. Then she opened her eyes." He ran his hands through his short hair. "You know how crazy her eyes are by now, right?"

Jess nodded.

"So I never snuck whiskey from the cabinet again."

Jess leaned toward him, waiting for the part of his story where Lucy levitated him with her broom or made his head spin in circles. It didn't come. "Wait, that's it? That's all that happened?"

"I was *fourteen*. And she was the Witch of Pine Lake. Scared the shit out of me."

She laughed. "You sound like Jeremy."

"How's that?"

"He acted the same way about Star today. You mountain men sure are scared of a bunch of little women."

His face lit with amusement, and he crossed the room, took a seat in the chair opposite her. "How's your niece doing?"

Jess took a sip of wine and another, then settled back on the couch and tried to sound casual. "Good. She likes it here." The wine buzzed through her body, making her fidget, and she searched for something to say to change the topic. "Lucy seems to really care about you."

He grunted and drained his whiskey. "We've known each other a long time."

"She seems concerned about you, though. Can't stop worrying about your loose end. What do you think she means by it?"

He stood, returned to the bar, and poured himself another glass. "What's that?"

"Your loose end. She's talked about it more than once, and it seems to upset her." His face had set like stone, and Jess worried that she'd crossed a line into something personal. Something that wasn't any of her business. She tried to switch tactics. "Sorry, it's just that she talks about loose ends a lot, not just yours, and as her caregiver I'm only trying to figure out what she means."

He took a sip before heading back to the chair. "Lucy gave me a job when I needed the money. Bought me practice gear for football. Things my parents didn't care about."

Ben's broad shoulders had shrunk, making him look defensive. He'd already told her that he'd had a less than perfect childhood, and she felt bad for prying. "Let me guess," she teased, hoping to lighten mood, "defensive lineman?"

He gave her a tight smile. "Quarterback."

"Did you play in college?"

His jaw tightened, and he gripped the sides of the tumbler. She half expected it to shatter. "I had a full scholarship to CU Boulder. Redshirted my freshman year, and by my junior year I was on track to be starting quarterback." He paused, and his jaw twitched. "I got injured before my junior year. Badly. The doctors prescribed me pain pills, too many of them, and I was young and stupid enough to think taking more than I needed was keeping the pain away. By the time I realized I was addicted, it was too late. I was missing practices, didn't show up for games, and I lost my scholarship." He knocked back the rest of the whiskey and met her eyes again. "I went through a rough patch after that, and by sheer strength of will I made it through in one piece. Lucy was there for me during that too."

She softened. Life was merciless and cruel. End of story.

"My son died when he was very young." She was surprised it came out so easily with someone she hardly knew, but she was touched that he'd shared his past with her. It wasn't easy to talk about failure. "I had nobody. It was"—she scratched her wrist through the cotton fabric of her shirt—"a very difficult time to get through, and I can't say I did it very well." She shook her head. "I'm not sure why I told you that, except I guess what I'm trying to say is that I'm glad you had Lucy."

He stared at her for a moment, his expression unreadable. "I'm sorry, Jess," he said in a soft voice.

She blinked rapidly and gave him a small smile. A part of her yearned to talk about her son, to share the lightness he'd brought into her world with someone else. But the shadow of how she'd found him that night stretched long and darkened the good memories with an ugliness that made it hard. "I'm not sure why Lucy would be concerned about your loose ends, because it seems to me like you overcame those days."

He shifted in his seat, ran a hand roughly through his hair. "That's why I'm worried about her. As she's gotten older, it's like she's lost track of time, forgets the past. Sometimes I swear she thinks I'm Ben from back then, not the guy who cleaned his life up."

"I'm really sorry for prying. It's none of my business."

His knee jiggled up and down, and he tapped the side of his tumbler with his fingers. "Lucy has a way of making everyone's business her own." His eyes scanned the room, ceiling to floor. "I know you're here to help her, Jess, but I'm serious about this house." As though in response to being talked about, the walls creaked and the light from the chandelier dimmed.

Jess blinked several times. Her eyes had grown dry at this higher altitude. "What about the house?"

"It's too big for her. I've been telling her that for years. Hell, she can barely make it up the stairs, and one day she's going to fall and break her hip."

Jess stiffened at Ben's tone. "That's what I'm here for, Ben," she reminded him. "If it puts your mind at ease, you're wrong. I've worked around many seniors her age and younger, and from what I've seen, Lucy is physically strong and manages those stairs like someone half her age. Personally, I think this house is exactly where she needs to be. Please don't take offense, but I truly believe that making her leave at this point is cruel and unnecessary."

He sat straight up, his broad shoulders almost wider than the wings of the chair, and held her gaze. "How long will you be here, Jess? Seems to me you're someone who doesn't like attachments or commitments. Where were you going the day your car broke down anyway?"

From somewhere within the house, a door banged against a wall. Jess stood, grateful for the interruption. The space between them was taut like a rubber band pulled too tight. She kept her head held high, her back straight. For now she was the caregiver, and she would make whatever decisions were in Lucy's best interests. "They're home," she said stiffly. "I'm sure Lucy will be pleased to see you, Ben, but she'll be tired from her evening out. Maybe you can come back tomorrow for a visit?"

The way he stared at her made Jess wonder if she'd gone too far. Then his face relaxed, and he smiled. "Of course. Thanks for the drink. I'll go say hello before I see myself out."

Her heart beat fast. The conversation about Lucy had turned into a tense standoff between them. Making an enemy out of someone who cared deeply for the older woman would be a mistake, and she needed to make it right before he left. "Hey, Ben," she said.

He hesitated in the doorway.

"I do see your point about the house, and I meant what I said the other day about helping her go through her things for when that time comes. We even started on a few boxes in the basement. We're starting on the attic next, and after that I thought we'd tackle the shed, but I can't seem to find a key that fits the lock. Lucy thought you might know. Do you?"

He stepped toward her, and even in the library with the arched ceilings and walls that stretched high above her head, his height and wide shoulders made the space feel small, claustrophobic. In that moment she wanted nothing more than to escape.

Lucy's red hair and stooped form appeared in the doorway just then, and Jess exhaled with relief.

"Benjamin!" she said. "This is an awfully late visit from you."

Star appeared silently behind her.

Ben's eyes widened at Lucy's voice, his shoulders slumped, and for a second Jess could see him as the teen boy who got caught drinking whiskey from the liquor cabinet.

"Ben saved me from a bear this evening," Jess offered.

"Is that so?" Lucy said.

Ben turned and gave Lucy a gentle smile. "If you're going to hire city folk up here, you need to teach them about mountain dangers."

Star's eyes widened, and she looked directly at Jess. "You saw a bear?"

Jess nodded but noticed how intently Ben stared at Star. It made the hair on the back of her neck stand on end, and she moved quickly to Star's side, leading her out of the library. "Tell me all about the movie," she said.

Star rolled her eyes, laughed. "I'm not sure I can. Lucy couldn't hear half of it and asked me or Jeremy to repeat just about every other sentence. Some kid behind me threw popcorn in my hair."

She smiled, half listening, because from the library she heard Ben say in a low voice, "Lucy, what do you know about Jess?"

CHAPTER THIRTY-TWO

STAR

For a few hours tonight, Star had almost felt like a regular teenager. Dinner and a movie with a friend, although she suspected most teenagers wouldn't dream of going to the movies with their grandmothers. Not that Lucy was her grandmother, but for a split second Star had let herself pretend she was, and it had felt good. Just like she'd let herself pretend that Jess was more than Lucy's hired caregiver and that she actually spent time with Star because she wanted to, not because it was a paid job. Pretending was easy for Star with as much sleep as she'd gotten and on a full belly.

A few days had passed since Star found the fort in the living room, and everything had been quiet, meaning no more things she couldn't explain. She bit her lip. One day she was a teenager with filthy clothes and nothing to lose, and the next she had a home, people who seemed to care about her, and the ghost of her friend haunting her. Star wanted to pretend she hadn't seen his picture, pretend she hadn't seen *him*. Then again, her life had been a shit show, and at this point, nothing really surprised her anymore. While the quiet made Star tense, it also gave her reason to hope that Chance didn't want anything bad to happen to her. Still, deep inside she knew she needed to talk to Jess, and that made her afraid—afraid saying anything out loud would end everything.

After Jeremy dropped her and Lucy off, they'd come inside and found Jess with Officer Ben in the library. Star's pulse had raced because she'd thought Jess had caved and finally told him, but from the way they faced each other, it looked to Star like they were in an old western standoff, and nobody said a thing about foster homes or caseworkers. She couldn't relax, though, because Officer Ben looked at her like he already knew something.

Jess was in an unusually talkative mood after her evening alone, asking Star about the movie and Jeremy and if Lucy had any concerning episodes. Star was desperate to avoid more conversation with the woman, afraid that it might all spill out. So she shrugged at her questions, yawned, and rubbed at her eyes until Jess suggested that she go to bed. It took her a while to fall asleep, and when she did it was fractured by dreams that pierced her with longing and fear.

Her mother stood in the hallway outside her bedroom, exactly how Star remembered her: dark hair, smooth skin, the hint of cinnamon in the air around her. Her heart nearly burst. Her mother was alive! She ran, reached out, her fingertips sliding over her mom's soft skin, but then she fell, and her mother slipped farther and farther away until Star was alone in the thick woods outside Lucy's house, her back pressed into the rough bark of a pine tree, her bare feet cold on the earth. Something blunt hit her shin, then another. Rocks, pelting her, bruising, painful. One glanced across her forehead; another bounced off the bone beneath her eye; trickles of blood ran down her face. The rocks kept coming, one after another until they piled up over her feet, up her legs, to her waist, burying her. She cried out, *Mommy!* From deep in the forest came a thrashing of leaves and branches and a growl that echoed around her. She screamed and tried to move, tried to wake herself, chanting, *Only a dream, only a dream.* But the rocks were up to her neck now, and out of the darkness something charged at her. A man, running hunched over like a bear until he pulled up even with her, and then he stretched to his full height, his head disappearing in the branches of the tree above her but his badge even with her eyes. A star, burning so bright it blinded her. Then she was back in her bed, small again, being held tight by her mother, who cooed softy in her ear, and Star never, ever, ever wanted to wake up.

"No, no, no, no," she sobbed, her body curled into a fetal position around her tangled and twisted sheets, her eyes tightly closed. "No, no, no."

Arms surrounded her, gently removing the pillow and pulling her up so that she lay cradled against a soft, warm chest.

"Sh-sh-sh-sh. It's okay, sweetie. You're okay." It was Jess, and the tenderness in her voice and the softness of her arms brought on another round of tears. Jess held her close, pressing Star's head against her chest and stroking her back in a circular motion. "Sh-sh-sh-sh-sh."

Star let herself be gently rocked, feeling small, protected, and safe, and she hiccuped a sob, thinking that now that she'd started, she'd never stop crying. When her eyes had dried and swollen, she pushed away from Jess, hanging her head to avoid looking at her. "I'm sorry," she said.

Jess pushed her chin up until Star met her eyes. "Don't apologize." She raised her eyebrows and didn't release her chin until Star nodded. "Okay then. Another bad dream?"

Star nodded again, unable to speak yet, afraid she might tell her everything.

Jess let her hands fall into her lap but stayed seated on the bed, her knee just touching Star's leg. Star swallowed; the physical contact, no matter how minimal, made her realize just how lonely she felt.

"I used to make cookies," Jess said.

"Cookies?"

"After a bad dream I could never go back to sleep, so I'd make cookies. Dozens of them. I'd give them to my neighbors, the bus driver, a stranger I passed on my way to the diner."

Star smiled. "What kind?"

"Chocolate chip, peanut butter, sugar—you name it."

"Oh," Star mumbled, twisting and untwisting her fingers.

Jess shifted, inhaled. "How long have you lived on the streets?" she said.

Thankful for a change of subject, Star said, "About six months."

Jess cleared her throat. "What happened?"

Star leaned against the bed frame and pulled her knees up to her chest. "My last foster family—" She hesitated, but it was spilling out on its own now, as though a gate had been opened and all she could do was talk. "You were right about me."

Jess raised her eyebrows. "How so?"

"You don't know me. I'm not *good*. I've never done drugs or anything like that, but I steal—er, I mean I've stolen before." She chewed on a fingernail. "From every one of my foster homes."

"What did you steal?"

"Anything. Mostly food, some cash, a few stupid trinkets. It didn't really matter; it was just something I could do." Her state-appointed counselor had said that it was a compulsion. She had been caught nearly every time, and every time she'd said she was sorry and that she'd never do it again. And then she would. "By my last foster family, I guess I was tired of saying I was sorry." She rubbed her eyes with the heels of her palms. "But you have to believe me. I'd never steal from you or Lucy. Ever."

"What happened before the foster families?" she said in a soft voice.

Star rested her chin on her knees, her eyelids dry and itchy. "My mom got sick and died, and I guess the hospital bills were too much, because my dad lost everything—our house, our money." She told her story in the same voice she might use to read the ingredients off a box of cereal. "And when I didn't think things could get any worse, he started dealing drugs, and then he died too." She was worn out, exhausted, and worried that at any moment the truth would be too much to hold in. "After that I landed in foster care." She tried to smile, but it stretched her lips too thin, felt unnatural. "There were some good families. A few that really wanted to make things better for me."

"But you didn't want their help, did you?"

A sob welled in Star's throat. She stopped, took a deep breath. "Everything sucked, the worst nightmare ever, and I wanted to wake up." Jess placed her fingers over Star's hand and squeezed. Star tried not to focus on the warmth that ran through her at the touch. "But there were awful foster homes too. And by my last one, when they discovered a twenty-dollar bill and the dad's worthless drugstore watch under my pillow, I'd had enough. I figured that I could take care of myself just as well, if not better. So I disappeared."

"How did you . . ." Jess faltered, pulled at the leg of her pajama pants. "Did anything happen to you on the street?"

Star shook her head. "Nothing too bad. I was lucky, I guess." She thought about the night of the attack, of Mel stopping it. What if he hadn't been there? She crossed her arms. "Until I wasn't. But then I came here."

Jess smiled. "And I'm glad you did." She touched Star's shoulder. "Thank you."

"For what?"

"For trusting me with your story. You're one brave smart-ass." She gave her shoulder a playful punch, eyed the bed. "Hop up. I think I'll wash your sheets today. There's nothing quite like clean sheets, is there?"

A lump hardened in Star's throat at Jess's offer, and before she could stop herself, Star blurted out, "I need to tell you something, Jess."

Jess had begun to pull off the fitted sheet and stopped, hovering over the bed, waiting. Star crossed and uncrossed her arms, trying to find the right words.

"You can tell me anything, Star."

Her eyes burned but no tears came, and the words she desperately wanted to say vanished. She was a coward. "It's nothing big," she said with a weak laugh. "Jeremy invited me to have dinner with his family tonight. I don't have to go or anything—"

"Go—of course you should go. I like that Jeremy. He's good for you."

Star stiffened. "How's that?"

"He makes you laugh."

CHAPTER THIRTY-THREE

STAR

"I'm nervous," Jeremy said.

"*You're* nervous?"

"That's what I said, isn't it?"

"Shouldn't I be the one who's nervous?" Star and Jeremy sat in the taxi in front of a beautiful two-story log home. After the movie last night, Jeremy had invited her over for dinner. He'd said his parents wanted to meet his mysterious new friend. Would they have invited the girl who'd stepped off the bus last week? Probably not.

She was surprised to find that she was curious about his big family. Did they hug? Did they laugh? She pulled at the tips of her hair. Her last foster family had been quiet and skittish. The mom barely spoke, and the dad hid in his home office. At dinner on the first night, Dawn, the mom with graying blonde hair, had said, "I hope you won't be any trouble."

The nervous thrumming of Jeremy's fingers on the steering wheel interrupted her thoughts. Could his family be that bad? "Why are you so nervous? Do they shoot strangers and ask questions later?"

Jeremy turned to stare at her. "You're not a boy."

"Huh?"

"Ever since I came out, they've been waiting. They never ask, and they've never said anything, but I know them too well. They're waiting to see what it will be like when I bring a boy home. But you're not a boy, and this might confuse them. I've talked about you a ton, told them all about you." He paused. "Well, not *all* about you, of course. Just that you're Jess's niece who's come up for the summer." His forehead dropped, resting against the steering wheel. "But you're not a boy, and now I'm afraid they'll think it was a phase."

"Did they have a hard time with it when you told them?"

Jeremy lifted his head from the steering wheel, a lock of hair falling over one eye. "Not at all. My parents are pretty great."

"So you're worried that your parents, who are pretty great and obviously love you, will meet me and think that you're not gay?"

"I knew you'd understand, Tuesday." His fingers moved to turn the keys, still hanging from the ignition. "And you're right—this was a terrible idea."

She slapped his hand away from the keys. "You know, downtown we have a name for people like you."

"You do?"

"Yeah, meth heads. They talk all kinds of crazy. You'd fit right in." She punched him on the shoulder, grabbed the keys, and hopped out of the van.

After a moment he climbed out and walked around the van to stand beside her. She'd known him only one week. And now she was going to meet his parents. How very small town of her.

He leaned down and whispered, "I suppose it does sound kinda crazy."

She laughed, and together they walked up to the house.

A covered porch stretched across the front with several rocking chairs, making Star want to sit down and take in the darkened mountains beyond. But the front door opened just then, bathing the wooden porch in a warm glow.

"We wondered when you'd get out of the car! Hello, Star, I'm Maryellen." Maryellen was tall with a mane of hair that fell in silvery-blonde curls to just below her ears. "And this is David."

David towered over all of them, thin like the stalk of a dandelion. He smiled warmly, taking her hand between both of his. "It's nice to meet you, Star."

Giggles and whispering came from inside the house, where Jeremy's ten younger brothers and sisters filled the doorway. Something tugged on her jeans, and she glanced down to find a very small boy peering up at her.

"You have funny hair," he said.

"Luke!" Maryellen shot him a stern look.

"He's right." Star ran her hands along the shaved section of her hair, then pulled at the long strands on top. "It is funny, Luke."

"Do you like it that way?"

"I do," Star said with a smile. She hadn't been around little kids much.

Luke crossed his arms and squeezed one eye shut. "Why would you want to have funny hair?"

"I'm not sure. I'll have to think about it."

"Okay." He turned and scurried inside the house, pushing through his throng of siblings to get inside.

"Do any of the rest of you have questions for Star?" Jeremy addressed the group. "No? Good. May we come in?"

They ate a dinner of roasted chicken and mashed potatoes around a long table constructed from old doors, scratched and worn from years of use. David explained that it was the first piece of furniture he had ever made and that Jeremy had been his helper.

"I was only two when you built this."

"Even so," David responded.

Conversation flowed throughout dinner. Star learned that David owned a successful business selling custom and refurbished antique furniture pieces. Most of his clients lived in Aspen and Vail, but he also had a small shop in Pine Lake. Maryellen had been a real estate lawyer, she told Star, until two years ago when she decided to homeschool the kids.

"So you just stopped being a lawyer?" Star asked.

Maryellen smiled. "In a way."

"But why? Don't you have to work hard to become one?" Star didn't know much about being a lawyer except that it took years of schooling and lots of books.

"I did." Here Maryellen looked at Jeremy. "But the kids needed me."

"Because you have so many?" Star said, and the table erupted into laughter. Her cheeks warmed, and she fidgeted in her seat, feeling out of her depth. She tried to explain. "The moms I knew with so many kids were, uh, different."

The chattering around her grew quiet. Star pressed her lips together and looked down at her lap. *Bonehead.*

But when Maryellen answered, her voice was warm. "I suppose that must be true for some families. But see, David and I were told we couldn't have a single child. We were so thrilled when Jeremy came along that I guess we just didn't know when to quit. Then we got to Luke, and well . . ." She gestured toward him as if in explanation.

Luke giggled, and Star looked his way. Crusty bits of mashed potato stuck to his cheeks. "That's 'cause Mommy said if I were first," he said around a mouthful of chicken, "then I would have been the last."

The entire table, including Star, broke out into laughter, leaving Star's awkward statement behind.

Warm apple pie topped with a scoop of vanilla-bean ice cream finished the dinner. Star's belly pushed against the waistband of her jeans, and she had to fight the urge to undo the top button to make room for more.

After dinner, Maryellen opened the windows, and a cool breeze brought the clean scent of pine into the family room. The children formed small groups to play board games. Star joined Luke and a few of the younger siblings in a game of Candy Land. When Luke sat down in her lap, Star stiffened, but he didn't seem to notice, and eventually she relaxed. He smelled like soap and mashed potatoes.

Not surprisingly, it was Luke who started the questions, but he was quickly joined by the other kids.

"Does everyone have hair like you where you come from?" That one was from Luke.

"Where are you from?"

"How long will you be here?"

"Are you scared of Lucy?"

"Have you seen a ghost yet?"

"Does she cook in a black cauldron?"

"Fly on a broomstick?"

Jeremy's hands shot up. "I've told you guys to leave Miss Lucy alone. She's not a witch."

"How long will you be in Pine Lake, Star?" asked Maryellen.

"Um, I don't know—maybe through the summer, I guess." She rubbed her arms, unsure and uncomfortable at the lie, convinced that Maryellen could see right through her. She shrugged. "Maybe longer?"

Maryellen raised her eyebrows. "Longer? Then will Jess enroll you in the public school?"

Star chewed on a nail. "Um, maybe? I, uh, well, I haven't attended a traditional school since, well, in a long time."

Maryellen brightened. "Have you been homeschooled?"

"Something like that." She shifted her eyes to Jeremy, hoping he could save her from digging a bigger hole.

"You're welcome to come here for school anytime you like. I home-school year-round, so we only have class in the morning. I'd be happy to fill in for your mom while you're here."

Maryellen's casual mention of her mom stabbed at her heart. She was searching for a response when Jeremy stood and motioned for Star to join him. "It's getting late," he said. "I should get you home."

Maryellen and David followed them to the door. "It was so nice to meet you, Star." She gave her a quick hug. "Let Jess know about school. I'd love to have you join our classroom."

"Thank you for dinner . . ." Star wanted to say more, but her thoughts filled with school and Maryellen's offer to come here on a regular basis, even if for a short while. She knew that most kids hated school, even the ones with families and nice school clothes and new backpacks every year. But she'd never hated it. Because when she'd been bouncing around foster homes, it was the only routine she could count on, the only place where she knew what to expect. Before she could stop herself, she blurted out, "I would love to come to your school!"

Maryellen laughed. "That's a first, huh, David? A teenager who wants to go to school."

"Unheard of," David responded.

"You're welcome here anytime, Star," she said, and the warmth of her words touched her eyes.

Luke pushed through the door. "You forgot to tell me why you have funny hair!"

Star laughed. "I guess because I can," she said.

~

"You have cool parents." It amazed her that families like his existed in the same world she'd grown up in. Would her life have been different if her mom had lived? She swallowed, looked out the window.

Jeremy pulled the van to a stop in front of Lucy's house. "Maryellen and David Foster are about as ordinary as you can get."

"Ordinary to you," she said quietly, then, "Thank you."

"For what?"

She studied a fingernail. Star couldn't remember what normal was anymore, but she was pretty sure that dinner with Jeremy's family was as close as she'd ever get. "Just thank you."

Jeremy coughed. "No thanks necessary."

She reached for the door.

"Star," he said, and his voice was more serious than normal.

"Yeah?"

His eyes turned skyward, and he blew out a breath. "I used to go to public school."

Star thought about the way Maryellen had looked at Jeremy when she talked about homeschooling. "When?"

"Two years ago." His jaw tightened.

The way he sat hunched over the wheel made her pause. She waited for him to continue.

"Small town, right? So of course everyone knew—or thought they knew—that I was gay. I hadn't even admitted it to myself until my freshman year. Then this new kid moved into town, and suddenly my world exploded. I had a friend, a boyfriend even, and for the first time I could be me. I didn't think I'd ever be so happy. Still, we met in secret until some dickhead from school saw us kissing, and like all repressed, close-minded, and scared pricks, he took it personally. School became a nightmare. And instead of staying, instead of not giving a fuck, I got sad and depressed and turned into a quivering, pathetic shell. I was a mess. I withdrew from everyone, even my family. I had convinced myself that the truth was worse than death."

Star's knee jiggled up and down. "You were going to hurt yourself?"

He nodded but didn't look at her. "My parents didn't know what was wrong, but they could see how I'd changed. They suggested Mom homeschool me for a year or so."

The van grew silent, dark, except for the sliver of bluish light coming from the half moon. She rubbed her arms.

"You have nothing to be ashamed of, Jeremy," she said.

"I do. I could have stayed. I could have waved my freak flag and painted my car with rainbows. I could have at least tried to be me without running away."

"You're happy now, though, right?"

Jeremy sighed. "That's not really why I brought this up. It's because of Lucy and Ben."

"What is?"

"Lucy sent Ben to the waterfall."

Star shook her head, trying not to get frustrated, but Jeremy was speaking in riddles. "You're sounding like those meth heads again."

"Have you been up to the waterfall?" he said.

She shook her head.

"That's because it's too steep for Lucy to climb. There's a trail that leads up to a narrow metal bridge that spans the dam. They installed a gate with a lock on it after me. But I wasn't the first."

Star opened her eyes wide, stunned. "How did she know?"

He shrugged. "How does she know anything? She just does. She called Ben and told him something bad was going to happen to me. He didn't even question her; he just ran out there as fast as he could."

"Oh," was all she could manage.

"Yeah," he said. "Oh."

She looked up at him. His story gave wings to the stubborn bit of hope that lived deep in her heart, and now it fluttered painfully against her chest. She kneaded her thighs with her fists, tried to squash the idea that Lucy really cared about her, like she did Jeremy. It couldn't be true. "So Lucy found us both," she said softly.

He nodded. "Looks that way, Tuesday."

She wanted to say something more, but she couldn't find the words. Instead she reached over, lightly touched his hand, and gave him a small smile before climbing out of the van.

Jeremy rolled down the passenger-side window. "School starts at eight. See you tomorrow."

CHAPTER
THIRTY-FOUR

JESS

"Have you found it?"

The question wormed into her mind, becoming part of her dream. *Have you found it?* The last word morphing to fit the nightmare. *Have you found him?* She stood in the middle of a darkened city street as white snowflakes danced in the air, melting into wet pools that reflected back the blinking red traffic light, the only sound her labored breath. She searched the empty road, her chest expanding when she saw the boy in the red sweatshirt standing on the sidewalk. But this time she could see him clearly, down to his caramel-colored curls. His hands reached for her, eyes wide, mouth stretched into a scream. She lunged forward, tears freezing on her skin, heart pumping painfully against her ribs. She could save him; she could finally save him. As her fingers nearly touched the round curve of his cheek, she jerked to a stop. She cried out, tried to move her legs, but her feet were encased in ice so cold it burned.

Mama! he screamed, and she turned to find the banana-yellow hood of a car hurtling toward her. Slush flew silently from beneath the tires, the driver's face obscured behind an ice-crusted windshield.

Relief shot through her veins. This was right. At last she smiled. She was exactly where she should have been.

She opened her arms wide and braced herself for the impact.

"Have you found it?" The car evaporated with Lucy's voice, taking with it the blinking light, the street, the snow, and lastly, the boy, smiling at her now, and then he too was gone.

Jess slowly opened her eyes to sunlight flooding her room. The dream faded, leaving her with an aching loss that made her want to close her eyes and go back to sleep.

Lucy stared at her from the doorway. It was odd for the older woman to be awake before her.

"Good morning, Lucy." Jess rubbed her face, pinched her cheeks, and tried to wipe away the heavy drowsiness that clung to her eyelids. The skin of her face felt tight and dry. It had been the worst kind of dream. The kind she couldn't remember but that left her with a desperate, painful longing for her son. She sank her head back into the pillow, closed her eyes, and breathed until the ache subsided enough for her to face a new day.

She opened her eyes again and for the first time noticed the sun angling in through her window the way it did in late morning. Had she overslept? She reached for her phone to check the time and cried out. A heart-shaped rock sat on the nightstand beside her phone. She jerked her hand away as though burned, and a tremor passed through her body. Lucy obviously collected the heart-shaped rocks too; it wasn't an uncommon thing for people to do. But between the local boy who was making a pastime of scaring her and the rocks she kept finding, reminders of her son seemed to be everywhere, and it made reality flimsy and unreliable.

Trying not to touch the rock, she slid her phone off the nightstand—ten forty-five. Her eyes widened. The last time she'd slept past five thirty she'd been five years old. She threw back the covers. "I'm so sorry I overslept," she said, and, struck by a thought, glanced once more at the rock. "Lucy, did you put this rock in my room?"

But Lucy swayed in the doorway, her eyes dull, mouth pulled down in a frown. She looked up at the ceiling, then down at her feet and wiggled her toes. "What rock?" she said.

"This one here, on my bedside table."

Lucy shook her head and smiled, but there was something vacant about it that set Jess's alarm bells ringing.

She slipped into a robe and hurried to Lucy's side. "You must be hungry. I'll fix you breakfast right away."

"No need."

"I think you need to eat."

"I already have. Star made me breakfast before she left."

Jess sat heavily on the edge of the bed, trying to catch up with the events of the morning. "Star made you breakfast before she left. Okay. Where did she go?"

"School."

"Right." She had mentioned it last night when she came home after dinner with Jeremy's family. Jess had felt a rush of happiness for Star, especially after seeing how excited she'd been, but a gnawing worry had developed at what it meant. Jess was afraid that Star was getting too attached, that they all were. She shook her head; right now she needed to focus on Lucy. "Why didn't she wake me up before she left?"

"You were sleeping," Lucy said in a tone she might use for a petulant toddler.

"I know, but by now Star knows I don't sleep in." She rubbed her face, yawned, and tried not to think about the rock. Lucy must have put it there. After the one in the library, Jess had already found several others in Lucy's room, even some in the sitting room. Maybe Jess could convince Lucy to keep them all in one place instead of scattered around the house.

"Seems to me like you needed to sleep in." Lucy turned to leave, and that's when Jess noticed something else wrong. Lucy still wore her nightgown, her skinny ankles protruding from beneath the hem. The woman never left her room without being fully dressed from head to toe.

Jess followed her. "Are you okay?"

Lucy looked up and down the hallway, her hands held suspended on either side of her as though her limbs disagreed on which way to turn. "She had to go back for it." She walked into Star's room, poking her head underneath the bed, pulling out drawers, opening the closet door. Then she retreated, pushing past Jess and into the hallway, where she stood again in the middle, hands held out on either side.

Jess turned back for her phone, her fingers tingling with a growing concern. The older woman's behavior was odd, even for Lucy. Should she call Ben? Didn't he mention something about finding her outside in her nightgown once?

"Where is it now?" Lucy moved back into Jess's room and looked under the bed, pulled out the top drawer of the bedside table, then turned, still frowning, and left the room. "She came back for it."

A dull ache began to spread behind Jess's eyes. She'd make Lucy a hot cup of tea and see if that might calm her. "Let's go downstairs." She took Lucy gently by the elbow.

But at the stairs, Lucy halted. "I need to check the calendar," she said, wobbling unsteadily on her feet.

Jess rubbed at her forehead, her concern momentarily overpowered by a rising staccato in her head. "Let's check the calendar, then, but please take my arm on the stairs." She hated how her words came out clipped and irritated, but she still felt disoriented from the dream, and Lucy's rambling only added to the feeling that she was a step behind.

At the bottom of the stairs, Lucy gripped her arm hard.

"She thinks it's her fault because she went back for it," Lucy said with an urgency that made Jess's heart skip a beat.

Nothing she said made sense, yet Jess couldn't ignore a nagging suspicion that Lucy spoke about Star. She opened her mouth to ask, but the woman had walked into the kitchen and sat down at the table, her shoulders rounded forward.

In the overhead light Lucy's skin looked pale, her face sad and defeated. Jess winced. She'd come to think of the older woman as strong and capable of just about anything. It wasn't easy to admit that Lucy's age was catching up to her.

Jess took a seat at the table. "Can you describe what it is you're looking for?" she said gently.

Lucy's blue eyes widened, and she leaned across the table to reach for Jess's hand. "Where's your mother?" she asked.

The muscles in Jess's face felt like they'd turned to stone. She hardly thought or talked about her mother. Maybe Lucy thought she was talking to Star? She rubbed at the back of her neck. Lucy must not have slept well the night before. "Why don't I make you some tea? Afterward you can go upstairs and rest for a bit."

Lucy pursed her lips. "I asked you a question, Jess," she said.

Her mouth turned dry. "My mother." The word stuck in her throat. Joann had been her name. Was still her name. "My mother kicked me out when I got pregnant at sixteen."

Lucy's brow furrowed, and she began to twist and untwist her fingers. "No, no, no. I didn't mean your mother. I meant you." She snapped her fingers. "I saw the picture of your little boy, the one in your room."

Jess slumped with relief. Lucy *had* taken her picture downstairs that day. And she must have been looking for it this morning when she got confused. Jess softened. Ben had been right about Lucy's episodes—they were increasing. She bit her lip. It was a subject she'd need to bring up with Lucy, but not today. "You must have taken the picture downstairs by accident. Don't worry; I found it and put it back."

Lucy shrugged. "He has your smile." She waved a dismissive hand. "Not that I see it much."

"See what?" The headache from earlier began a drumbeat against her skull.

"Your smile."

Her lips felt thick. "I don't have a reason to smile anymore."

"Neither does he." Lucy rested her elbows on the table, her hands clasped in front of her. "You're a good mother."

Jess curled her fingers into claws. "Was. I *was* a mother," she said through clenched teeth. A good mother would never have left her son alone. A good mother would have been there when he needed her the most. Jess had once been a mother, but she had never been a good one.

"You still can be."

Jess stood frozen to the spot. Was Lucy talking about Star? Star needed a mother, but that part of Jess's life was over. Chance had died cold, alone, and scared; she didn't deserve to be in that role ever again. Jess pressed a hand to her cheek. Her skin felt clammy and cool. "I had a son and he died, Lucy."

Lucy settled back in the chair and picked up her reading glasses, resting the plastic rims across the bridge of her nose. Lying on the table, folded over into a rectangle, was her crossword puzzle. Her eyes lit up when she spied it. "There it is!"

"Your crossword puzzle?" Lucy's behavior was alarming. Could she have had a stroke?

Lucy peered at Jess over the rim of her glasses. "It's a tough one, multiword, but I think you might be ready for it now."

Jess reached out and put two fingers across Lucy's wrist. Her pulse was strong. If Lucy was experiencing the onset of dementia, Jess had learned that sometimes it was better and less stressful for them to just play along than to keep trying to convince them otherwise. "How many letters?"

The paper rustled. "Three words, nine letters. It's good when a batter does it on the field, but not on the road."

Jess remembered the puzzle question from her first day in Pine Lake. She opened her mouth to remind Lucy that she didn't know the answer, but then it came to her in a wave of nausea that turned her stomach inside out. The floor tilted beneath her feet, and she clung to the table, taking in small sips of air. "Hit-and-run," she said.

Lucy slid her glasses off, her eyes soft. "Oh dear."

Jess covered her face with her hands, trying to breathe in before she passed out. She felt Lucy's hand on her fingers, patting gently.

"Is that how he died?"

She stood with such force she smashed her knee into the table. Shock waves of pain rushed up her thigh, and her eyes stung. Lucy stayed seated, hands folded on the table in front of her, head tilted to the side.

"What did you say?" Jess said through her teeth.

"I'm so very sorry, dear. I had no idea." The lines and wrinkles around Lucy's bright-blue eyes were wet with tears.

Jess felt her body deflate at the tenderness in the old woman's voice. "Of course you didn't know, Lucy. I've never told you. It's not something I talk about with anyone. That crossword puzzle just shocked me, I guess."

It was silent for a few minutes, and despite the absurdity of the morning, it was a comfortable silence that helped Jess regain her composure. After a while Lucy took in a deep breath and stood. "I need you to run an errand for me," she said.

"Of course. What do you need?"

"It's something for Star, actually. It should be . . ." She twisted around, glanced toward the calendar. "Ah yes, just check the calendar." She picked up the paper and the pencil lying beside it, readjusted her reading glasses, and turned back to her crossword puzzle.

Jess stood in the middle of the kitchen, digging her fingernails into her palms. Her dream from the night before flashed through her mind, and she nearly crumpled to the floor. She'd give anything to go back to that night and choose Chance instead of work. Jess scratched at her wrist until she felt a raw pain spiral across her arm. But she couldn't go back—she studied her wrist—and she couldn't give up. Her only option was to move forward until she couldn't move forward anymore.

CHAPTER THIRTY-FIVE

STAR

The clock read seven o'clock. Star smiled and poured herself a mug of coffee. It was only her second morning of school, but she couldn't wait to start the day, hopping out of bed as soon as her eyes opened.

She wandered out to the front steps to take in the sunrise and sat down, placing her mug on the step beside her. The eastern sky was cobalt except for a sliver of raspberry across the horizon. She sipped her coffee and thought about Chance. Every Saturday they used to meet in the fort. It was the only thing she had to look forward to, and Jazz was always there. Except once.

She'd made him a card for his birthday. One she'd decorated at school with markers and glitter and colored glue. She'd never given anybody a birthday card before, and she remembered how her chest had puffed up with pride. She couldn't wait to give it to him.

But her father had stopped her from leaving. *If you're lying to me, Star, we're both dead.* His eyes bugged wide open and darted between her and a pile of baggies and money on the couch. He inhaled a cigarette, and the red embers danced up and down in the bluish dark.

She looked away. It was always better to look away.

Her father grabbed her chin between his fingers and squeezed until she met his eyes. The skin around his fingertips was yellow and cracked, and his fingers smelled gross. She tried not to wrinkle her nose.

We need the money, understand? If I don't get the money he owes me, we're dead either way. So tell me again, are you sure?

He squeezed her face so hard she felt something pop in her cheek, and her eyes filled with tears. She didn't want to answer him because her father was mean and the man was nice. *Please don't hurt him.*

When he released her, she grabbed her card and one of the bonsai trees and ran out of the apartment, feeling sick and looking over her shoulder in case he chased her. Chance wasn't at the fort, so she sat on the quilt and waited, hiding the card and tree behind her. When he finally showed up, it was only for a moment, and what Star remembered the most was how his smile stretched from ear to ear and that her throbbing cheek hurt too much to smile back.

I can't play today, Star. My mom's taking me to breakfast, and then we're going to a movie. Can you come over later and make cookies with us?

He looked so happy that Star almost started to cry. She pushed her stupid card under her legs and shook her head.

His face fell. *Oh, okay, but if you change your mind, come over.* And he left.

Happy birthday, Jazz, Star called softly, except the door had already closed, and he didn't hear her.

The sky had lightened, and Star wiped a hand across her eyes. She did change her mind, but it had made everything worse.

The sun arced above the horizon then, shattering the night sky with rays of color. She kept fooling herself thinking that Chance would want her to have anything to do with his mother. She knew better. And sooner or later she was going to have to face the truth.

She sipped the last of her coffee and stood. Jeremy would be here soon, and Star wanted to go to school.

She was heading for the kitchen to refill her cup when Lucy's muffled voice called to her.

"In the library, Star," she said.

When she reached the library door, it swung open before her fingers touched the wood. Star breathed out and took a step inside. Lucy sat on the couch, the curtains on the window behind her drawn tightly closed. The chandelier burned bright, thick fingers of light reaching into the corners.

"You're awake early," she said, and sat down opposite Lucy, stuffing her hands under her thighs to hide the shaking. Lucy knew something; otherwise, Star and Jess and Chance wouldn't all be here together, and it was only a matter of time before it would all come out.

"Do you have any questions for me?" Lucy said.

Star shrugged.

Lucy folded her blue-veined hands loosely in her lap. She wore the black dress Star remembered from the first day they met. Her hair was not in its typical bun but was brushed out until it lay flat against her head. She raised her eyebrows. "I'm not going to ask the questions."

Star cleared her throat. "I'm a loose end."

Lucy nodded.

"And m-my friend is one too."

Lucy nodded again.

"But how do you know when the loose ends are tied up?"

Lucy threw her hands in the air. "What a wonderful question!"

Star waited expectantly, but Lucy didn't say anything more. Her nerves felt shot. "Well?"

"It's not my job to tell you, only to bring you together. But I can tell you with certainty that you already know."

A bead of sweat ran down her back. "Know what?"

"What he wants."

"I'm not sure I do," she said. "Does he t-talk to you?"

"Not the way you think. I know very little about him. But he's shrouded in shadow, which means he's angry about the way he died."

"It was an accident," she said, and her voice shook.

Lucy pursed her lips. "He disagrees."

She hunched forward, chewed on a nail.

"Questions, Star."

She sat up straight. *Fuck it.* It was time she stopped being a coward. "Am I supposed to tell Jess—"

Lucy held up her hand. "Not yet."

Star wrinkled her forehead, angry that she was being silenced after she finally got the nerve to ask, but also relieved. "Why not?"

"She was cut so deep, poor thing. It takes time to heal."

She inhaled through her teeth. "But I'm ready to talk about Chance."

"Of course you are." Lucy waved a hand as though to dismiss Star's protests. "I was wrong to be so rash. These things take time."

A soft knock on the door interrupted them.

"Come in," Lucy said.

Jess poked her head around the door. "Are you sure?"

"Yes, yes. Bring it here."

Star narrowed her eyes.

Jess entered the room, a frown tugging at the corners of her mouth. Lucy opened her palm, and Star watched as Jess laid something silver and shiny in her hand.

"I only made the one copy," Jess said. "So don't lose it."

"Lose what?" Star tried not to sound defensive, but she felt oddly exposed, vulnerable. She squinted, trying to see what Lucy held, but Lucy closed her fingers around the object.

"Close your eyes and open your hand, Star," she said.

She did, trying to push down a swell of anticipation. *Don't be silly,* she chided. *It's probably a bus ticket back to the city.* But Lucy made everything exciting, and Star couldn't stop her toe from tapping the floor. Something cold and light dropped into her palm.

"For you."

She opened her eyes, and her skin tingled. A key. Small and silver with tiny grooves along the top. It hung on a short key chain that connected to a tiny charm of a blue star.

"A key?" she said, looking from Lucy to Jess. "What does it open?"

Lucy laughed. "The house, silly girl! So you don't have to wait for me or Jess to open the door for you."

Jess stood above them, her arms crossed, a slight wrinkle in the space between her eyebrows. "This doesn't change anything, okay? At some point we'll need to contact somebody—"

Lucy interrupted her with a long, winded sigh that came out with surprising volume and seemed to grow as it traveled up the library's high ceilings. Star had to press her lips together to keep from giggling.

"Enough of that for now, Jess, please," Lucy said. "I think we all get the point."

"Okay, okay."

Star let her eyes fall back to the key in her hand, felt a lump inch its way up her throat until she thought she might choke.

"I've never had a key before," she said.

Lucy patted her knee before rising slowly to her feet.

Star fingered the tiny medallion. "You put a star on it too."

Lucy smiled. "I only asked for a key. Jess is the one who dressed it up." She turned, and her skirts whispered around her when she walked out of the library.

Star let her eyes roam back to Jess, who hadn't moved from where she stood by the couch. But Star saw something soften in her eyes, a brightness that quickly disappeared. "Don't lose it," she said, and left the room.

~

She ran upstairs to her bedroom with the key still grasped in her hand, liking the way the metal felt cool against her skin. A pink-and-green camo backpack rested against her doorframe with a sticky note attached to the front. *For school*, it read. Star picked it up, slid her arms into the straps, and pulled it snug to her back. Her heart pushed against her chest, like it might grow too big for her body. She breathed in and tried to get a grip on the excitement that made her rock back and forth on her heels. *Time for school.*

She turned to leave, hesitated. Out of habit she still put the rock from Chance in her sock, but today it felt heavy and uncomfortable. She held the key in one hand, the rock in the other. The key made her smile. She squeezed her palm around the rock until it felt like the bones of her hand might splinter with the effort. Then she opened the drawer of her bedside table and tossed the rock inside. It landed with a thump on top of the note.

Almost immediately her breath seemed to flow easier, like the rock had sat on her chest. She closed the drawer with a smile, readjusted her backpack, and hopped down the stairs. In her heart she knew she couldn't ignore Chance forever, but for now she had to get to school.

~

"Star, what do you want to be when you grow up?" Maryellen Foster asked the question from where she stood by the window of the classroom. If it could be called a classroom, since it was like no class that Star had ever seen. The walls were painted a vivid purple with hand-drawn flowers in bright orange and soft pinks. Beanbags covered the floor, along with yoga mats and blankets. There were desks, too, but as Mrs. Foster had pointed out on her first day, desks were for writing, not for learning. There was even a small trampoline in the corner where Jeremy said Luke jumped up and down while multiplying numbers in his head.

"Mom," Jeremy pleaded. "We're not toddlers."

Mrs. Foster smiled warmly. "I'll rephrase. What career path are you considering?"

Star hadn't come up with an answer yet, because she hadn't given that part of her life much thought. "I don't know," she said at last.

"Then answer this question first: What do you love?"

Without hesitation, Star said, "To read." And then a thought came to her that made her lower her eyes, suddenly shy. "A writer?" she said so quietly she hardly heard herself.

"The kind who writes books?"

"Um, maybe? Or maybe someone who does the news or writes the news." She reddened. "Whatever that's called." Star looked down at her hands on the desk, unsure and a little embarrassed by how stupid her answer sounded.

"A journalist?" Mrs. Foster said, tapping her finger on her chin. "Do you mean someone who interviews people and writes articles?"

Star shrugged. "I guess."

"I can see that," Jeremy said.

"Me too. You've got the curiosity and I suspect the tenacity for that kind of job." Mrs. Foster clapped her hands. "Okay, your assignment then. I want you to read articles. And not the kind you find online. I want you to read articles from actual newspapers."

"Mom, what do you have against the internet?"

"Not a thing. But if Star wants to be a journalist, then she needs to have an appreciation for how it used to be done before tweets, news bites, and Facebook."

Jeremy groaned. "Facebook, Mom? Who even uses that anymore?"

Star giggled.

Mrs. Foster ignored her son and looked to Star. "I bet Lucy has a bunch of old papers lying around in that house of hers."

CHAPTER THIRTY-SIX

JESS

The days since Star's arrival had melted into one another, creating a routine both natural and bizarre. The front door opened, then slammed shut, rattling the dishes Jess had set to dry on a rack by the sink.

"Sorry!" Star called, appearing in the kitchen. She flopped into a chair, flinging her bag onto the table, where its contents spilled across the surface.

"Algebra already?"

"I know!" Star giggled. "Apparently I have"—she curled her fingers into air quotes—"a natural ability."

Jess had reservations about Star going to Jeremy's homeschool, knowing that it was only one more attachment that would hurt the girl when she had to leave. But Lucy had shamed her when she brought it up.

You'd deny the girl an education?

Jess had reddened, and she'd tried to switch tactics. *What if Jeremy's parents find out who Star really is?*

Lucy shook her head, looking disappointed. *Star is happy. Can't you see that?*

Jess couldn't argue with her. Lucy was right. Star *was* happy. When she came home from school, she attacked her books, often reading and studying until late into the evening. When Jess asked if she'd always been this serious at school, Star had shrugged and said, "I don't know." Last night she had fallen asleep sitting up with a pencil in her hand. Jess had woken her with a tap on the shoulder, sending her off to bed with a gentle admonishment to get more sleep.

Jess set a bowl of popcorn and a can of soda on the table beside where Star sat hunched over her mess of papers, her finger tracing the lines of text in her math book.

A few papers slipped off the edge and fluttered quietly to the floor. As Jess knelt to retrieve them, she studied Star. Sleep and regular meals had filled in the hollowness of her cheeks, erased the dark smudges beneath her eyes. Apart from her hairstyle, she looked much like any other teen living in this mountain town.

Star cleared her throat, her forehead wrinkling. With a start, Jess realized she still knelt on the floor, the papers grasped in her hands.

"What's wrong with your mouth, Jess?" Star slid a pencil behind her ear.

"What do you mean?" She pushed to her feet, dropping the pages on the table.

"The corners. They started to curl upward." Star's hands flew to her chest. "I-I-I think it was the beginning of a smile. Quick! Run to the mirror! You might catch the tail end of it."

"If only I'd known that school would make you an even bigger smart-ass." Jess swatted her playfully with a dish towel, and Star threw her head back with a laugh.

With a lingering grin, Star turned back to her work, the tip of her tongue peeking out from between her lips as she concentrated on a math problem. But Jess found herself rooted to the floor, wringing the dish towel between her hands and staring at the back of Star's bent head. Star was fifteen. An in-between age, she could tell from the days she'd spent around her. How she flipped so easily between a wisecracking young woman to a girl who giggled like a child. She brought the dish towel to her heart, held it there in a crumpled ball.

And then she was standing behind Star's chair, looking down at the spiky ends of her hair, the smooth skin of her neck. Jess tried to turn away, but her hand was already reaching out, her fingers brushing the hard curve of Star's bony shoulder.

Star jumped, and her pencil clattered onto the table. "You scared me!" she said, turning around in her seat.

Jess gently took hold of Star's thin arm and pulled her to her feet until she stood opposite her.

Star narrowed her eyes. "This is weird."

It was. But Jess couldn't stop herself, and without a word she put her hands on either side of Star's shoulders. Star stiffened, but Jess only wrapped her arms around her, pulling her in until she enveloped Star's small frame in an awkward hug. They stood like that, frozen, stiff armed, until after another moment Star relaxed, leaning her full weight into Jess.

Jess exhaled and laid her chin on top of Star's head. They didn't move or speak, the light *plink* of water dripping slowly from the kitchen faucet the only sound in the small kitchen.

Their breathing synchronized. It felt natural: the feathery weight of Star in her arms, the sinkful of dishes behind them, the math book lain open across the worn kitchen table. She squeezed her wet eyes shut and fought an overwhelming urge to tell Star that everything was going to be okay. But that would be nothing more than a cruel joke, because she couldn't promise her anything. And Jess was not the type to lie.

"You were a great mom, Jess."

Star's words, spoken into her shoulder where her face rested, doused the intensity of her thoughts like she'd slipped into an icy snowbank.

She pulled away, wiping her hand across her face, and turned her back to Star, busying herself with washing a bowl she'd already cleaned. Lucy must have said something to Star, and Jess couldn't help but feel violated by it.

"I'm sorry. I didn't mean—"

Jess turned. Star leaned against the counter by the sink, her arms folded, her chin raised slightly, and her face echoing the toughness from when she'd first arrived. Jess softened. The girl could have no idea how much it hurt, and she certainly couldn't blame her for Lucy's blabber-mouth. "It's okay. I didn't tell Lucy to keep it to herself. It's just . . . it's hard for me to talk about him."

"Well, thank you," Star said softly.

"For what?"

"You know."

"You looked like you needed a hug," Jess said, her voice hoarse. "Algebra can be frustrating."

Star glanced down at the floor and then back up, looking almost shy for a moment. "I want to show you something."

Jess followed her into the sitting room, where she stopped in front of the large window by the antique radio.

Star fidgeted, her eyes big and dark, face devoid of emotion, and Jess realized that she was nervous. Then she moved to the side, and Jess gasped. Chance's bonsai tree and Mr. Kim's, all three of them, were alive. More than alive—they looked like they had made a marked improvement. She looked from the trees to Star, but she found she couldn't speak right away, so she cleared her throat. "Did you do this?"

Star nodded, biting her lip.

"How?"

"They just needed to be watered every day. And I've been trimming the new growth to give them back their shape. This one especially." Star touched Chance's tree and rubbed her fingers gently along the delicate trunk. "It had gotten really out of hand. I think we should repot it."

Jess touched the shiny leaves, thought of Mr. Kim and how much he would have appreciated this. Thought of Chance and the friend she'd never met who'd given him a tiny tree for his birthday. Her eyes grew wet, and she coughed to hold back the tears. "How did you know what to do?"

"I used to watch my mom, and sometimes she'd let me try too." She looked at the trees, shrugged. "I guess I just remembered."

It was a gift, Jess knew, and she was touched by the sincerity in it. "Your mom sounds lovely."

"She was."

The skin around Star's mouth had turned white, as though she wanted to say more but stopped herself. Jess pressed on, feeling like their losses gave them common ground. "Do you mind if I ask . . . what happened to your dad?"

"He was murdered," Star said flatly.

Jess pressed a hand against her chest. "Oh, honey, I'm . . ." She trailed off, having no idea what to say. "How, er, no, um, what happened?"

Star looked at her for a long moment, her lips pressed into a thin line. Then she seemed to decide something, because she took in a deep breath and said, "It was just another night at the Lancaster."

Jess felt as if the wind had been knocked out of her. Star had lived at the Lancaster too?

It wasn't completely out of the realm of possibility; she and Star came from similar backgrounds, and the Lancaster was a catchall for many people with little income and no savings. But Lucy's voice echoed softly in her head. *Loose ends.* What were the odds, really? She tilted her head. Star was about Chance's age. Jess's heart skipped a beat. "I lived there too. Did you . . ." She swallowed. "Did you know a boy named Chance?" The idea that Star might have known her son was both painful and sobering. Why would it matter? Nothing would bring him back.

Star shook her head, and Jess exhaled. She'd been a fool to even ask, but one thing was for sure: Lucy was getting to her. "Thank you so much, Star, for making them better. It means more to me than you know. One of the trees, it belonged to my son." Jess let the words rush out of her. After everything that had happened since Star arrived, it felt right to share something with the girl; even more than that, it felt good.

But the color seemed to drain from Star's cheeks, and her eyes widened, shifting to the plants and back to Jess. She stepped close to Jess, her hands out, staring up at her with a look in her eyes that Jess couldn't decipher. "Star?" she said.

As Star opened her mouth to speak, there was a knock at the door, and she jerked back, shaking her head. "That's Jeremy. I—" She bolted from the room.

Jess followed her, feeling the crinkle form in her forehead at the girl's odd behavior.

Jeremy stood in the doorway; he waved. "Hi, Jess."

Jess gave him a smile, then trained her attention on Star. "Is everything okay?"

Star crouched on the ground next to him, shoving a book into her backpack. "Yeah, we just need to get going or we're going to be late."

"What are you up to this afternoon?" Jeremy's mom held school only in the mornings, leaving the afternoons free for more studying or other activities.

Jeremy turned to show his backpack. "We're going to the library to study like real students."

Jess snorted. "You are real students."

"Yeah, but like the real ones who go to school and stuff," he said.

For the first time in many years, Jess's laughter felt real, not the bland variety she forced out when it was expected. It bubbled up from someplace deep inside and spread warmly throughout her body. "Have fun being real students, then." She smiled down at Star, who fiddled with the zipper of her bag. "And thanks again for saving my bonsai trees, Star."

Star pushed to her feet, slung her backpack across one shoulder, and gave Jess a long look that made her think she was about to say something. Instead she shrugged and turned to leave, punching Jeremy in the shoulder as she did. "C'mon," she said, and walked out the door.

Jess stood alone in the foyer, shaking her head, her smile fading, fingers running back and forth across her wrist.

CHAPTER
THIRTY-SEVEN
STAR

Jeremy and Star returned from the library that afternoon to find the house empty. A note from Jess had been stuck to the refrigerator.

At Ebee's house, staying for dinner. Box of newspapers in basement.

The night before, Star had asked Lucy if she had any old newspapers lying around. Lucy had tilted her head to the side and jabbed the air with her finger. "That's the right question, Star!" And then she left the room. Star had planned on asking her again today, but now she had her answer.

"In the basement," Jeremy said in a deep voice. "Spooky."

"We'll bring it upstairs." Star headed down the hallway, forcing herself to keep away from the sitting room and the bonsai trees. It had shocked her to hear that one of Jess's bonsai trees was the one Star had given to Chance. Star had assumed they all came from the old guy Jess had taken care of in her nursing home job. Part of her had wanted to take back her mother's bonsai and put it in her own room, but she hadn't because it didn't belong to her anymore. Besides, with Jess and Star together and the bonsai still alive, Star feared that too many things were falling into place, and she didn't like how it was adding up, because she didn't think it was in her favor. She rubbed her face with her hand, trying to stop thinking about it.

"Are you coming?" she said to Jeremy, and winced at the irritation in her voice. He didn't deserve that. She tried to soften it with a smile.

He nodded, and she led him past the library to a short and narrow hallway behind the staircase. She took hold of the crystal knob, hesitated. Cool air drifted up from the crack beneath the door, tickling her ankles. Star had every reason to avoid the basement: the spirit of her dead friend was hanging out underneath Lucy's bed, and she was a teenager who thought basements, period, were scary. But the thought that glued her feet to the floor was a growing certainty that Chance wanted her to go down there. She hung her head. Her whole life people had made decisions for her. This felt like more of the same, and she was powerless to change it.

Jeremy stood so close his toes clipped the backs of her heels, and she could feel his breath on her neck. She glared at him over her shoulder. "A little space, please."

"Sorry," he said, his eyebrows raised high. "Basements are scary."

"Not to me," she said, and, steeling herself, pulled open the door. It resisted at first and then opened with a whoosh, bringing up air that smelled damp and stale.

"Ew," Jeremy said from behind her.

She squinted, trying to see beyond the second stair, but all that met her was darkness. She bit on a cuticle. Chance was down there too. She knew it in her bones.

"Can you find the lights?" Jeremy whispered.

She inched her fingers along the exposed studs of the wall until she found a plastic switch and flipped it up. Thin light stretched from a single bulb, bathing the stairs but leaving the basement floor in shadows. Star had been clinging to a hope that Chance wanted her to be happy, that he had brought her here for something good. She breathed through her teeth and walked down the stairs. Another switch for the basement lights was affixed to a stud at the bottom. But if he wanted her to be happy, then why had he waited so long? She'd been miserable since his death, lonely and angry and sad all the time. With a sinking feeling, she knew that he wanted something else. And once she found out what, Star believed that it would change everything she had come to love in Pine Lake.

In the dark, her foot missed the last stair, and she stumbled, landing on the basement floor. Dust motes coated her tongue, and she sneezed.

"Star?" Jeremy called.

She looked up. Jeremy had not moved from the top of the stairs. She frowned. "You wuss."

"Hey, you've slept outside for the last six months. I'm soft, Tuesday, and I'm not ashamed to admit it." He squinted down at her. "It'll be easier to find the box if you turn the light on."

"Great idea, genius, if I can find it." She was reaching back to search for the switch when her shoe hit something small. It clattered across the cement floor, landing in the small crescent of light coming from the top of the stairs. She let out a strangled scream that she quickly muffled. Her rock. The one she knew for certain she'd left in her drawer with the note.

"Star?" came Jeremy's voice from halfway down the stairs.

Her breath came in panicked huffs, and her skin prickled. What did he want? She was grasping the railing when the room exploded in a bright light that made purple spots dance in her eyes.

"And then there was light!" Jeremy stood at the bottom of the stairs, smiling. He peered past Star. "I don't know why you're so scared. This place isn't so bad." He looked down. "You already found the box?"

A large cardboard box lay at her feet with a yellow sticky note clinging to the water-stained top. In Lucy's unmistakable handwriting, it read *Old Newspapers*. Star shoved the rock into her pocket. "Let's bring it to the library," she said quickly. "We can spread out in there."

They walked with the box held between them, and when they reached the top of the stairs, the light was bright and reassuring, but the rock felt heavy in her pocket.

They settled on the thick rug in front of the couch and placed the box between them. Jeremy slipped his finger under the packing tape and brought it up in even strips. The top popped open, emitting the peppery smell of ink and paper.

Jeremy lifted a newspaper out. "This one is from January 5, 2001. Think that's old enough for my mom?"

Her scalp tingled. "That's my birthday," she said, and began pulling the papers out one by one. Her fingertips turned black and shiny from the newsprint. A familiar yellow square was attached to almost every paper. "Lucy has notes on all of these." She examined several squares. "But they're all blank."

Jeremy held out a *Denver Post*. "Not this one."

"Loose end?" She met Jeremy's eyes. "That's what she said to me when I first met her."

Lucy had scrawled the two words in thin black ink. The note teased her with its vagueness. Then she saw the date. *May 1, 2008.*

Her mouth went dry. It couldn't be. She grabbed the paper and laid it flat on the floor in front of her, fumbling to open the pages. Her eyes scanned every page until there, she found it—a small headline in the middle of the page.

Eight-Year-Old Boy Killed by Hit-and-Run Driver

Knifelike pain twisted in her belly.

"Star? What's wrong?" Jeremy's voice sounded like it came from the end of a tunnel.

She pulled her legs up, laid her chin on her knees, and pointed to the article. "What does it say?"

The paper rustled when Jeremy picked it up. He scanned the article. "It's about a kid who was killed outside some apartment complex in Denver." His eyebrows wriggled together. "Oh man, that's terrible. It was a hit-and-run. Nobody saw anything, except one person on the other side of the building who saw a small red car with a yellow hood speeding down the street, but the police never found it or any other witnesses . . ." He squinted, his eyes moving back and forth across the small columns until he paused and gave a soft gasp. "Oh my God. His mother was coming home from work when it happened." He looked up, his face stricken. "She was the one who found him."

The walls shifted inward, and Star couldn't breathe. Jess had *found him*. She dragged her nails down her arms, leaving red trails deep in her flesh. "Oh, poor Jess," she whispered.

"Poor Jess?" Jeremy said. The paper rustled again, and he said in a choked voice, "That was her *son*?"

Star nodded, unable to utter a word.

"His name was Chance," she said. "We were best friends."

Jeremy swallowed so hard she heard it as an audible gulp. "Oh, Star."

The chandelier flickered, the light dimmed and then grew bright, and a rusty creak echoed from above them, like a wooden ship battered by waves.

"I think you should go," she said.

Jeremy had turned white, his eyes wide as he looked above them. "Why?"

"Because Chance is here."

CHAPTER THIRTY-EIGHT

JESS

Ebee set a bowl of almonds and a plate of cookies on her square table. They'd eaten a hearty stew made with summer vegetables she'd canned from her garden, along with thick buttered slices of her homemade bread. It all tasted amazing, and Ebee promised to teach Jess how to can that summer. Her life in Pine Lake, which was how Jess had begun to think of it, had taken on an unfamiliar shape. One made up of friends and work and a life that hinted at deeper levels of connection. She found that it wasn't only a job that kept her in Pine Lake—she wanted to stay because she liked the person she was becoming here.

Ben had shown up for dessert and, as Ebee put it, *because we need a fourth to play euchre.* Jess had never played euchre, but they were into their sixth round, and she'd caught on quickly, enjoying the banter and what Ben had already pointed out was blatant table talk between Ebee and Lucy.

"So they're cheating," Jess clarified, laying down the lead card, an ace of diamonds.

"Yup," he said.

"I beg your pardon." Lucy studied her cards, pulled one, hesitated. "We don't cheat." Ebee popped an almond into her mouth. "We merely encourage each other to *be nimble and quick* and strong of *heart*," she said, emphasizing the words in a way that made Jess narrow her eyes.

Lucy pushed back the card, pulled another one, and laid it down. A nine of diamonds. Jess tried to keep from smiling; she and Ben might actually win this round.

Ben tossed his card on the pile, a ten of hearts. Damn, she thought he had a jack or a trump at least. "They cheat," he said.

Beside her, Ebee smiled and played the second-to-highest trump, a jack of hearts, making Lucy whoop and gather the cards. They'd won another round.

Jess wrinkled her forehead. "Wait a minute."

Ben raised his eyebrows. "Told you."

Ebee shuffled the deck, laughing. "So, Jess, Lucy told me about your little boy."

Her breath caught in her throat. Jess had talked about him more in the last few days than she had since he died, but still, his absence was a sucking hole in her chest that never got smaller. And it seemed that Lucy was now telling everyone about him. She rubbed the back of her neck.

But maybe talking about him, sharing memories of him, would fill the hole with something other than pain and regret.

"His name was Chance."

Ebee covered Jess's hand with her palm, looked her directly in the eye. "I lost my niece when she was quite young too. There are some things that time can't touch."

Jess squeezed her hand, nodded, and Ebee let go, went back to shuffling the cards. "What was he like?" Ebee asked as she dealt.

Jess hesitated, her mouth hanging open. This was foreign ground to her, and she was afraid that if she answered, her heart might crack open. She breathed in and heard the echo of his laugh, the way it sounded like it started deep in his belly until he couldn't hold it in anymore. She smiled and began to talk. "He was a terrible baby, colicky and cried all through the night. I was so young, and I had no idea what I was doing. Those were the hard days. But that only lasted for a little while. As a little boy, he was kind and sweet and stubborn as an ox—oh, but he was funny. I remember he used to tell this joke about an anteater." She sniffed, smiled again. "I can't remember the punch line. Just how much we laughed whenever he said 'anteater.'"

Lucy tilted her head to the side, nodded like she remembered too.

Now that she'd started, she didn't want to stop. "He was creative and fun and had an amazing imagination. He built this fort in the stairwell where he loved to play, and he spent every Saturday morning there." Suddenly she was flooded with bits and pieces of those days that made her want to remember more. "When we first moved into the apartment, he was so worried about meeting a friend. I told him that if anybody could make a friend in a place like the Lancaster, then it would be him." Her thoughts went to Star, and she rubbed her arms, wishing their paths had crossed. Star would have made him a nice friend.

The entire table jerked upward, sending the cards fluttering to the floor and upending the bowl of almonds. Lucy's and Ben's water glasses tumbled over, too, and water rushed under the cards and almonds, soaking everything. Ebee grabbed a towel and began to wipe the table down. "Sorry," Ben mumbled.

"Benjamin!" Lucy admonished. "You're too tall for your own good."

Ben stood, looming over the table. He was a tall man and must have knocked the table with his knee by accident, Jess realized. "Sorry about that," he said again.

"Are you okay?" Jess asked.

"Yeah, I'm sorry." He wiped a hand across his forehead, looked at Lucy again. "I have the late shift tonight, covering for a buddy of mine, and in all the cheating fun I let the time get away from me." He walked around the table, grabbed his coat by the door. "Thanks for dessert, Ebee, but we'll have to finish this game another time."

"Ha!" Ebee winked at Jess. "Are you sure it's not because of the euchre ass kicking Lucy and I just gave you?"

"Ebee!" Lucy said. "Language."

Ben smiled at Ebee, but the comfortable ease that had filled the kitchen all evening had disappeared. He stood in the doorway, his eyes glued to the back of Lucy's head. "How did your son die?" he asked.

Jess sucked in a breath at the abrupt, almost rude question. She folded her arms, felt the warmth of the good memories fade from her skin, the blackness of that night rise up and turn her stomach. "Hit-and-run."

"Oh, Jess," Ben said, but she noticed how he kept looking at Lucy, his face pale. "I'm so sorry. I—uh, I'm sorry I have to go." He tipped his head, then stepped outside. The door clicked shut after him.

The kitchen was silent after he left, Ebee and Lucy staring at Jess with equal compassion and quiet patience. She dragged her nails across her wrist, over and over, wanting to feel her skin open up again. "I never knew why."

"Why what?" Ebee said.

She met Ebee's gaze. "Why he was outside that night, alone and not even wearing a coat. He knew he wasn't supposed to leave the apartment." She felt her cheeks grow wet as she talked. She started to wipe them away, then stopped. *Fuck it.* Lucy had been telling her it was okay to cry. "I think—" She swallowed. "I think he was on his way to find me, but I never found out why." As soon as the words left her mouth, a door opened somewhere in her mind.

She hadn't been able to concentrate during her shift at the diner, mixing up orders, dropping dishes, and the entire time trying to ignore the prickling that ran down her spine, curled into her stomach. The certainty that she shouldn't have left him ate away at her until she couldn't take it anymore, and she hurried from the diner, her apron still tied around her waist. She ran, despite the icy streets, throat tight, heart pounding. Before she even turned the corner and saw his limp form dusted in snow, she knew that it was too late. Knew it in the way a mother just knows. He was gone.

"Give her some water."

A cold splash on her face shocked Jess back to the warm light of Ebee's kitchen.

"I meant give her some to drink, not baptize her with it," came Ebee's voice.

Jess opened her eyes to Lucy and Ebee, staring at her, their faces etched with deep lines of concern.

She rubbed the back of her neck. "What happened?"

"You went elsewhere," Lucy said.

Ebee gave Lucy a look, touched Jess on the shoulder. "You don't talk much about Chance, do you?"

Jess shook her head, stood from the table. "I think I need to get back. Is that okay, Lucy?"

"Of course, dear."

CHAPTER THIRTY-NINE

STAR

"Chance is here." Jeremy had been repeating the same sentence over and over, looking around the room as he did. "Here. Like, right beside me?" He pointed to a spot on the floor by his knee. "Chance is right here."

The flickering lights stopped, but the walls continued creaking, along with the sensation that the room had unanchored from the house.

Star nodded.

Jeremy's hair flopped forward over his forehead. He blew it away with a long breath. "What does he want?" His voice was pitched high when he spoke.

"I don't know." But that was a lie. After the bonsai and now this article, she knew what he wanted, and she was too chickenshit to do it. She hung her head, shame burning her cheeks and bringing tears to her eyes. She was a coward, just like her father. When it came down to it, she was no better than him, maybe even worse.

Jeremy's cheeks puffed up when he blew out a sigh. "Wow, that Lucy. She's something, isn't she? Does Jess know yet?"

Her hands curled into fists. "Does Jess know what?"

"About you and Chance? Lucy brought you two together, obviously, for a reason." His eyes widened. "Oh man, could it be so you can have a home now too?"

Star pushed to her feet, wrapped her arms tight across her chest, and glared down at Jeremy. "You're so stupid, Jeremy. You think Jess wants to know about me? That once she does we'll all live happily ever after? That's your kind of fairy-tale world, not mine!" She was shouting now, fueled by an anger that churned in her belly. "If Jess finds out who I am and what I did, I'll—she'll—" Her nostrils flared as she fought against tears. Feeling sorry for herself was pointless. She collapsed to the floor and sat cross-legged, letting her head fall into her hands. "She'll want nothing to do with me."

"Oh, Star. What did you do?"

She looked at him over the tops of her fingers, felt it begin to spill out, and she couldn't stop herself. "It was all my fault."

Chance hadn't opened the door until her fourth knock, and when he did, she'd only meant to give him the card and bonsai tree and then leave, maybe hang out in the fort until she thought it was okay to go back home. She pulled at her sleeve, the memory so clear it could have happened yesterday. "I remember he smelled clean, like dryer sheets, and when I saw the two little cows behind him, I just couldn't make myself leave."

Jeremy cleared his throat. "What?"

It was such a stupid thing, but she was only a little girl and was starving for something good to come into her life. "There was a small light that glowed yellow, right above the stove. At the very edge of the light I saw a pair of tiny ceramic cows on the counter. They stood on their back hooves, one with an apron that said *S* and the other wearing an apron with a *P*."

"Salt and pepper shakers?"

"Yeah. I know it's stupid, but his apartment was nothing like mine. I mean, it was shabby and the carpet was frayed and later I noticed worse water stains on the ceiling than mine, but it was . . . um, it was—"

She heard Jeremy make a noise in his throat. "A home," he finished for her, and her eyes burned because he understood. And then she was thinking about Jess and how she had hugged Star in the kitchen. That, too, had felt comfortable in a way that hurt now, when she was about to lose it all. She sniffed and pushed down the tears that tried to cloud her vision.

"I asked him if I could come inside, and I only meant to stay until it was safe to go home."

"Safe?"

She met Jeremy's gaze and for a moment saw herself through his eyes. A girl who had lived a life he'd only read about. A girl with a father who didn't love her enough to stay sober. Jeremy waited patiently for her to answer, his eyes soft. She lifted one side of her mouth in a half smile. "My dad was a drug dealer. Sometimes they came to our apartment, and I didn't like to be there when that happened because they scared me."

"Oh man," he said, and Star could see in the way his shoulders slumped that it was hard for him to hear, hard for him to picture her in that kind of situation. Chance had been like that. It made her want to hug Jeremy for his compassion. She stuck her hands under her legs instead.

Chance had smiled and led her to the kitchen table, where she ate oatmeal raisin cookies until her stomach hurt, and the thought of going back to her cold apartment with her dad and his cigarettes that burned and the needles and white plastic baggies made her stomach hurt worse. "Then I asked if I could live with him." She hung her head at the memory.

"Oh, Star."

Chance had responded like any eight-year-old kid with a heart like his. *What? Wow, yeah! You can be my sister! My mom is so great, and I'm sure she'll say yes.* He'd made a face. *Especially if you tell her about your dad.*

"He set up a bed for me on the couch with a fuzzy blanket. I don't remember thinking how impossible it all was; I just remember how happy it made me to think of living with Chance and his mom. There was just one thing I needed to get, one thing I wanted to take with me into my new family—my mom's other bonsai. One for Chance and one for me, that's how I imagined it. Like one of those friendship necklaces I'd seen girls wear with the stupid half of a heart, but tiny trees instead of a useless necklace. My father never cared about her trees, and I knew it would die without me, so I told Chance I'd be right back." Here she paused, wrapped her arms across her stomach, and squeezed. What she wouldn't give to do it all over again.

"Star?"

She ignored Jeremy and kept talking, letting her gaze settle on the floor. "He wouldn't let me go by myself. He said that Jazz—that was his favorite Transformer—would never let a girl walk around the Lancaster at night by herself." He'd taken her hand, and together they left his apartment.

Star had started to cry as she spoke, so hard she was gulping for air. "If only we'd waited for his mom to come home. If only I'd never gone down there in the first place." Jeremy had moved close, his hand rubbing small circles across her back. "If only my mom had never died, Chance would still be alive," she ended in a hoarse whisper.

From the hallway came the sound of the front door closing and the soft murmur of voices. Lucy and Jess were home. Star wiped at her face with the sleeve of her shirt; a low humming had started in her ears.

"I don't see how Chance dying was your fault, Star," Jeremy said quietly.

She stood, her leg muscles twitching. She wasn't ready to face Jess, didn't want to leave Pine Lake or Lucy or Jess; even if it was a dream she could never have and didn't deserve anyway, she wasn't ready for it to end.

"Star?" Jeremy's voice was edged in concern.

Her eyes shifted wildly about the room, looking for an escape. Jeremy stood, touched her shoulder. "I'm not going to say anything. It's not my business, and I don't think it's how Lucy works, anyway." His eyebrows met in the middle of his forehead. "It's your loose end, Star—that's what Lucy would say. But only when you're ready."

"You won't think of me the same when you know."

Jeremy stared at her, his mouth hanging open slightly.

The library door opened. "I see you found my box of newspapers!" Lucy said.

Jeremy closed his mouth and gave Lucy a wide grin. "We had to go into your basement!" he said.

Lucy laughed.

Jeremy looked at Star. "I'd better get going. I'll see you at the usual time tomorrow for school." He gave her a quick hug and left.

Lucy stood by the door, a folded-up crossword puzzle in one hand. She tilted her head and locked eyes with Star.

She rubbed at the skin on her face. Crying had made her eyes dry and puffy, and her body suddenly ached for sleep. "Where's Jess?"

"She went on up to bed. It was a tiring evening, I think." Lucy cleared her throat, slid her glasses on, and held up the crossword puzzle. "A four-letter word for a small building used to store things. Have you got an answer yet, Star?" She peered at Star over the rim of her glasses, her eyes a brilliant blue.

She shifted her weight, struggled to come up with something that didn't include Chance or Jess or the accident. "I'm going to clean up here and then head up to bed."

"Very well. Good night, then." Her black skirts swung when she turned, but at the door she paused, looked again at Star. "It's been a pleasure having you stay here with us, Star. I hope you've enjoyed it too."

Star's heart seemed to shrink in her chest. Was Lucy saying good-bye? She stretched her mouth into a weak smile. "I have, Lucy," she said. She wanted to drop to her knees and beg Lucy to let her stay, but Star knew better. "It's the first place that's felt like home." She hated herself for how pathetic it sounded, but the truth was just that.

Lucy's eyes grew bright, but all she said was "Exactly!" and left the library.

Star stood for a few moments, unable to move or shake the feeling that it was all ending. She felt fragile, like she might shatter at any moment, and at the thought of returning to the streets she sank to her knees. Paper crinkled, and her eyes caught an article she hadn't noticed before on the opposite page.

Residents Complain Lancaster Apartments Not Safe

Her heart thumped against her chest as she read the first few lines.

> After a violent night at the Lancaster, residents demand increased police presence and a crackdown on the rampant drug problem that they say has made living in this downtown Denver apartment complex a nightmare.

The article didn't specifically mention her father's murder, but then again, a drug deal gone bad at the Lancaster was not breaking news. She found a pair of scissors in a small rolltop desk and cut out both articles, folding them in half and sliding them into her pocket.

CHAPTER FORTY

STAR

The house was quiet when she woke up the next morning. She found a note from Jess in the kitchen, next to a slow cooker full of steel-cut oatmeal and between small bowls of brown sugar and raisins. *Forgot to tell you that Lucy has a doctor's appointment this morning. Have a good day at school. See you this afternoon.*

She stared at the note, one sentence in particular. *Have a good day at school.* Something a mother would say to her kid. She swallowed hard and pulled out the silverware drawer, her hand hovering over the spoons. A note from Lucy lay on top. *Check the calendar.* Star did. In the square for today it read, *School canceled, stomach flu.* She wrinkled her nose. *Ew.*

She ate slowly, thinking about the free time stretching ahead of her now. There was a writing assignment she could finish, math homework. Maybe she could even do some laundry for Jess. She'd like that, Star was sure of it, and she'd do anything to stay on Jess's good side.

The oatmeal lost its flavor. How long could Star go on pretending that this was her new normal? She washed the rest down with a few sips of milk and rinsed the bowl out in the sink. Jeremy had echoed exactly what she'd been secretly hoping: that Lucy had brought them together to give Star a new family. But when she thought of Jess and the scars that ran across her wrist, Star knew that would never work. Once she knew the truth, Jess would never be able to see Star as anything more than the reason her son died.

Star rubbed her arms, sat down at the table. There was nothing she could do now, so she spread out her math book and began to work. A few minutes later, she noticed Lucy's crossword puzzle lying on the kitchen table. She picked it up, studied the page. Most of the puzzle had been completed, and the answers, written in Lucy's neat handwriting, made her skin break out in goose bumps: *Star, Bonsai, Hit-and-run, Suicide.*

Her throat turned dry. How was this possible? A few squares were still blank. She checked the clues on the side, her eyes landing immediately on four down, a six-letter word for *accidental, serendipitous.* The lead scratched the newsprint before she realized she knew the answer. Chance. Her fingers tingled. She read the next clue, one that Lucy had asked her last night, four letters, *a small building used to store things.* The pencil felt heavy in her hand, and she let it fall to the table. Whatever answers were left, Star didn't want to know.

From behind her came a light clacking sound. She turned, heart racing. The small serving bowl of raisins lay upside down. She gripped the back of the chair, glanced into the foyer. Empty. The rubber soles of her shoes squeaked loudly when she approached the counter. She lifted the bowl. The raisins were clumped in the middle of the counter. Her eyes bugged wide. Was she seeing things? She blinked rapidly. No, the shriveled fruit had formed a crude shape. A five-pointed star.

A low moan escaped her lips, and she backed away from the counter. Her heel hit something on the floor, and she stumbled, turned. The foyer was covered in rocks, and the rocks had formed into dozens of five-pointed stars. She screamed and ran for the door, tugging on the handle, fear making her skin itch, throwing open the inner door, reaching for the outer door just as it was flung open, and she found herself staring directly into a uniformed chest. The small silver name tag said WATTS. She looked up and almost cried with relief. Officer Ben.

He held her by the elbows. "Are you okay? I was just outside when I heard you scream."

"Yes, I'm fine." Her breathing was jagged, so she took a deep breath, smiled. What could she possibly tell him that wouldn't make her sound like a lunatic? "I-I thought I saw a bear, or something, through the window."

"And you were running outside to see it closer?" He shook his head. "You and your aunt have a lot in common."

"Ha ha, yeah." She glanced over her shoulder. The rocks were gone. Had she imagined it? She shook her head, turned back to Officer Ben. "Lucy's not here. Jess took her to a doctor's appointment."

He leaned heavily against the doorway, and from the way he pressed his lips together, Star thought he was going to be sick. She took a step back, but the light from the foyer glinted off his badge, making her gasp. A five-pointed star.

She stared at it, then up at his face, lined in a different way than she remembered, then back to his badge. Memories that before had seemed like an unfinished quilt, scattered pieces of cloth with no connection, began to pull together into a pattern that she understood.

The hospital, her dad, the kind police officer—Ben. Lucy's words from that first day in Pine Lake echoed in her head. *It takes time for all the loose ends to be in one place, but once they are, things tend to move very quickly.*

She began to laugh so hard she almost started to cry. For a moment, she felt the thinnest strand of hope tug on her heart. She'd found Ben's loose end.

"Officer Ben?"

"Yeah?" He looked sad, his eyes, his mouth pulled down by a deep frown.

She studied him a moment longer, trying to remember his face from back then, but her childhood memories were patchy, and the ones that stuck were mostly the ones that hurt. This one, however, had stuck for a different reason. Because he'd been kind to her when she needed it most.

"I think you knew my dad," she ventured. They still stood in the doorway, both doors open. Cold air hit the backs of her legs, flowing from inside the house and through the open doors. "Would you like to come inside?" she asked.

He shook his head, the lines in his forehead deep. "Your dad?" he echoed, sounding confused.

The first time she'd seen Ben was at the hospital after her dad's overdose. The next time had been when she'd glimpsed him coming into the apartment before she hid in the bathroom. She was amazed she recognized him now, but she understood why she did. Chance. He'd been trying to get her to remember Ben. Was it to reassure her that not all adults were bad? An unfamiliar feeling fluttered in her belly. Could Chance want something good for her? She inhaled; maybe it was time she told the truth. Maybe Chance wanted her to be happy after all. "I was really young, but I think you were trying to help him."

He stared at her, his eyes dull and tired. "I'm not following, Star."

"We lived at the Lancaster. You visited my dad a few times. He was a—" Her face burned, and she lost her words. "He wasn't a good man. He was a drug dealer. But I told him I'd met you before and that you were trying to help him." Ben looked at her, his expression blank. A bead of sweat slipped down her back. "I thought if anybody could help him get clean it would be a nice police officer like you."

Still no reaction from Ben, and then Star realized why. She felt her shoulders relax. He still thought she was Jess's niece with the hippie parents. But Ben was a part of this, too, and he needed to know who she was. "Oh, I'm not actually Jess's niece. We only said that because we didn't know yet."

"Know what?"

"That I'm your loose end."

Ben's eyes shifted, and he seemed to be staring behind her now. His jaw slackened, and for a second Star thought he looked scared.

"Officer Ben, do you want to come inside?"

He coughed, shook his head as though to clear it, and backed out of the door until he stood on the top step. "No, thanks, I have to go." He gave her a long look. "But don't go running after any more bears, okay?"

CHAPTER FORTY-ONE

JESS

The dirt path around the lake was about a mile long, and the afternoon warmth gave her the perfect excuse to take a break and go for a walk. The doctor's appointment had been short and uneventful, and they'd returned home to find Star in an upbeat mood doing laundry and cleaning her bathroom.

Jess had raised her eyebrows at Star's sudden enthusiasm for household chores. "Did you smoke weed with the kids by the boathouse again?"

Star threw her head back and laughed. "Nah, I've moved on. It was meth this time."

Jess smiled. "Smart-ass." And they both laughed.

Now Jess was halfway around the lake and enjoying the fresh air and exercise. Last night at Ebee's had left her feeling heavy with memory but also strangely liberated, as though talking about Chance had freed her in some way.

In the woods surrounding the path came the crunch of dead leaves. Her head shot up at the sound, and she scanned the shaded depths. A squirrel clicked at her from the low branch of a pine tree, disturbing a large black raven. The bird lifted above the leafy canopy, the flapping of its wings heavy in the wooded silence. She shuddered, thinking about the bear. Having been a city girl her entire life, nature was an unfamiliar partner that she didn't quite understand yet.

The path ended in a set of wide metal stairs that led to the bottom of the waterfall. She jogged down the stairs and followed a narrow trail to a bench that sat facing the plunging water. To her surprise, a familiar form already occupied the bench, his large shoulders hunched forward, head in his hands.

She approached quietly. "Ben?"

His head jerked up, and he seemed to recoil at first. He sat up straight. "Afternoon, Jess." He fell silent, eyes trained on the ground in front of him.

Jess took a seat on the far side of the bench, shivered. A day of full sun had left the air warm, but the bench sat under the shadow of a pine tree where the frigid air of winter seemed to take refuge regardless of the season. She crossed her arms, wishing she'd remembered to grab a jacket.

Far above her, water plummeted over the concrete lip of the dam and onto the sharp boulders scattered across the shallow pool in front of them. Spray misted the air, dampening her clothes and adding to her chill.

"So Lucy's bloodwork from the last visit came back good. Dr. Patel says she's the perfect specimen of health. I told Lucy not to let it go to her head."

Ben snorted.

The silence between them lengthened until Jess shifted, uncomfortable. "Is everything okay?"

He leaned back on the bench and looked up. In the shadows of the pine tree, his skin had a gray tinge. "When I was a little boy, I wanted to jump over that waterfall."

His comment caught her off guard, and she studied the top of the dam. A narrow metal walkway spanned the length of the concrete lip, with high metal sides that stretched up and over like a cage. "From up there?"

"It was an open bridge then. They installed the gate a few years ago."

The waterfall was high, maybe sixty feet, and with the ragged points of the boulders below, a jump from that height would be suicide. "Bad idea," she said.

One side of his mouth lifted. "It sure was. My plan was to rent a paddleboat, take it past the buoys, step onto the concrete lip, and then when the entire town had appeared, execute a perfect dive." He stared at the top, a wistful expression pulling the edges of his mouth down.

"What happened?"

"I didn't have enough money to rent a paddleboat in the first place."

She smiled. "Swimming is free."

He sighed. "The thought did cross my mind, and except for one major obstacle I would have done it."

She pictured him as a small boy standing on the muddy banks of the cold lake. "What's that?"

"I didn't know how to swim," he said.

"And you were going to dive sixty feet into a pool of rocks?"

He gave a rueful smile that didn't touch his eyes. "Eventually I lost interest in the whole plan."

Jess fidgeted in the silence that followed. He hadn't looked her way since she first sat down, and he spoke almost as though she wasn't there.

"I reinjured my back not long after college."

She stole another glance at him, wondering where he was going with this, but his eyes were glued to the waterfall. "And then one night I found myself standing at the top of the waterfall, just like I'd planned all those years before. Except I wasn't a kid anymore."

He hunched forward, his elbows resting on his knees, head hanging.

"And that's when Lucy showed up and told me to get down." He laughed but it was grim, humorless. "She just has a way of knowing."

Jess touched the scars on her wrist, her mind flashing to the burning agony of the ragged blade across her skin. It took an enormous amount of pain for anyone to contemplate suicide. Ben's confession softened her, made her wonder what demons he had struggled with, made her want to share her own.

"A year after my son died, I stopped trying to pretend that I could live without him."

Ben's head swiveled around, and he looked at her as though seeing her for the first time.

"What I'm trying to say is that I get it. I understand what it's like to want an end." She held out her wrist, the scars pale white, jagged lines across her skin, then pulled down her sleeve to cover it back up. "I saw him everywhere, to the point where I thought it meant I was supposed to join him. Chance was my only purpose in life, and I couldn't see my purpose without him. So I tried."

"What happened?"

She inhaled sharply. "He wouldn't let me."

A cloud passed over the sun, turning the light blue and bringing shadows out of hiding.

"Why did you lie to me about Star?" His voice was gruff, his question abrupt.

"Who told you?"

"Star."

Jess was taken aback. Star had told Ben. "She must trust you."

He met her eyes, but his gaze seemed unfocused. "Does she."

He said it as a statement, and Jess shifted on the bench, uncomfortable. Was he going to call social services? But if Star had told Ben, maybe she was ready to face her past. Jess rubbed at her arms. The afternoon had slipped away, turning the sky a stormy blue. A cool breeze whispered through the pine needles.

Maybe it was time to help Star the way they should have at the very beginning.

CHAPTER FORTY-TWO

STAR

"I made fajitas!" Star announced to Jess the minute she returned from her walk.

Jess paused in the doorway to the kitchen. Her hair was down and around her shoulders in long brown waves. Star couldn't remember when she'd stopped wearing her tight ponytail every day, but she liked her better this way.

Jess was looking at her with a little wrinkle in her forehead. "You told Ben."

Star bit her lip. "I did."

"Does this mean you're ready to go home?"

Star stiffened. "What? No!" How could Jess still think Star wanted to go anywhere? "I recognized him."

Jess's eyebrows rose. "From where?"

"From when I was a kid." She could feel the excitement from this morning growing again. "You know how Lucy gets so upset about Ben's loose end and all that?"

Jess nodded.

"Well, I think I figured it out. I remembered Ben as this police officer who tried to help get my dad clean."

Jess's jaw dropped open. "Have you talked to Lucy about this?"

"Not yet—she's still sleeping."

"Still?" Her voice sounded alarmed. She headed up the stairs, not even bothering to take her coat off.

Star followed, her throat tight. She should have thought to check on Lucy. What if something had happened?

Jess opened the door without even knocking and entered the room, with Star so close that when Jess stopped suddenly, Star stumbled into her.

"Sorry," she mumbled.

Lucy sat in the chair facing the window, her red hair brushed out until it was a frizzy halo around her head. The glow of the late-afternoon sun shot through her window, lighting her hair on fire.

"Hey, Lucy," Jess said softly. "Would you like to come down for dinner? Star made fajitas."

Lucy didn't move, and Star felt her heart stop for a beat. "Lucy?" she said, and her voice trembled.

Jess moved swiftly to her side, knelt down by the chair, and placed her hand on Lucy's back. Lucy's neck craned forward, giving her the look of a vulture.

"I think I missed something important," Lucy said, and her voice came out as a croaking whisper.

Star hugged her arms to her chest, afraid to move any closer. Lucy always sounded old, but she'd never sounded weak before.

Jess took Lucy by the elbow and helped her to rise. "We had to get up so early this morning, I think it wore you out. Why don't you settle in here for the night. I'll bring your dinner up, maybe one of your crossword puzzles too?"

Lucy nodded, her thin fingers gripping Jess's arms and her eyes trained on every step she took.

"I made fajitas," Star offered.

Lucy looked up, but her eyes were a dull blue, and she seemed to be looking through her. She lifted the hand not holding on to Jess and pointed at Star.

"I take care of all of my loose ends," she said.

Star moved closer to the bed. "Oh, I know! That's what I want to tell you. Ben—"

"Stopped by earlier to see you." Jess shot Star a look that said, *Stop talking.*

She shut her mouth, confused.

Lucy yawned, smiled at Jess. "That's nice of Benjamin." She lay back against the pillows and closed her eyes. "Mother always said I could be blind when I wanted to be."

Jess nodded her head toward the door, and together they left the room and walked silently to the kitchen.

"What's wrong with her?" Star chewed nervously on a nail. What if something happened to Lucy?

Jess filled a glass with tap water and drank the entire thing before answering. "I think she's just tired, Star. It was a long day, and while she doesn't act it, her age does catch up with her from time to time. C'mon, let's eat."

They fixed their plates and sat across from each other at the table.

"Why didn't you let me tell her about Ben?"

Her mouth opened and closed, and Star tensed. This was the way people broke bad news.

"Lucy does good things for people here, and she definitely has a talent for figuring people out. But I think . . ." Jess looked down at her plate, and her face soured like she'd lost her appetite. She put her fork down. "I think Ben is right about her. She doesn't have magical powers or supernatural sight, and letting her believe she does isn't good for her."

Jess was wrong, but she didn't know everything. If Star could get her to see how they were all connected, then maybe there was a chance. "But what about you and me?"

The frown line between her eyes deepened. "You and me? We happened to live in the same building at the same time. Honey, given our backgrounds, that's not so unlikely."

Star felt her chest tighten; she'd forgotten that Jess didn't know about Chance and her. "But what about Ben? I know he's the same police officer who was so nice to me and who tried to help my dad. I *remember* him." Plus Chance had been trying to tell her with all the five-pointed stars, so she knew she wasn't making things up in her head. She crossed her arms, rolled her shoulders. Lucy was the real deal.

Jess gave her a soft smile. "Did Ben say he remembered you?"

When she thought back to this morning, she realized that he hadn't really said much. She shrugged, feeling tears well in her eyes.

"You would have only been what, seven or eight?"

Star nodded.

"I'm sorry, Star, I just think we're caught up in some pretty unique circumstances, and we've let Lucy's imagination get the better of us." She reached out, touched Star's arm. "Lucy is struggling with some memory issues. The doctor wasn't sure if it's early-onset dementia, but I don't think it's a good idea to encourage her."

Star chewed on the fajita meat. Jess didn't know what Star knew, hadn't seen the things that Star had, but there was something about her tone that made the meat turn rubbery in her mouth. It seemed like Jess was leading up to something that Star had been expecting since she'd first arrived in Pine Lake. She could tell in the way she sat in the chair, straight back, the tight lines around her mouth.

Jess cleared her throat, and Star's leg muscles cramped. She'd been here before, and she'd been such a fool to think this time was different.

"I was thinking, Star, that since Ben knows who you are now, maybe it's time for you—for us—to reach out to your social worker. I can, you know, help in some way. Make sure we find you the kind of family who deserves you."

A hard lump filled the base of her throat. Leave Pine Lake? Her stomach churned at the thought of crawling under a bench to sleep. Coming here had stripped her of her hard layer, made her soft. Her eyes burned, and she felt a sob building in her chest. But then she thought of Chance pointing her toward Ben, and a rush of optimism spread inside her. Maybe, just maybe, if she was brave enough to say it out loud, maybe she could get what she really wanted.

She took in a deep breath, lifted her eyes. "Everyone around here thinks Lucy's a witch. Maybe she could adopt me, and I'll become known as the Little Witch of Pine Lake." She shoved her shaking hands under her thighs, but her knee jiggled up and down under the table.

"Oh, Star," Jess whispered. Her eyes grew bright, and Star had to look away. "I don't think the state would ever consider . . . Lucy's very old."

It was all slipping away; Star could feel it. This was her chance, and as humiliating as it was to have to ask, if she didn't, she'd regret it for the rest of her life. And maybe Jess felt the same way. Her words spilled out in a strained whisper. "What about you?"

Jess's eyes widened, and her mouth opened and closed again, like a fish gasping for air, but she didn't make a sound, didn't say a word.

She didn't need to.

Star pushed up from the table, abandoning her half-eaten fajita. Her stomach was in free fall, but she did her best to ignore the sensation, and with her chin held high she walked out of the kitchen, leaving Jess and her fishhook face behind.

CHAPTER FORTY-THREE

JESS

She stared at her hands. They were on the small side, her fingers a tad long to be called stubby. She studied the creases in her knuckles, the cracked tips beneath her short, unpainted nails, the deep lines that crisscrossed the dry skin of her palms.

She curled them into fists, banged them on the table. She was a coward. As cracked and dry as her hands. Sat there with nothing to say after Star asked what Jess knew took every ounce of courage the girl probably had left.

She pressed her palms against her eyes and let her head fall to the table, overcome by a memory of one of the last afternoons she'd spent with Chance.

She'd grasped the end of the banana-shaped seat of the bike she'd given him for Christmas. The day was cool but with a hint of spring in the light breeze. They stood underneath the only two trees in front of the Lancaster; thin branches held stubbornly to a handful of dry brown leaves. The cracked pavement in front of their apartment building made it hard to ride, but it was the first warm afternoon since Christmas, and he was determined to learn. Chance balanced on the pedals, making the bike wobble in her hand.

Ready? she said.

He gave a single nod, and they took off. Jess ran beside him for a few feet, one hand holding the back of the seat, the bike stuttering over the pavement. Both of them laughing.

Tell me when to let go . . .

I got this, Mama!

She released the seat, and he pedaled a few feet on his own, his little legs pumping up and down until the front of the bike began to jerk from side to side.

Put your feet down! she called to him, and he did, coming to an abrupt stop.

Chance let the bike fall to the ground before he turned to her, laughing. *Did you see me?*

When she picked him up, he clasped his legs around her waist. *I saw you. You're a real bike rider!*

Afterward they'd rested against the spindly trunk of one of the trees, her arm slung around his small shoulders, his head of light-brown hair resting against her chest. She pressed her lips into his curls and inhaled, and his little-boy scent filled her nostrils—the sweet, sweaty musk of a boy still years away from the hardness of manhood.

A hand squeezed her shoulder, and Jess's head shot up, her face wet. The cold remains of the fajita sat on the table in front of her, filling her nose with the tangy smell of room-temperature salsa. Night had fallen outside, and without any lights turned on, the kitchen was dark except for the dim light above the stove.

Lucy stood above her, and in the darkness the wrinkles lining her face caught the light, making her cheeks look caved in, hollow.

"I'm so sorry, Lucy!" She sprang to her feet, wiped the wetness from her face, and checked the clock. Her eyes widened; she'd slept for a couple of hours. "I'll pull dinner together for you now. Are you feeling better?"

"Yes and no," Lucy said, and began to pace the kitchen, walking in a small circle, checking the calendar with each pass she made. She picked up her crossword puzzle from a pile under the phone, squinted down at it. "The problem is that it's too close. I can't see when it's too close."

Jess set a full plate on the table, handed Lucy her glasses. "Here, come and eat. It's been hours since lunch."

The chair scraped across the floor when Lucy sat down. She slid her glasses on and read, "Nine letters, a confirmed habit."

That damned crossword puzzle seemed more like Lucy's tool for evading conversation. Jess sighed and set a napkin with silverware beside the plate. "Iced tea?"

"Yes, dear. Hmmm, one covering tracks, perhaps."

"Excuse me?"

Lucy pursed her lips, studied Jess over her glasses. "Four letters. Come now, I thought you'd gotten better at this."

The ice cracked when she poured the tea, making a popping sound. Sometimes it was also good policy to ignore what she couldn't answer. She stirred in a couple of heaping teaspoons of sugar and returned to the table, handing it to Lucy. "Star told Ben the truth." She hoped the change of subject would help.

Lucy's eyebrows rose. "Is that so?"

"Yes, and I think it was the right thing to do. I know you like to help people, and what you've done with her is so great, but I think . . ." She swallowed, thinking of Star's face when she'd asked if Jess would adopt her. "She needs a home, Lucy."

The tip of the older woman's pencil rested against her cheek, and her eyes moved across the puzzle, widened, and then she scribbled something across a row of boxes. "She has one," she said without looking up from the paper.

A flush spread up her neck at Lucy's stubbornness. "This is not a permanent home, and you know it."

Lucy's pencil hovered over the squares of the crossword puzzle, and her mouth turned down at the corners. "Six-letter word." She brought the paper closer to her face. "A clock." Her eyes finally met Jess's over the edge of the newspaper. "Do you know the answer?"

Jess rubbed at her temples. "We're talking about Star," she said.

"About Star." Lucy sat back in her chair, tapped the table with the pointed end of the pencil. "I don't like loose ends." Her words were clipped, businesslike. "You of all people should know that."

Something snapped in her then. "God dammit, Lucy!" Anger boiled in her gut. She breathed deeply. "With all due respect, I think you've let this idea of yours get in the way of seeing things clearly. Like Star. That girl"—she brought her fist down onto the table with a thump—"she's the one who gets hurt when your games are over."

Lucy's attention had drifted back to the puzzle in front of her.

Jess continued anyway, speaking as much to convince herself as Lucy. "She wants to stay. Did you know that? She thinks you'll adopt her." Jess laughed shrilly. "Or me. She thinks that this house, this town, you and me, that we're her new family. You're promising her something she can't have, Lucy. Loose end or not, there's nothing more cruel than that." She finished in a whisper, like her words had been the helium, her body a balloon. And now she was empty.

The scratch of graphite on paper was loud in the stillness that followed.

Jess closed her eyes, covered her face with both hands. With a sigh she pushed up from the table and began to clean the kitchen.

The crinkle of newsprint sounded from behind her. "A six-letter word for an unnatural ending," Lucy said. "It's time for answers, Jess."

Jess hung her head, inhaled through her nose; she was on her own. Tomorrow she would talk with Star, help her to understand that while she cared deeply for her, this situation wasn't right. She needed a home with a mom and a dad who could love her the way she deserved.

CHAPTER FORTY-FOUR

STAR

Star lay against the headboard of her bed with her knees drawn up, trying to remember the girl she'd been before. But all that came to her was the sadness and the filth. Slogging through each day like a zombie, numb and single minded, keeping her heart hard. Like her father.

Maybe they hadn't been so different after all.

She shifted on the bed and noticed the drawer to her bedside table was partially open. She pulled it out all the way. The rock lay inside, on top of Lucy's note. She stared at it, thinking. When Chance had first given it to her, she'd taken it as a sign that her mother was watching over her.

She picked up the stone and closed her fist around it until the bones of her palm hurt and the skin around her knuckles turned white. Her fist opened, and she let it drop onto the bed. She opened the note, reread the first line. *You watched your best friend die.* The words blurred, and her hands crumpled the worn paper into a ball. She'd been such a fool. She didn't deserve to be here. Chance probably hated her for living.

She curled up on her side as hot tears fell down her cheeks. She'd leave tomorrow. Screw Lucy and her loose ends and Jess and her stupid face. Star didn't need them. And screw Chance. She'd never asked him to save her stupid, worthless life in the first place.

Her eyes grew dry and heavy, and she climbed under the covers, thinking about the next day. Jeremy and the other half of his siblings were sick now, and Mrs. Foster had canceled school again tomorrow. Then she thought of the pity that had welled in Jess's eyes when she asked if she'd adopt her, and Star felt her body ache like she had a fever. *Stupid, stupid, stupid.* Lucy was too old; Jess didn't want her. What was the point in staying around?

She pulled the sheet up and over her head. Lucy and Jess were going over to Ebee's house tomorrow. As soon as they were gone, she'd pack her bag and leave.

Her eyes closed, and she pushed away thoughts of where she'd be sleeping tomorrow night.

~

A cool breeze tickled her face, bringing with it the woodsy scent of pine trees and earth and pushing the folds of her nightgown around her ankles. Star opened her eyes to a glowing black night and felt a jolt that tingled her fingertips. She stood outside the front door. How had she gotten here? The moon shed a clean white light over everything. Her heart raced. The last thing she remembered was falling asleep; the conversation with Jess had played a constant loop in her mind and unsettled her dreams.

A child's laughter echoed from behind the house and sent chills racing up her spine. She tried the door, but it was locked. Was this a dream? No, the cold air that wrapped itself around her bare ankles felt too real, made her shiver.

More laughter floated on the breeze, accompanied by the crunch of grass. A dark form flitted behind the trunk of a thick tree. She yanked at the door with both hands, whimpering as she fought against a rising hysteria.

"Let me in, let me in," she whispered.

But the house was dark and silent. Nobody could hear her. She turned around, pressing her back against the door, her hand still grasping the curved handle. There was nowhere to hide, no curtains to close, no lights to turn on. The figure slipped around the tree and walked toward her. In the shadows, she could just make out the tint of red in his sweatshirt. Her heart thumped loudly in her ears. She tried the door again, but her fingers slipped from the handle.

She rested her forehead against the door, wrapped her arms across her belly, and turned to face him. The darkness surrounding his small form rippled like a wave, and he disappeared around the side of the house.

She balanced on the balls of her feet and followed, wincing at the panicked huff of her breath. When she reached the stone patio, her back tensed. Empty. The library window towered above the patio, reflecting the glare of the moon.

A feathery breath tickled the bare skin of her neck. Her hands clenched into fists, and she whirled around. Gnarled branches of a young aspen tree reached for her like fingers. She let out a muted groan.

Boyish laughter seemed to come from all around her, but when she covered her ears it didn't stop. There was a flash of red in the night, and she looked up to where an old shed sat on a small rise behind the house.

He wanted her to follow. A bead of sweat coursed down her neck. She wiped it off and started on the overgrown trail that led up the hill. Rocks and small pinecones dug into the soft skin of her feet. The crooked trail rose above the house and passed through a weed patch of purple thistle, and the tall stalks nipped at her nightgown with thorny teeth. She quickened her pace.

The shed was before her, rusted metal walls sloped inward, grass stretching waist high up the sides. Brown vines twisted through the ridges of corrugated metal and over the sagging roof, making it look as though the earth itself wanted to swallow the shed whole.

A metallic scratch sounded from inside, and as she watched, the door swung open. Her breath stuck in her chest, and she gasped for air, wishing she could wake up from this nightmare. Nothing but darkness waited for her inside the shed, and more than anything she wanted to be in her room with her head buried under a pillow.

"What do you want, Chance?" Her voice sounded pathetic and small.

The door swung in the night breeze, hitting hard against the metal walls.

She felt cold all over. With one hand pressed against the rough metal doorframe, she peered inside.

CHAPTER
FORTY-FIVE

JESS

Sleep refused to come, and Jess tossed and turned, her wrist aching, her dreams tormented. She dreamed of Star as a baby in the arms of her mother. Star as a small girl carrying a bonsai tree in her arms. As a kid with haunted eyes watching her father pierce his skin with a needle. A teen, huddled under a city bench, her legs drawn up and into her belly.

When she woke up, her pillow was wet from her tears. She sat on the edge of the bed, waiting for the dreams to fade, but all she could think about was Star. She cried out suddenly, smothering it with her hand. How could she have let Star leave the kitchen like that? She slipped on her thin cotton robe and opened the door. A cold draft shot into her room, raising the hair on her arms.

Star's door was open, and from inside came the soft creak of the floorboards. Good, she was awake too. Jess hesitated when she stepped into the hallway. The look on Star's face when she'd fled the kitchen had been one of naked vulnerability and hurt. What promises could Jess make her? The girl deserved to be loved and cared for, and that wasn't something Jess could give her. Her calves hardened with a desire to turn away. *Don't be ridiculous. Go and talk to her before it's too late.*

But when she peered inside, she gasped. The room was empty. She gritted her teeth. The sound had probably been from that mouse she'd seen under Lucy's bed. Or another just like it. The traps hadn't caught anything yet, and the critters most likely had a whole network of holes in this house. She searched the empty room, checked the corners for signs of droppings. Nothing. Bright moonlight poured through the window, lying across the floor in a white rectangle. She stared at the moon; it stared back.

She was halfway out the door when she noticed the drawer to Star's bedside table lay open, nearly falling off the rails. When she bent to close it, she saw the note. The one that Jess had delivered from Lucy. But it wasn't the note that dried her mouth. It was the rock sitting beside it—painted red, the color faded and flaking off so that chunks of the black stone beneath it showed through.

Her legs wobbled, and she sank onto the bed, bracing her hands on her knees and breathing hard. It couldn't be the same rock.

She snatched the note from the drawer, opened it. The paper was soft and limp. Star had read it often. Jess's heart pounded loudly in her ears. She shouldn't be in here. This was Star's room. This was her note. Her eyes darted to the stone, then back to the paper. All she had to read were the first few lines:

Dear Girl,
Here is what I know:

1. You watched your best friend die.

The paper shook, and the rest of the note blurred. She let it fall back into the drawer and clasped her hands together, squeezing her eyes shut. It couldn't be. But when she opened her eyes, all she saw was the rock.

And his small hands with dimples on the knuckles drawing the tiny gold stars that were almost all rubbed off now. Her own hands holding the rock steady when he wrote his initials on the back.

Her fingertips pinched the stone, turned it over, and Chance was there, right beside her, the memory of that moment washing over her, when they'd stood in front of the Lancaster, Chance holding her hand, their meager possessions packed in a black duffel bag at their feet. They'd stared up at the five-story low-income housing complex before them, the sky gray against the drab brown of the building's exterior.

Is this our new home, Mama? Her son's voice was sweet and small.

For now.

The Lancaster catered to single moms like her, along with addicts and dealers. It was the best she could do on her meager salary.

What do you think, buddy?

He tilted his head to look up at her with soft brown eyes. *It's not a car, and it's not a couch.*

It's better than that. Police sirens sounded in the distance, growing louder as they approached the Lancaster. The sirens stopped, but the rotating lights painted the sides of the building red and blue.

Do we have our own room?

She nodded. *And our own kitchen.*

And our own bathroom?

Only the best, right, buddy? She tweaked his nose, and they both laughed. He understood how bad things had gotten, but he was an unflagging optimist. She adored that about him.

Hey, look at that. He knelt to the pavement. His small fingers dug into a crack, rooting around in the dirt beneath until he extracted something small and dark gray. *Cool!*

What is it?

He held out his hand. Lying in the center was an ordinary rock, small and dull.

A rock?

Not just any rock, Mama. Look.

As she squinted the sun shifted, peeking out from behind a building. In its soft golden light, the small rock shimmered. *It's pretty,* she said.

Can't you see it? He shot her an impatient look before turning back to his prize.

See what?

It's a heart. He pointed to a slight indentation.

She studied it again and could almost make out the faint outline of a heart. But the sun disappeared behind the next tall building, turning the rock a flat black, and it was gone. *I don't see it. But that doesn't mean you don't. I think you're just better at seeing things for what they could be.*

His shoulders slumped in disappointment. *I thought it was special.*

It is! She picked up their bag and slung it over her shoulder. *Put it in your pocket. I bet it brings you good luck.*

He brightened immediately. *Like for meeting a friend here?*

Well, that wouldn't surprise me one bit. You're the best at making friends.

Can I paint it?

Of course. How do you want to paint it?

He rubbed the rock and thought for a moment. She reached out and touched the curls that clung close to his head. *Red with stars.* He looked up at her with an excited smile. *And I'll give it to the first friend I make here.*

She held the rock to her chest and dug up another memory, so vague that at first it was only the outline of one. She squeezed her eyes shut and tried to let it grow richer, darker, like a Polaroid, and when it did her tears made small wet spots on her robe.

Chance had sat at the kitchen table, drinking milk and eating a chocolate chip cookie. He dunked the cookie in the milk, making puddles of white liquid and crumbs on the place mat. *I met my friend today, Mama. And we're gonna meet in my fort on Saturdays.* She remembered how the cookie crumbs had stuck to the milk mustache above his lips.

But Jess had been distracted and missed what he was telling her because she'd noticed the way the hem of his pants rose to his calves. She'd already let the hem out on this pair of pants once. A knot formed in her stomach like it always did when the bills were due—maybe she could find something at a secondhand shop. Then she noticed the rubber sole of his shoe had come away from the side. Shoes first.

What's his name? Her attention had returned to the electric bill, the total higher than she'd expected.

She's Star.

She'd written out the check while he talked, knowing there wasn't enough in the bank to cover it. But she had to hide her worry from him—he didn't need to know how tight it was. So she'd smiled vaguely. *A girl, huh? I'm sure she is a star, buddy. Just like you.*

Her head hung, and her hands sat lifeless in her lap. Star had been Chance's best friend. The one he met in the fort. Her mind turned back to the day she'd found Star staring at the picture of Chance, and she felt a jolt rush through her chest. Star had lied to her about knowing her son. Why?

A familiar sound outside made her heart beat faster. She hurried to the window. Star's room faced the side patio, and from here Jess had a clear view of the overgrown path leading up to the shed. The structure's metal door was open, flapping against its frame as though caught in a gust of wind. Movement below the window. Her nails bit into her palms. A small figure picked her way through the patch of thistles. The moon made her billowing white nightgown glow against the grayness of everything else. Star.

She hurried through the weeds, her nightgown rippling when it caught on the thorns, stumbling when she reached the top. And her eyes never seemed to leave the shed. Jess inhaled sharply. What was Star doing?

She flew from the room and down the stairs, hurling open the door. It smashed into the wall with a loud bang. The image of the bear and the boy and the knowledge that Star had lied to her twirled around in her head until it became a tangle of thoughts too twisted to understand.

CHAPTER
FORTY-SIX

STAR

Inside, the shed was a wall of blackness so dense she couldn't tell where the floor or walls or ceiling met or began or ended. She shivered. It was like a giant mouth. A squat, hulking shape with wide-set eyes began to form. She whimpered, but as her eyes adjusted she saw it was only a car. It filled the shed, leaving about a foot of space between the doors and the slanting walls. Her curiosity momentarily overcoming her fear, she walked all the way inside. The car didn't appear to be anything special, just a two-door hatchback—maybe a dark red or blue. But it was the hood that was unusual, painted a different, lighter color from the body.

She backed away, but the door behind her closed with a thud, plunging the shed back into darkness. The stench of burning rubber snaked inside her nose, and her breathing turned ragged.

In the dark her foot turned, twisting her ankle, and she pitched forward, flailing in space until she landed face-first onto the cold metal hood. The walls groaned and creaked around her. When she pressed her palms down to push herself up, she felt that the metal curved inward. She ran her hands across the hood, and her mind filled with flashes of the car before the door had closed. A shattered windshield, dent in the hood. She jerked her hands away, felt her mouth go dry.

There could be only one reason that Chance wanted her to see this car. Her legs gave out, and she fell to the ground. Her thoughts turned to Lucy. She pressed her palms on either side of her head and rocked back and forth. *No, no, no. Not Lucy.*

The walls seemed to shrink, and she couldn't breathe. She pulled open the door and scrambled out of the shed, sucking in a lungful of cool air as behind her the door slammed shut. The sky above was a dark gray; it was almost morning.

"Star?"

She jumped. Jess stood at the top of the hill.

"What are you doing out here?"

The words would not come. She stood rooted to the ground, mutely rubbing her arms. She understood now. Chance wanted his mom to know everything.

"Please answer me, Star." Jess stood in front of her, looking past Star's shoulder. "Were you inside the shed?"

"I couldn't sleep," she said. "And I thought I heard a bear."

Jess eyed her feet. "So you came all the way up here to scare it off in your nightgown and bare feet?" She looked again at the shed. "How did you get in there?"

Before she could answer, a scream came from inside the house. Jess's eyes widened, and her mouth opened. "Oh my God!" She whipped around and ran down the path, and Star followed close behind, her heart pounding in her ears.

Jess was inside before her, but her cry sent a ripple of fear down Star's back. A figure lay sprawled at the bottom of the stairs—frail ankles, skinny calves poking out of her black nightgown.

"Call 9-1-1," Jess said, her voice hoarse with panic.

As Star ran to the phone, a man's voice stopped her.

"I already have," Ben said, jogging down the stairs.

Star gasped. What was Ben doing here?

Jess's head shot up. "Ben?" She didn't wait for his response. Turning back to Lucy, she put two fingers on her wrist. "Lucy? Can you hear me?"

But Lucy made no sound.

Star hovered behind them, biting one fingernail after another, her eyes glued on Lucy's still form. The wail of sirens drifted up from Main Street, getting louder as the ambulance pulled up in front of the house.

And then the foyer was full of people in uniform, and Star saw Jess stand to the side, holding her hands out in front of her like they didn't work anymore. Star moved so that she stood just behind her, fighting the urge to reach out and touch her.

Ben leaned down and hissed at Jess, "I told you something like this would happen."

Jess stared at him, and her face was so sad, Star looked down at her feet.

"Why are you here, Ben?"

His jaw tensed. "I was just getting home from a late shift when I heard voices from my driveway. When I came down to investigate, I found the front door wide open and Lucy standing at the top of the stairs, confused and very upset."

"But how did she fall down the stairs?" Jess said through her teeth.

Ben ran a hand roughly through his hair. The skin beneath his eyes was puffy and dark, like he hadn't slept well, and dark stubble covered the sharp edges of his cheeks and jaw.

"When she saw me, she started to come down the stairs, and she must have tripped on her nightgown or—" He made a choking sound like a sob, pressed a fist into his mouth, his eyes suddenly wet.

Star swallowed. He looked so lost right then.

Jess visibly softened, placed her hand on his arm. "She's not always steady on her feet. Things happen."

The paramedics had loaded Lucy onto a stretcher and wheeled her outside.

Ben inhaled, sniffed, and his face turned serious again. "I'll follow the ambulance." He left quickly, and Jess ran upstairs, returning a few minutes later dressed in sweatpants and a long-sleeved shirt. Star stood in the empty foyer, her bare toes cold on the hardwood floor.

"Ma'am?" A paramedic stuck his head through the door. "You can ride with us if you'd like."

"Thanks," Jess said, then paused and turned to face Star as though just now remembering that she was there. She slid her hand inside her pocket and pulled something out, took Star's hand, and placed it in her palm. It was smooth and cool and round. Star blinked rapidly, looked down, thought her heart might shrivel in her chest.

It was her rock, red with gold stars.

Jess didn't let go of her hand right away, squeezed it a little. "We need to talk," she said hoarsely, and released her hand.

CHAPTER FORTY-SEVEN

STAR

The sirens faded into silence. She didn't move from the foyer, the rock pressed to her heart, until the sky began to lighten into strips of pink and blue. A light breath of cold air brushed across her bare arms. She looked up and felt the hair on her neck stand on end. Chance stood at the bottom of the stairs, hands hanging by his sides, his hair as curly, eyes as brown as the first day she met him.

She reached out. "I'm—" she croaked, but he turned, ran down the hallway, and disappeared into the sitting room. Her feet dragged across the floor when she followed. What did he want to show her this time? She turned the corner into the sitting room—empty, but something moved by the window. She gasped and sprinted across the room, dodging couches and end tables. She was too late.

"No!" The center bonsai crashed to the floor, scattering dirt, small rocks, and pottery pieces across the rug. Star dropped to her knees and began to scoop up whatever she could, tears making paths down her cheeks even though it wasn't her mother's tree. She hunched forward over the mess and cried out to the empty room, "I'm sorry, Chance.

I'm so sorry." She squeezed the broken pottery, sending sharp spikes of pain up her arm, and felt warm drops of blood skim down her palm. He deserved to be here instead of her, to be with his mom. She deserved none of it. With a sob, she released the pottery and fell to her knees, letting the memory of that night unfold.

At night, the stairwell at the Lancaster felt like another world. The light made everything green, and the floors looked even dirtier, caked with layers of muck, the corners full of cigarettes, potato chip bags, and other stuff Star never touched. Chance had bounded ahead of her like usual, taking the stairs two at a time. Star's stomach flip-flopped with excitement, making her out of breath. She was going to live with Chance and his mom. Her feet hardly touched the stairs; she was flying.

When they got to her apartment, Star put her ear to the door, and the whooshing sound that echoed back made her think of the ocean. Soon she picked up other sounds—Mr. Ahmed's television from next door turned up loud because he didn't hear well, a woman yelling cusswords, and then grunting or shuffling or something like that. She wasn't sure, but she didn't hear her father's voice. He must be passed out by now.

She gave Chance a thumbs-up, put her finger to her lips. He mouthed *O-K*, making his lips really big with the *O* and wide with the *K*. She covered her mouth with her hand, giggled without sound. Chance put his hand on the knob, turned, and pushed so that he was standing in front of her, blocking her view. She would never forget the way his shoulders stiffened, how his hand reached back to clamp onto her arm, strong like one of those robots he always talked about. He stood in front of her, and when she tried to look around him. he held her back, stiff armed. All she could see was the top of her father's head from where he lay on the floor, his shiny scalp pointed toward the door.

At first she thought he'd overdosed again, because there was someone else on top of him, doing something with his hands like a paramedic. But her father's body flailed, and the person's hands were on his neck, squeezing, squeezing, squeezing. A wet choking sound came from her father, and his arms shot up, his hands curled into claws.

Chance moaned softly and grabbed her hand, pushing her in front of him as they whirled and sprinted toward the stairs.

A man's deep voice shouted at them. *Hey! Get back here, boy!*

They stumbled down the stairs, and Star scraped her face against the cement wall, drawing blood in a line across her cheek. When they passed Chance's apartment on the first floor, she tried to turn him, thinking he had forgotten where he lived.

Instead he pulled her toward the entrance to the building, out the glass door, and into a night so cold her lips stuck to her teeth and her wet face froze. She was crying and so was Chance. His tears were red, though, reflecting the stoplight. *The diner isn't far. My mom will know what to do.* Her legs were shorter than his, and she had trouble keeping up. He yanked at her arm, sending a sharp pain into her elbow. *Hurry!*

They crossed the street, but the road was thick with slush and ice that splattered her ankles, and she slipped and stumbled, nearly falling, but Chance wouldn't let go of her hand. There was no sound, the snow making everything quiet on the empty streets. Her heart pounded so fast she thought her chest was going to burst, trying to keep up with him.

A car engine cut through the heavy silence. And then Chance pushed her so hard she flew backward, sliding easily in the slush until her spine crunched against something hard and she stopped.

She looked up. His face glowed white like the moon. And then he was gone.

She couldn't feel her feet or her legs, but somehow she pushed up from the pavement, her cold hands scraped and bloodied, numb. The next thing she knew she was standing outside her apartment again. The door was wide open. Her father's body lay sprawled across the floor, unmoving. She curled into a ball on her cot, stuck her thumb in her mouth, and lay there until Mr. Ahmed found her sometime the next day.

Star wiped the tears from her face, her hands stinging from where slivers of pottery stuck to her palms. She began to pick them off, her face hot and dry, the room cold and empty. The sun had risen and filtered in through the window, bleak and unpromising. She finished scooping up the bonsai and, not wanting to throw it away, put it back on the table—dirt, limbs, and pottery.

In the foyer she paused, stared at the floor, her hands curled into fists. What was her plan? She clenched her jaw and ran up the stairs to her bedroom. From her backpack, she took the two newspaper articles and a package of Post-it notes that Lucy had given her. She wiped a hand across her eyes. Lucy. Her hand hovered above the small square of paper, and then she scribbled everything she could, taking up two sides of the note. She took the articles and notes to Jess's room and slid them all under her pillow.

She breathed out, feeling a small bit of peace. This was what she was meant to do; she knew it in her heart. She was never supposed to have a happy ending; she'd never deserved one, but Jess did. And this, however painful, would give Jess the closure Star knew she needed.

She threw only the warmest of her clothes into her backpack, leaving the two dresses and the nightgown from Lucy lying across her bed. She looked at the clothes with a pang, slung her bag over her shoulder, and left.

CHAPTER FORTY-EIGHT

JESS

Lucy was pissed. She sat up in the bed, her back hovering off the pillow, looking ready to leave the hospital at any minute. Jess didn't think she'd ever seen her this amped up before. Ebee perched on one end of the bed, her hand resting on top of the covers. They'd been at the hospital for most of the day, waiting for a room to open up, and all Lucy wanted was to go home.

Jess wrung her hands. "I'm so sorry, Lucy, for not being there when you needed me."

"Yes, about that. Where were you?"

Jess pressed her palms into her thighs. The coincidences had piled up to an unbelievable height, but still, she didn't want to burden Lucy with everything she'd found out. Not yet. Once she made sure that Lucy was stable, Jess was going straight back to the house to talk with Star. "I saw Star outside, and I was worried about her being out there in the middle of the night with all the bears. I'm just glad that Ben was there."

Lucy raised her eyebrows, her eyes growing that bright blue that made Jess's toes curl. "Benjamin was there?"

Jess wrinkled her forehead. "You don't remember?"

Lucy frowned. "I'm not sure." The deep wrinkles around her temples moved inward with her narrowed eyes. "Jess, where were you?" she asked again.

"I was outside because Star—"

"Where?" Lucy tilted her head, looking annoyed.

"She was up by the shed. Well, actually, she was in the shed. I don't know how because that old padlock looks like you'd need a crowbar to open it."

"The shed?" Lucy sat all the way up, bending forward until her curved fingers touched the soft spot beneath Jess's chin.

It was like being trapped in the sights of a rifle. She couldn't move, mesmerized by the color of Lucy's eyes.

"The shed," Lucy said again as if feeling the word out on her tongue. She patted the bed, glanced at the bedside tray table. "Now, where is my crossword puzzle? A small building . . ." She trailed off, and Jess grew alarmed.

"You're not making a lot of sense," she said softly. "Should I call a doctor?"

Lucy ignored her, turning to Ebee. "If Star *was* in the shed, then that means . . ."

Ebee stood abruptly. "Do you think it's happening?"

Jess looked back and forth between the two women. Maybe Ebee needed to be admitted too. "What's happening?" she asked.

Lucy sighed heavily, looking at Jess with exasperation. "Oh dear. Are we still on page one? The loose ends, Jess. I bring them close, but they always tie themselves."

Ebee was at the door to the hospital room. "I'll keep watch out here."

Jess gaped at her and turned around to find Lucy struggling to get out of bed. "Now's your time, Jess."

"My time?" Jess scrambled over to her, feeling clumsy, like a small puppy with big paws.

"To do what I hired you to do. Now help me get dressed, and let's leave this place."

"You just fell down a flight of stairs, Lucy! I can't let you leave." Miraculously, the older woman had not broken a single bone. The ER doctors had called her the bionic granny and said she probably wouldn't need to be in the hospital for more than a night, maybe two, considering her age.

Outside the window a horn beeped once, and Jess turned to see the Foothills Taxi van pull to a stop along the curb, Jeremy hunched over behind the steering wheel, a black cap covering his normal mop of curls, and wearing a black turtleneck and gloves. Jess sucked her cheeks in. "Why does he look like he's driving the getaway car for a bank robbery?"

Lucy slipped her arm into the sleeve of her black dress, one that Ebee must have brought with her, and Jess began to help her. Lucy was stubborn as an ox. Besides, the doctor did say she was fine, and Jess really wanted to get home and talk with Star. In all the excitement of last night, she'd hardly had time to think about what she had discovered—that Star was Chance's best friend. Tears welled in her eyes, but she wiped at them with the back of her hand.

Lucy smiled, looked out the window. "Ah, Jeremy—always there when we need him."

"Coast is clear," Ebee hissed from the doorway.

Lucy grasped the crook of Jess's elbow. "It's time," she said softly.

"Time for what?"

Lucy's face softened with compassion. "For your part, dear. It's all up to you now."

CHAPTER
FORTY-NINE

STAR

It was after nine on a weeknight, well past rush, dinner, and happy hours, so the streets were quiet. She'd been able to scrounge up enough in change, plus a twenty-dollar bill she'd found in the basket underneath the phone, to purchase a bus ticket. She'd hesitated, but without it she couldn't leave Pine Lake, so she'd grabbed it and stuffed it into her backpack, telling herself that Lucy wouldn't mind. After Jess found the note, Lucy would be happy that Star was gone. Before she left the house, though, she ran upstairs and put her rock on Lucy's pillow, wishing that she could have said goodbye or sorry or anything, and hating that the last she saw of Lucy was her body strapped to a hospital stretcher.

By the time she'd gotten to Denver, it had been late afternoon, and she'd sat in a yellow plastic seat and hugged her backpack tightly to her chest, trying to build up the courage to leave the bus station. It was hours later when she looked up through the skylights and found a black night staring back at her. Panic squeezed her throat; she didn't want to sleep out there tonight. She wished she'd had time to say goodbye to Jeremy; then again, he would have only tried to talk her into staying.

She spied an empty bus idling in the bay area, the warm gleam of its inside lights beckoning to her. She slipped through the glass doors and into the bus, taking a seat in the very back, where she slid way down. If nobody noticed her, she could sleep here tonight and use the daylight tomorrow to come up with a plan.

The bus swayed, and footsteps sounded from the aisle until she saw the tips of black shoes standing even with her row. The driver. "Young lady." The toe of his shoe tapped the floor.

She ignored him, turning to stare at her reflection in the window.

He tapped her shoulder. "This is my last stop of the night. You have to get off." He seemed kind; then again, she looked like a teenager on a field trip. She knew the game; his caring manner wouldn't extend to her after a month on the streets. "Do you have somewhere to go?" He was worried. "I can call . . ." And nosy.

She pushed to her feet, sidling out of the row and past him. "I'm fine, thank you." She waved to him from the front of the bus. "My family's meeting me here. Thanks for the ride!"

He didn't look like he believed her, but she hopped to the pavement before he could say anything.

Resigned, she stood and trudged back inside, this time heading for the escalator that would take her to the street above. Her boots squeaked against the floor, and the sound bounced off the walls of the empty terminal.

Outside, the fluorescent lights of Union Station made the night seem unnaturally bright. But at the line where the light ended and the night began, Star paused. The last time she'd made the decision to try her luck on the streets she'd been a very different person.

Pine Lake had been a dream—everything she could have wanted in a home. It was nothing normal like Jeremy's family, not with Lucy and her loose ends and crossword puzzles or Jess with her grief that ran through her like a current. But it was the first place Star had felt wanted. Her arms felt the firmness of Jess's hug, the bowls of buttery popcorn she left out when she was studying, the way she paused outside her door every night. Star pressed her lips together. None of that belonged to her; it was meant for Chance, and Star was better off on her own.

She breathed in the layered smells of the city: oil-stained pavement, fryer grease from a fast-food restaurant across the street, the sweet pungency of piss-soaked gutters. Laughter bounced against the brick sides of the buildings.

There was nothing left for her in Pine Lake. She'd left everything that Jess needed to know under her pillow; it was up to her to figure out what to do about Lucy.

With a final look behind her, Star stepped into the night.

~

The scraping sound of skateboard wheels reached her as soon as she turned the corner to begin her long trek down the mall. She hunched her shoulders, lowered her head, and walked. But the disorganized chatter, the howls of laughter, and the skunky smell in the air made her heart race. She pressed a hand to her chest.

A group of six or so kids hung out in the center section of the mall. Ball caps pulled low, large hoodies cinched tight. Star tensed. Some lounged on metal benches and nailed-down chairs, and one or two rolled around on skateboards, flipping tricks against a low stone wall. She kept to the opposite side and trained her eyes on the glow of the clock tower a few blocks away.

But the smooth whir of wheels came up from behind her. "Hey there, baby girl. You got some change?"

She stiffened at the voice. It was the boy who had attacked her, Shred. She picked up her pace, hoping that if she ignored him, he would give up and leave her alone.

He rolled ahead and stopped, popping the board up and into his hands. Her pulse thundered in her ears. She tried to move past him, but he jigged first to one side and then to the other, cutting her off. "Hey now, what's the rush?"

Her chin jutted out, and she looked up at the kid who stared down at her with red-veined eyes and yellow teeth. Large welts pitted his skin, the flesh stretched tight across his cheekbones. She remembered the feel of his body pinning her to the ground, and her legs began to shake. He leaned down, moving his face close to hers as though he needed a magnifying glass to see clearly. A smile pulled his lips into thin white lines, ghoulish. "Oh, it's you." He ran a finger along her collarbone. "Where you keeping your money these days?"

With her hair buzzed short and wearing only jeans and a sweatshirt, she felt exposed and vulnerable. But there was one thing she had learned during her months on the street: never show fear. She stood as tall as she could. "Don't touch me, asshole," she said through clenched teeth.

He leaned close until the stench of his breath blew across her face. "Crazy bitch."

A hot rage built within her from his touch, his rotting breath. The taste of a life with walls and locks and friends like Jeremy had changed her. She didn't belong here. She put her palms against his bony chest and pushed. He stumbled backward, landing hard on the pavement. He raised his eyes, but instead of anger he was laughing, so hard it shook his body. The sound chilled her to the core.

"Girl, you must have a fucking death wish." He stood up, one foot on his skateboard, pushing it back and forth, and glanced over at the kids who watched the exchange, still as statues. One girl, her hair long and stringy under a wide-brimmed baseball cap, shook her head slowly from side to side.

Star squared her shoulders and began to walk away. *No fear,* she chanted, but he grabbed her elbow hard, and the force whipped her around until she faced him again. "You don't scare me," she said, her voice quavering.

He squeezed harder and twisted her arm until she cried out. "You know what's funny?"

She didn't answer.

"What's funny is there was some dude looking for you this afternoon. Showing your picture around, sayin' you were his long-lost daughter," he said.

She was so surprised that for a second she forgot where she was and who she was talking to. A man was looking for her. Her heart fluttered. Could Jess want her to come home? The hope that flared with the thought died just as quickly. It left an empty feeling inside her chest.

The only reason they would want her to come back would be because of Lucy and the car. And she didn't want anything to do with that.

"You don't seem surprised. Where have you been, Star?" Shred smiled. "Said he'll be back tomorrow. Offering dough to anyone with information." He touched her shoulder, and the contact made her stomach turn. "Should I tell him where you'll be, baby girl?"

There was only one reason he was telling her this. "What do you want, Shred?"

He shrugged and bent over to pick up his skateboard. "What I've always wanted."

"I won't sell for you." Despite her words, her voice sounded small and weak.

"This is my street." He poked the center of her chest with his finger. She tried not to wince.

"And you can't stay if you don't play." He poked her again, so hard it sent a wave of pain through her chest. "You need me."

Her eyes watered, but she breathed deeply, crossed her arms. She might be back to where she'd started, but there was one thing that would never change. "I don't need you," she said. "I'm nothing like you."

His laugh was a high-pitched howl. "Shit, right, 'cause you'll be dead in a week."

She shrugged. "Maybe."

"What's funny is you think you have a choice." He stared at her for a long moment before reaching around to grab the strap of her backpack and jerking so hard she fell, landing on her side. He yanked the strap hard again until the whole thing slid off her arms, and then he jumped on his skateboard with it slung over one shoulder.

She watched him roll across the street, her eyes glued to his rail-thin form. When he reached the middle island with the other kids, he spun, pinning her with his glare. His hand shot up, and he waved it slowly in the air. "Sleep well tonight, Star," he called. The girl from before sniggered loudly.

CHAPTER FIFTY

JESS

"It won't open, Lucy." Jess had been pushing against the heavy outer door to Lucy's house for a few minutes, and it still wouldn't budge. "It's never stuck like this before."

She buzzed the doorbell, rattled the handle. Where was Star? She checked her phone once more. No messages. She hadn't spoken to the girl or been able to get hold of her since early that morning when they left in the ambulance. Star hadn't mentioned doing anything this afternoon, and when Jess had quizzed Jeremy during the car ride over here, he'd just shrugged, not meeting her eyes. He was acting suspicious, and Jess wondered what Star might have told him. Before she got the chance to ask, he'd left to drive Ebee home.

"Oh dear." Lucy's eyes rose to the top of the house. "Oh dear." She wrung her hands, the lines around her mouth deepening into a frown.

"Lucy?"

"It's empty," Lucy said.

"What's empty?"

Lucy pointed her curved index finger. "She's gone."

From behind Jess came a soft click. She turned and stared. A crack allowed a shaft of light from the foyer to peek out. The door was open.

Lucy pushed the door all the way open, and Jess was hit by the smell. Like someone had lit a match and then blown it out.

"Oh dear," Lucy said again.

Something clattered down the stairs, hitting each step with a loud whack before skittering across the floor of the foyer and coming to rest at Jess's feet. She bent to pick it up, and the hair on her arms stood on end. Chance's rock.

"Star," she called again, but the air absorbed her voice, making it too small for the big house.

"I told you—she's gone."

Jess raced upstairs, her stomach in free fall, and opened Star's door. The room was empty, the bed made, and the dresses and the white nightgown had been laid across the edge. Her eyes scanned the room. No backpack. Jess sank onto the bed. Star was gone. But where? And why? Her gut twisted, and she doubled over, heart sinking.

Lucy stood in the doorway, pulling at the hem of her black sleeves.

"How did you know?" Jess asked.

Lucy backed away from the door and into the hallway, looking left, then right. "Oh dear."

Jess shot up off the bed. Lucy's eyes were wide and glassy, her soft cheeks pale. "Lucy?" Before she could reach her, Lucy turned and disappeared into her own bedroom. Jess hurried after her and found her sitting in her chair by the window, looking toward the lake. Her hands trembled, rattling the table in front of her.

Jess rushed to her side. "Lucy?" She sucked on her bottom lip, felt the rock snug in her palm. A chill crept up her back. "If Star's not here, how did the rock roll down the stairs like that?"

Lucy whirled around, and her eyes were wide and bright blue.

"I suspect that was our other guest." She rested her hands in her lap, one on top of the other.

"Other guest?" Jess's voice trembled.

"Come now, Jess. You don't know?"

"Know what?" But her mind was already on heart-shaped stones and a boy in a red sweatshirt.

"He made quite a racket under my bed that day." Lucy sighed, looked down at her crossword puzzle. "But he doesn't want to be here anymore without her."

Jess opened her mouth to speak, but nothing came out. Something cold and feathery brushed across the nape of her neck. And she inhaled the familiar scent of soap and coconut shampoo. Her heart thudded loud in her ears.

"A six-letter word for serendipitous, accidental," Lucy said in a soft voice.

Jess's palm flew to her chest. "Chance," she whispered, even as a small part of her protested. It wasn't possible.

Lucy laid the paper onto the table with a small smile and walked over to Jess. She touched her forearm. "That's the right answer, Jess," she said.

It came together like one of Lucy's puzzles, and for the first time she allowed herself to see. The boy, her wrist, the rocks, her dreams. "He's here?" she croaked.

"Yes." Lucy looked around the room and seemed to sniff the air. "Not for long, though."

Jess grabbed for the door to keep from falling to her knees, but it swung outward, and she landed with a thud on the wooden planks. Exhaustion settled like a blanket, weighing her down, and a headache formed as a stabbing pain behind her eyes. She pressed her palms against her head.

Lucy touched her shoulder. "Let's get you up," she said.

With great effort, Jess pushed up from the floor. Lucy led her to the big chair by her bed, and Jess sank deeply into the cushions. She laid her head back, closed her eyes, overcome. Her fingers tingled with the sudden longing to touch the smooth skin of her son's cheeks, but the yearning to have something that was forever gone was unbearable. Tears ran unchecked down her face.

"You're ready now, dear," Lucy said quietly. "I'll make us some tea." Her footsteps sounded light on the rug.

Jess's thoughts drifted from Chance to Star, each face overlapping the other until all she could see was Star, alone and huddled under a bench. Her eyes flew open. *He doesn't want to be here without her.*

She tore out of the room and into the hall, her eyes searching the corners, the stairs, the bathroom, Lucy's bedroom, for something, anything. Nothing. Was he gone? She leaned against the doorframe to her bedroom and clutched at her chest. She couldn't lose him again.

"Please," she cried. "Help me." As if in response, the door to her bedroom was flung open, and she locked eyes with her son.

He sat on her bed, the curve of his jaw, the brown of his eyes, everything in heartbreaking detail. His feet dangled just above the floor, and she pressed a palm to her chest, pushed back against the painful beating of her heart.

For an achingly brief moment she could pretend they were back in their apartment. Like the past eight years had been a terrible dream. Like the accident had never happened. Her arms itched with memory. Of holding him, hugging him. She stepped into the room, her hand stretched out. If she could touch him one last time. Feel the softness of his curls. The smooth skin of his cheek.

"Chance?" she whispered.

He didn't move. Not a twitch, a single blink. An unearthly stillness. She pressed a hand to her heart, felt the soft thump below her skin and ribs. Moved farther into the room. "Honey?"

Dust motes glittered like crystals in the air, and her breath shot out of her nose in white wisps. "Chance?" she repeated through frozen lips. Around her shadows twirled in a coordinated dance. She moved as though through water. With each step he grew fainter, and by the time she reached the bed he was gone. She cried out when her hand passed easily through the emptiness, and she crumpled onto the bed.

"What do you want, baby?" she croaked as she twisted the comforter in her hands. "Tell me, sweetheart," she begged.

As she watched, a depression formed in the center of her white cotton pillow. She wiped her eyes and shifted closer, resting her palm into the soft indentation. Another one appeared beside her hand, small and round like the shape of a fist. She laid her head on the pillow, wanting nothing more than to feel his small body curled into her own.

"Chance?" she said, but the room absorbed his name. Shadows pulled from the corners, and the walls groaned around her. Her hands shook. From under the pillow, beneath her head, came the crinkle of paper that sounded too loud in the still room. She sat up, and then she saw it. A gray piece of newsprint peeking out. She pulled. Two newspaper articles paper clipped together. She flinched when she saw the headline.

Eight-Year-Old Boy Killed by Hit-and-Run Driver

In the other article, someone had underlined a quote from one of the residents. Just another night at the Lancaster. It was the same thing Star had said when she talked about her father's death.

Stuck to the newspaper was a yellow Post-it. Star had written a note in small print that filled both sides of the square note.

I'm sorry I lied to you, Jess. Chance was my best friend. I came to your apartment, and he let me in because I was scared and sad. He said I could live with you. I'm so sorry, Jess. I forgot my other bonsai tree, the one from my mom that I kept for myself, so he came upstairs with me, but when we opened the door my dad was on the floor and something bad was happening to him. We ran as fast as we could. I think Chance was taking us to where you worked, but when the car came he pushed me out of the way. He saved my life. I don't know how to say I'm sorry for taking your son away. It should have been me.

There was a small space, almost as though she'd been finished, and then it picked up again.

I think you are the one who's supposed to check the shed. Lucy was right about everything except one thing. She's the loose end. I hope you can forgive her; she's a good person. Star

The shadows retreated, and the room lapsed into stillness, warmth returning. He was gone. She clutched the article, tears blurring her eyes so that she couldn't read. He'd left the apartment to help his friend, and he'd been running to Jess. She covered her face with her hands, breathing out long ragged breaths until her tears eased.

She read the note again. *She's the loose end. Check the shed.*

She scanned the article, but nothing about it was new to her. Nobody could identify the car except for one man, who told the police he saw a red car with a banana-yellow hood. Her nails dug into her thigh, and she gripped the article. *Check the shed.*

She hurried from the room and down the stairs. Ebee and Lucy sat across from each other at the kitchen table, each holding playing cards. Jeremy sat hunched in a chair by the window, head in his hands, looking sad.

Jess pulled at her earlobe, feeling sluggish, her body reluctant to do what Star had asked her to do. She was afraid to see what was inside the shed, afraid it would tear her apart all over again. She looked at Ebee. "I thought Jeremy took you home."

Ebee's eyes crinkled. "Jeremy's dad thought he saw Star get on a bus this morning." She gave Jeremy a warm smile. "We thought you two might be needing us."

Jess felt as though she teetered between two worlds, and she didn't know how to balance. She cleared her throat and pointed upstairs. "My son," she began. "He was . . ." She trailed off.

Lucy pressed her lips into a thin line. Ebee put her cards facedown and folded her hands in her lap. Jeremy looked out the window. Their silence added to the swirl of emotion that tied her tongue.

She waved the article in the air. "What's in the shed?"

Lucy's eyebrows drew together. "I haven't gone in that shed for years."

"Why?"

Lucy rose from the table and walked slowly toward Jess. "You need to understand, Jess. He couldn't come to you on his own. It's too hard for them to communicate with the ones they left behind." Lucy closed her eyes. "Painful even." When she opened her eyes again, Jess stiffened. The flecks of color spun around her pupil. "They come to me for help, and I do what I can." She patted Jess on the back before returning to her seat at the table.

Ebee reached over and touched Lucy on the arm. "You do good," she said quietly.

Jess's eyes darted from Lucy to Ebee, but they stared back at her with unreadable expressions. The ticking of the clock in the foyer grew loud and began to grate in her ears. She stared at the article in her hand. The shed. The boy—she cleared her throat—no, her *son* had been trying to tell her all along.

Jess tore out of the house. She ran past the library window and through the weed patch. The door of the shed stood open. Dying sunrays lit the inside through cracks in the rusted ceiling, splashing across the yellow hood of the car parked inside.

Bile stung her throat. Her legs weakened, and she gripped the shed to steady herself. The hood curved inward into a crater, and a spiderweb crack ran across the windshield. *Oh God, not Lucy.* A stabbing sensation in her chest made it difficult to focus. Star's note. *I hope you can forgive her. She's the loose end.* Everything blurred. Jess wiped her hand across her eyes and stumbled down the dirt path to the house.

Lucy and Ebee sat at the table, playing cards in hand and eyeing her expectantly. She gasped for breath, her lungs bursting from her effort to breathe and speak at the same time.

Ebee's chair scraped against the kitchen floor when she stood. She took Jess by the elbow and led her to the table. "Come now, sit down. How about some tea?"

A warm mug was pressed into her hands. Jess stared into the amber liquid and let the heat seep into her skin, but it couldn't touch the coldness in her heart. The car that had killed her son was in the shed. Lucy had killed her son.

When they'd thrust Chance into her arms in the delivery room, covered in white paste and streaks of blood, his eyes and lips swollen, she couldn't think, couldn't blink, couldn't utter a single word. He lay with his cheek pressed against her breast, and all she could do was stare. She reached down to stroke the velvet skin of his face, and the contact made him turn his head and stare up at her with wide black eyes.

The nurse who held her hand patted her on the shoulder. *What's his name, sweetheart?*

Chance. Jess locked her gaze onto his face. *He's my Chance.*

Rage turned the muscles of her face into stone, and she slammed her mug onto the table. Brown water sloshed over the lip and collected in dark pools. "Did you kill my son, Lucy?"

Lucy's gaze slid away, landing on the folded-up crossword puzzle in front of her. She leaned over, pushed her glasses onto her nose. "A clock," she read.

Jess's stomach lurched, and she pounded the table with her fist. "No! No more! You have to answer me. That car in your shed killed my son." Her shoulders slumped forward, the fire that had fueled her spent. *Not Lucy, please, not Lucy.* She breathed in. "Tell me. I have to know."

From behind her came a soft rustling. She looked over her shoulder. The pages of the calendar fluttered wildly up and down, and the walls appeared to shift inward, giving the room an unnatural slant. The overhead light fell into the creases in Lucy's face, turning her hair blood red. She looked older, frailer, as though her very bones had shrunk. "I can see them now," she said, her voice a raspy whisper.

Jess's hands clenched into fists on the table. "See who?"

"The loose ends."

"Enough!" When she stood, she knocked her chair over. It clattered to the floor.

"Easy there, kiddo," Ebee said in a low voice.

Jess curled her hands into fists. "What did you do, Lucy?" she asked in a small voice.

Lucy sighed. "All I know is that he doesn't regret it. Do you understand that?"

Air rushed from her lungs like she'd been punched in the gut. She sat back down in the chair, laid her forehead on the table. "How do you know?" she whispered.

Lucy touched Jess's arm. "Regret burns. But your son . . ." She paused, cleared her throat. "He's in shadow and very angry."

Jess thought of the shed, and a bitter taste flooded her mouth. "Is he angry with you?"

No response. Jess lifted her head. Lucy's mouth twisted as though she fought whatever she wanted to say.

"We're here together. Me, Star, Chance, you, and that car." She pointed toward the back of the house. "All the loose ends." She breathed through her teeth. "Please just tell me—did you kill my son?"

"No, I didn't," she said quietly.

Jess felt a sob catch in her throat. She desperately wanted to believe that Lucy was telling the truth, even as a part of her questioned how much the old woman could remember from that long ago.

Lucy slid her hand into a pocket in her dress and pulled out something small and black and in the shape of a heart. "Take it." She held it out to her. "It's always something small at first. A sign that they want to communicate. He began with stones. I think it's what connects them."

Jess's heart thumped loud in her ears. "He gave her one when they first met."

Lucy's face tightened. "But I don't always understand what they want."

"I think he wants me to know the truth about that car. Can you tell me that, Lucy?"

Lucy's eyes grew bright blue, the chunks of color spinning. "That's the right question. It was mine." A frown deepened her wrinkles into ruts. "But it's not mine anymore. I gave it away."

Jess knelt in front of Lucy, feeling a surge of hope rush through her body. "You gave it away?"

"That's right, I did." Lucy stared down at her hands. "Sometimes my memories have holes, you know. This one is a big hole, or it's too close. I think . . ." Her gaze lifted, but now it looked unfocused, confused. "Nine letters, a confirmed habit," she murmured.

Jeremy spoke for the first time. "Addiction," he said.

Her skin tingled.

"A six-letter word for an unnatural ending."

"Murder," Ebee answered quietly.

The words began to jumble around in her head, puzzle pieces. She waited for them to fall into place, to make a picture she understood.

"Six letters, a clock," Lucy said, then again, "Six letters, a clock."

Jess leaned close. "What did you say?" But her heart pounded because she already knew the answer. "Big Ben."

CHAPTER
FIFTY-ONE

STAR

There it was. Her bench, caught in the greenish light of a nearby streetlamp. She approached it, her boots dragging across the cement. Once it had been her refuge; now it looked like her coffin.

In the years since her father's death, at each foster home and every dark night on the street, she had never felt so alone. She'd never had anything to lose before either. It had been a different story in Pine Lake. And here she was, back in her pathetic life, having lost it all.

She huddled on the bench; the cold cement seat felt hard through the fabric of her jeans, and she thought about the old army coat she'd left hanging in the closet. She shivered. Concrete was never warm, especially at night.

Down the street she caught sight of a familiar hunched figure in a coat with ragged tails that dragged along the ground. He pushed a small shopping cart with wobbly wheels. It stopped at her bench. Mel. He studied her, his bushy, overgrown eyebrows drawing together in disappointment, his cheeks sucking in and over his toothless gums.

He stuck his hand into a small black garbage bag inside the cart, rummaging around until he found what he wanted—a green wool coat. He held it out to her, the skin of his small hands laced with deep and painful-looking cracks.

"Thank you," she said.

He nodded—his mouth curling up at the ends, his lips pressed together—and shuffled down the mall until he came to a doorway with a large awning. The cart quieted, and Star watched as Mel spread his own coat across the ground, easing his withered frame onto it until his back pressed against the doorway.

The streetlight pulsated, growing bright before it shut off. They did that, she remembered, turning on and off at random times. She felt exposed in the darkness that followed and quickly crawled inside. But as she tried to find a comfortable position, her thoughts went to the night before she'd left: Shred, his hands, the knife.

Tremors racked her body, and she scrambled out from under the bench. She couldn't sleep here. A cool wind whipped down from the mountains, rushing over her exposed skin. She slid her arms into the coat, pulled it tight around her, and tried to ignore the musty smell that rose from the wool. She scanned the area. Cones of light illuminated benches and trash cans. She squeezed her shaking hands into fists and began to walk in the direction of the chocolate shop.

When she got closer, her heart sped up, and her eyes searched the area. Empty. She spied another bench, this one made of metal and not nearly as long, but it would do. She crawled underneath and curled into a ball. Maybe she'd wake up to those two girls playing their guitars.

She tried closing her eyes, but they sprang open at the slightest sound. She thought of her bed at Lucy's. The door that locked. A lump settled in her throat. How was she going to make it alone?

The scrape of shoes on pavement, of a body settling onto the ground beside her head. She peeked out. Soft brown eyes stared back at her, and she gasped, hitting the back of her head so hard that stars pitted her vision. A small hand appeared and flicked something toward her. It landed by her elbow. She inched her fingers across the cool concrete until she felt it. Her breath caught, and she brought it close to her face.

A heart-shaped rock. Small and perfect.

She tightened her palm around the rock, made a pillow with her hands, and laid her head on top.

~

She awoke to Chance's voice and the feel of his breath tickling her ear. *Star!* Her eyes sprang open, and her body turned rigid. A bright light shone under the bench. She covered her face with her hand.

"Star?"

The light shifted, and Officer Ben's face appeared, peering at her from outside the bench.

"How did you find me?"

"Girl with that skateboard kid said you hung out here." He shifted on his knees. "Come on out."

She crawled out and stood. He loomed over her.

"You okay?" he asked softly.

Tears pricked her eyes. "Not really. Are you here because of my note?"

"What note?" He held out a bottle, but she couldn't see what it was in the dark. He shone the light on it. "Apple juice. Thought you might be thirsty."

A bead of condensation slipped down the cold glass. Thirst burned her throat. She hadn't had a sip to drink since the day before in Pine Lake.

He opened the bottle and handed it to her. The sweetness of the juice exploded in her mouth and slid down into her empty stomach. It tasted so good she almost choked. It had been only one night, and she was so hungry and thirsty her stomach ached.

She gulped the rest of the juice, not minding the liquid that dribbled down her chin. Officer Ben cleared his throat, and she wiped a sleeve across her mouth. "Thank you," she said, and handed the bottle back to him. "How's Lucy?"

"She's going to be okay," he said. "Can I ask you something?"

She flicked her eyes up at him. A nearby streetlight kicked on, and in the blue glow she noticed that he wasn't in uniform. Instead he wore a plaid shirt over jeans with a ball cap pulled low over his eyes.

Sugar from the juice rushed through her, momentarily buoying her mood. "Yeah."

"You said you remembered me trying to help your dad. I'm not sure I follow."

She smiled. "I remember you coming over to our apartment. When my dad dealt, he'd make me hide in the bathroom, but one night I saw you before I went in. I remembered how nice you were to me at the hospital, and I figured you'd come to help my dad."

"Did you tell your dad that I was a cop?" He craned his neck forward like he was trying to see her more clearly.

The movement made her uneasy, and Star hugged her arms across her chest. "Um, yeah. I did. I thought he already knew." She wrinkled her forehead. "Why are you looking for me?"

Ben tilted his head to the side, but with the ball cap Star couldn't see his eyes. "Jess asked me to bring you back," he said.

A faint fluttering of hope rose in her chest. Did Jess want her after all? She slumped. No, nothing had changed, and she couldn't go back. Not with Lucy and the car in the shed. She didn't know why Lucy had that car, and she didn't want to find out.

"I'm not going back." She stood tall, but even at her full height, the top of her head barely reached his chest. She pulled at her sleeves and stepped away. "I know what's in that shed."

He stared at her until she began to fidget in the silence.

"Tell Jess I'm fine and thanks for trying to help me, but I'm better off on my own." When she turned to go, his hand gripped her elbow.

"You need to come with me, Star."

She yanked her arm out of his grasp, and the effort sent him wobbling backward, where he stumbled over the curb behind him. He must be a lousy cop if it was that easy to push him over.

"You have to come with me, Star." He advanced toward her, his mouth set in a grim line.

"Or what?" The hair on the back of her neck stood on end.

He let his hands fall by his sides. "Or I'll call social services," he said in a resigned tone. "And after running away like you did, your next foster home will be something with locked windows and guards."

She shifted from one foot to the other, legs twitching with an urge to run. He loomed above her, tall and muscular. She'd never outrun him. "Fine. I'll go with you." She'd wait for the first opportunity to get away from him and disappear for good. She'd done it before, and she could do it again. And this time she'd get on a bus and never look back.

"Good girl."

She cringed, his tone making her feel like an obedient puppy.

He rested his big hand at the small of her back, pressing lightly into her spine. The pressure made her lurch forward. He walked her to a white pickup and opened the door with one hand, the other still pressing into her back. She slid into the cab, surprised at the wrappers at her feet and the stale stink of cigarettes clinging to the upholstered seats. When he climbed into the driver's seat, she caught the dull gleam of his gun poking out from under the hem of his shirt.

"I thought you were off duty," she said.

He looked down, staring at the gun for a long moment before pulling the hem over the weapon. Without a word he started the engine, and when he pulled forward the truck swerved and nearly hit a parking meter. She grabbed the door handle with both hands to keep from sliding across the seat, looking at Officer Ben through the corner of her eye. He drove with both hands gripping the wheel, shoulders rounded forward.

She turned to her window and stared at the dark and empty streets, part of her relieved that Officer Ben had found her. At least this time she'd make sure she said goodbye to Jeremy.

CHAPTER FIFTY-TWO

JESS

"Ben," Jess said again.

Lucy's body crumpled, her stooped back rounding forward until all Jess saw was the top of her head where glimpses of her white scalp showed through the delicate red strands.

"I understand now," Lucy said.

"I don't understand. Star thought she was Ben's loose end."

"She is." A single tear worked its way in and out of the deep creases in Lucy's cheek. "I thought I had helped Benjamin, but I was too close to see. Mother always said I could be blind when I wanted to be."

Jess felt her stomach heave, and she squeezed her eyes shut, shaking her head back and forth. "He told me he was addicted to pain pills from an old football injury. That he tried to hurt himself."

Lucy nodded. "The second time was when I found him at the waterfall, and that was . . ." She trailed off, and her eyes shifted to the calendar. It seemed like all of them held their breath. "Eight years ago."

Jess sat up straight. "The car in the shed is the one he fixed up when he was a kid."

"That's right." Lucy straightened up suddenly. "He's gone after her."

Jeremy scrambled to his feet, his eyes wide. "After Star? We have to find her."

"I'll stay in case she shows up here," Ebee offered.

"I'll drive." Jeremy hustled out the door.

The pages of the calendar fluttered wildly in the air. "We have to go now," Lucy said. "We have to find them. Time is running out."

"Is he going to hurt her?" Jess's voice cracked as she hurried to keep up with Lucy.

Jeremy helped Lucy into the van, and Jess climbed into the back, feeling panic settle deep inside, writhing and twisting in her stomach. She bit her lip so hard it bled.

Jess saw Jeremy's eyebrows scrunch together. "Where to?"

Lucy pointed a curved finger ahead of them. "Just drive, Jeremy. He'll help us."

"But I thought Ben—"

"Chance," Jess said in a low voice. "My son. He'll help us."

As the van lurched forward, Jess clutched at her chest.

Lucy twisted around. "He's been trying to keep her safe."

She nodded, swallowed. She understood that now. She gritted her teeth and turned to look out the window. The mountains were black shadows that loomed over the van, making Jess feel hemmed in, claustrophobic. Star needed her, and she would not fail this time.

Jeremy's eyes kept meeting hers in the rearview mirror. Finally, he said, "She loved him, you know."

Her eyes burned. "I know."

Jeremy turned to Lucy. "Will we find her?" His voice was hoarse.

Lucy pursed her lips. "Drive fast, Jeremy."

CHAPTER FIFTY-THREE

STAR

The drive into Pine Lake twisted and curved up the mountain. Pine trees bordered the narrow road, a dense canopy that shaded the moon and made weird shadow patterns across the pavement. Star breathed in the clean smell of wood and earth and smiled despite herself. It felt good to be back.

Officer Ben hadn't spoken since the city, which suited her just fine. She didn't want to make small talk. A sign appeared around a sharp curve in the road: PINE LAKE.

Her fingers twisted the fabric of her leggings. Why did Jess want her back? What if Lucy was really hurt? The thought made it hard for her to breathe, so she pushed it away. Lucy was the strongest person she knew.

But if Ben didn't know about the note, then Jess might not have found it yet. If that was true, then maybe Star should try to talk to Lucy herself. She straightened her shoulders and looked out the window. For all she knew, that car had nothing to do with the accident.

The truck slowed, and Ben made a quick turn onto a dirt lane that was hidden from view. It curved sharply up the hill, and Star had to grab the door handle to keep from sliding across the seat. Deep crevices in the road caused the cab to jerk violently back and forth as it climbed.

"Where are we going?"

His jaw tightened, but he didn't say anything or look at her.

Trees crowded the road, the forest beyond deep in shadow. Branches scratched the sides of the truck. She flexed her feet, stretched out her fingers. Something was wrong. "This isn't the way to Pine Lake." Her voice quavered.

The road opened into a meadow ringed by trees. The truck jerked to a stop.

"Get out," he said.

The hairs on her neck stood on end. "What?"

He hefted himself out of the truck and slammed the door shut; the truck swayed from the force. Her vision blurred. She needed to get out, but her body wasn't obeying. Her thoughts fogged, one bleeding into the next. *Get out.* She reached for the door handle. Her fingers missed, flopping like fish onto her lap. What was wrong with her?

The door flew open with a rusty squeal, and Ben's plaid shirt was in front of her, filling her line of sight. Then his hands gripped her arms, and she was flying through the air until her body hit the ground and she heard a crack. She cried out from the impact. Above her, the full moon looked like someone had punched a hole in the sky, and she stared at it, her body relaxing despite a muffled voice screaming at her. *Get up! Get up!* She pushed up onto one arm, but it buckled under her, and she collapsed, her arm stretching unnaturally away from her body.

Hands grabbed her ankles and pulled. She lifted her head. Ben. Sticks scratched her skin, and rocks poked into her spine. She tried to kick, but he squeezed her ankles. "Stop it," she cried. "Please! What are you doing?"

He pulled her like a sack of rice through the meadow. She brought her head up again, tried to look past him, but all she saw was dark sky.

"Please," she begged. "Let me go." He must have known about her note. He loved Lucy. Maybe he'd been protecting her all this time. "If this is about the car—" A rock cracked her skull. White spots pockmarked her vision.

"He said his *kid*." His voice was low, almost a growl, making it hard for Star to understand him. He grunted, and her body stopped moving. "The boy opened the door. Where were you?"

Star felt cold all over. "I don't understand."

He turned around, stared at her. His hat was missing now, and Star could see his eyes, red-veined and wet. "It was your father's fault." He rubbed his eyes.

"My father?" *What does he have to do with any of this?*

"The bastard threatened me." He squeezed her ankles so hard she felt the pain this time as a dull sensation that traveled up her spine and to her head. "I never knew how he found out I was a cop, until now."

Her head spun, and she tried to piece her thoughts together; they scattered easily.

He dropped her ankles and eased himself beside her on the ground. Star tried to lift her body, curl her fists, anything to protect herself, but he swatted her hands away and pushed her into the ground. The air rushed from her lungs, and she fell back into a fetal position.

He pulled a bottle of amber liquid from his pocket and took a long sip. "Everything was going to work out. She was going to give me the house." He took another sip. "Every goddamn day I've worried about someone opening that shed, and then you two show up and I can't sleep—I start seeing things." His body seemed to shrink, and Star thought he looked scared. "Since you came, I've been watching that shed every fucking night."

He wasn't making sense, and she struggled to understand. She coughed, tried to get a full breath.

He drained the rest of the bottle and hurled it across the meadow. Star watched it fall, but instead of landing on the ground it disappeared behind it. From somewhere below them she heard the rush of water. Her stomach lurched. The waterfall?

"Lucy thinks she can save everybody." The lines around his mouth hardened. "But she didn't save me, and she can't save you."

He wasn't making sense. She blinked against the tiredness, terrified that if she fell asleep she might not wake up. Her mouth was dry; her eyelids lifted too slowly. "Did you put something in my juice?"

His gaze flicked to her. "Pain meds," he said. "Maybe too many. It'll be easier if you're calm."

She touched her lips. They'd gone numb. Nothing made sense. "Why're you doing this to me?"

Ben sat with his knees bent, staring at the ground, his face hard, impassive. "You should never have told him," he said, as though speaking to the ground at his feet.

Told who? She struggled to sit up, and the trees spun with the effort. The sky had begun to lighten with the dawn. She stole a glance at Ben. His skin was pasty and gray, puffy, like her father in the months before he died. Slowly the pieces fell together, not perfectly, some overlapping or in the wrong place, but enough for her to understand a little. Ben hadn't come over to help her dad get clean; he'd been buying from him. He was an addict too.

Her stomach heaved, and she threw up into the grass.

His biceps flexed against the sleeves of his T-shirt. "I'm not a bad guy, Star. You know?" His voice cracked, and Star saw wet streaks running down his face. "I'd gotten clean once; I knew I could do it again. But if they had found out, I would have lost my job—I would have lost everything."

Her lips pulled away from her teeth, and she huffed out air through her mouth and nose. Did he want her to feel bad for him? "Did you kill my father?"

He barked a laugh. "I thought you knew. When you said you remembered me, I thought you knew. If you hadn't told your dad in the first place, then none of this would have happened." He rubbed his face, and she heard his beard scratch his palms. "Fucking Lucy!" he roared, and lurched to his feet, pacing back and forth in front of her.

"Did you hurt her?" she tried to say, but her tongue wasn't moving well, and it sounded garbled and slurred.

"If she'd let me buy that house from her when I first offered," he said without looking in Star's direction, "nobody else would have been hurt. But when I saw you and Jess at the shed, I could feel that it was all about to come out. I thought if I could just talk to Lucy, convince her to let me buy the house, then I could get you two to leave." He swung his head back and forth. "But I never had the time. She was already on the stairs. I think I startled her or . . ." He stopped pacing, hovered over her, glaring down with wide eyes. "She tripped on her nightgown." His face contorted, and he pounded the top of his thigh with his fist. "I should have taken care of that car years ago!"

She swallowed, and her throat felt like sandpaper. "You know about the car?"

"I hid it right away, never drove it again. Nobody ever knew. Not even Lucy, because I kept the keys to that shed." He looked away and sat down beside her on the grass, hung his head between his knees.

Bile stung Star's tongue, and she tried again to sit up, but whatever he had given her had turned her limbs to mush. A dull stabbing sensation ran down the arm she'd fallen on when Ben threw her out of the truck. Star tried to use the pain to clear her head. Ben had killed her father. Her body started shaking. Why did he keep talking about Jess? Chance's face loomed large in her mind. His smile. His laugh. But she couldn't hold on to the image, and tears leaked from her eyes when it dissolved.

He took a bag of white pills from his pocket, stuffed a few into his mouth, and swallowed them dry. "He saw me, and then he was there in the middle of the goddamn road. It seemed so easy." Ben's body twitched, and he clenched his hands into big fists. She flinched when they brushed her side.

Her heart thumped painfully. "You killed Chance?"

His back shook, but he made no sound. "So much is blurry about that night. I-I thought I'd hit a pothole instead of the kid." Ben's hands fiddled with the plastic bag. He dried his face with the back of his sleeve. Several pills tumbled from the bag when he did. "That poor woman. She didn't deserve any of this."

Star lifted her head to see where she was. An empty meadow, the edges blurring into a thicket of pine trees. They were alone. Sweat trickled from her armpits. She tried to put together everything he said, but his words flitted away, making it hard to concentrate. Her body shook, racked by shivers.

Ben sighed and shifted so that he was kneeling on the ground beside her. He looked down at her, his eyes soft and wet and full of compassion. "I thought you knew." He scooted his arms under her knees and back and picked her up, cradling her body to his broad chest. She wanted to kick and bite the flesh of his shoulder; instead her body hung limp in his arms. She was going to die. Tears ran down her face.

The crunch of leaves sounded from beyond the meadow. She twisted her head, straining to see around the curve of Ben's shoulder. A small form stood in the shadows of the trees. Red sweatshirt, hands hanging by his sides. The air shimmered, and darkness snaked around his body.

Ben walked her across the meadow; her head bobbed, and she lost sight of Chance in the blur of trees and sky. The meadow ended abruptly in a steep cliff that rose high above the lake and waterfall. Ben teetered at the edge. How was she going to get away when they were so far from town? A thick haze settled behind her eyes, making her thoughts feel detached, like those of another person.

The shrill ring of a cell phone opened her eyes wide. Ben set her down, holding her arm firmly with one hand while he dug for his phone. He looked at the screen, tightened his grip on her arm. "Damn it," he said.

"Please let me go," she whimpered.

He gazed down at the waterfall, pointed. "They put that gate up after Jeremy," he said as though she hadn't spoken. He kicked a rock, and Star watched it plummet over the side and bounce off the sharp point of a boulder that lay half-submerged in the lake.

He pushed her roughly against a large boulder. Her ribs crunched from the impact. "Stay there," he growled.

The effort of leaning against the rock took every bit of strength she had. Strong winds rushed up the valley, hitting Star in the face and whipping her shirt. She turned her head away from the wind, and her breath caught in her throat. A small dark figure moved fluidly through the open meadow. The wind swirled, bending tree limbs low, flattening the grass like a giant hand. Gray clouds raced across the sky. A fluttering in her belly. Could Chance save her again?

Ben faced the cliff and didn't notice the figure coming toward them. He fumbled with something small and clear, and it took her a moment to realize what he held in the blue light of early dawn. A syringe. She shook her head, let out a low moan.

Ben's head shot up at the sound. "Heroin. It won't surprise anyone. Heroin's become a big problem here." He shook his head. "Kids start with pain pills, but it's an expensive habit to keep up." He tapped the syringe. "The affordable solution. A street kid like you? I'm sure you know all about this."

Her body began to shake uncontrollably. He'd make it look like she'd overdosed or killed herself.

He smiled, and for a moment he was the man who'd sat with a little girl in the hospital when she was scared. "Don't worry. It won't hurt."

Tears wet her face; she didn't want to die. Could Chance help her? Her skin prickled. Or was he waiting for her? She scanned the meadow, but it was empty, and Star felt her body deflate.

She was alone.

CHAPTER FIFTY-FOUR

JESS

Jeremy flew down the two-lane road out of Pine Lake, the bloated van hurtling like an awkward toddler around sharp corners. Jess slid back and forth on the seat, her fingers clutching the handrail. She dialed Ben's number again. No answer. She rubbed her arms, watched the trees race past the van. In any other circumstance, she would have yelled at Jeremy to slow down. "Can you drive any faster?" she asked.

The light outside was a dull gray that submerged the thick stands of pine trees into a deeper gloom. The road curved sharply, and she cried out. Chance stood on the side of the road, staring straight at her.

Jeremy braked hard, making the seat belt cut into Jess's chest and stomach.

Her hands shook when she unbuckled her belt. She scooted forward, pointed to the road. "There," she said. "Turn right there."

Jeremy swung his head back and forth. "Where?"

She couldn't breathe. Chance stood within feet of the bumper, his brown eyes locked on to her own. "There's a road." She stabbed a finger in the air. "Right there!"

Lucy placed her palm on top of Jess's hand, and the contact settled her.

"She's right, Jeremy," Lucy said. "Turn here."

When Jeremy turned, the trees opened up, revealing a narrow dirt lane that climbed up and over a steep embankment. The engine roared as the van climbed, spewing dust and rocks behind them. At the top of the hill, the trees opened up, and the van pulled into the middle of a clearing, nearly colliding with a white pickup truck.

Jess was out of the van before the wheels had stopped turning. Her heart leaped into her throat. At the end of the meadow, where it looked like the ground disappeared into the sky beyond, Star stood swaying on her feet, Ben holding her by her arm, his fingers squeezing tight. At the sound of the van, he jerked Star like a rag doll, and when he saw Jess, his face contorted.

"Ben!" she cried. "No!"

Fear trickled across her skin, but before she could move, something cool brushed against her arm, dry and thin, like if she reached out it would scatter in the air. Her pulse thumped in her throat, and the wind tickled her face, bringing with it the scent of her son's skin after a bike ride. Sun warmed and sweet.

She breathed in and ran. Ben's eyes widened, and he fumbled for something at his waist. A gun appeared, the tip pointed at Jess. She halted several feet from where Star perched on the rocky edge of a steep drop. The girl hung from Ben's grip, her face slack. The tip of the gun wavered in the air. Jess looked from the gun back to Star, narrowed her eyes. What was wrong with the girl? She stepped forward, her hand outstretched, fingers desperate to touch Star's face, pull her body in for a hug. But Ben stepped backward until his heels neared the edge, and he yanked Star with him.

"Don't come any closer," he said.

Jess stopped moving.

"Let her go, Ben." She spoke softly, but the wind picked up her voice and swept it through the grass until it seemed to twirl with the leaves in the air. Her heart beat against her chest, and she held her hands out, palms up. "I just want to talk," she said.

Footsteps moved the grass behind her, and out of the corner of her eye, Jess caught the swing of Lucy's black skirts. The old woman could do little in the face of Ben and his gun, but her presence was a comfort nonetheless. "Stay behind me, Lucy," Jess said in a low, calm voice.

Ben swung the gun, pointing to the space beside Jess. "Do you . . . can't you see . . ." Saliva flew from his lips, and his cheeks turned ashen. "Oh, Jesus. Don't you see him?" His gaze implored Jess to say yes. To acknowledge the boy in the red sweatshirt with butterscotch skin and soft brown eyes standing beside her. The boy who stared, unblinking, at Ben.

But Jess didn't respond, and Lucy and Jeremy stayed a silent few feet behind her. "How have you lived with yourself all these years?"

Her question must have taken him by surprise, because he tightened his grip on Star's arm. At the girl's soft whimper, Jess dug her nails deep into the skin of her palms. With Ben's gaze locked on the silent figure by her side, Jess inched forward. Should she grab the gun? Try to pull Star away? Every plan seemed futile. With Ben's size and weapon, she stood no chance. Ben let out a low moan, and the hand holding the gun trembled violently.

She felt a strange calm wash over her. There were memories she kept buried because they hurt too much, but remembering might be the only way to get Ben to listen. "His favorite color was red," she said, and her voice cracked on the words.

Ben dragged his eyes away from Chance and stared glassy-eyed at Jess.

Her chest ached. "He loved pancakes with whipped cream smiley faces." She was crying, her tears running over her jaw and down her neck. But she couldn't stop. "He loved his stuffed bear with the missing ear, and his favorite Matchbox car was a '67 Chevelle." She gulped for air and felt a light pressure by her side.

Ben's face had lost all color, his body hunched. The gun flopped forward until the barrel pointed at the ground. He swung his head from side to side. "I didn't mean . . ." He trailed off. Even he seemed to understand how futile it was.

"You killed my son, Ben. You took everything I had. Everything Star had." She felt Lucy touch her lightly on the shoulder and had to gulp in air to push down a sob.

Ben slumped as though she'd knocked the wind out of him, but just as quickly he whirled the gun around until the tip of it pressed into Star's temple.

Star's eyes widened, and Jess felt her stomach twist into knots. "Why Star?" she said quickly. "She's got nothing to do with this."

His eyes shifted wildly from Jess to Chance.

"Let her go, Ben." Jess's eyes slid to Star. The girl struggled to stay on her feet, her face pale, eyes glassy. What had he done to her? The thought sent hot anger through her veins. Standing next to Ben, Star looked so small and helpless. Jess clenched her hands into fists and tried to ignore the panic that clutched at her throat.

Ben gripped Star's arm with one hand, the gun in the other, his eyes locked on Chance. "I didn't mean to kill anyone." He spoke as though to someone else, and when he shifted his feet, a loose rock skittered over the side and dropped soundlessly into the canyon below. Jess's heart stopped. She was too late.

The figure beside her moved, held out his hand, palm up. Chance's presence thinned the air, turned the wind into a stinging bite on her skin. She shivered.

Ben's face crumpled, and the gun dropped to his side. "What's he doing?"

"You need to turn yourself in."

"What's he got in his hand?" He wiped at his forehead with the back of the hand holding the gun. "Can't you see him?"

"Jeremy?" Jess called without taking her eyes from Ben. "Can you call the police?"

She heard Jeremy clear his throat. "Already have, Jess."

She nodded. "Good, maybe you two should wait in the van."

Ben fidgeted, yanking on Star's arm, shifting his weight from foot to foot. "You see him, don't you? What's happening?" He looked behind her. "Lucy?" When he said her name, he sounded hopeful.

"Oh, Benjamin," she said quietly.

When she didn't say anything more, Ben appeared to deflate, his body rounding forward. He released Star's arm to pull a small liquor bottle from his pocket, and Jess lurched for Star, her heart in her throat. Without his support, Star crumpled backward toward the edge. Jess stretched her arms out as far as she could until her fingertips brushed Star's shoulders. But Star's heel slipped on the loose earth, and her body tipped backward.

Not again.

Jess dove forward, wrapped her arms around Star's shoulders, and pulled hard. They both stumbled away from the drop, and Jess cried out in relief when the solid weight of Star's body leaned into her. Jess would have crumpled to the ground if not for Jeremy, who slid his hands under her armpits. He hauled her to her feet and moved them quickly toward the van.

Her eyes shot to Ben. He and Chance stood as before, Chance with his hand stretched out, and Ben with his head hanging, eyes trained on the rock. The gun dangled from his fingertips.

The wail of sirens muffled by the dense forest pushed up from the road below. Ben still hadn't moved. At the van Jeremy worked quickly, laying Star on the back seat and helping Lucy in beside her.

"Jess," he hissed, climbing into the driver's seat. "Let's go."

She turned to leave, but a sudden ache spread across her wrist. Her scalp prickled. Chance wasn't finished. And then she was striding back through the meadow, coming to a stop beside the silent and still figure of her son.

Her breath huffed loudly in her ears. "It's a heart-shaped rock," she said.

Ben looked up at her through heavy-lidded eyes. "Heart shaped?"

She nodded. "I told him they were special."

Chance turned his hand over, and the stone tumbled to the ground. "He wants you to have it."

"Why?" Ben slumped forward, and to Jess he was a shell of the man she thought he'd been. A ghost of the man he'd wanted to believe he was. Her heart swelled with pity.

"Because he forgives you, Ben." She felt a feathery lightness brush over her hand, cool fingertips against her palm. At last she understood what Chance wanted for her. It stung her eyes, made her chest tighten painfully, but it was exactly what her boy with the coppery curls and the toothless grin and the heart that saw the good in everything and everyone would want. "I-I forgive you too," she said.

As soon as the words left her mouth, Chance vanished, leaving behind nothing but a faint shimmer in the air. Her throat squeezed shut, and the edges of her vision blurred. He was gone. A part of her wanted to lie down on the grass, curl into a ball, and join him. With great effort, she tore her gaze from the empty spot beside her and back to Ben. He fell to his knees and picked up the rock.

"I'm sorry . . ." His words dropped off, but Jess didn't need to hear any more.

She backed away and hurried across the meadow to the van. Inside she pulled Star's head into her lap and stroked the long strands of her black hair away from her face. Lucy sat on the other side of Star, hands resting across the girl's small ankles.

"Drive away from here, Jeremy," Lucy said.

The engine roared to life. Jess took one more glance over her shoulder.

Ben stood at the edge of the cliff, his face tilted up at the sky, his foot hovering in the air.

And then he jumped.

The van jerked forward, and the meadow disappeared behind the trees. Jess turned her gaze to Star's face and silently stroked her hair.

CHAPTER FIFTY-FIVE

STAR

Star was afraid to open her eyes. The bits and pieces she remembered made her want to curl up in a ball and never wake up. Most of it blurred together, but Jess and Lucy and Jeremy had been there and taken her away in the van. Or had that been a cruel dream? Star had finally given in to the drugs and fallen asleep to the swaying of the van.

She dreamed that the arms that cradled her, the hands that brushed the hair from her face, the voice that begged her to wake up belonged to her mother. And she didn't want to wake up and find herself alone.

"Star, honey, please wake up." Jess, her voice hoarse like it had been raked over coals. "Wake up." It was raining in fat drops that tickled the skin on her cheeks. They ran into the corners of her mouth. Salty raindrops.

She opened her eyes.

Jess, her face drawn into tight lines, her eyes red rimmed, stricken.

"Hi," Star whispered, and winced at the pain it brought to her head. She shifted, taking in the white walls of her small hospital room and the black sling that kept her right arm glued to her chest.

"You broke your arm and your collarbone," Jess said. She perched on the edge of the bed, twisting and untwisting her hands.

"He was going to kill me."

Jess nodded.

Star scrunched her eyes closed, tried to remember. But only one question came to mind. "Chance?"

Jess took hold of Star's shoulders and pulled her into a gentle but firm hug. They stayed like that for a few quiet moments. Star let her head rest against the soft curve of Jess's chest. Then Jess pulled away, just enough to look her in the eyes but not enough to let her go. "I know everything," she whispered.

Star's body went limp, and tears rushed down her face. "I'm sorry," she gulped. "I'm so sorry."

Jess's eyes were unreadable.

Star hesitated, waiting for her voice to steady. "He saved my life." Her vision swam, and Star closed her eyes, laid her head back on the bed. Her heart felt like it might break through the bones in her chest. It hurt to breathe. She waited to feel the bed shift from Jess standing, for the door to click when she left.

"He loved you, Star."

Then Jess put something small and cool into her hand. Star opened one eye. Red with gold stars. She brought it to her heart. Jess was smiling and crying at the same time, tears running unchecked down her face.

And then she was laughing. A sound that didn't fit, except it did. And then Star was laughing, too, until she was sobbing, and Jess took her back into her arms, and they cried together.

CHAPTER FIFTY-SIX

JESS

She sat at the kitchen table, her knee bouncing up and down, and glanced out the window to the road in front of the house. Empty. She got up, paced the small kitchen, checked the calendar. Empty.

It had been eight months since that terrible morning. Social services had swooped in afterward, thrusting Star into foster care. But Jess had visited her every week, sometimes bringing Lucy, whose black dresses and unsettling eyes drew odd looks from the foster family. Other times bringing Ebee, whose easygoing nature and good humor put everyone at ease.

Jess sat down, drummed her fingers across the surface of the table. She looked out the window again, but all that greeted her was the empty road and beyond it the lake. It lay frozen, frosted white from the recent snowfall and reflecting the sun in a million tiny sparkles.

"She'll be here." Lucy walked into the kitchen, touching Jess lightly on the shoulder. Thin strands of white twisted through her hair. It had happened suddenly, and when Jess asked her about it, she'd waved her away and said, "I suppose they're all tied for now." Jess didn't bother to ask again.

Through the kitchen window came the crunch of tires climbing the dirt road, the squeal of brakes. Jess stood, swallowing past a tight knot in her throat, and peered out the window. A black SUV pulled to a stop in front of the house. In the passenger seat was a small figure, her hair shaved close to the sides, the top growing out in silky black strands to her chin.

Star.

Jeremy, who had kept a patient guard at the front door, scrambled down the stairs, his mop of curly hair flopping around his face. He opened the door with one hand, extending the other when he bowed deeply. A grin swept across Star's face, and she took his hand.

Jess pulled at the cuff of her sleeve, flicked a small bit of fuzz from her shoulder, and waited for the thumping of her heart to slow. The slam of the car door was followed by the tinkle of young laughter floating through the thin kitchen windows. The muscles in her arms tingled with anticipation, and a slow smile spread across her face.

It was a Tuesday. A warm winter day when white clouds like cotton balls flitted across the ice-blue sky. Jess turned from the window and checked the paper calendar hanging on the wall by the phone. Small and neat script filled the once-empty square.

Our girl comes home.

The doorbell rang.

ACKNOWLEDGMENTS

I decided to write a book, and so I did. And then I wrote that same book again and again until it was just right. Writing is an exciting, painstaking, laborious, pull-out-your-hair kind of process, but I didn't do it alone. In fact, without the guidance and enthusiasm and patience—oh, the patience—of the people around me, I'd still be on page one. So while words can't convey the true depth of my gratitude, I want to say thank you to those who are a part of my journey.

To my husband and best friend, Sean, who believed in me despite the years of rejections and rewrites and, okay, maybe a few tears. Thank you for reading the same story too many times to count and for loving it every time. Thank you for your honesty, insight, and unflagging optimism. Here's to putting the pen to paper, babe.

To my mom, Phyllis, who still takes my phone calls even after our lengthy and exhausting conversations about this character or that scene, who both lifted me up and told me to toughen up when I needed it. And to my dad, Charlie, whose pride in me and my work still makes me feel like his little girl, even at this very mature age. Thank you both for your bottomless well of love and unending support for the accomplishments of all your children. I hit the parent jackpot.

To my children, Ella, Keira, and Sawyer, whose sweet support of my writing efforts and enthusiasm for celebrating the small successes along the way kept me moving forward if for nothing else than to make them proud. You three are my heart.

And to my agent, Jessica Faust, for taking a chance on me and for loving this story as much as I have. Your expertise, wisdom, and love for this industry make it an absolute joy to be your client. Thank you to my editor, Chris Werner, who connected to this story in the way I had hoped and for believing it was something worth sharing. And to the insightful Tiffany Yates Martin for eloquently guiding me through editing rounds that brought us to a fuller, smoother, and richer version of what I had set out to tell in the first place. Many thanks to the entire team at Lake Union, who patiently and expertly shepherded this book to publication.

To my sister and brother, Jennifer and Scott, for your encouragement and love. And to my Ohio University crew, Taryn, Sara, and Kelly, for reading and supporting and being my lifelong friends and my chosen family who will always make me laugh.

Where, oh where, would I be without the many friends and writing partners who supported and worked with me through all the stages of this book? To my critique partners, Mary Johnson and Elizabeth Richards: thank you for your honesty and investment in Star and Jess and for making sure that the eggs were cooked in a cast-iron skillet. And to my friend and gifted writer Sara Miller, for the many coffee dates, phone calls, and massively long texts where you patiently helped me work out the kinks. To Matt Adams, for inspiring me to write in the first place and for your encouragement and especially for your merciless but insightful red pen. And many thanks to my early readers: Christi Clendenon, Mindy Pellegrino, Annahita de la Mare, Alex Harpp, Emma Young, Samaria Stovall, and Denise Boeding.

ABOUT THE AUTHOR

Photo © 2018 Eric Weber Studios

For as long as she can remember, Melissa Payne has been telling stories in one form or another—from high school newspaper articles to a graduate thesis to blogging about marriage and motherhood. But she first learned the real importance of storytelling when she worked for a residential and day treatment center for abused and neglected children. There she wrote speeches and letters to raise funds for the children. The truth in those stories was piercing and painful and written to invoke in the reader a call to action: to give, to help, to make a difference. Melissa's love of writing and sharing stories in all forms has endured. She lives in the foothills of the Rocky Mountains with her husband and three children, a friendly mutt, a very loud cat, and the occasional bear. *The Secrets of Lost Stones* is her first novel.